Tom Sharpe

Tom
Sharpe

Riotous
Assembly

Wilt

CHANCELLOR
PRESS

Riotous Assembly first published in Great Britain
in 1971 by Martin Secker & Warburg Limited
Wilt first published in Great Britain
in 1976 by Martin Secker & Warburg Limited

This edition first published in Great Britain in 1984 by

Chancellor Press
an imprint of the Octopus Publishing Group p.l.c.
59 Grosvenor Street
London, W.1.

in association with

William Heinemann Limited
10 Upper Grosvenor Street
London, W.1.

and

Martin Secker & Warburg Limited
54 Poland Street
London, W.1.

ISBN 0 907486 56 8

Printed in Great Britain at The Pitman Press, Bath

Tom Sharpe

Contents

Riotous Assembly

Wilt

Tom
Sharpe

Riotous
Assembly

For all those members of the South African Police Force whose lives are dedicated to the preservation of Western Civilisation in Southern Africa

Chapter 1

Piemburg is deceptive. Nothing about it is entirely what it seems to be. Huddled among the foothills of the Drakensberg and crouching at the feet of a great flat-topped hill it has few of the marks of a capital city. Travellers whose trains to Johannesburg stop, if they bother, beneath the rusting sheet-metal gingerbread of its station roof, or who whisk past on the National Highway, glimpse a tiny town that seems to have died and been embalmed. For Piemburg is by popular accounts quite dead. Sleepy Hollow they call it, and an American visitor is reported to have looked at Piemburg and said, 'Half the size of New York Cemetery and twice as dead.' And certainly at a first glance the city's lack of animation seems complete. It lies curled in its valley under the African sun and sleeps. Its red iron roofs and wrought-iron balconies bespeak a distant age of long-forgotten enterprise. Its roads are lined with jacarandas and its gardens are lush with flowering dark verandahs. Everything grows immediately and just as immediately stands still. Time and the climate both combine to growth and growth's suspension.

And Piemburg grew with the garrison, and with the garrison's departure died. Or fell asleep. The capital of Zululand, it sprang up with the British Empire's conquest of the Zulu nation. In the first flush of that resounding victory, Piemburg was transformed from a tiny settlement long deserted by its Afrikaaner founders into a capital city. Civic buildings multiplied in a rash of colonnade and red Victorian brick. The governor's mansion bloomed with Italian marble floors, Venetian glass and all the trimmings of imperial splendour. The railway station, a paragon of metal fretwork and faïence, provided a suitable staging post for the Viceregal trains that passed through Piemburg on their way to further and less attractive imperial dominions in the hinterland of Africa. And as the great steam engines blustered up the winding gradient to Empire View, the hill above Piemburg, carrying with them their august burden to an early death by tsetse fly or malarial mosquito, monocled and moustached men would gaze serenely down on the capital of Zululand and murmur, 'A gem, a gem set in a green and yellow ring,' and then turn back to study the wholly inaccurate survey maps of their new territories.

Piemburg would salute their passing with a governor's greeting on the station platform and an exchange of statesmanlike admonitions made inaudible by the military band playing under the iron roof. And Piemburg would pay its respects a few months later when the Viceregal Coffin borne in a carriage draped in black and drawn by a locomotive adorned with wreaths halted a moment while the band played a death march with a gusto that made once more inaudible the governor's condolences to the aide-de-camp. And in the intervals between imperial progress and imperial retreat, the capital of Zululand would adorn itself with new bandstands and botanical gardens and the amusements of a tiny metropolis. In Fort Rapier the great parade ground would echo to the bellowed commands of sergeant-majors. Thousands of putteed legs would stamp or turn about, and the glittering bayonets would eddy to and fro across the brilliant square.

In the town itself the streets were prickly with waxed moustaches. Blanco and brass polish stood high on the list of life's necessities. In the Imperial Hotel the mornings and afternoons were liquid among potted plants and wicker chairs with the music of a Palm Court orchestra. Sam Browne belts and whalebone waist-pinchers restrained the officers and their wives who listened to the whine of the violins and recalled the shires and parishes of England with thankful melancholy. Many would never return and those who stayed and were not buried in the military cemetery in Fort Rapier would build their houses as close to the Governor's Mansion as their seniority and overdrafts allowed.

While the garrison stayed Piemburg prospered. Piemburg was even, briefly, gay. The Garrison Theatre was made brilliant by performances of plays and revues that bred one great English actor and playwright and charmed the governor and his wife. Bazaars and garden parties were bright with the parasols and bustles of wives who had been swept from the terraced suburbs and semi-detached houses of South London to the grandeur of the lawns and shrubberies of Piemburg by the surprising good fortune of having married husbands whose mediocrity won for them the reward of being posted to this distant sliver of the Empire. The taste of the Victorian lower middle class imposed itself indelibly upon Piemburg and has stayed there to this day. And with the taste there came an immutable sense of hierarchy. Viceroys, governors, generals, vice governors, colonels, down the ranks swept, broadening as they went, through nuances too subtle to enumerate, where schools and wives' fathers' professions and a dropped aspirate or one retained 'g' could cause a major to step in an instant up above a lieutenant-colonel. At the bottom of the scale came private soldiers in the pay corps. Below these pariahs there was nothing left. Zulus competed with Pondos, Coloureds with Indians. What happened down there was simply nobody's concern. All that one had to know was that somewhere even lower than the loyal Zulus and the treacherous Pondos there were the Boers. And so it went until the war. Boers didn't wash. Boers were cowards. Boers were stupid. Boers were an excrescence that blocked the way to Cairo. Piemburg ignored the Boers.

And then came the Boer War and as the Boers shot the monocles out of the eyes of the officers of Fort Rapier, waiting deliberately for a semaphore reflection of the sun to signal a suitable monocled target, a new respect was born in Piemburg. The Boer could shoot straight. The Boer was cunning. The Boer was now the enemy.

And but a moment later the Boer was the enemy no more. The obstacle to Cairo and the gold mines quite removed, Piemburg began its swift decline. As the garrison departed and the bands played 'Goodbye Dolly Gray' for the last time, Piemburg fell asleep. Like a replete puff-adder coiled and bloated it lay under the African sun and dreamt of its brief days of glory. Only a sense of precedence remained to multiply in the luxuriant climate of its own mediocrity. The houses stood and gazed at the ring of hills and on their stoeps the sons and grandsons of the sergeant majors, quartermaster sergeants and warrant officers pretended to a grandeur their ancestors had never known. In Piemburg time stood still, marked only by the dust that gathered on the heads of the stuffed lions that mouldered in the Alexandra Club and by the drip of snobbery. Piemburg's mediocrity was venomous and waited gently on events.

Chapter 2

Kommandant van Heerden had few illusions about himself and a great many about everything else. And it was thanks to his illusions that he found himself in charge of the Police station in Piemburg. It was not a very onerous position. Piemburg's mediocrity was not conducive to more than petty crime and it had been felt at Police Headquarters in Pretoria that, while Kommandant van Heerden's appointment might push the city's crime rate up, it would at least serve to lower the waves of violence and theft that had followed his postings to other more enterprising towns.

Besides, Piemburg deserved the Kommandant. As the one town in the Republic still to fly the Union Jack from the Town Hall, Piemburg needed to be taught that the Government could not be challenged without taking some revenge.

Kommandant van Heerden knew that his appointment was not due to his success in the field of criminal investigation. He fondly imagined it had come to him because he understood the English. It was in fact due to the reputation of his grandfather, Klaasie van Heerden, who had served under General Cronje at the Battle of Paardeberg and had been shot by the British for refusing to obey the order of his commanding officer to surrender. He had instead stayed put in a hole in the bank of the Modder River and shot down twelve soldiers of the Essex Regiment who were relieving themselves there some forty-eight hours after the last shot had been fired. The fact that Klaasie had been fast

asleep throughout the entire battle and had never heard
the order to cease fire was discounted by the British during
his trial and by later generations of Afrikaans historians.
Instead he was accounted a hero who had been martyred
for his devotion to the Boer Republics and as a hero he was
revered by Afrikaans Nationalists all over South Africa.

It was this legend that had helped Kommandant van
Heerden to his present rank. It had taken a long time for
his incompetence to live down the reputation for cunning
that had been bequeathed him by his grandfather, and by
that time it was too late for Police Headquarters to do
anything about his inefficiency except put him in command of Piemburg.

Kommandant van Heerden imagined that he had got the
post because it was in an English town and certainly it
was just the post he wanted. The Kommandant believed
that he was one of the few Afrikaaners who really understood the English mind. In spite of the treatment the
British had meted out to his grandfather, in spite of the
brutality the British had shown to the Boer women and
children in the concentration camps, in spite of the sentimentality the British wasted on their black servants, in
spite of everything, Kommandant van Heerden admired
the British.

There was something about their blundering stupidity
that appealed to him. It called out to something deep within his being. He couldn't say exactly what it was, but deep
called to deep and, if the Kommandant could have chosen
his place of birth, its time and nationality, he would have
plumped for Piemburg in 1890 and the heart of an English
gentleman.

If he had one regret, it was that his own mediocrity had
never had the chance to express itself with anything like
the degree of success that had attended the mediocrity

and muddleheadedness of the rulers of the British Empire. Born an English gentleman in Victorian Britain he might well have risen to the rank of field marshal. His military ineptitude would surely have been rewarded by constant and rapid promotion. He was certain he could have done as well as Lord Chelmsford, whose forces had been massacred by the Zulus at Isandhlwana. Stormberg, Spion Kop, Magersfontein, might have been even more appalling disasters had he been in command. Kommandant van Heerden had been born out of nation, time and place.

The same could not be said of the Kommandant's second in command, Luitenant Verkramp, nor of Konstabel Els. That they should never have been born at all, or, if their births could not have been aborted, that their nation, place and time should have been as distant as possible from his own, was Kommandant van Heerden's most fervent and frequent wish.

Luitenant Verkramp hated the English. His grandfather had not suffered as had the Kommandant's for the sake of the Boer Republics. Instead he had proclaimed peace and friendship for the British Empire from the pulpit of his Church in the Cape and had made a small fortune on the side by supplying the British army with the Basuto ponies it needed for its mounted infantry. Verkramp's childhood had been spent in the shadow of that pulpit and little Verkramp had inherited a marked eschatological bent from his grandfather and a hatred for all things English from his father who had spent his life trying to live down the name of 'traitor' which had clung to the Verkramp family long after the Boer War. Luitenant Verkramp brought both inheritances with him to his work. He combined his inquisitorial tendencies with his antipathy for the English by becoming head of the Security Branch in Piemburg, a post which allowed him to send reports on the political reliability of the citizens of Piemburg to his superiors in BOSS, the Bureau of State Security in Pretoria. Even Kommandant van Heerden was the subject of Luitenant Verkramp's suspicions and the Kommandant had taken good care to read the reports about himself that Verkramp had submitted. In one of these he had detected the innuendo that he was insufficiently active in pursuit of Communist cells.

In the week following, the Kommandant had sought to rebut the accusation by a series of lightning raids on likely Communist groups. A playreading of Shaw's *Arms and the Man* at the Piemburg Amateur Dramatic Society had been interrupted by the entrance of the Kommandant and his men who confiscated all copies of the play and took the names of all present. *Black Beauty* had been removed from the shelves of the Public Library on the Kommandant's orders. The showing of the film *The African Queen* had been banned at the local cinema, as had an article on weather forecasting in the Piemburg News entitled 'Red Sky at Night'.

All in all the Kommandant felt satisfied that he had made significant moves to combat the spread of Marxism in Piemburg and the public outcry that followed would, he felt, go a long way to convince BOSS that he was not as soft on Communists as Luitenant Verkramp's report had suggested. Besides he had Verkramp's report on Konstabel Els to fall back on.

The gulf that separated fact from fiction in all the Luitenant's reports on political life in Piemburg widened to a cosmic abyss in the report he had submitted on Konstabel Els. In it Els was described as a regular attendant at the Dutch Reformed Church, an ardent member of the Nationalist Party and a determined opponent of 'liberalistic and communistic tendencies to pollute racial purity by social, economic and political methods of integration'.

Since Els neither went to church nor belonged to the
Nationalist Party and was a living exponent of mixed
sexual intercourse, Kommandant van Heerden felt that he
had Luitenant Verkramp's reputation for accuracy by the
short hairs.

With Konstabel Els matters stood rather differently. For
one thing Els constituted no sort of threat to the Kommandant though a very considerable one to nearly everyone else in Piemburg. His natural aptitude for violence
and particularly for shooting black people was only
equalled by his taste for brandy and his predilection for
forcing the less attractive parts of his person into those
parts of African women legally reserved for male members
of their own race. Kommandant van Heerden had had to
speak quite severely to him about the illegality of this last
tendency on several occasions, but he had put Els's taste for
black women down to the undoubted fact that the Konstabel was of mixed race himself.

No, Konstabel Els had his virtues. He was conscientious,
he was an excellent shot and he knew how to operate the
Electrical Therapy Machine which had proved such a boon
in extracting confessions from suspects. Luitenant Verkramp had brought it back from one of his visits to
Pretoria and Els had immediately made himself extraordinarily proficient with it. It had originally been intended for
political suspects only, but Luitenant Verkramp's efforts
to find any saboteurs or Communists in Piemburg to try
the gadget out on had failed so hopelessly that Els had
finally had to arrest a native boy he had caught early one
morning with a bottle of milk in his hand. The fact that
Els knew him to be the milk delivery boy hadn't prevented
the Konstabel proving the efficacy of electric shock
therapy and after five minutes treatment the boy readily
confessed that he had stolen the milk, while after ten

minutes he admitted administering poisoned milk to fifty European households that very morning. When Els proposed transferring the terminal from the boy's toe to his penis, the suspect admitted to being a member of the Communist Party and agreed that he had been trained in milk sabotage in Peking. At that point Luitenant Verkramp confessed himself satisfied with the experiment and the milk delivery boy was charged with being out without a Pass, obstructing the police in the course of their duties and resisting arrest, which charges got him six months hard labour and satisfied the magistrate that his injuries were justified if not actually self-inflicted. Yes, Els had his virtues, not the least of which was a deep if obscure sense of devotion to his commanding officer. Not that Kommandant van Heerden was in the least interested in Konstabel Els's regard for him, but it made a change from the abiding dislike that emanated from Luitenant Verkramp.

All in all Kommandant van Heerden felt well satisfied with life in Piemburg. Things would go on as they had in the past and he would have time to continue his private hobby, the intellectual puzzle of trying to understand the English, a puzzle he knew to be impossible to solve but for that very reason endlessly fascinating.

If Piemburg was the garden of Kommandant van Heerden's soul where he could wander happily dreaming of great men and great deeds done, Miss Hazelstone of Jacaranda Park was the key plant, the corner tree of this interior landscape. Not that she was young or beautiful or charming or even in any sense likeable. She was none of these things. She was old, ugly, garrulous and abrupt to the point of rudeness. Hardly alluring qualities but to the Kommandant they were filled with extraordinary attractions. These were all the attributes of the English. To hear Miss Hazelstone's voice, high-pitched, loud and utterly unselfconscious, was to hear the true voice of the British Empire. To be chided, nay, trounced by Miss Hazelstone for infringing his authority by cautioning her chauffeur for driving at 80 mph through a built-up area in a 1936 Hudson Terraplane with defective brakes was a pleasure almost too great to be borne. He treasured her refusal to grant him any title. 'Van Heerden,' she would snarl from the back of the sedan, 'you exceed your authority. Driver, proceed,' and the car would drive off leaving the Kommandant marvelling at her savoir-faire.

Then again on the rare occasions that he could find an excuse to visit Jacaranda House, Miss Hazelstone would receive him, if she deigned to see him at all, at the servants' entrance and would despatch him with an economy of incivility and an abundance of implicit contempt that left the Kommandant breathless with admiration.

With Luitenant Verkramp she was even ruder, and when the Kommandant could endure the Security Branch man's insolence no longer he would invent reasons for him to call at Jacaranda House. Luitenant Verkramp had made the mistake on his first visit of addressing Miss Hazelstone in Afrikaans and ever since she had spoken to him in Kitchen Kaffir, a pidgin Zulu reserved only for the most menial and mentally retarded black servants. Luitenant Verkramp returned from these penitential trips speechless with rage and vented his spleen by submitting security reports on the Hazelstone family accusing the old woman of subversion and of fomenting civil disorder. These memoranda he sent to Pretoria with the recommendation that Miss Hazelstone's activities be brought to the attention of the State Attorney.

The Kommandant doubted that the reports enhanced Verkramp's reputation for accuracy or for political reliability. He had forgotten to tell his second-in-command that Miss Hazelstone was the only daughter of the late Judge Hazelstone of the Supreme Court who was known in the legal world as Breakneck Bill and who, in a Minority report of the Commission on Traffic Congestion, had advocated that flogging be made mandatory for parking offences. With such antecedents, it seemed unlikely to the Kommandant that BOSS would question Miss Hazelstone's patriotism. English she might be, subversive and criminal never.

It came therefore as all the more of a shock when he heard Konstabel Els answer the phone in the outer office and the strident tones of Miss Hazelstone vibrating from the receiver. Interested to see how Els would suffer at her hands, the Kommandant listened to the conversation.

Miss Hazelstone was telephoning to report that she had just shot her Zulu cook. Konstabel Els was perfectly capable of handling the matter. He had in his time as a police officer shot any number of Zulu cooks. Besides there was a regular procedure for dealing with such reports. Konstabel Els went into the routine.

'You wish to report the death of a kaffir,' he began.

'I have just murdered my Zulu cook,' snapped Miss Hazelstone.

Els was placatory. 'That's what I said. You wish to report the death of a coon.'

'I wish to do nothing of the sort. I told you I have just murdered Fivepence.'

Els tried again. 'The loss of a few coins doesn't count as murder.'

'Fivepence was my cook.'

'Killing a cook doesn't count as murder either.'

'What does it count as, then?' Miss Hazelstone's confidence in her own guilt was beginning to wilt under Konstabel Els's favourable diagnosis of the situation.

'Killing a white cook can be murder. It's unlikely but it can be. Killing a black cook can't. Not under any circumstances. Killing a black cook comes under self-defence, justifiable homicide or garbage disposal.' Els permitted himself a giggle. 'Have you tried the Health Department?' he enquired.

It was obvious to the Kommandant that Els had lost what little sense of social deference he had ever possessed. He pushed Els aside and took the call himself.

'Kommandant van Heerden here,' he said. 'I understand that there has been a slight accident with your cook.'

Miss Hazelstone was adamant. 'I have just murdered my Zulu cook.'

Kommandant van Heerden ignored the self-accusation. 'The body is in the house?' he enquired.

'The body is on the lawn,' said Miss Hazelstone. The Kommandant sighed. It was always the same. Why couldn't people shoot blacks inside their houses where they were supposed to shoot them?

'I will be up at Jacaranda House in forty minutes,' he said, 'and when I arrive I will find the body in the house.'

'You won't,' Miss Hazelstone insisted, 'you'll find it on the back lawn.'

Kommandant van Heerden tried again.

'When I arrive the body will be in the house.' He said it very slowly this time.

Miss Hazelstone was not impressed. 'Are you suggesting that I move the body?' she asked angrily.

The Kommandant was appalled at the suggestion. 'Certainly not,' he said, 'I have no wish to put you to any inconvenience and besides there might be fingerprints. You can get the servants to move it for you.'

There was a pause while Miss Hazelstone considered the implications of this remark. 'It sounds to me as though you are suggesting that I should tamper with the evidence of a crime,' she said slowly and menacingly. 'It sounds to me as though you are trying to get me to interfere with the course of justice.'

'Madam,' interrupted the Kommandant, 'I am merely trying to help you to obey the law.' He paused, groping for words. 'The law says that it is a crime to shoot kaffirs outside your house. But the law also says it is perfectly permissible and proper to shoot them inside your house if they have entered illegally.'

'Fivepence was my cook and had every legal right to enter the house.'

'I'm afraid you're wrong there,' Kommandant van Heerden went on. 'Your house is a white area and no kaffir is entitled to enter a white area without permission. By shooting your cook you were refusing him permission to enter your house. I think it is safe to assume that.'

There was a silence at the other end of the line. Miss Hazelstone was evidently convinced.

'I'll be up in forty minutes,' continued van Heerden, adding hopefully, 'and I trust the body—'

'You'll be up here in five minutes and Fivepence will be on the lawn where I shot him,' snarled Miss Hazelstone and slammed down the phone.

The Kommandant looked at the receiver and sighed. He put it down wearily and turning to Konstabel Els he ordered his car.

As they drove up the hill to Jacaranda Park, Kommandant van Heerden knew he was faced with a difficult case. He studied the back of Konstabel Els's head and found some consolation in its shape and colour.

If the worst came to the worst he could always make use of Els's great gift of incompetence and if in spite of all his efforts to prevent it, Miss Hazelstone insisted on being tried for murder, she would have as the chief prosecution witness against her, befuddled and besotted, Konstabel Els. If nothing else could save her, if she pleaded guilty in open court, if she signed confession after confession, Konstabel Els under cross-examination by no matter how half-witted a defence attorney would convince the most biased jury or the most inflexible judge that she was the innocent victim of police incompetence and unbridled perjury. The State Attorney was known to have referred to Konstabel Els in the witness box as the Instant Alibi.

Chapter 3

It was with these thoughts in mind that Kommandant van Heerden drove down the drive to Jacaranda House. They interrupted only briefly the aesthetic pleasure he always felt in the presence of relics of the British Empire, for Jacaranda House was pure Cecil Rhodes and Bishop Colenso.

Rambling and stuccoed, the massive edifice had been jerry-built to last. In style it managed to combine elements of both East and West. In Jacaranda House the twain had met. At first sight it looked as though Windsor Castle had been used for the artificial insemination of the Brighton Pavilion and from its crenellated gables to its tiled and columned verandah it succeeded with an eclecticism truly English in bringing more than a touch of the durbah to a building as functionally efficient as a gents. Whoever had built Jacaranda House might not and almost certainly did not know what he was doing, but he must have been a positive genius even to have known how.

As the police car drew up, the great Gothic front door was opened by an Indian butler, wearing white gloves and a red sash, who led the Kommandant and his assistant through a vast hall whose walls were patinaed with the mouldering heads of one warthog, sixteen buffaloes, ten lions and numerous lesser fauna, which heads the late Judge Hazelstone had purchased at an auction to sustain his totally unwarranted reputation as a big-game hunter. To add to the impression that they were in the jungle a profusion of potted plants and ferns reached their dusty fronds up to the plaster fan-vaulting. The corridor and the great sitting-room through which they passed were similarly decorated with the portraits of long-dead Hazelstones, and when at last they came out on to the verandah at the back of the house, Kommandant van Heerden's regard for Imperial Britain had increased by leaps and bounds.

Miss Hazelstone had chosen the scene of her crime with a sense of propriety and occasion which belonged to a distant and leisurely age. The body of Fivepence lay on an immaculate lawn and was huddled in a suitably obeisant rigor at the foot of a pedestal on which had stood the bust of Sir Theophilus Hazelstone, G.C.R., G.C.S.I., G.C.I.E., D.S.O., and one-time Governor of Zululand and Viceroy of Matabeleland; which bust had been erected at the conclusion of the Zulu Rebellion to commemorate Sir Theophilus's victory at Bulundi over 17,000 unarmed Zulus who had misguidedly assumed that Sir Theophilus had invited them there for an indaba as the representative of the Great White Queen. The ensuing massacre was noted in military history as the first occasion on which ten-inch naval guns had been fired at the point-blank range of twelve yards with the resultant deaths by shrapnel of half their gun crews. In later stages of the battle this mistake had been rectified and the naval guns had been used at long range to decimate the fleeing Zulus to such good effect that they had destroyed four farmhouses and a British blockhouse on the Tugela River some seven miles beyond the actual battlefield. These innovations in the art of military strategy had earned Sir Theophilus his knighthood and a bar to his D.S.O., not to mention the admiration of his surviving officers and men, and had added to his reputation for scrupulous honesty and fair play among the tribesmen who, maimed and mutilated, managed to survive the holocaust. During his reign as Governor, Zululand knew a decade of untroubled peace and on his death a generation of Zulu widows came out of mourning.

It was on the reputation of such heroes as Sir Theophilus that Kommandant van Heerden's admiration for the British and their Empire had been formed. Reputation, it seemed to the Kommandant, was all that remained to Sir Theophilus. Certainly his bust had disappeared from its pedestal and lay fragmented over half an acre of otherwise spotless lawn. Beyond the lawn the trunks of the gum trees were gashed and splintered and the azalea bushes looked as though they had been the subject of the concentrated attention of some very large and desperately hungry animal. Branches and leaves lay scattered and torn in a gap some twenty yards across.

For a moment the Kommandant drew fresh hope that Fivepence's sudden death must have been the result not of any human agency but of some natural cataclysm in the order of a freak tornado which had passed without a shadow of a doubt well noticed through Jacaranda Park but unremarked in the rest of Piemburg. This brief spasm of optimism died almost as soon as it was born. It was all too obvious that whatever other gifts Miss Hazelstone had inherited from her illustrious Imperial forebears, Sir Theophilus had left her with a marked propensity for enormous firearms and their use at quite unnecessarily close range.

She sat, a thin, angular, almost frail, elderly lady dressed in dark chiffon with lace to her throat, in a frail, elderly wicker chair complete with an unnecessary antimacassar and cradled in her lap lay a weapon which startled Kommandant van Heerden and even Konstabel Els and which explained all too readily the scene of devastation that lay beyond the contorted figure of Fivepence and the bustless pedestal. It was a four-barrelled rifle, some six feet in

length and its bore was of a diameter so large that it suggested one of Sir Theophilus's favourite weapons, the ten-
inch naval gun. Kommandant van Heerden's experienced
eye told him immediately that this was no standard fire-
arm licensed for self-defence.

'This is the murder weapon,' said Miss Hazelstone,
evidently reading his thoughts. She patted the four barrels
and van Heerden noted that she was obviously determined
to leave no part of the gun free of fingerprints.

The Kommandant eyed the rifle cautiously. 'What is
it?' he enquired at last.

'It's a magazine-loaded multi-barrelled elephant gun,'
Miss Hazelstone replied. 'It was designed by my father,
the late Judge Hazelstone and made to his own specifica-
tions. Its rate of fire is forty bullets a minute and it can
incapacitate a charging elephant at a thousand yards.'

Van Heerden volunteered the opinion that it seemed
unnecessary to kill elephants at a thousand yards. He
couldn't bring himself to use the word 'incapacitate'. It
seemed inappropriately modest. Evaporate seemed more
likely.

'My father was a lousy shot,' Miss Hazelstone continued.
'Besides, he was a dreadful coward.'

'No man who fired that gun could be called a coward,'
said the Kommandant both gallantly and truthfully. He
was beginning to find the interview quite relaxing. Murder
had evidently brought a new touch of humanity to Miss
Hazelstone. She was treating him with unaccustomed
civility. The Kommandant decided that the time had come
to resume his defence of Miss Hazelstone's innocence.

'That rifle is far too heavy for a woman ... I beg your
pardon ... for a lady to use,' he said and regretted the remark almost as soon as it was made. It was evident that
Miss Hazelstone would respond to any challenge. She rose

from her chair and aimed the great rifle into the garden.

The Kommandant had discounted any possibility that she might fire the thing. Konstabel Els, for once, acted with greater resourcefulness and threw himself to the ground. That the ground he chose was already occupied by a large Dobermann Pinscher and that the dog chose to dispute the right of Konstabel Els to lie prone on it and that in any case all South African dogs are trained to bite persons of negro extraction and that Konstabel Els was of sufficiently mixed blood to justify biting on suspicion, all this was lost to Kommandant van Heerden as Miss Hazelstone, aiming now at the ground and now at the sky, pulled the trigger.

The Kommandant, who was standing some eighteen inches to the right of the four barrels and almost level with their muzzles and who, but an instant before, had been a rational thinking human being in full possession of his senses, found himself as it seemed to him, in a vast and rapidly expanding bubble of flame. The sensible world of garden, sky, twittering birds, even the screams of Els being savaged by the Dobermann, all disappeared. Kommandant van Heerden knew only the absolute silence at the still heart of an enormous explosion. There was no pain, no anxiety, no thought, only the certain realization, not that the end of the world was at hand, but that it had already been irremediably accomplished. For one brief, illuminating moment Kommandant van Heerden experienced the highest form of mystical understanding, total bodily dissolution. It was some time before he returned to the world of physical sensation and too late for him to hear anything of the thunderclap that volleyed forth from Jacaranda Park in the direction of the Drakensberg Mountains. With the glazed eyes of an awakened sleepwalker and the singed moustache that comes from standing too close to an enormous gun barrel, he looked at the scene around him. It was not one to reassure a man doubtful of his own sanity.

Konstabel Els's contretemps with the Dobermann had been exacerbated, to put it mildly, by the broadside. It was doubtful which of the two animals had been more maddened by the roar of the elephant gun. The dog, which had at first bitten Konstabel Els's ankle to the bone, had transferred its attentions to his groin and once there had developed all the symptoms of lockjaw. Els, conservative as ever, and having nothing else to bite on except the Dobermann's backside, was applying his knowledge, gained in several thousand interrogations of Africans, of what he cheerfully called 'ball-bashing' but which in the autopsy reports on some of his patients was termed severe contusions to the testicles.

Kommandant van Heerden turned what remained of his attention away from this unpleasant spectacle and tried to look at Miss Hazelstone who lay stunned but satisfied in the wicker chair where the kick of the rifle had thrown her. Through his singed eyelashes the Kommandant could partially see that she was addressing him because her lips were moving but it was some minutes before he recovered his hearing sufficiently to be able to make out what she was saying. Not that he found her remarks at all helpful. It seemed positively gratuitous to repeat, 'There you are. I told you I could fire the gun,' and the Kommandant began to wonder if he had not been a trifle unjust to Luitenant Verkramp. Miss Hazelstone was after all a woman who would stick at nothing.

Her second firing had destroyed what remained of the pedestal on which Sir Theophilus's bust had stood and, being aimed at ground level, had almost obliterated all traces of Fivepence's recently obeisant corpse. Almost but not entirely, for the fragmentary and dispersed remains of Sir Theophilus's bust had been joined on their widely separated patches of lawn by the no less fragmentary and dispersed remains of the late Zulu cook, while patches of black skin had attached themselves limpet-like to the blasted trunks of the gum trees that fringed the once immaculate lawn. Kommandant van Heerden couldn't bring himself to focus on the round black object that kept trying to draw attention to itself by swinging wistfully from a branch in the upper reaches of an otherwise attractive blue gum. Down the centre of the lawn the elephant gun had cut a straight trench some eight inches in depth and fifteen yards long from whose serrated edges arose what the Kommandant despairingly hoped was steam.

Feeling that the afternoon's work and his recent transcendental experience had released him from the standards of politeness he had previously maintained in Miss Hazelstone's company, the Kommandant sat down uninvited in a chair well outside any likely arc of fire from the terrible elephant gun, and watched Konstabel Els's gladiatorial conflict with the Dobermann with the air of a connoisseur.

On the whole he thought they were pretty well matched both in physique and in intellectual grasp of the situation. Certainly Els suffered the disadvantage of a smaller jaw and fewer teeth, but what he lacked in biting power he made up for in concentration and experience in castration. The Kommandant did think, momentarily, of intervening but Miss Hazelstone had already acted with that decisiveness he had always found so admirable in persons of her class. She sent the Indian butler into the house and a moment later he returned with a bottle of ammonia and a large wad of cotton wool.

'The best way of separating dogs,' she shouted above

the growls and groans, 'is to hold a pad of cotton wool soaked with ammonia over their muzzles. They gasp for air and you pull 'em apart,' and so saying she clamped the wad over Konstabel Els's already purple face. The Kommandant wondered at her choice of Els as the first to be forced to release his grip, but he put it down to the English love of animals and, to be fair to Miss Hazelstone, he knew her to be particularly fond of the Dobermann.

It was immediately apparent that the method was remarkably efficacious. With a muffled scream and all the symptoms of imminent asphyxia, Els released his grip on the dog's reproductive organs and was assisted in discontinuing the struggle by the Indian butler who, hanging on to his ankles, attempted to drag the Konstabel away.

Unfortunately for Els the Dobermann was less intimidated by the threat of death by suffocation, or else it had developed an immunity to ammonia and it took several minutes to persuade the beast not to pursue the advantage it naturally assumed it had won by the intervention of its mistress. It may well have thought that Miss Hazelstone had joined it on the ground because Konstabel Els had transferred his quite appalling mandible attentions to her, which would at least have been more natural although, considering her age and lack of physical charm, not altogether understandable. Whatever the reasons for the Dobermann's continuing attachment to Els's groin, the interval allowed the Kommandant to concentrate his attention, interrupted only by the agonized screams of his assistant, on the case he had been forced to investigate.

By the time peace and tranquillity had once more been restored to Jacaranda House and Miss Hazelstone had sent Oogly, the Indian butler, to serve tea in the drawing-room, Kommandant van Heerden had sufficiently recovered his faculties to begin the investigation of the case. But first

he ordered Konstabel Els to retrieve the remains of Fivepence from the lawn and from what was clearly an un-
scaleable blue gum, an order which the Konstabel tended
to dispute on the grounds that he was in need of immediate and prolonged hospital treatment for multiple and
severe dog bite, not to mention battle fatigue and shell
shock.

In the end the Kommandant was able to resume his
interrogation of Miss Hazelstone to the accompaniment of
an old-fashioned tea with smoked-salmon sandwiches and
cream scones and the almost equally enjoyable observa-
tion of Konstabel Els suffering severe vertigo some forty
feet up the blue gum.

'Now about this cook,' the Kommandant began. 'Can I
take it that you were dissatisfied with his cooking?'

'Fivepence was an excellent cook,' Miss Hazelstone de-
clared emphatically.

'I see,' said the Kommandant, though he didn't, either
literally or metaphorically. He had been having difficulty
with his vision ever since he had been enveloped in that
ball of flame. It sort of came and went and his hearing was
behaving erratically too.

'Fivepence was a culinary expert,' Miss Hazelstone went
on.

'Was he indeed?' The Kommandant's hopes were raised.
'And when did he do this?'

'Every day of course.'

'And when did you first discover what he was up to?'

'Almost from the word "Go".'

The Kommandant was amazed. 'And you allowed him
to go on?'

'Of course I did. You don't think I was going to stop him,
do you?' Miss Hazelstone snapped.

'But your duty as a citizen—'

'My duty as a citizen fiddlesticks. Why in the name of heaven should my duty as a citizen oblige me to sack an excellent cook?'

The Kommandant groped in the recesses of his shell-shocked mind for a suitable answer.

'Well, you seem to have shot him for it,' he said at last.

'I did nothing of the sort,' Miss Hazelstone snorted. 'Fivepence's death was a *crime passionelle.*'

Kommandant van Heerden tried to imagine what a Cream Passion Nell looked like. Fivepence's death had looked more like an exploded blood pudding to him and as for the portions that Konstabel Els was still attempting to dislodge from the blue gum, even a dog butcher would have been hard put to it to think of an adequate description for them.

'A Cream Passion Nell,' he repeated slowly, hoping that Miss Hazelstone would come to his rescue with a more familiar term. She did.

'A crime of passion, you fool,' she snarled.

Kommandant van Heerden nodded. He had never supposed it to have been anything else. Nobody in his right mind would have inflicted those appalling injuries on Fivepence in cold blood and without some degree of feeling being involved.

'Oh I can see that,' he said.

But Miss Hazelstone had no intention of allowing him to remain under this comforting misapprehension. 'I want you to understand that my feelings for Fivepence were not those which normally obtain between mistress and servant,' she said.

Kommandant van Heerden had already reached that conclusion off his own bat. He nodded encouragingly. Miss Hazelstone's old-fashioned and formal way of expressing her thoughts delighted him. Her next remark had quite the opposite effect.

'What I am trying to tell you,' she continued, 'is that I was in love with him.'

It took some time for the full implications of this statement to sink into the Kommandant's overloaded mind. By comparison his experience of bodily dissolution at the muzzle of the elephant gun had been a mere sighing of the breeze in distant meadow grass. This was a bombshell. Speechless with horror he gazed unfocused in Miss Hazelstone's direction. He knew now what the face of madness looked like. It looked like a frail elderly gentlewoman of illustrious and impeccable British descent sitting in a winged-back armchair holding in her delicate hands a china teacup on which in gilt transfer the crest of the Hazelstones, a wild boar rampant, was underlined by the family motto 'Baisez moi', and openly confessing to an Afrikaans policeman that she was in love with her black cook.

Miss Hazelstone ignored the Kommandant's stunned silence. She evidently took it for a mark of respect for the delicacy of her feelings.

'Fivepence and I were lovers,' she went on. 'We loved one another with a deep and undying devotion.'

Kommandant van Heerden's mind reeled. It was bad enough having to try, however hopelessly, to comprehend what, in God's name, Miss Hazelstone could have found in any way attractive in a black cook, let alone trying to imagine how a black cook could be in love with Miss Hazelstone, but when to crown it all, she used the expression 'undying devotion' while what was left of Fivepence was splattered over an acre of lawn and shrubbery or hung sixty feet up a blue gum tree as a direct result of his lover's passion for him, then Kommandant van Heerden knew that his mind was seriously in danger of utter derangement.

'Go on,' he gasped involuntarily. He had intended to say, 'For God's sake shut up,' but his professional training got the better of him.

Miss Hazelstone seemed happy to continue.

'We became lovers eight years ago and from the first we were delightfully happy. Fivepence understood my emotional needs. Of course we couldn't marry, because of the absurd Immorality Act.' She paused and held up a hand as if to silence the Kommandant's shocked protest. 'So we had to live in sin.' Kommandant van Heerden was past shock. He goggled at her. 'But if we weren't married,' Miss Hazelstone continued, 'we were happy. I must admit we didn't have much of a social life, but then by the time you reach my age, a quiet life at home is all one really wants, don't you think?'

Kommandant van Heerden didn't think. He was doing his best not to listen. He rose unsteadily from his chair and closed the french doors that led out on to the stoep. What this ghastly old woman was telling him must on no account reach the ears of Konstabel Els. He was relieved to note that the redoubtable Konstabel had finally made it to the top of the tree, where he seemed to be stuck.

While Miss Hazelstone mumbled on with her catalogue of Fivepence's virtues, the Kommandant paced the room, frenziedly searching his mind for some means of hushing the case up. Miss Hazelstone and Jacaranda House were practically national institutions. Her column on refined living and etiquette appeared in every newspaper in the country, not to mention her frequent articles in the glossier women's journals. If the doyenne of English society in Zululand were known to have murdered her black cook, or if falling in love with black cooks was to come into the category of refined living and the fashion spread, as well it might, South Africa would go coloured in a year. And what about the effect on the Zulus themselves when they learnt that one of their number had been having it off with the granddaughter of the Great Governor, Sir Theophilus Hazelstone, in Sir Theophilus's own kraal, Jacaranda Park, freely, practically legally, and at her insistence? Kommandant van Heerden's imagination swept on from wholesale rape by thousands of Zulu cooks, to native rebellion and finally race war. Luitenant Verkramp had been right in his reports to Pretoria after all. He had shown astonishing perspicacity. Miss Hazelstone and her Zulu bloody cook were indeed capable of ending three hundred years of White Supremacy in Southern Africa. Worse still he, Kommandant van Heerden, would be held responsible.

At last, after gazing long and prayerfully into the face of a moth-eaten hyena which, in his distracted state of mind, he assumed to be a portrait of Sir Theophilus in his younger days, the Kommandant mustered his last remaining faculties and turned back to his tormentor. He would make one last attempt to make the old bitch see her duty as a lady and a white woman and deny that she had ever entertained anything more lethal or passionate than mildly critical thoughts towards her Zulu cook.

Miss Hazelstone had completed her catalogue of Fivepence's virtues as a sentimental and spiritual companion. She had begun to describe the cook's attributes as a physical and sensual lover, a sharer of her bed and satisfier of her sexual appetites which were, the Kommandant was to discover to his disgust, prodigious and, in his view, perverse to the point of enormity.

'Of course, we did have our little difficulties to begin with,' she was saying. 'There were little incompatibilities in our attitudes, not to mention our physical attributes. A man of your experience, Kommandant, will naturally know what I mean.'

The Kommandant, whose experience of sex was limited to an annual visit to a brothel in Lourenço Marques on his summer holiday, but whose experience of Zulus was fairly extensive, thought that he knew what she meant and hoped to hell that he didn't.

'To begin with Fivepence suffered from *ejaculatio praecox*,' Miss Hazelstone continued clinically. For a brief, all too short moment the Kommandant's lack of Latin and his limited knowledge of medicine spared him the full implications of this remark. Miss Hazelstone hastened to explain.

'He used to have emissions prematurely,' she said, and when the Kommandant ventured to suggest incomprehendingly that, in his humble opinion, Fivepence could not have gone to mission prematurely enough considering his filthy habits in later life, Miss Hazelstone stooped to the level of the stable and explained in language the Kommandant was forced, however unwillingly, to recognize as all too intelligible.

'He used to ejaculate almost as soon as I touched him,' she continued remorselessly, and mistaking the Kommandant's look of abject horror for an indication that he still didn't grasp her meaning, she administered the coup de grâce to his dumbfounded sensibilities.

'He used to come before he could get his prick into me,' she said, and as she said it, the Kommandant seemed to be aware, as in some ghastly nightmare, that the corners of Miss Hazelstone's mouth turned upwards in a slight smile of happy remembrance.

He knew now that Miss Hazelstone was clean out of her mind. He was about to say that she had blown her top, but the phrase, being all too reminiscent of Fivepence's disgusting propensity, not to mention his ultimate fate, was throttled on the threshold of his consciousness.

'In the end we got over the problem,' Miss Hazelstone went on. 'First of all I got him to wear three contraceptives, one on top of the other, to desensitize his *glans penis* and that was quite satisfactory from my point of view though it tended to restrict his circulation a teeny bit and he did complain that he couldn't feel very much. After an hour I would get him to take one off and that helped him a bit and finally he would take the second off and we would have a simultaneous orgasm.' She paused and wagged a finger mischievously at the stupefied Kommandant who was desperately trying to raise enough energy to call a halt to these appalling disclosures. 'But that wasn't the end of it,' she went on, 'I want you to know that I finally arrived at an even better solution to dear Fivepence's little trouble. I was having my six-monthly checkup at the dentist and Dr Levy gave me an injection of local anaesthetic to deaden the pain.' She hesitated as if ashamed to confess to a weakness. 'Of course in the old days we never bothered with such nonsense. A little pain never hurt anyone. But Dr Levy insisted and afterwards I was so glad I had had it. You see I suddenly realized how I could stop Fivepence being overcome by the intensity of his feelings for me.' She paused. There was indeed no need for her to continue.

Kommandant van Heerden's lightning intellect had raced ahead and had grasped the point quite firmly. Besides he was beginning to understand, though only fitfully, the train of thought that Miss Hazelstone was bound to follow.

At this moment he visualized the scene in court which would follow the disclosure that Miss Hazelstone had made

it a habit to inject her black cook's penis with a hypodermic syringe filled with novocaine before allowing him
to have sexual intercourse with her. He visualized it and
vowed that it would never happen, even if it meant he had
to kill her to prevent it.

Despairingly his gaze wandered round the assembly of
long-dead Hazelstones adorning the walls of the drawing-
room and he hoped they appreciated the sacrifices he was
prepared to make to save their family name from the
shame that Miss Hazelstone seemed hell-bent on bestow-
ing on it. The bit about the novocaine injections was an
innovation in sexual techniques of such a bizarre nature
that it wouldn't just hit the national headlines. The newspapers of the world would splash that titbit in foot-high
letters across their front pages. He couldn't begin to think
how they would actually word it, but he had every confidence in their editors' abilities to make it sensational. He
tried to imagine what sort of sensation Fivepence had
found it to be and reached the conclusion that the cook's
death at the muzzle of that awful elephant gun must have
seemed a relatively comfortable release from the continual
practice of Miss Hazelstone plunging the needle of her
hypodermic syringe into the top of his cock. The Kommandant wondered idly if Fivepence had had a foreskin.
It was a fact that they would never be able to ascertain
now.

The thought caused him to glance out of the window to
see how Konstabel Els was getting on. He noted, with
what little astonishment Miss Hazelstone's confession had
left in him, that Els had regained his head for heights, not
to mention Fivepence's, and had somehow managed to
reach the ground where he was busily seeking promotion
by kicking the Indian butler into collecting the scattered

remains of the Zulu cook and putting them into a pillow-case. Els was, as usual, the Kommandant thought, being a bit optimistic. They didn't need anything as large as a pillowcase. A spongebag would have done just as well.

Chapter 4

Behind him Miss Hazelstone, evidently exhausted by her confession, sat back silent in her armchair and gazed happily into her memories. Kommandant van Heerden slumped into a chair opposite her and gazed with less satisfaction into his immediate future. What Miss Hazelstone had revealed to him he had no doubt she would reveal to the world if he gave her half a chance and at all costs those revelations had got to be stopped in their tracks. His own career, the reputation of Zululand's leading family, the whole future of South Africa clearly depended on Miss Hazelstone's silence. His first duty was to ensure that no word of the afternoon's events leaked out of Jacaranda Park. Kommandant van Heerden had little faith in his own ability to prevent that leak. He had none whatsoever in Els's.

The Kommandant knew from bitter experience that Konstabel Els was incapable of keeping anything, money, wife, penis, prisoners, let alone gossip, to himself. And what Miss Hazelstone had to recount wasn't in the nature of mere gossip. It was political, racial, social, you name it, dynamite.

It was just at this point in his musings that the Kommandant caught sight of Konstabel Els approaching the house. He had the air of a good dog that has done its duty and expects to be rewarded. Had he possessed a tail he would undoubtedly have been wagging it. Lacking that appendage he dragged behind him a terrible substitute which, Kommandant van Heerden noted thankfully, he had the decency not to wag. What remained of Fivepence were not things that anybody, not even Els, would wish to wag.

Kommandant van Heerden acted swiftly. He stepped out on to the stoep and shut the door behind him.

'Konstabel Els,' he commanded. 'These are your orders.' The Konstabel dropped the pillow case and came to attention eagerly. Tree-climbing and body-snatching he could do without, but he loved being given orders. They usually meant that he was being given permission to hurt somebody.

'You will dispose of that ... that thing,' the Kommandant ordered.

'Yes sir,' said Els thankfully. He was getting tired of Fivepence.

'Proceed to the main gate and remain there on guard until you are relieved. See that nobody enters or leaves the grounds. Anybody at all. That means Europeans as well. Do you understand?'

'Yes sir.'

'If anyone enters you are to see that they don't get out again.'

'Can I use firearms to stop them, sir?' asked Els.

Kommandant van Heerden hesitated. He didn't want a bloodbath up at the main gateway to Jacaranda Park. On the other hand the situation was clearly such a desperate one and one word to the press would bring hordes of newspapermen up—that he was prepared to take drastic measures.

'Yes,' he said at last. 'You can shoot.' And then remembering the fuss there had been when a wounded reporter had been taken to Piemburg Hospital, he added. 'And shoot to kill, Els, shoot to kill.' Complaints from the morgue were easier to refute.

Kommandant van Heerden went back into the house

and Konstabel Els started off to guard the main gate. He hadn't gone very far when the thought crossed his mind that the elephant gun would certainly ensure that nothing larger than a cockroach got out of Jacaranda Park alive. He turned back and collected the gun from the stoep and then, after adding several packets of revolver ammunition from the police car, set off up the drive with a light heart.

Back in the house Kommandant van Heerden was glad to see that Miss Hazelstone was still in her stupor in the armchair. At least one problem had been solved. No word of the injections would reach Konstabel Els. The thought of what would follow should Els get wind of that diversion had been haunting the Kommandant's mind. There had been enough complaints lately from local residents about the screams that came from the cells in Piemburg Police Station without Konstabel Els practising penal injections on the prisoners. Not that Els would have been content to use novocaine. He would have graduated to nitric acid before you could say Apartheid.

With Els out of the way, the Kommandant decided on his next step. Leaving Miss Hazelstone in her chair, he made his way to the telephone which lurked in the potted jungle in the hall. He made two calls. The first was to Luitenant Verkramp at the Police Station.

In later life Luitenant Verkramp was to recall that telephone conversation with the shudder that comes from recalling the first omens of disaster. At the time he had merely wondered what the hell was wrong with his Kommandant. Van Heerden sounded as though he were on the brink of a nervous breakdown.

'Verkramp, is that you?' his voice came in a strangled whisper over the phone.

'Of course it's me. Who the hell did you think it was?' Verkramp couldn't hear the answer but it sounded as if the Kommandant was trying to swallow something very unpleasant. 'What's going on up there? Is something wrong with you?' Verkramp enquired hopefully.

'Stop asking stupid questions and listen,' the Kommandant whispered authoritatively. 'I want you to assemble every single officer in Piemburg at the police barracks.'

Luitenant Verkramp was appalled. 'I can't do that,' he said, 'the Rugby match is on. There'll be a riot if—'

'There'll be a fucking riot if you don't,' the Kommandant snarled. 'That's number one. Second, all leave including sick leave is cancelled. Got that?'

Luitenant Verkramp wasn't sure what he had got. It sounded like a frantic Kommandant.

'Assemble them all at the barracks,' continued the Kommandant. 'I want every man jack of them fully armed up here as soon as possible. Bring the Saracens too, and the guard dogs, oh and bring the searchlights too. All the barbed wire we've got, and bring those Rabies signs we used in the epidemic last year.'

'The Rabies signs?' Luitenant Verkramp shouted. 'You want the guard dogs and the Rabies signs?'

'And don't forget the Bubonic Plague signs. Bring them too.'

Luitenant Verkramp tried to visualize the desperate outbreak of disease that had broken out at Jacaranda Park that necessitated warning the population about both Rabies and Bubonic Plague.

'Are you sure you're all right?' he asked. It sounded as if the Kommandant was delirious.

'Of course I am all right,' snapped the Kommandant. 'Why the hell shouldn't I be all right?'

'Well, I just thought—'

'I don't care a stuff what you thought. You're not paid to think. You're paid to obey my orders. And I'm order-

ing you to bring every bloody sign we've got and every
bloody policeman and every bloody guard dog....' Kommandant van Heerden's catalogue continued while Verkramp desperately searched his mind for the reasons for
this emergency. The Kommandant's final order trumped
the lot. 'Come up here by a roundabout route. I don't want
to attract any public attention.' And before the Luitenant
could enquire how he thought it possible to avoid public
attention with a convoy of six armoured cars, twenty-
five lorries and ten searchlights, not to mention seventy
guard dogs, and several dozen enormous billboards announcing the outbreak of Bubonic Plague and Rabies, the
Kommandant had put down the 'phone.

Kommandant van Heerden's second call was to the
Commissioner of Police for Zululand. Standing among the
flora and fauna of the hall, the Kommandant hesitated
some time before making his second call. He could see a
number of difficulties looming up ahead of him when he
made his request for Emergency Powers to deal with this
situation, not the least of which was the sheer disbelief
that was certain to greet his considered opinion as a
police officer that the daughter of the late Judge Hazelstone had not only murdered her Zulu cook but that
prior to this act had been fornicating with him regularly for eight years after rendering his reproductive
organs totally numb and insensitive by intramuscular
injections of massive doses of novocaine. Kommandant
van Heerden knew what he would do to any subordinate
officer who rang him up in the middle of a hot summer
afternoon to tell him that sort of cock-and-bull story. He
decided to avoid going into the details of the case. He
would stress the likely political consequences of a murder
case involving the daughter of an extremely eminent
judge who had, in his time, been the country's leading

exponent of capital punishment, and he would use Luitenant Verkramp's report to Pretoria on Miss Hazelstone's
subversive activities to justify his need for Emergency
Powers. Plucking up courage, Kommandant van Heerden
picked up the telephone and made his call. He was surprised to find the Commissioner raised no objections to his
request.

'Emergency Powers, van Heerden? Of course, help
yourself. You know what you're doing. I leave the matter
entirely in your hands. Do what you think best.'

Kommandant van Heerden put down the phone with a
puzzled frown. He had never liked the Commissioner and
he suspected that the feeling was reciprocated.

The Commissioner in fact nourished the ardent hope
that one day Kommandant van Heerden would perpetrate
an error so unforgivable that he could be summarily reduced to the ranks and it seemed to him now from the
Kommandant's hysterical manner on the phone that his
day of vengeance was at hand. He immediately cancelled
all appointments for the next month and took his annual
holiday on the South Coast, leaving orders that he was not
to be disturbed. He spent the next week lying in the sun in
the certain knowledge that he had given van Heerden
enough rope with which to hang himself.

Armed now with Emergency Powers that made him the
arbiter of life and death over 70,000 Piemburgers and gave
him authority to suppress newspaper stories and to arrest,
detain and torture at leisure all those he disapproved of,
the Kommandant was still not a happy man. The events
of the day had taken their toll of him.

He turned for relief from his problems to a full-length
portrait of Sir Theophilus Hazelstone in the full panoply of
his regalia as Knight of the Royal Victorian Order and Viceroy of Matabeleland that hung at the foot of the great

staircase. Sir Theophilus stood, robed in ermine, his scarlet uniform encrusted with jewelled stars and the medals
of disastrous campaigns, each medal representing the
deaths through their General's incompetence of at least
ten thousand enlisted men. The Viceroy's left hand rested
arthritically upon the hilt of a sword he was far too pusil-
lanimous ever to have withdrawn from its scabbard, while
his right hand held the thonged leash of a wild boar which
had been specially imported from Bohemia to share the
honour of representing the Hazelstone family in this great
work of art. Kommandant van Heerden was particularly
struck by the wild boar. It reminded him of Konstabel
Els and he was not to know that the poor beast had had
to be strapped to an iron frame before the Viceroy would
enter the same room as the animate family emblem, and
that only after being cajoled by the artist and the administration of half a bottle of brandy. All this escaped the
Kommandant and left him free to hold firmly to his faith
in the great qualities of the Imperial statesman whose
granddaughter he had made it his mission to save from the
consequences of her own folly. Spiritually resuscitated by
his perusal of this portrait and a similar one of the late
Judge Hazelstone looking as remorseless as the Kommandant could remember him to have looked in court on the
day he had sentenced eleven Pondo tribesmen to death for
stealing a goat, the Kommandant slowly ascended the
staircase to look for somewhere to rest until Luitenant
Verkramp arrived with reinforcements.

Once the park had been isolated from the outside world,
he would set about the business of convincing Miss Hazelstone that she had never murdered her cook and that she
had invented the whole business of the injection needle
and the love affair. He felt sure that he could bring the old
lady to see reason and if that failed the Emergency Powers

entitled him to hold her indefinitely and without recourse
to a lawyer. If need be he would invoke the Terrorist Act
and keep her incommunicado for the rest of her life,
which life could be shortened by suitable treatment and
a regimen of necessary harshness. It was hardly the method
he would like to have applied to a lady of her descent but
for the moment he could think of nothing better.

He paused at the top of the staircase to regain his breath
and then made his way along the gallery that ran the
length of Jacaranda House. If the hall downstairs had been
filled with stuffed heads and portraits, the gallery walls
were likewise lined with trophies of past battles. On either
side of him the Kommandant was startled to find weapons
of all shapes and sizes, weapons of all ages and types,
united by only one common feature as far as the Kommandant could make out, that they were all in perfect
working order and lethal to a degree he found positively
hair-raising. He stopped and examined a machine-pistol.
Well-oiled and complete, it hung beside an ancient blun-
derbuss. Kommandant van Heerden was amazed. The
Gallery was a positive arsenal. Had Miss Hazelstone not
telephoned to acknowledge her contretemps with Fivepence and had she decided to defend Jacaranda House,
with these weapons at her disposal, she could have held
the entire Piemburg police force at bay for weeks. Thank-
ing his lucky stars for her co-operation, Kommandant van
Heerden opened one of the doors that led off the gallery
and looked inside.

As he had expected, it was a bedroom and was furnished with a sense of taste and delicacy appropriate to
the home of South Africa's leading expert in soft furnish-
ings. Chintz curtains and a matching bedspread gave to
the whole room a gay and floral air. What lay on the bed
had the opposite effect. There was nothing tasteful or deli-

cate about it at all and nobody could call it furnished. For there, its incongruity emphasised by the daintiness of the other appointments, lay the body of a large, hairy and completely naked man. Worse still, for the Kommandant's disturbed state of mind, the body bore all the signs of having only recently bled to death. It was practically coated with blood.

Shaken by the appalling discovery of yet another corpse, the Kommandant staggered into the gallery and leant against the wall. One body in an afternoon he could just about cope with, particularly if it was black, but two, and one of them white, filled him with despair. Jacaranda House was taking on the qualities of an abattoir. Worse still, this second corpse destroyed any chances of hushing the case up. It was one thing to persuade Miss Hazelstone that she hadn't murdered her black cook. The disappearance of Zulu cooks was a routine matter. The murder of a white man would simply have to be made public. There would have to be an inquest. Questions would be asked and one thing would lead to another until the full story of Miss Hazelstone and her Zulu cook came out into the open.

After a moment's agonizing thought, Kommandant van Heerden recovered his nerve sufficiently to peer round the door into the murder room again. The corpse was still there, he noted miserably. On the other hand it had certain attributes which Kommandant van Heerden found unique in his experience of corpses. One quality in particular struck his attention. The corpse had an erection. The Kommandant peered round the door again to confirm his suspicion, and as he did so the corpse stirred and began to snore.

For a moment Kommandant van Heerden was so relieved by this evidence of life, that he felt inclined to

laugh. The next moment he realized the full importance
of his discovery and the smile died on his face. He had no
doubt at all that the man whose body lay before him on
the bed was the true murderer of Fivepence. The Kommandant peered down at the figure on the bed and as he
did so he became aware of the smell of brandy in the air.
A moment later his foot banged against a bottle lying on
the floor. He reached down and picked it up. Old Rhino
Skin Brandy, he noted with disgust. It was a brandy that
Konstabel Els was partial to and if anything was needed
to confirm his suspicion that the fellow on the bed was a
dangerous criminal it was the knowledge that if he shared
one of Konstabel Els's depraved tastes, he was almost certain to share others even more vicious.

 With the bottle still in his hand Kommandant van Heerden tiptoed from the room. Outside in the passage he tried
to consider how this discovery affected his plans. That the
man was a murderer, he had no doubt. That he was now
drunk to the world, no doubt either. What remained a
mystery was why Miss Hazelstone had confessed to a
crime she had never committed. More of a mystery still,
why she had embroidered her confession with the gratuitous filth that she had been sleeping with her Zulu cook
and injecting him with novocaine. Kommandant van
Heerden's head reeled with possibilities and, not wishing
to remain in the vicinity of a dangerous killer, he made his
way along the passage to the landing at the top of the
stairs. He wished now that he hadn't sent Els off to guard
the main gateway and at the same time he began to wonder when Luitenant Verkramp would arrive with the
main force. He leant over the balustrade and stared down
on the tropical mausoleum in the hall. Hard by him the
head of a stuffed rhinoceros peered myopically into
eternity. Kommandant van Heerden peered back and

wondered which of his acquaintances it reminded him of, and as he did so he had the sudden insight into the true meaning of Miss Hazelstone's confession which was to alter his life so radically.

He had suddenly realized that the face of the murderer on the bed reminded him of someone. The realization sent him stumbling down the stairs to stare up at the great portrait of Sir Theophilus. A moment later he was back in the bedroom. Tiptoeing to the edge of the bed Kommandant van Heerden peered cautiously down at the face on the pillow. He saw there what he had expected to find. In spite of the gaping mouth and the bag-bottomed eyes, in spite of years of dissipation and sexual overindulgence and gallons of Old Rhino Skin brandy, the features of the man on the bed bore an unmistakable resemblance to those of Sir Theophilus and to the late Judge Hazelstone. He knew now who the man was. He was Jonathan Hazelstone, Miss Hazelstone's younger brother.

With new understanding dawning on him, Kommandant van Heerden turned to leave the room. As he did so the murderer stirred again. The Kommandant froze in his tracks and watched with a mixture of fear and disgust as a bloodstained hand groped up the man's hairy thigh and grasped the great erection. Kommandant van Heerden waited no longer. With a gasp he dashed from the room and hurried along the corridor. A man who could put away a bottle of Old Rhino Skin and still survive in no matter how comatose a state was undoubtedly a maniac, and if on top of all that he could lie there with an erection while his body fought off the appalling injuries being inflicted on it by the brandy, he was undoubtedly a sex fiend whose sexual appetite must be of such an intensity as to leave nothing safe. Kommandant van Heerden remembered Fivepence's posture at the foot of the pedestal and he began to think he knew how the Zulu cook had died and in his calculations there was no place for the elephant gun.

Without a moment's hesitation he hurried down the stairs and left the house. He must fetch Konstabel Els before he tried to arrest the man. As he strode up the drive, he understood why Miss Hazelstone had made her outrageous confession and with this understanding there grew in the Kommandant's breast a new and deeper respect for the old family ties of the British.

'Chivalry. It's pure chivalry,' he said to himself. 'She is sacrificing herself to protect the family name.' He couldn't quite see how confessing to murdering your black cook was saving the family name, but he supposed it was better than having your brother confess to having buggered the said cook into an early grave. He wondered what the sentence for that sort of crime was.

'Deserves to be hanged,' he said hopefully, and then remembered that no white man had ever been hanged for murdering a black. 'Buggery's different,' he thought. Anyway they could always get him for 'actions calculated to excite racial friction', which crime carried with it ten strokes of the heavy cane, and if buggering a Zulu cook wasn't calculated to excite racial friction, then he for one didn't know what was. He would have to ask Konstabel Els about it. The Konstabel was more experienced in that sort of thing than he was.

Chapter 5

At the main gateway to Jacaranda Park, Konstabel Els was
not finding the afternoon as enjoyable as he had expected.
Nobody had tried to enter or leave the Park and Els had had
very little to shoot at. He had taken a pot shot at a
native delivery boy on a bicycle, but the boy had recognized Els in time and had thrown himself into the ditch
before Els had time to take proper aim. Missing the native
hadn't improved Els's temper.

'Miss one and you miss the fucking lot,' he said to himself, and it was certainly true that once word got round
that Kaffir-Killer Els was in the district, white housewives
could scream blue murder at their servants and threaten
them with every punishment in the book, and still no sane
black man would venture out of the house to water the
lawn or fetch the groceries.

So, for want of anything better to do, Els had explored
the area round the gateway and had closed and bolted
the great wrought-iron gates. In the course of his explora-
tions he made the exciting discovery that what he had at
first sight taken to be a well-clipped square privet hedge
concealed in fact a concrete blockhouse. It was clearly
very old and just as clearly very impregnable. It dated in
fact from the days of Sir Theophilus who had ordered its
construction after the battle of Bulundi. The Governor's
victory on that occasion had done nothing to diminish
his natural cowardice and the accusations of treachery
levelled against him by the Zulus and by the next of kin of
the officers killed by their own shells had turned what had

been previously natural anxiety into an obsessive phobia that thousands of vengeful Zulus trained in the use of ten-inch naval guns by the surviving members of his old regiment, the Royal Marines Heavy Artillery Brigade, would storm Jacaranda Park one awful night. Faced with this imaginary threat, Sir Theophilus had begun the collection of weapons that had so startled Kommandant van Heerden in the gallery of Jacaranda House, and also the construction of a series of formidable blockhouses around the perimeter of the park, all of which had been designed to withstand a direct hit from a ten-inch naval shell fired at point-blank range.

It was a tribute to the Governor's skill as a military engineer that the blockhouses were still standing. Judge Hazelstone, as great a coward as his father but more convinced of the deterrent effect of capital punishment, had cnce employed a demolition firm to remove the blockhouses. After blunting scores of drills, the demolition crew had decided to try blasting, and conscious that the bunker was no ordinary one they had practically filled it to the roof with dynamite before lighting the fuse. At the inquest that followed the survivors of the demolition crew described the resulting explosion as being like four gigantic tongues of flame issuing from the gun ports of the blockhouse and the noise had been heard in Durban thirty-five miles away. In view of Judge Hazelstone's legal standing the firm had replaced, free of charge, the gateway their zeal had destroyed, but had refused to continue the work of demolishing the blockhouse. They suggested hiding the unsightly building by planting a privet hedge round it as being a less costly way of getting rid of the thing, and contributed to the cost of the operation as a tribute to the men they had lost in the dynamite explosion.

Konstabel Els knew nothing of all this, but having found

the doorway to this impregnable fortress, amused himself by mounting the elephant gun in a gun port and aiming it down the road. He wasn't optimist enough to suppose that anything worthy of the fearful weapon was likely to try to enter the Park, but the tedium of his duties persuaded him that there was no harm in being prepared for the most unlikely eventualities.

He had no sooner done this than he spotted an Alsatian dog which had stopped for a pee against one of the gateposts. Konstabel Els was not one to miss opportunities and besides he was still feeling the effects of his encounter with the Dobermann Pinscher. One well-aimed revolver shot and the Alsatian lost all interest in the events of the afternoon. Other people in the neighbourhood of Jacaranda Park were not so fortunate. Five plain-clothes detectives whom Luitenant Verkramp had sent straight up to Jacaranda Park, and who were walking with the utmost discretion and at intervals of twenty-five yards between them, heard the shot, consulted together and began to approach the main gate with drawn revolvers and a degree of furtiveness calculated to excite the suspicions of Konstabel Els in the blockhouse.

Kommandant van Heerden, trudging happily up the drive, also heard the shot, but he was so engrossed in calculating the exact number of strokes Jonathan Hazelstone would receive before being hanged that the sound of one shot coming from Els's direction hardly penetrated his consciousness. He had besides never solved a case before with such rapidity and he had just discovered fresh reasons for justifying his assumption that Jonathan Hazelstone was the murderer. He had recalled that Luitenant Verkramp's report on the Hazelstone family had included the information that Miss Hazelstone's brother had a criminal record involving embezzlement and fraud, and that the family had paid him to live in a remote part of Rhodesia.

It was only when the Kommandant heard a volley of shots ring out from the direction of the gate, followed by the screams of wounded men, that he began to suspect that Els was exceeding his instructions. He hurried on in an attempt to reach the gate before the situation got wholly out of hand, but the density of the firing had by that time reached such dangerous proportions and its aim was so wild that he was forced to take cover in a hollow beside the drive. Lying there out of sight Kommandant van Heerden began to regret that he had given Els permission to shoot to kill. The agonized screams suggested that Els was having at the very least some moderate degree of success. As stray bullets ricochetted overhead, the Kommandant racked his brains to imagine who on earth was trying to shoot it out with his assistant.

In the blockhouse Konstabel Els was faced with the same problem. The five sinister figures who had crept round the corner of the road with revolvers in their hands had been so clearly bent on entering the Park illegally that he had shot the first two without hesitation. The answering spatter of bullets through the privet hedge had seemed fully to justify his action and, safe within the blockhouse, Konstabel Els broke open the ammunition packs and prepared for a long battle.

After ten minutes the plain-clothes men were reinforced by a dozen more and Els settled down to the business of defending the gateway with a relish that fully justified his early expectations that the afternoon would prove interesting.

Luitenant Verkramp had been having his own troubles. In trying to put into effect Kommandant van Heerden's

orders he had run into a host of problems. It had been difficult enough to marshal the entire complement of the
Piemburg Police force, including the sick and the walking
wounded, at the barracks on their Rugby afternoon. But
when that had been accomplished he was faced with the
problem of explaining where they were going and why,
and since Kommandant van Heerden had omitted to explain the purpose of the expedition he was left to draw
his own conclusions. The only two certain facts he had
gleaned from the Kommandant's garbled instructions were
that an outbreak of Rabies at Jacaranda Park had coincided
with the appearance of Bubonic Plague, a combination of
disease so lethal that it seemed positively insane to send six
hundred healthy men anywhere near the place. Far better
in his opinion to send them in the opposite direction. Nor
could he understand why six armoured cars were necessary to help abate the outbreak unless it was that the Kommandant thought they might be useful to control the riot
that would certainly break out when the news became
public knowledge. The order to bring the searchlights
added to the Luitenant's confusion and he could only
suppose that they were to be used to search out any infected animals at night so that they could be hunted across
country by the armoured cars.

The speech that Verkramp finally made to the assembled
policemen was not one to inspire them with any confidence in their own futures and it was only after he had
stamped out several incipient signs of mutiny that the
column of lorries and the expedition finally got under
way. As it was the entire force, headed by six armoured
cars bedecked with signs announcing the epidemic of
Bubonic Plague and the Rabies outbreak, wound its way
slowly along side roads and through the country town
of Vlockfontein exciting a degree of attention exceed-

ingly gratifying to the policemen crowding the lorries, but hardly achieving the purpose Kommandant van Heerden had hoped for.

The Bubonic Plague signs caused a degree of alarm in Vlockfontein only surpassed by the Rabies billboards which immediately preceded the lorries containing the untrained German guard dogs, one of which in the excitement broke loose and leapt from the lorry to bite a small boy who had been pulling faces at it. In the panic that ensued the guard dog went berserk, bit a number of other people, several other dogs and finally disappeared up a back alley in pursuit of a cat. Within minutes the convoy had been halted at the request of the Mayor who had insisted that the dog be shot before it could infect anyone else. Verkramp's assurances that the animal was perfectly healthy convinced no one and there was a delay of some twenty-five minutes until it was finally shot by an irate householder on the other side of town.

By that time its desperate search for safety had driven it through back gardens and across lawns, and for almost all the time it had managed to stay out of sight so that its pursuers could only judge its probable whereabouts by the barks and snarls of the dogs belonging to the householders of Vlockfontein. It was therefore not altogether surprising that the notion gained ground that the guard dog had infected the entire canine population of the town, a belief that was confirmed beyond any shadow of doubt by the strange behaviour of the Vlockfontein dogs who, sharing in the general excitement, yelped and barked and strained at their leashes and in general behaved in just that unusual manner that the Rabies notices had warned people to look out for.

As the police convoy wound out of Vlockfontein the afternoon quiet was punctuated by the sound of shots as the massacre of the entire dog population began, while the boy who had caused the whole business was testifying to the extremely painful nature of the anti-rabies injections by adding his screams to those of the dying dogs. The discovery later that evening of several dead rats, which had been killed by dogs desperately trying to prove their utility, only added to the general sense of impending disaster among the Vlockfonteiners. Dead rats, they had learnt from the Bubonic Plague notices, were the first sign that the Black Death had arrived. By nightfall Vlockfontein was a ghost town littered with the corpses of unburied dogs while the roads into Piemburg were jammed with cars whose drivers were exhibiting all the symptoms of mass hysteria. It was clear that the aim that Kommandant van Heerden had hoped to achieve by the detour was not being realized.

The same thing could hardly be said of Konstabel Els. His aim, always accurate, had by this time become positively unerring. The casualties among the plain-clothes men were mounting so rapidly that they fell back from their more advanced positions and huddled in the hedgerow trying to think of some way of circumventing the deadly privet bush which was obstructing them so successfully in the course of their duty. Finally while some of them crept into the thick bushes that covered the hillside directly facing the gateway and far enough away to ensure the deadly revolver couldn't reach them, others decided to try to outflank the murderous bush.

To Konstabel Els it was beginning to become fairly clear that this was no ordinary gun-battle, but something quite new in his experience as an upholder of law and order. He listened with quiet confidence to the hail of bullets that flattened themselves against the walls of the blockhouse. Every now and again he peered out of the gun port that overlooked the park to make sure that no one had worked his way round behind him, but the park was clear. He need not have worried. Sir Theophilus had prepared for just such an eventuality by constructing an extremely deep ditch which ran between the blockhouses that fringed the park. As with so many of the Governor's devices this defensive haha was unexpectedly treacherous and so well camouflaged that anyone approaching it from the road was quite unaware of its existence until he was already impaled on the terrible iron spikes that lined its concrete bottom. The plain-clothes men lost two of their number in the haha before they gave up the attempt to outflank the concealed blockhouse.

The screams that followed this attempt heartened Konstabel Els who imagined that he had scored two new hits in what he had no doubt were extremely painful portions of the human anatomy. He was a little surprised at his success as he had not fired for several minutes and certainly not in the direction from which the screams came. He decided to check his rear again, and peering out of the gunport that overlooked the park was just in time to see Kommandant van Heerden leave his hollow and scuttle towards the house with an astonishing turn of speed for a man of his age and sedentary habits. Kommandant van Heerden had also heard the screams that came from the haha and had reached the frantic conclusion that the time had come to leave the security of his hollow at no matter what cost to life and limb and return to Jacaranda House to try to find out what had happened to the cretinous Luitenant Verkramp.

Whatever the Kommandant's reasons, and they were unknown to Konstabel Els, the sight of his only possible ally scuttling away and leaving him in the lurch convinced

the desperate Els that the time had come to use the elephant gun if he were not to die alone and deserted at the
hands of the desperados down the road. He could see
movement in the bushes on the hillside opposite him and
he decided to try a volley there. He mounted the great
multi-barrelled rifle in the gun port, aimed at the bushes
concealing the plain-clothes men and gently pulled the
trigger.

The detonation that followed was of an intensity and
had about it a seismic quality which came, when he could
pick himself off the floor of the blockhouse where the re-
coil had thrown him, as a complete surprise to Konstabel
Els. Not that he hadn't heard it before, but on that occasion he had been slightly distracted by the attentions of the
Dobermann. This time he could appreciate the true qualities of the weapon.

With a white face and with his eardrums reverberating
quite astonishingly, he peered through the gun port and
observed his handiwork with a sense of satisfaction that
he had never known before, not even on the day he had
shot two kaffirs dead with the same bullet. That had been
a triumph. This was a masterpiece.

The four barrels of the elephant gun erupting simul-
taneously had opened up a vista before him he would
never have believed possible. The great wrought-iron gates
of Jacaranda Park lay a twisted and reeking heap of partially molten and totally unidentifiable metal. The stone
gateposts had disintegrated. The boars rampant sculpted in
granite that had surmounted the posts would ramp no
more, while the roadway itself bore witness to the heat of
the gases propelling the shells in the shape of four lines
of molten and gleaming tarmac which pointed down to
what had once been the thick bushes that had obscured
his view of his adversaries. Konstabel Els had no need now

to complain that he couldn't see what he was shooting at.

The cover his enemies had used was quite gone. The hill-side was bare, barren and scorched and it was doubtful if it would ever regain its original look. There was no such doubt about the five objects that remained littering the ground. Bare, barren and horribly mutilated, the five plain-clothes policemen who had sought cover from Els's fire in the bushes needed far more cover now than mere bushes could provide. Dying instantaneously, they had in some sense been luckier than their surviving comrades, some of whom, Els noted with satisfaction, were wander-ing about naked and blackened and clearly in a state of mental confusion. Els took advantage of their defenceless and shocked state to wing a couple with his revolver and wasn't very surprised that they seemed to take little notice of these new wounds which were obviously an anti-climax after the ravages of the elephant gun. The rest of the plain-clothes men who had been spared the effects of the volley, having dragged their naked and bemused colleagues out of the way of Els's gratuitous target practice, fell back down the hill and awaited the arrival of the main convoy before resuming their attack on the privet bush.

Standing in the turret of the leading armoured-car, Lui-tenant Verkramp had heard the enormous explosion and had immediately jumped to the conclusion that the maga-zine at the police barracks had been blown up by sabo-teurs. Coming as it did in the wake of the chaos and panic that had marked the progress of the convoy through the countryside, it came as no great surprise. But looking down over the town he could see nothing to support this supposition. Piemburg lay in its quiet and peaceful hollow under a cloudless and azure sky. The only unusual feature he could spot through his binoculars was an unbroken chain of cars moving slowly along the main road from

Vlockfontein.

'Funeral down there,' he muttered to himself, and, puzzled by the enormous length of the cortege, wondered what great man had died. It was only when he turned the next corner and saw the tiny group of naked and hysterical plain-clothes men that he realized for the first time that Kommandant van Heerden's frantic instructions had not after all been unwarranted. Whatever was going on at Jacaranda Park deserved the extraordinary show of force the convoy presented.

He held up his hand and the task force ground to a halt. 'What the hell has been going on?' he asked. There was no need to ask what had been coming off. Naked and blackened, the little group of plain-clothes cops presented a pitiful sight.

'Something has been shooting at us,' one of them managed to blurt out at last.

'What do you mean, something?' Verkramp snarled.

'It's a bush. A bush up by the gateway. Every time anyone goes anywhere near it, it shoots them.'

'A bush? Someone hiding behind a bush you mean. Why didn't you fire back at them?'

'What the fuck do you think we've been doing? And it's not anyone behind a bush. I'll take my oath on that. We've pumped hundreds of rounds into that fucking bush and it still goes on firing back. I tell you it's bloody well bewitched, that bush.'

Luitenant Verkramp looked up the road uncertainly. He certainly wasn't going to fall for any crap about bewitched bushes but on the other hand he could see that something pretty extraordinary had reduced the men to their pitiful condition. It was on the tip of his tongue to say, 'You're out of your minds,' but since they were out of just about everything else he thought it better not to. The question of morale was important and it had been at the back of his mind ever since they had left the station. One false move now and there would be a panic in the convoy. He decided to set the men an example.

'I want two volunteers,' he told Sergeant de Kock and while the Sergeant went off to dragoon two mentally retarded konstabels into volunteering, Luitenant Verkramp turned back to the plain-clothes men.

'Where is this bush?' he asked.

'Just inside the gateway. You can't miss it,' they told him, adding, 'And it won't miss you either.'

'We'll see about that,' muttered the Luitenant and clambering off the Saracen he began to prepare for the reconnaissance. Luitenant Verkramp had attended an anti-guerilla course at Pretoria and was well versed in the art of camouflage. By the time he had finished the three men who began crawling up the ditch towards Konstabel Els's privet bush resembled nothing so much as three small bushes themselves. They were not so well trimmed, it was true, and certainly not so bullet-proof, but whatever else their camouflage served to conceal it was quite impossible to tell even at close range that here were three uniformed men of the South African Police.

Chapter 6

Kommandant van Heerden had just paused for breath under an oak tree in the middle of Jacaranda Park and was trying to pluck up courage to return to the house when Konstabel Els fired the elephant gun. In the wake of the detonation that followed the Kommandant had his mind made up for him. For one thing a vulture which had been waiting with evident prescience in the branches above him was startled into flight by the roar of the gun and flapped horribly up into the sky. For another the Kommandant reached the immediate conclusion that the company of Jonathan Hazelstone was infinitely less murderous than the holocaust Konstabel Els was generating at the main gate. He left the cover of the tree and raced ponderously towards the house, looking for all the world like the maddened pachyderm the elephant gun had been designed to incapacitate.

Behind him the silence of recent death hung sombrely over Jacaranda Park. Ahead he could just make out the tall elegant figure of Miss Hazelstone standing on the stoep. She was looking tentatively up into the cloudless evening sky. As the Kommandant plunged past her into the drawing-room he heard her say, 'I thought I heard a clap of thunder just now. I do believe it's going to rain.' It was good to be back in a world of sanity, the Kommandant thought, as he dropped limp and exhausted into an easy chair.

Presently Miss Hazelstone turned from her study of the sunset and entered the room. She carried with her an

atmosphere of tranquillity and an acceptance of life as it
came to her unique, or so it appeared to Kommandant van
Heerden, among the people who were living through the
events of the afternoon at Jacaranda Park. The same
could hardly be said of Konstabel Els. Whatever life was
coming his way he certainly wasn't accepting with anything faintly approaching tranquillity. The only consolation Kommandant van Heerden could find was the
thought that by the sound of it Els had blown himself and
half the neighbouring suburb up.

Miss Hazelstone moved pensively and with an air of
gentle melancholy to her wing-backed armchair and seating herself in it turned her face with a look of the pro-
foundest reverence towards a painting that hung above
the fireplace.

'He was a good man,' she said at last in a low voice.

Kommandant van Heerden followed her gaze and
studied the painting. It portrayed a man in long robes and
carrying a lantern in his hand at the door of a house,
and the Kommandant supposed it to be yet another portrait of Sir Theophilus, painted this time, to judge by the
robe he was wearing, while the great man had been serving in India. It was entitled, 'The Light of the World',
which even the Kommandant for all his admiration of the
viceroy, thought was going a bit far. Still he felt called
upon to say something.

'I'm sure he was,' he said sympathetically, 'and a very
great man too.'

Miss Hazelstone looked at the Kommandant gratefully
and with new respect.

'I had no idea,' she murmured.

'Oh, I practically worship the man,' the Kommandant
continued, adding as an afterthought, 'He knew how to
handle the Zulus all right,' and was surprised when Miss

Hazelstone began to sob into her handkerchief. Taking her tears to be a further indication of her devotion to her grandfather, van Heerden ploughed on.

'I only wish there were more of his sort about today,' he said, and was gratified to notice Miss Hazelstone once more gazing at him gratefully over her handkerchief. 'There wouldn't be half the trouble there is in the world today if he were back.' He was about to say, 'He'd hang them by the dozen,' but he realized that hanging wasn't a tactful subject to bring up considering the likely fate of Miss Hazelstone's own brother, so he contented himself by adding, 'He'd soon teach them a thing or two.'

Miss Hazelstone agreed. 'He would, oh, he would. I'm so glad, Kommandant, that you of all people see things his way.'

Kommandant van Heerden couldn't quite see the need for her emphasis. It seemed only natural that a police officer would want to follow Sir Theophilus's methods of dealing with criminals. After all, Judge Hazelstone hadn't sucked his known preference for hanging and flogging out of his thumb. Everyone knew that old Sir Theophilus had made it his duty to see that young William early developed a taste for corporal punishment by inflicting it on the boy practically from the day he was born. The thought of duty recalled the Kommandant to his own distasteful task, and he realized that this was as good a moment as any to break it to her that he knew that Fivepence had been murdered not by her, but by her brother Jonathan. He rose from his chair and relapsed into the formal jargon of his office.

'I have reason to believe....' he began, but Miss Hazelstone wouldn't let him continue. She rose from her chair and gazed up at him enraptured, a reaction van Heerden had hardly expected and certainly couldn't admire. After all, the fellow was her own brother, and only an hour before she had been willing to confess to the murder herself just to shield him.

He began again, 'I have reason to believe—'

'Oh, so have I. So have I. Haven't we all?' and this time Miss Hazelstone gathered the Kommandant's large hands into her own tiny ones and gazed into his eyes. 'I knew it Kommandant, I knew it all the time.'

Kommandant van Heerden needed no telling. Of course she had known about it all the time, otherwise she wouldn't have been covering up for the brute. To hell, he thought, with formalities. 'I suppose he's still upstairs in the bedroom,' he said.

The expression on Miss Hazelstone's face suggested a certain wonder which the Kommandant assumed must be due to her sudden recognition of his talents as a detective.

'Upstairs?' she gasped.

'Yes. In the bedroom with the pink floral bedspread.'

Miss Hazelstone's astonishment was obvious. 'In the pink bedroom?' she stammered, backing away from him.

'He's not a very pleasant sight, I'm afraid,' the Kommandant went on. 'He's as drunk as a lord.'

Miss Hazelstone was verging on hysteria. 'As the Lord?' she managed to gasp at last.

'Soused,' continued the Kommandant. 'Blind drunk and covered with blood. Guilt's written all over him.'

Miss Hazelstone could stand no more. She made for the door but Kommandant van Heerden was there before her.

'Oh no you don't. You're not going upstairs to warn him,' he said. 'He's got to take what's coming to him.' Kommandant van Heerden had private doubts if the fellow was still upstairs. Even a blind drunk must have been jerked awake by that explosion. Still the man was a maniac and one never knew with lunatics. Their actions were likely to be unpredictable. There were symptoms too, he now noticed, of irrationality and unpredictability in Miss Hazelstone's behaviour, and signs that she could behave in a manner neither sweet nor gentle.

'Come, come, my dear Miss Hazelstone. There are some things we must learn to accept,' he said reassuringly, and as he said it, Miss Hazelstone knew only one thing for certain, that nothing on God's earth would persuade her to come anywhere within striking distance of this fat perspiring policeman who thought that Jesus Christ was lying dead drunk and covered with blood upstairs in the pink floral bedroom. There might be, she conceded generously, certain irrational tendencies in her own psyche, but they were as nothing to the inescapable symptoms of insanity that the Kommandant was displaying. She sprang back from him white and gibbering and, seizing an ornamental scimitar that hung on the wall, held it above her old grey head in her two hands.

Kommandant van Heerden was taken totally by surprise. One moment he had been confronted by a dear old lady who held both his hands in hers and gazed tenderly up into his face, and the next she had turned herself into a dancing dervish evidently intent on slicing him in half with a terrible knife.

'Now, now,' he said, unable to adjust his pattern of speech to his new and terrifying predicament. A moment later it was clear that Miss Hazelstone had taken his 'Now, now' as an indication that he wanted his death to be immediate. She was moving crablike towards him.

Miss Hazelstone was, in fact, trying to reach the door into the hall. 'Stand aside,' she ordered, and the Kommandant, anxious to avoid causing her the slightest pretext for bifurcating him with the scimitar, leapt to one side, colliding as he went with a large Chinese pot which toppled from its stand and crashed to the floor. For a second time the expression on Miss Hazelstone's face demonstrated that capacity for rapid change the Kommandant had already noticed. Now she was clearly mad with rage.

'The Ming! The Ming!' she yelled and brought the scimitar crashing down from above her head. But Kommandant van Heerden was no longer there. He was charging across the room leaving in his wake the shattered art treasures of several millennia of Chinese history.

As he plunged across the verandah he could still hear Miss Hazelstone screaming to her brother.

'The Ming! The Ming!' she yelled and judging the Ming to be some indescribably powerful weapon hanging ready to hand on the wall of the gallery, the Kommandant raced across Jacaranda Park yet again, but this time in the direction of the sound of renewed gunfire at the gate, a sound he now welcomed as indications of normal healthy violence. And as he ran, he thanked his lucky stars that dusk was already turning into night, to obscure the path of his flight.

The first indication that Konstabel Els, still smirking at the effects of his marksmanship, had that several new factors had entered the little patch of Western civilization he was defending so manfully, came as dusk began to fall over the Park's contorted gates. He was just having a swig of Old Rhino Skin brandy to keep out the night chill, when he heard a strange scratching noise outside. He thought at first that a porcupine was scratching itself against the armoured door of the blockhouse, but when he opened it there was nothing outside, while the sounds were getting closer. They seemed to emanate from a hedge down the road, and he had just begun to think that they could only be explained by supposing that a rhinoceros suffering from impetigo was seeking relief from its irritation by rolling in a thorn tree when he saw three remarkably agile agglomerations of vegetable matter scuttle across the road. Evidently the next attack was about to begin.

Konstabel Els sat back and considered the position. He had repelled one attack with his revolver. He had decimated a second with the elephant gun. It was time, he felt, to go over to the offensive. In the deepening dusk Konstabel Els left the shelter of the blockhouse, and clutching his revolver crawled silently towards his attackers, whose polyphonic progress drowned any slight noises he might make.

By the time Luitenant Verkramp and his two volunteers had crawled three-quarters of a mile to the top of the hill, Verkramp had begun to wish that he had come up in the armoured car after all, and to doubt the value of the whole exercise. It was already so dark that while he might not be able to miss the bush that was giving so much trouble, he probably wouldn't be able to see it. His hands were scratched and torn, and he had come within spitting distance of two puff-adders and a cobra, which had been an undoubted tribute to his skill in camouflage, but one that he could well have done without. He had never realized before what a profusion of wild life there was in the hedgerows of Piemburg.

The spider that had bitten him on the nose as he tried to disentangle himself from its web had been of a size and malevolence he would never have believed possible if he hadn't seen it with his own one eye, the other being obscured by the spider's three feet which it had fastened there to give it a good foothold while it injected

50 cc of toxic venom into his left nostril. He had almost turned back at that point because the poison spread so fast and with such evident effect that even after the giant spider had been good enough to let go of his cornea he still couldn't see out of it. That side of his face was pulsating alarmingly and his sinus appeared to be filled with some caustic liquid. Realizing that the expedition must proceed with some urgency before his breathing apparatus seized up for good, Luitenant Verkramp and his two men crashed on through the infested undergrowth towards their quarry.

Konstabel Els, crawling with less haste and more anonymity, had, in the meantime, discovered Sir Theophilus's terrible haha and had observed with considerable satisfaction its effects on its latest victims. Els lay back in the grass and debated some further means of satisfying the clearly insatiable appetite of this offspring of Sir Theophilus's anxiety. The sounds reaching him from the hedgerow seemed to indicate that his enemies were already suffering some trepidation. To the sounds of breaking twigs that had accompanied their progress were now added the occasional whimper and what appeared to be chronic catarrh. Konstabel Els waited no longer. Crawling soundlessly he avoided the murderous haha and stationed himself in the grass beside the road.

To Luitenant Verkramp crawling doggedly in the hedge nothing seemed ominous or unusual. His nose was giving him trouble, it was true, and the spider's venom had spread alarmingly so that now his eyes were playing him up and now his ears, but if his interior world was full of flashing lights and strange drumming noises, outside all seemed peaceful and quiet. The night was dark, but overhead the stars shone and the lights of Piemburg in the valley below gave to the sky an orange glow. The lights of Jacaranda House twinkled invitingly across the park. Crickets sang and the distant murmur of traffic wafted gently to him from the Vlockfontein road. Nothing in the world prepared Luitenant Verkramp for the horror that was to strike him so suddenly.

Not that anything struck him physically. It was worse than that. There was an almost spiritual quality about the scream that exploded in his damaged ear, and about the appallingly crooked and malignant shape that suddenly loomed above him. He couldn't see what it was. He knew only its disgusting breath and with it a banshee yell, malignant beyond belief, and coming, he had no doubt at all, from the very depths of hell. Any doubts Luitenant Verkramp had entertained about the story of the be-witched bush disappeared in a trice, and in another trice Verkramp, hurling himself sideways, dropped into the very pit of hell he suspected the scream came from. Lying impaled on the iron spikes at the bottom of the haha, his screams echoing across the park, Luitenant Verkramp, half dead with fear and pain, stared upwards and knew himself eternally damned. In his delirium he saw a face peer down into his grave, a face diabolically satisfied: the face was the face of Els. Luitenant Verkramp passed out.

His two companions had by that time reached the foot of the hill. They had fled, leaving behind them not only the Luitenant but a trail of leaves, branches, helmets, and all the impedimenta of their profession. They need not have hurried. The news of the encounter had preceded them. Konstabel Els's yell, terrible even *diminuendo*, had wafted like some fearful confirmation of doom to the cars that still jammed the Vlockfontein road.

The policemen lounging by the lorries and armoured cars grew rigid at its import. Men who had been erecting some of the Rabies and Bubonic Plague billboards stopped work and stared into the darkness trying to make out what new horror had sprung from the deadly bush. Even the guard dogs cringed at the sound. And in the middle of Jacaranda Park, Kommandant van Heerden, in terror of his life from the ming, halted involuntarily at the sound. No one who heard that scream was ever likely to forget it.

If Konstabel Els had been astounded at the effect of the elephant gun, he was even more astounded at the results of his experiment in psychological warfare. His imitation of the awakened dead had borne fruit among his vegetable enemies to an extent he wouldn't have believed possible, but as he stood listening to the ebbing screams from the ditch, a momentary shadow of doubt crossed his mind. There was something about those screams, something about their tone that was vaguely familiar. He went over to the haha and peered down, and was just able to make out through the foliage that covered it, a face, and again there was something familiar about that face. If it hadn't been for the bulbous nose and the puffed-up cheeks, he might have thought it was Luitenant Verkramp down there. He grinned to himself at the thought of the Luitenant lying on those spikes. Serve the bastard right if he had been down there for keeping him hanging around all night when he should have been relieved hours ago, he thought as he entered the blockhouse.

He took another swig of brandy and was just putting the bottle back in his hip pocket when he heard a sound that sent him hurrying to the gun port. Something was coming up the road. Some vehicle, and a touch of familiarity caught his ear. It sounded for all the world like a Saracen armoured car. 'About bloody time too,' Els thought, as the headlights swung round the corner and lit up for a second the bodies lying on the hillside opposite. A moment later a fresh light was thrown on the scene. A searchlight probed through the night and turned the privet hedge into one brilliant spot in an otherwise dark world.

'All right, you bastards, enough's as good as a fucking feast,' Els yelled into the night, and before he could say more the privet hedge began to disintegrate around his shelter. As the bullets tore into the blockhouse walls and the gun port was aflame with tracer bullets, Els knew that he was about to die. This wasn't the relief he expected. In one last desperate move to avert tragedy, Konstabel Els aimed the elephant gun at the armoured-car. He held his fire until the Saracen was only ten yards from the gate and then pulled the trigger. Again and again he fired, and with a mixture of awe and satisfaction saw, silhouetted against the searchlight, the great armoured vehicle grind to a halt and begin to disintegrate. Its guns were silenced, its tyres were shreds of rubber and its occupants trickled gently but persistently through a hundred holes drilled in its sides. Only one man was even capable of trying to leave the thing and as he emerged convulsively from the turret top, Els saw with appalling clarity the familiar uniform and cap of the South African Police. The body slumped back inside the turret, and Els, understanding dimly for the first time the enormity of his offences, knew himself but a stone's throw from the gallows. He fired his last shot. The searchlight exploded into darkness and Els, with desperate energy, gathered up all evidence of his recent occupation and stumbled out of the blockhouse and dragging his awful accomplice, sneaked off across the park.

Behind him the armoured colander burst into flames and as Els hurled himself towards Jacaranda House the night sky was bright with the flames and the delicate tracery of exploding ammunition.

Chapter 7

In Jacaranda House, Jonathan Hazelstone was singing in his bath. He was wearing a rubber bathing-cap to protect his delicate ears from the water, and partly because of the cap and partly because he was rather deaf, he was singing rather more loudly than he imagined. As a result he heard nothing of the noises of battle that accompanied his rendering of 'Onward Christian Soldiers'. Around him the pink water eddied and swirled, assuming strange intricate patterns as the percussion of the elephant gun reached it. But Jonathan Hazelstone had no time for observing such trifles. His mind was preoccupied with his own shortcomings. Shame and a guilty pride at his own achievement mingled in his thoughts and over them both there hung the awful remembrance of things past.

He tried to put the dreadful business out of his mind but it came back insistently. Still, in spite of his remorse he had to smile to himself a little. After all, he thought, there couldn't be many men still alive who could say that they had done what he had and got away with it. Not that he was given to boastfulness, and he certainly was not going to go about broadcasting his deed. On the other hand he had been provoked quite horribly, and in the event he felt that his action had to some extent been excusable. 'Old Rhino Skin,' he thought, and shuddered, and was about to remind himself that he must tell the cook never to use the beastly stuff for cooking again, when he remembered that there was in fact no cook to tell.

He looked sadly at the pink ring on the sides of the
bath and then hurriedly got out and emptied the water.
He sluiced the bath clean, refilled it and added bath salts
and then lay down in the hot water to consider what to do
next to erase the effects of the afternoon's events. He was
faced, he knew, with a terrible problem. True, his sister
had promised to make a full confession to the police and
that was all right as far as it went, but it wasn't going to
help him to escape scot-free. There were bound to be
repercussions, and the whole episode was hardly calculated to help his career. It was a ghastly business altogether.
Not that he had a great fund of sympathy for that damned
cook. If it hadn't been for him, none of this would have
happened. Besides, there were some things that Jonathan
Hazelstone could never forgive. Perversion was one of
them.

Kommandant van Heerden would have shared all these
sentiments had he known about them, but by this time
his faculties were all focused on one simple realization,
that his career as a police officer and probably as a free
man had almost certainly been ended by his handling of
the Hazelstone Case. The explosion that heralded the end
of the armoured car had made that clear as daylight to
him. Disgraced, cashiered and convicted of being an
accessory before, during, and after the murder of the
policemen who had undoubtedly fallen before Els's
tornado of gunshot at the main gate, he would share the
rest of his life in prison with men who bore him debts of
ingratitude no amount of suffering would ever repay. The
day he entered Piemburg Prison might not be his last, but
it would undoubtedly be his worst. Too many men had
signed confessions after being tortured by Konstabel Els
in the cells of Piemburg Police Station for him to relish

the prospect of their company in prison.

After a brief spell of sobbing Kommandant van Heerden tried to think of some way out of the mess Els had got him into. Only one thing could save him now and that was the successful capture of the murderer of Miss Hazelstone's Zulu cook. Not that he placed much hope in that achievement and it wouldn't help to explain the bloodbath Els had initiated. No, Els would have to stand trial for wholesale murder and there was just a chance that he could be persuaded to plead insanity. Come to think of it, there was no need for the bastard to have to plead. He was obviously insane. The facts spoke for themselves.

Urged forward by this faint hope and certainly not by the exploding ammunition in the once-mobile incinerator, Kommandant van Heerden reached the park gates. Clambering over the pile of contorted metal the Kommandant stood and looked about him. A pall of black smoke darkened the night sky. It poured from the open turret of the Saracen and issued from the holes in its sides. Even the distracted Kommandant was aware of its smell. It smelt like nothing on earth. Taking a deep breath of the disgusting stuff, Kommandant van Heerden bellowed into the night.

'Konstabel Els,' he yelled, 'Konstabel Els, where in fuck's name are you?' and recognized the stupidity of the question as soon as it was uttered. Els was hardly likely to come forward at this juncture. More likely he would consign his commanding officer to eternity with the same relish he had employed on his other comrades. After a moment's silence punctuated only by the bang and whizz of bullets ricochetting round the interior of the Saracen the Kommandant shouted again.

'This is your commanding officer, I order you to cease fire.'

Down the road the sound of Kommandant van Heerden's strange order puzzled the men in the convoy and brought a warm glow of admiration to their hearts. The Kommandant was up there by the gates and had evidently captured the maniac who had been slaughtering them. They were amazed at this development, for the Kommandant was not known for his physical courage. Slowly but surely in little groups they made their way hesitantly up the road towards him.

Konstabel Els was making off in quite a different direction and racking his brains for a way of getting out of the mess he was in. First of all he had to conceal the elephant gun and then he would have to concoct an alibi. Considering the size of the gun he wasn't sure which was going to be the more impossible task, and he was just debating whether or not to put it back on the stoep, where he had found it, when he ran across another privet hedge. His recent experience of privet hedges had taught him that they were ideal places for hiding things in. In this case the privet hedge hid a swimming-bath. Els peered round the hedge, and after reassuring himself that the swimming-bath was what it purported to be and not yet another of Sir Theophilus's little traps, he stole into the enclosure and across to a small and elegant pavilion which stood at one end. He groped round in the dark for a moment and then struck a match. By its light he saw that the pavilion was a changing-room with pegs along its wall for hanging clothes. To his horror he saw that one of the pegs was being put to good use. A suit of dark clothes was hanging there.

Els doused the match and peered out at the pool. The owner of the black suit must be out there watching him, he thought. But the surface of the swimming-bath was unbroken by anything more sinister than reflections of the stars and a new moon which had just begun to rise. The edges of the pool held no unaccountable shadows and Els knew himself to be alone with a suit of dark clothes, an elephant gun, and the need to concoct an alibi.

'Privet hedges seem to bring me luck,' he said to himself and promised himself to plant one in his front garden if he ever got out of this scrape alive.

He lit another match and examined the clothes. He thought at first that he might be able to use them as a disguise but the trousers were much too large for him, while the jacket which he tried on would have done as a winter coat. He was a little puzzled by the black waistcoat with no buttons on it until he spotted the attached dog-collar. Konstabel Els gave up all thought of using the clothes as a disguise. He had too much respect for religion to profane the garments with his own person. Instead he used them to wipe the elephant gun clean of his fingerprints. An expert in removing vital evidence, by the time he had finished there was nothing to connect him with the gun.

Twenty minutes later Konstabel Els stepped jauntily out of the pavilion and sauntered cheerfully across the park towards Piemburg. Behind him he had left everything that connected him with the massacre at the main gate. The elephant gun was concealed under the clergyman's clothes. In a back pocket of the trousers was his revolver while the jacket pockets bulged with the empty cartridge cases he had carefully collected from the floor of the blockhouse. Each and every article had been meticulously polished. No fingerprint expert could prove that they had been used by Konstabel Els. Finally, and with a touch of whimsy, he had put the half bottle of Old Rhino Skin into the inside breast pocket of the jacket. It had been quite empty and he had no use for empty bottles anyway.

It was while he was shoving the bottle into the pocket that he made another useful discovery. The pocket contained a wallet and comb. Konstabel Els searched the other pockets and found a handkerchief and several other objects.

'Nothing like doing a job properly,' he thought pocketing the things and set off for the blockhouse for one final visit. By the time he reached it his confidence had returned. Policemen were wandering around looking at the burning Saracen and no one took any notice of the Konstabel who nipped for a second behind the privet hedge before strolling off down the road in the direction of Piemburg. On the way he stopped to read a notice which was being hammered into place by a group of policemen.

An hour later, foaming at the mouth and exhibiting all the symptoms of rabies, Konstabel Els presented himself at the casualty department of Piemburg Hospital. Before they could get him into bed he had bitten two nurses and a doctor.

At the entrance to Jacaranda Park Kommandant van Heerden was exhibiting similar symptoms to the men who gathered round him under the pall of smoke. The disappearance of Luitenant Verkramp particularly incensed him.

'Missing? What do you mean missing?' he yelled at Sergeant de Kock.

'He came up here to reconnoitre, sir,' answered the Sergeant.

'Any chance he came in that?' asked the Kommandant more hopefully, looking at the burnt out Saracen.

'No sir. In disguise.'

'In what?' yelled the Kommandant.

'He was disguised as a bush, sir.'

Kommandant van Heerden couldn't believe his ears. 'Disguised as a bush? What sort of bush?'

'Difficult to say, sir. Not a very big one.'

Kommandant van Heerden turned to the men. 'Any of you men seen a small bush round here?'

A hush fell over the policemen. They had all seen a small bush round there.

'There's one just behind you, sir,' a konstabel said.

The Kommandant turned and looked at what remained of the privet hedge. It was obviously nothing like Verkramp disguised or not. 'Not that you fool,' he snarled. 'A walking fucking bush.'

'I don't know about that bush fucking, sir,' said the konstabel. 'And I daresay it can't walk, but I do know the bloody thing can shoot straight.'

'What the hell are you talking about?' snapped the Kommandant as a nervous giggle ran round the crowd.

Sergeant de Kock enlightened him. 'The fellow who knocked out the Saracen took cover behind that bush.'

A moment later Kommandant van Heerden was peering through the doorway into the blockhouse. The interior was still filled with the fumes of burnt powder, but even so Kommandant van Heerden's olfactory nerve could detect a pervasive familiar smell. The blockhouse stank of Old Rhino Skin. On the floor there was further evidence. A wallet, a comb, and a handkerchief lay in the middle of the bunker. The Kommandant picked them up and gingerly held them to his nose. They were practically soaked in brandy. He opened the wallet and saw stamped in gold letters a name he was also familiar with, 'Jonathan Hazelstone'.

Kommandant van Heerden wasted no more time. Leaving the bunker, he gave his orders. The Park was to be surrounded. Road blocks were to be set up on all roads in the vicinity. Searchlights were to illuminate the entire area of the park. 'We're going in to get him,' he said finally. 'Bring up the other Saracens, and the guard dogs.'

Ten minutes later the five remaining Saracens, a hundred men armed with sten guns and the sixty-nine tracker dogs were assembled at the Park gates ready for the assault on Jacaranda House. Kommandant van Heerden climbed aboard a Saracen and addressed the men from its turret.

'Before we start,' he said, 'I think I had better warn you that the man we are after is a dangerous criminal.' He paused. The policemen who had seen the burnt-out armoured car and the corpses littering the hillside needed no telling. 'The house is practically a fortress,' continued the Kommandant, 'and he has at his disposal an armoury of lethal weapons. At the first sign of resistance you have my permission to open fire. Are there any questions?'

'What about the Black Death?' Sergeant de Kock asked anxiously.

'The black's death? Oh yes, caused by gunshot wounds,' replied the Kommandant enigmatically, and disappearing inside the turret slammed the lid. The convoy moved off cautiously down the drive to Jacaranda House.

Chapter 8

Jonathan Hazelstone's musings on his next sermon had taken his mind off the tragic death of Fivepence. He had just decided on the title, 'The Rhinos of Wrath are Whiter than the Horses of Destruction', for a peroration on the evils of alcohol and was drying himself after his bath when he remembered he had left his clothes in the bathing-pavilion. Still groggy from the effects of the brandy he wandered absent-mindedly downstairs wearing the bathing-cap and wrapped only in a voluminous towel. On the steps of the front door he stopped and took a deep breath of cool night air. Headlights were moving slowly down the drive.

'Visitors,' he thought to himself. 'Mustn't be caught like this,' and wrapping the towel more firmly round himself trotted across the drive and disappeared behind the privet hedge as Kommandant van Heerden's convoy approached the house. He went into the bathing-pavilion and a moment later came out again feeling worse than ever. The smell of Old Rhino Skin in the pavilion sent a wave of nausea over him. Standing on the edge of the swimming-pool, he uttered a silent prayer to the Almighty to help him by no matter what drastic methods to avoid the repetition of his wickedness, and a moment later the Bishop of Barotseland plunged through the moon's reflected image into the cool water of the bath. He swam the length of the pool underwater, surfaced momentarily and then

swam back and forth along the bottom of the swimming-
pool and as he swam it seemed to the Bishop that the Lord
was calling to him. Faintly, very faintly it was true, but
with a distinctness he had never before experienced he
heard through his bathing-cap the voice of the Lord,
'Jonathan Hazelstone, I know you are there. I don't want
any resistance. Give yourself up quietly,' and six feet beneath the surface of the water the Right Reverend Jonathan Hazelstone knew for the first time that he was truly
destined for great things. The call he had waited so long
to hear had come at last. He turned on his back and gave
himself up quietly and without any resistance to meditation under the night sky. He knew now that he had been
forgiven his lapse of the afternoon.

'O Lord, thou knowest I was provoked,' he murmured,
as he floated on the still surface of the pool, and a sense
of peace, sweet forgiving peace, descended on him as he
prayed.

Peace had not descended on the rest of Jacaranda House.
Ringed by one hundred armed men who crouched in the
shadows of the garden fingering the triggers of their sten
guns, by sixty-nine German guard dogs snarling and slobbering for a kill and by five Saracen armoured-cars which
had been driven heedlessly over flowerbeds and lawns to
take up their positions, Jacaranda House stood silent and
unanswering.

Kommandant van Heerden decided to have one more go
at getting the brute out without trouble. The very last
thing he wanted was another gun-battle. He peered out of
the turret and raised the loudhailer again.

'Jonathan Hazelstone, I am giving you one last chance,'
his voice amplified a hundred times boomed into the night.

'If you come out quietly you will be safe. If not, I am coming in to get you.'

The Bishop of Barotseland, lying on his back meditating quietly and staring up into the night sky where a great bird drifted slowly above him, heard the words more distinctly than before. God manifested Himself in many mysterious ways, he knew, but vultures he had never thought of. Now the Almighty had spoken again and more clearly, much more clearly.

The first part of the message had been quite unequivocal. 'Come out quietly and you will be saved,' but the second part had been much less easy to interpret; 'If not, I am coming in to get you.' Jonathan Hazelstone swam to the edge of the pool and climbed out quietly as instructed. Then pausing to look back at the water to see if the Lord had even begun to get in to fetch him out, he noticed the vulture turn and flap horribly away over the blue gums.

'He chased me down the nights and down the days,' he murmured incorrectly, remembering the Hound of Heaven, and he knew that he had been witness that night not only to the voice of God but to his shape as well. If God could come as Doves and Hounds why not as a Vulture? And murmuring another poem his grandfather had taught him as a child, one which he had never understood until these last few minutes, he began to dry himself.

'The harbingers are come. See, see their mark;
Black is their colour, and behold my head.
But must they have my brain? Must they dispark
Those sparkling notions, which therein were bred?
Must dulnesse turn me to a clod?
Yet have they left me, Thou art still my God.'

It was called 'The Forerunners', by George Herbert, and while old Sir Theophilus had revised it by changing white to black in the second line, and had assumed that 'sparkling notions' referred to his murderous haha, the Bishop now saw that it applied perfectly to the vulture and was grateful to note that the harbinger had indeed left him. With a silent prayer to the Lord to assume a less ominous form in future, the Bishop of Barotseland entered the pavilion to fetch his clothes.

Fifty yards away Kommandant van Heerden was making up his mind to give the order to storm the house, when Miss Hazelstone appeared in the main entrance.

'There's no need to shout,' she said demurely. 'There is a bell, you know.'

The Kommandant wasn't in the mood for lessons in etiquette. 'I've come for your brother,' he shouted.

'I'm afraid he's busy just at the moment. You'll have to wait. You can come in if you wipe your boots and promise not to knock anything over.'

The Kommandant could imagine just how busy Jonathan Hazelstone must be and he had every intention of knocking things over if he had to come into the house. He glanced uneasily at the windows on the upper floor.

'What is he so busy about?' as though there was any need to ask.

Miss Hazelstone didn't like the Kommandant's tone of voice. 'He's about his ablutions,' she snapped, and was about to turn away when she remembered the breakage. 'About that Ming....' she began. With a slam of the turret-top Kommandant van Heerden disappeared. From inside the armoured car came the muffled sound of his voice.

'Don't talk to me about the ming,' he yelled. 'You go in

and tell your brother to unblute the fucking thing and come out with his hands up.'

Miss Hazelstone had stood as much as she could take. 'How dare you speak to me like that,' she snarled. 'I'll do no such thing,' and turned to re-enter the house.

'Then I will,' screamed the Kommandant, and ordered his men into the house. 'Get the bastard,' he yelled, and waited for the roar of the deadly ming. He waited in vain. The men and dogs pouring over Miss Hazelstone's prostrate body encountered no further resistance. The Dobermann, knowing now what lack of foresight it had shown by disputing its patch of lawn with Konstabel Els, lay on the drawing-room floor pretending to be a rug. Around it policemen and dogs charged, searching the house for their quarry. There was no human obstacle to the policemen who dashed upstairs and along corridors into bedrooms in search of the killer. Disconsolate, they reported to the Kommandant who was still cowering in the Saracen.

'He's not there,' they yelled.

'Are you absolutely certain?' he asked before opening the lid. They were, and the Kommandant clambered out. He knew there was only one thing left to do, one slim chance of capturing Jonathan Hazelstone that night.

'The dogs,' he ordered frantically. 'Bring the tracker dogs,' and dashed despairing into the house and up the stairs followed by the pack of breathless and eager Alsatians. The pink floral bedroom was just as the Kommandant had seen it last—with the notable exception of the naked man. Grabbing the bedspread from the bed he held it out to the dogs to smell. As the dogs sniffed the cloth and passed off down the corridor they read its message loud and clear. The thing reeked of Old Rhino Skin brandy. Ignoring the odour of bath salts on the stairs the dogs bounded down into the hall and out on to the drive. A

moment later they had picked up the trail Konstabel Els
had left and were off across the park towards the blockhouse.

Behind them in the privacy of the pavilion the Bishop of
Barotseland was having some difficulty in getting dressed.
For one thing his clothes seemed to have wrapped themselves round some heavy metallic object and when at last
the Bishop had disentangled the thing and had carried it
out into the moonlight to see what it was, he was so dis-
tressed by its associations with the murder of Fivepence
that in his agitation he dropped it and the great gun
splashed into the pool and disappeared. Consoling himself
with the thought that it could do no more harm down
there, he went back into the pavilion to put on the rest of
his clothes.

He had some more difficulty with his trousers. There
was something large and heavy in his back pocket, and
it took him some time to get it out.

'Ah well,' he said to himself as he struggled to pull the
revolver loose, 'these things are sent to try us,' and was
trying to imagine how on earth the weapon could have
found its way into his trouser pocket when he became
aware that he was no longer alone.

With the departure of the dogs in pursuit of Konstabel
Els, Kommandant van Heerden found himself with time
on his hands. His mood of melancholy had returned with
the disappearance of the murderer and, not wishing to
share what promised to be his lonely vigil with an irate
and unpredictable Miss Hazelstone, he left his hostess still
recovering from the novel experience of being used as a
doormat by 200 hobnailed boots and 276 paws and wandered miserably out into the garden. As the Kommandant

sauntered about the lawn viciously kicking the pieces of Sir Theophilus's shattered bust, he came near to cursing the great hero of his yesteryears for having spawned the line of progeny that had brought his career crashing to the ground as effectively as they had the bust of Sir Theophilus himself.

He was just considering what the Viceroy would have done had he found himself in a similar situation when his attention was drawn to one of the blue gums. An odd sort of knocking and ripping sound was coming from its trunk. Kommandant van Heerden peered into the gloom. Something strange was moving there. By bending down so that the creature was silhouetted against the orange glow that coloured the night sky, the Kommandant could make out its shape. In imitation of a woodpecker, the great vulture hung to the trunk of the tree and contented itself with scraps of the late Zulu cook.

For the second time that night the vulture brought a message to a watcher in the garden of Jacaranda House, but if the Bishop of Barotseland had mistaken the bird for the shape of God, Kommandant van Heerden made no such error. What he had seen of the scavenger's hooked profile reminded him too closely for comfort of several prisoners in Piemburg gaol who would welcome his arrival there with just such relish. The Kommandant shuddered and turned hastily away from this vision of his future. And as he turned away he heard a loud splash coming from the back of the house. Loud splashes played no part in the regime he had imposed on Jacaranda Park. There was something, he felt, positively sinister in loud splashes at this time of night, a view which was evidently shared by the vulture which flapped hopefully away from its hors d'œuvres to see if its next course was going to be something drowned.

Kommandant van Heerden followed it less optimistically and found himself beside a privet hedge on the other side of which he could hear something going about some grim business. Whatever was busy behind the hedge was reciting to itself as it worked, work which necessitated the dropping of large heavy objects, weighted no doubt, into deep water. The Kommandant couldn't hear much of the song because from behind him across the park there came the sound of running feet and a slobbering and snuffling noise which gained intensity from moment to moment. He glanced over his shoulder and saw racing towards him the pack of tracker dogs and dozens of policemen. A few seconds later they were on him and, pinned to the hedge, he watched the tide of animals and men wash past him and round the corner. He sighed with relief and followed in their wake.

The Bishop of Barotseland was less fortunate. His poor hearing and the fact that he was still wearing the bathing cap prevented him hearing the approach of the dogs. One moment he was standing by the pool looking down at the revolver, and reciting from his grandfather's favourite poem, and the next he was engulfed in dogs. Muzzles raised, fangs bared, with slobbering jowls they came, and the Bishop, overwhelmed by their rush, fell backwards into the swimming-pool, still clutching the revolver. As he went he involuntarily pulled the trigger and a single shot disappeared harmlessly into the night sky. The Bishop surfaced in the middle of the pool and looked around him. The sight was not one to reassure him. The pool was filled with struggling Alsatians and, as he watched, others launched themselves from the edges and joined the hordes already in the water. A particularly ferocious hound just in front of him opened its mouth and the Bishop had just

enough time to take a gulp of air and disappear before the
dog bit him. He swam the length underwater and surfaced. A dog snapped at him and he swam back. Above him
paws thrashed the water into foam as the Bishop pondered this new manifestation of the Almighty. Evidently
he had not got out of the pool quietly enough the first
time, and God had come in to get him in the shape of
dozens of dogs and he was just wondering how this col-
lective appearance could be reconciled with the notion
that God was one and indivisible when his arm was seized
and he was dragged out of the pool by several policemen.
Thankful for this deliverance and too bewildered to wonder how policemen fitted into this spectacle of divinity he
stared back at the water. Hardly a foot of the surface of
the pool was free of dog.

The next moment his wrists were handcuffed behind
him and he was swung round.

'That is the swine all right. Take him into the house,'
said the Kommandant, and the Bishop was frogmarched
by several konstabels across the drive and into the family
home. Naked and wet, Jonathan Hazelstone stood among
the potted plants in the great hall still wearing the bathing
cap. From a great distance and far beyond the frontiers
of sanity he heard the Kommandant whisper, 'Jonathan
Hazelstone, I charge you with the wilful murder of one
Zulu cook and God knows how many policemen, the wilful destruction of Government property and being in unlawful possession of weapons calculated to harm life and
limb.'

He was too dazed and too deaf to hear the Kommandant
tell Sergeant de Kock to take him down into the cellar and
keep him safely under guard until morning.

'Wouldn't he be safer down at the police station?' the
Sergeant suggested.

But Kommandant van Heerden was too exhausted to leave Jacaranda House and besides he was looking forward to spending the night in a house renowned throughout South Africa for refined living.

'The place is ringed with men,' he said, 'and besides, we've been having complaints from the neighbours about the screams from the cells. Up here nobody will hear him when he yells. I'll cross-examine him in the morning.'

And as the Bishop of Barotseland was led down into the cellar of Jacaranda House, Kommandant van Heerden wearily climbed the staircase to find himself a nice comfortable bedroom. He chose one with a blue bedspread on an enormous double bed, and as he stepped naked between the sheets, he considered himself a lucky man.

'To think that I can commandeer the house that once belonged to the Viceroy of Matabeleland,' he said to himself and turning on his side between the remarkably smooth sheets, promptly fell asleep.

Chapter 9

Few other people in Piemburg dropped off to sleep so
easily that night. Too many disturbing things were happening around them for their sleep to be anything but fitful.
In Upper Piemburg the searchlights swung slowly to and
fro around the perimeter of Jacaranda Park, illuminating
with quite astonishing brilliance the great hoardings that
announced the arrival of death by two of its most awful
means. Designed originally for the army before being
turned over to the police force, the searchlights did a
great deal more than that. As they traversed the Park, the
neighbouring suburbs and the city itself, they turned night
into brilliant day with some remarkable results, particularly in the case of a number of chicken farms whose bat-
tery hens were driven to the verge of nervous breakdown
by finding their already short nights suddenly diminished
to something like four minutes.

Families which had taken the precaution of locking
their dogs in the backyard and of sprinkling their sheets
with DDT and whose bedrooms lay in the path of the
searchlights found dawn break upon them with a rapidity
and brilliance they had never before experienced, to be
succeeded by a duskless night, and the process repeated
endlessly while they tossed and turned in their itching
beds. Outside along the roads rumbled the armoured cars
and trucks of the police and bursts of firing interrupted
the silence of the night, as the crews followed the Kommandant's instructions to shoot any small bush resembling

Luitenant Verkramp.

The switchboard at the Piemburg Hospital was deluged with calls from agitated callers who wanted to know the symptoms of Bubonic Plague and Rabies and how to treat the diseases. In the end the frantic telephonist refused to take any more calls, a dereliction of duty that had fatal results in two cases of heart attack.

Only Konstabel Els slept soundly in the isolation hospital. Occasionally he twitched in his sleep but only because he was dreaming of battle and sudden death. On the Vlockfontein Road families whose cars had broken down in the long queue trudged towards Piemburg. It was a hot night and as they walked they sweated.

Kommandant van Heerden sweated too but for a rather different reason. He had been too exhausted when he climbed into bed to take much notice of his surroundings. He had noticed that the sheets felt peculiar but he had put their smoothness down to the fact that Miss Hazelstone's bedlinen would naturally be of the finest quality and unlike his own ordinary sheets.

Kommandant van Heerden slept like a babe for an hour. When he awoke it was to find the bed dripping with moisture. He climbed out of bed horribly embarrassed.

'It isn't as though I've been on the booze,' he muttered as he grabbed a handtowel from the washbasin and began to mop the bed out, and wondered how he was going to explain the mishap to Miss Hazelstone in the morning. He could imagine the sort of caustic comments she would make.

'Thank heaven the sheets seem to be waterproof,' he said and climbed back into bed to dry them out. 'It's a terribly hot night,' he thought tossing and turning. He

just couldn't make himself comfortable. As he drifted off
and woke again and drifted off he gained the definite impression that the bed was getting no dryer. If anything
it was getting wetter. He could feel the sweat running
down his back as he slithered from side to side in the in-
fernally slimy sheets.

He began to wonder if he had fallen sick with a fever
brought on by the strain of the day. He certainly felt
feverish and his thoughts bore all the marks of delirium.
Uncertain whether he was dreaming or recalling what had
actually happened, pursued by elephant guns, Miss Hazelstone with a scimitar, mings and a demented Konstabel Els,
Kommandant van Heerden thrashed on through the night
in a froth of agitation.

At two in the morning he took the blankets off the bed.
At three he mopped the bed out again. At four, convinced
that he was dying in a raging fever and with a temperature
of 110 he stumbled to the bathroom in search of a ther-
mometer. He had begun to think that he had shown remarkable foresight in ordering the plague notices to be put
up round the park. Whatever disease he had caught he had
no doubt it must be both infectious and fatal. But when he
took his temperature he found it to be subnormal.

'Odd,' he thought. 'Very odd,' and after drinking several
pints of water out of a tooth-mug went back to his room
and climbed back into bed. At five o'clock he gave up all
idea of sleeping and went along to the bathroom and had
a cold bath. He was still debating what was wrong with
him as he began to dress. He noticed that the room had a
funny sort of smell about it, and for a moment he looked
suspiciously at his socks. 'It isn't that sort of smell,' he
said to himself and crossing to the windows pulled back
the curtains.

Outside the sun was up and the jacaranda trees bright
with flowers in the morning light. But Kommandant van
Heerden wasn't interested in the view from his window.
He was much more concerned with the curtains. They felt
just like the sheets. He felt them again. 'The bloody things
stretch,' he thought, and found that the sheets were elastic
too. He smelt them closely and recognized the smell now.
The sheets and the curtains were made of latex. Everything in the room was made of thin blue rubber.

He opened the wardrobe and felt the suits and dresses
that hung there. They too were made of rubber. Kommandant van Heerden sat down on the bed astonished. He
had never run across anything like this in his life. Certainly
his annual acquaintance with latex had hardly prepared
him for this encounter, and as he sat there he began to
think that there was something definitely sinister about
the room. Finally he examined the contents of the chest
of drawers and found the same thing there. Shirts, pants,
and socks were all made of rubber. In one small drawer he
found several latex hoods and two pairs of handcuffs. Very
definitely the room had a sinister purpose, he thought and
went downstairs to have breakfast.

'How's the prisoner?' the Kommandant asked Sergeant
de Kock when he had finished his toast and coffee.

'Looks insane to me. Keeps talking about animals all
the time. Seems to think God is a guard dog or a vulture
or something,' said the Sergeant.

'Won't do him much good. How many men did we lose
yesterday?'

'Twenty-one.'

'Twenty-one and a Zulu cook. Say twenty-one and a
quarter. No man who shoots twenty-one policemen can
plead insanity.'

Sergeant de Kock wasn't convinced. 'Any man who shoots twenty-one policemen and leaves his wallet behind at the scene of the crime sounds insane to me.'

'We all make mistakes,' said the Kommandant, and went upstairs to begin his cross-examination.

Down in the cellar the Bishop of Barotseland had spent the night chained to a pipe. He had slept even less than the Kommandant and had been guarded by four konstabels and two dogs. During the sleepless hours he had wrestled with the intellectual and moral problem implied by his predicament and had finally come to the conclusion that he was being punished for not getting out of the swimming bath fast enough. For a while he had even considered the possibility that what was apparently happening to him was a symptom of delirium tremens brought on by drinking a bottle of bad brandy neat. When finally he was dragged to his feet and taken upstairs and down the corridor to his father's study he was certain that he was having hallucinations.

Kommandant van Heerden had not chosen Judge Hazelstone's study for interrogating the prisoner by accident. His unerring sense of psychology had told him that the study, redolent with judicial severity and the associations of childhood, would prepare Jonathan Hazelstone for the grilling the Kommandant intended to give him. Seating himself at the desk in a large leather-covered chair, the Kommandant assumed a posture and mien he felt sure would remind the prisoner of his father. To this end he toyed with a miniature brass gallows complete with trap and dangling victim which he found on the desk serving as a paperweight. It was a gift, he noted, from 'The

Executioner in gratitude for Judge Hazelstone's many favours.' Confident that he looked very much as the great lawmaker must have done when he interrogated his son about some childish misdemeanour, the Kommandant ordered the prisoner to be brought in.

Whatever resemblance there might have been between the Kommandant and Judge Hazelstone of the Supreme Court, and it was practically non-existent, there was absolutely none between the manacled and naked creature that hobbled into the study still wearing the absurd bathing-cap, and any high church dignitary. Staring wild-eyed at the Kommandant, the Bishop looked the picture of depravity.

'Name?' said the Kommandant putting down the paper-weight and reaching for a pen.

'I'm hard of hearing,' said the Bishop.

'So am I,' said the Kommandant. 'Comes of firing that bloody elephant gun.'

'I said I can't hear what you're saying.'

Kommandant van Heerden looked up from the desk. 'What the hell are you wearing that cap for?' he asked, and signalled to a konstabel to take it off. The konstabel laid the bathing-cap on the desk and Kommandant van Heerden looked at it suspiciously. 'Do you make a habit of wearing rubber clothes?' he enquired.

The Bishop chose to ignore the question. It had too much of the nightmare about it and he wanted to get back to the everyday world.

'I must protest against the assaults made on my person,' he began, and was surprised at the reaction this simple statement provoked.

'You want to do what?' yelled the Kommandant.

'I have been assaulted by several of your men,' went on the Bishop. 'They have treated me absolutely abominably.'

Kommandant van Heerden couldn't believe his ears. 'And what do you think you were doing to them yesterday afternoon, playing kiss-in-the-fucking-ring? You butcher half my bloody men, ruin a perfectly good Saracen and murder your sister's Zulu bleeding cook and you've got the nerve to come in here and protest at the assaults on. . . .' Kommandant van Heerden was at a loss for words. When he recovered his temper he went on more quietly. 'Anything else you would like to ask me?' he said.

'Yes,' said the Bishop. 'I demand to see my lawyer.'

The Kommandant shook his head. 'Confession first,' he said.

'I'm entitled to see my lawyer.'

Kommandant van Heerden had to smile. 'You're not.'

'I am entitled by law to consult my lawyer.'

'You'll be bleating about Habeas Corpus next.'

'I most certainly will unless you bring me before a magistrate in forty-eight hours.'

Kommandant van Heerden sat back in his chair and grinned cheerfully. 'You think you know your law, don't you? Being the son of a judge, you'd know all about it, wouldn't you?'

The Bishop wasn't going to be drawn. 'I know my basic rights,' he said.

'Well, let me tell you something now. I'm holding you under the Terrorism Act and that means you can see no lawyer and there's no Habeas Corpus, nothing.' He paused to let this sink in. 'I can detain you till the day you die, and you never so much as get a whiff of a lawyer, and as for charging you before a magistrate, that can wait for forty-eight years or four hundred and eighty, for that matter.'

The Bishop tried to say something, but the Kommandant

continued, 'I'll tell you something else. Under the Terrorism Act you have to prove yourself innocent. I don't have to go to the bother of proving you guilty. Really rather convenient from my point of view,' and the Kommandant picked up the paperweight with what he hoped was a meaningful gesture.

The Bishop groped for something to say. 'But the Terrorism Act doesn't apply to me. I'm not a terrorist.'

'And what would you call a person who went round murdering twenty-one policemen if not a bloody terrorist?'

'I've no idea what you're talking about.'

'I'll tell you what I am talking about,' shouted the Kommandant, 'I'll spell it out for you. Early yesterday afternoon you attempted to destroy the evidence of a bestial crime committed upon the person of your sister's Zulu cook by shooting him with a monstrous elephant gun. You then forced your sister to confess to the crime to save your skin, while you went up to the main gate and shot down twenty-one of my men as they tried to enter the Park.'

The Bishop looked wildly round the room and tried to pull himself together.

'You've got it all wrong,' he said at last, 'I didn't kill Fivepence—'

Kommandant van Heerden interrupted him quickly, 'Thank you,' he said, and started to write, 'Confesses to killing twenty-one police officers.'

'I didn't say that,' screamed the Bishop. 'I said I didn't kill Fivepence.'

'Denies killing Zulu cook,' continued the Kommandant painstakingly writing it down.

'I deny killing twenty-one policemen too,' shouted the Bishop.

'Retracts previous confession,' said the Kommandant.

'There was no previous confession. I never said anything about killing the policemen.'

Kommandant van Heerden looked at the two konstabels. 'You men heard him confess to killing twenty-one police officers, didn't you?' he said. The two konstabels weren't sure what they heard but they knew better than to disagree with the Kommandant. They nodded.

'There you are,' the Kommandant continued. 'They heard you.'

'But I didn't say it,' the Bishop yelled. 'What would I want to kill twenty-one policemen for?'

The Kommandant considered the question. 'To hide the crime you'd committed on the Zulu cook,' he said at last.

'How would killing twenty-one policemen help to hide Fivepence's murder?' wailed the Bishop.

'You should have thought of that before you did it,' said the Kommandant smugly.

'But I didn't do it, I tell you. I never went anywhere near the main gate yesterday afternoon. I was too drunk to go anywhere.'

The Kommandant started to write again. 'Claims he acted under the influence of alcohol,' he said.

'No I don't. I said I was too drunk to go anywhere. I couldn't have got up to the gate if I had wanted to.'

Kommandant van Heerden put down his pen and looked at the prisoner. 'Then perhaps you'll be good enough to tell me,' he said, 'how it was that sixty-nine tracker dogs when put on your trail followed your scent up to the main gate and then back to the swimming-pool where you were disposing of the murder weapons?'

'I don't know.'

'Expert witnesses, tracker dogs,' said the Kommandant. 'And perhaps you'll explain how your wallet and handkerchief came to be inside a blockhouse from which my men had been shot down.'

'I've got no idea.'

'Right, then if you'll just sign here,' said the Kommandant holding out the statement to him.

The Bishop bent forward and read the statement. It was a confession that he had murdered Fivepence and twenty-one police officers.

'Of course I won't sign it,' he said straightening up at last. 'None of the crimes you mention there have anything to do with me.'

'No? Well then just you tell me who committed them.'

'My sister shot Fivepence. . . .' the Bishop began, and realized he was making a mistake. In front of him the Kommandant's face had turned purple.

'You sordid bastard,' he yelled. 'Call yourself an English gentleman, do you, and try and shift the blame for a murder on your poor dear sister. What sort of a man are you? Doesn't the family name mean a bleeding thing to you?'

At a signal from the Kommandant the two konstabels grabbed the Bishop and hurled him to the floor. In a flurry of boots and truncheons, the Bishop rolled about the floor of the study. Just as he thought he was about to die, he was hauled to his feet in front of the desk.

'We'll continue this conversation when you feel up to it,' the Kommandant said more calmly, and the Bishop thanked the dear Lord for sparing him another encounter with Kommandant van Heerden. He knew he would never feel up to it. 'In the meantime I am sending for Luitenant Verkramp. This is clearly a political case, and in future he

will interrogate you,' and with this dire threat the Kommandant ordered the two konstabels to take the prisoner
back to the cellar.

As Kommandant van Heerden waited for Miss Hazelstone to be brought to him, he fingered the bathing-cap
thoughtfully and wondered what had happened to Luitenant Verkramp. He had no great hope that the Luitenant
was dead. 'The crafty swine is probably holed up somewhere,' he thought and idly poked his finger into the bathing-cap. He was beginning to wish that the Luitenant was
around to consult about the case. Kommandant van Heerden was no great one for theories and the cross-examination had not turned into a confession quite as easily as he
had expected. He had to admit, if only to himself, that
there were certain aspects of Jonathan's story that had the
ring of truth about them. He had been dead drunk on the
bed in Jacaranda House. The Kommandant had seen him
there with his own eyes and yet the shooting at the gate
had started only minutes later. The Kommandant could
not see how a man who was dead drunk one minute half a
mile from the blockhouse, could the next be firing with
remarkable accuracy at the plain-clothes men. And where
the hell had Els disappeared to? The whole thing was a
bloody mystery.

'Oh well, never look a gift horse in the mouth,' he
thought, 'After all my whole career is at stake and it
doesn't do to be choosy.'

The Kommandant hadn't been far wrong in his assess-
ment of Luitenant Verkramp's position. He was indeed
holed up. Of all the people who slept in Piemburg that
night, Luitenant Verkramp was perhaps the least restless
and certainly the least refreshed when dawn broke. His

sleep had been disturbed, very disturbed, but in spite of his discomfort he had not dared to move. Below him and in some cases actually inside him, the dreadful spikes made the slightest movement an exceedingly unrewarding experience.

Above him the moving finger of an enormous light swung eerily back and forth through a great pall of greasy smoke. A nauseating smell of burning flesh filled the air, and Luitenant Verkramp in his delirium began to believe in the hell his grandfather's sermons had promised for sinners. At intervals during the long night he woke and considered what he had done to deserve this dreadful fate, and his mind was filled with visions of the prisoners he had tortured by tying plastic bags over their heads, or by administering electric shocks to their genitals. If only he were given another chance in life, he promised he would never torture another suspect and realized as he did so that it was a promise he would never be able to keep.

There was only one portion of his anatomy he could move without too much pain. His left arm was free and as he lay staring up into the smoke and flames of hell, he used his hand to feel about him. He felt the iron spikes and underneath him he discovered the body of another damned soul stiff and cold. Luitenant Verkramp envied that man. He had evidently passed on to some other more pleasant place like oblivion, and he envied him all the more a moment later when an extremely unpleasant sound further down the ditch drew his attention to new and more horrible possibilities.

He thought at first that someone was being undressed in a great hurry, and by a person with little respect for his clothes. Whoever was busy down there certainly wasn't bothering to undo buttons very carefully. It sounded as if some poor devil was having the clothes ripped off him very unceremoniously indeed. Luitenant Verkramp was sure they would never be fit to wear again. 'Probably preparing some poor devil for roasting,' he thought and hoped that his camouflage would help to prevent them finding him for some time.

Raising his head inch by inch he peered down the moat. At first it was too dark to see anything. The sound of undressing had ceased and was followed by noises more awful than anything he had ever heard. Whatever was going on down there didn't bear thinking about, but still horribly fascinated he continued to peer into the darkness. Above him the great probing light swung slowly back towards the moat, and as it passed overhead Luitenant Verkramp knew that his encounter with the wildlife of the hedgerow in the shape of the giant spider had been as nothing to the appalling agonies death held in store for him. Down the ditch a great vulture was up to its neck in plain-clothes policemen. Luitenant Verkramp passed out yet again.

When dawn broke over the varied remains of Konstabel Els's defence of Jacaranda Park, the policemen guarding the gate discovered the haha and its inhabitants living and dead and clambered gingerly down to collect what had not already flapped gorged out of the moat. They had some difficulty at first in recognizing Luitenant Verkramp under his vegetation and when they had decided that he was at least partially human, they had even more difficulty deciding whether he was alive or dead. Certainly the creature they hauled onto the grass seemed more dead than alive, and was clearly suffering from a pronounced persecution complex.

'Don't roast me, please don't roast me. I promise I won't do it again,' Luitenant Verkramp yelled and he was still screaming when he was lifted into the ambulance and driven down to the hospital.

Chapter 10

As Luitenant Verkramp was being admitted to Piemburg Hospital, Konstabel Els was being discharged.

'I tell you I've got rabies,' Els shouted at the doctor who told him there was nothing physically wrong with him. 'I've been bitten by a mad dog and I am dying.'

'No such luck,' said the doctor. 'You'll live to bite another day,' and left Els standing on the steps cursing the inefficiency of the medical profession. He was trying to make up his mind what he should do next when the police car that had accompanied the ambulance carrying Luitenant Verkramp to hospital stopped next to him.

'Hey, Els, where the hell have you been?' said the Sergeant next to the driver. 'The old man has been yelling blue murder for you.'

'I've been in hospital,' said Els. 'Suspected rabies.'

'You'd better hop in. We'll go by the station and pick up your little toy.'

'What little toy?' asked Els, hoping it wasn't the elephant gun.

'The Electric Shock machine. You've got a customer up at Jacaranda House.'

As they drove up the hill Els sat silent. He wasn't looking forward to seeing the Kommandant and having to explain why he had left his post. As they passed the burnt-out Saracen, Els couldn't restrain a little giggle.

'I don't know what you're laughing at,' said the Sergeant sourly. 'Might have been you in there.'

'Not me,' said Els. 'You wouldn't find me in one of those

things. Asking for trouble they are.'

'Safe enough normally.'

'Not when you're up against a good man with the right sort of weapon,' Els said.

'You sound as though you had something to do with it, you know so much about it.'

'Who? Me? Nothing to do with me. Why should I knock out a Saracen?'

'God alone knows,' said the Sergeant, 'but it's just the sort of stupid thing you would get up to.'

Konstabel Els cursed himself for opening his mouth. He would have to be more careful with the Kommandant. He began to wonder what the symptoms of bubonic plague were. He might have to develop them as a last resort.

Kommandant van Heerden's examination of Miss Hazelstone had got off to a bad start. Nothing that he could say would convince her that she hadn't murdered Fivepence.

'All right, suppose for the moment that you did shoot him,' he said for the umpteenth time. 'What was your motive?'

'He was my lover.'

'Most people love their lovers, Miss Hazelstone, yet you say you shot him.'

'Correct. I did.'

'Hardly a normal reaction.'

'I'm not a normal person,' said Miss Hazelstone. 'Nor are you. Nor is the konstabel outside the door. We are none of us normal people.'

'I would have said I was fairly normal,' said the Kommandant smugly.

'That's just the sort of asinine remark I would expect you to make and it only goes to prove how abnormal you are. Most people like to think that they are unique. You evidently don't and since you seem to consider normality to consist of being like other people, in so far as you possess qualities that make you unlike other people, you are abnormal. Do I make myself clear?'

'No,' said the Kommandant, 'you don't.'

'Let me put it another way,' said Miss Hazelstone. 'Normality is a concept. Do you follow me?'

'I'm trying to,' the Kommandant said despairingly.

'Good. As I have said, normality is a concept. It is not a state of being. You are confusing it with the desire to conform. You have a strong urge to conform. I have none.'

Kommandant van Heerden groped his way after her. He couldn't understand a word of what she was saying but it didn't sound very complimentary.

'What about motive?' he asked, trying to get back on to more familiar ground.

'What about it?' Miss Hazelstone countered.

'If you killed Fivepence you must have had a motive.'

Miss Hazelstone thought for a moment. 'It doesn't follow,' she said at last, 'though I suppose you could argue that a motiveless act is an impossibility because it inevitably presupposes an intention to act without motive which is a motive in itself.'

Kommandant van Heerden looked desperately round the room. The woman was driving him mad.

'You didn't have one then?' he asked after counting to twenty slowly.

'If you insist on my having one, I suppose I'll have to supply it. You can say it was jealousy.'

The Kommandant perked up. This was much better. He was getting on to familiar ground again.

'And who were you jealous of?'

'No one.'

'No one?'

'That's what I said.'

Kommandant van Heerden peered over the edge of an abyss. 'No one,' he almost screamed. 'How in the name of hell can you be jealous of no one?' He paused, and looked at her suspiciously. 'No One is not the name of another kaffir, is it?'

'Of course not. It means exactly what it says. I was jealous of no one.'

'You can't be jealous of no one. It's not possible. You've got to be jealous of somebody else.'

'I haven't, you know,' Miss Hazelstone looked at him pityingly.

Beneath him the Kommandant could feel the abyss yawning. It was the abyss of all abysses.

'No one. No one,' he repeated almost pathetically, shaking his head. 'Someone tell me how somebody can be jealous of no one.'

'Oh it's really quite simple,' Miss Hazelstone continued, 'I was just jealous.'

'Just jealous,' the Kommandant repeated slowly.

'That's right. I didn't want to lose dear Fivepence.'

Teetering above the unfathomable void of abstraction the Kommandant clutched at Fivepence. There had once been something substantial about the Zulu cook and the Kommandant needed something substantial to hang on to.

'You were frightened you were going to lose him?' he pondered aloud, and then realized the terrible contradiction he was stepping into. 'But you say you shot him. Isn't that the best way of losing the brute?' He was almost beside himself.

'It was the only way I had of making sure I kept him,' Miss Hazelstone replied.

Kommandant van Heerden pulled himself back from

the void. He was losing control of the interview. He started again at the beginning.

'Let's forget for the moment that you shot Fivepence so that you wouldn't lose him,' he said slowly and very patiently. 'Let's start at the other end. What was your motive for falling in love with him?' It was not a topic he particularly wanted to investigate, not that he believed for a moment that she had ever been in love with the swine, but it was better than harping on about no one. Besides he felt pretty sure she would give herself away now. The Hazelstones couldn't fall in love with Zulu cooks.

'Fivepence and I shared certain mutual interests,' said Miss Hazelstone slowly. 'For one thing we had the same fetish.'

'Oh really. The same fetish?' In his mind the Kommandant conjured up a picture of the little native idols he had seen in the Piemburg Museum.

'Naturally,' said Miss Hazelstone, 'it provided a bond between us.'

'Yes, it must have done, and I suppose you sacrificed goats to it,' the Kommandant said sarcastically.

'What an extraordinary thing to say,' Miss Hazelstone looked puzzled. 'Of course we didn't. It wasn't that sort of fetish.'

'Wasn't it? What sort was it? Wooden or stone?'

'Rubber,' said Miss Hazelstone briefly.

Kommandant van Heerden leant back in his chair angrily. He had had about as much of Miss Hazelstone's leg-pulling as he could take. If the old girl seriously supposed that he was going to believe some cock-and-bull story about a rubber idol, she had another think coming.

'Now listen to me, Miss Hazelstone,' he said seriously, 'I can appreciate what you are trying to do and I must say

I admire you for it. Family loyalty is a fine thing and trying to save your brother is a fine thing too, but I have my duty to do and nothing you can say is going to prevent me doing it. Now if you will be good enough to get to the point and admit that you had nothing whatever to do with the murder of your cook and were never approximately in love with him, I will allow you to go. If not I shall be forced to take some drastic action against you. You are obstructing the course of justice and you leave me no alternative. Now then, be sensible and admit that all this talk about fetishes is nonsense.'

Miss Hazelstone looked at him icily.

'Are you easily stimulated?' she asked. 'Sexually, I mean.'

'That has got nothing whatever to do with you.'

'It has got a lot to do with this case,' said Miss Hazelstone, and hesitated. Kommandant van Heerden shifted uneasily in his chair. He had come to recognize that Miss Hazelstone's hesitations tended to augur some new and revolting disclosure.

'I have to admit that I am not easily aroused,' she said at last. The Kommandant was delighted to hear it. 'I need the presence of rubber to stimulate my sexual appetite.'

The Kommandant was just about to say that in his case the presence of rubber had quite the opposite effect, but he thought better of it.

'You see I am a rubber fetishist,' Miss Hazelstone continued.

Kommandant van Heerden tried to grasp the implications of the remark.

'You are?' he said.

'I have a passion for rubber.'

'You have?'

'I can only make love when I am dressed in rubber.'

'You can?'

'It was rubber that drew Fivepence and me together.'

'It was?'

'Fivepence had the same propensity.'

'He did?'

'When I first met him he was working in a garage re-treading tyres.'

'He was?'

'I had taken my tyres in for a retread and Fivepence was there. I recognized him at once as the man I had been looking for all my life.'

'You did?'

'I might almost say that our love affair was cemented over a Michelin X.'

'You might?'

Miss Hazelstone stopped. The Kommandant's inability to say more than two words at a time and those two in the form of a question she had already answered was beginning to irritate her.

'Do you have any idea what I am talking about?' she asked.

'No,' said the Kommandant.

'I don't know what more I can do to make my meaning plain,' Miss Hazelstone said. 'I have tried to explain as simply as I can what I found attractive about Fivepence.'

Kommandant van Heerden closed his mouth which had been hanging open and tried to focus his mind on something comprehensible. What Miss Hazelstone had just told him so simply had not, he had to admit, been in the least abstract, but if just before he had hovered over a void of unfathomable abstractions, the simple facts she had placed before him now were so far beyond anything his experience had prepared him to expect that he began to think that on the whole he preferred the conceptual abyss. In an effort to regain his sense of reality, he resorted to healthy vulgarity.

'Are you trying to tell me,' he said, picking the bathing-cap off the desk and dangling it from his finger a few inches in front of Miss Hazelstone's face, 'that this rubber cap gives you an overwhelming desire to lay me?'

In front of him Miss Hazelstone nodded.

'And if I were to wear it you wouldn't be able to control your sexual impulses?' he went on.

'Yes,' said Miss Hazelstone frantically. 'Yes, I would. I mean, no I wouldn't.' Torn between a raging torrent of desire and an overwhelming aversion for the person of the Kommandant, she hardly knew what was happening to her.

'And I suppose you're going to tell me that your Zulu cook had the same taste for rubber?'

Miss Hazelstone nodded again.

'And I suppose all those rubber clothes I found in the bedroom upstairs belong to you too?' Miss Hazelstone agreed that they did. 'And Fivepence would put on a rubber suit and you would wear a rubber nightdress? Is that right?'

Kommandant van Heerden could see from the expression on Miss Hazelstone's face that at long last he had regained the initiative. She was sitting mute and staring at him hypnotized.

'Is that what used to happen?' he continued remorselessly.

Miss Hazelstone shook her head. 'No,' she said, 'it was the other way round.'

'Oh really? What was the other way round?'

'The clothes were.'

'The clothes were the other way round?'

'Yes.'

'Inside out I suppose, or was it back to front?'

'You could put it like that.'

Kommandant van Heerden's experience of rubber clothing during the night hadn't induced in him any desire to put it like anything.

'Like what?' he said.

'I wore the men's suits and Fivepence wore the dresses,' Miss Hazelstone said. 'As you've probably noticed I have some marked masculine characteristics and Fivepence, poor dear, was a transvestite.'

The Kommandant staring at her with increasing disgust could see what she meant. Masculine characteristics indeed! A taste for tall and revolting stories for one thing. And if for one moment he really believed that a fat Zulu cook had been dressing up in his missus's clothes then he was a very lucky Zulu to have gone the way he had. The Kommandant knew what he'd do to any houseboy of his he found prancing around in ladies' clothes, rubber or not, and it included pulling more than his vest tight too.

He dragged his attention back from the prospect and tried to think about the case. He had known there was something sinister about the bedroom with the rubber sheets, and now Miss Hazelstone had explained its purpose.

'It's no good your going on trying to cover up for your brother,' he said. 'We've enough evidence to hang him with already. What you tell me about the rubber clothes merely confirms what we already know. When your brother was arrested last night, he was wearing this cap.' He held it up in front of her again.

'Of course he was,' said Miss Hazelstone. 'He has to when he goes swimming. He has trouble with his ears.'

Kommandant van Heerden smiled. 'Sometimes listening to you, Miss Hazelstone, I fancy there's something wrong with my ears too, but I don't go around with a rubber bathing-cap on all the time.'

'Nor does Jonathan.'

'No? Well then perhaps you'll explain how it came about that when he was brought before me this morning, he was still wearing it. Your brother evidently likes wearing rubber things.'

'He probably forgot to take it off,' Miss Hazelstone said, 'He's very absent-minded you know. He's always forgetting where he's left things.'

'So I've noticed,' said the Kommandant. He paused and leant back in the chair expansively. 'The pattern of the case seems to go like this. Your brother comes home from Rhodesia, probably because things got too hot for him up there.'

'Nonsense,' interrupted Miss Hazelstone. 'Barotseland does get very hot, I know, but Jonathan's used to the heat.'

'You can say that again,' said the Kommandant. 'Well, whatever the reason, he comes home. He brings with him all the rubber clothes he's so fond of and he starts trying to seduce your Zulu cook.'

'What utter rubbish,' said Miss Hazelstone. 'Jonathan wouldn't dream of any such thing. You're forgetting that he is a Bishop.'

The Kommandant wasn't forgetting anything of the sort since he had never known it.

'That's maybe what he has told you,' he said. 'Our information is that he is a convicted criminal. There is a file on him down at the station. Luitenant Verkramp has the details.'

'But this is insane. Jonathan is the Bishop of Barotseland.'

'Probably his alias,' said the Kommandant. 'Right. We've got to the part where he tries to make Fivepence. The cook objects and runs out on to the lawn, and your brother shoots him down.'

'You're mad,' Miss Hazelstone shouted and stood up. 'You're quite mad. My brother was in the swimming-bath when I shot Fivepence. He came running when he heard the shot and tried to administer the last rites.'

'Last rites is one way of putting it,' said the Kommandant. 'And I suppose that's how he got blood all over himself?'

'Exactly.'

'And you honestly expect me to believe that a nice old lady like you shot your cook, and that your brother whom I find dead drunk on a bed, naked and covered with blood, is a Bishop and had nothing to do with the killing? Really Miss Hazelstone, you must take me for an idiot.'

'I do,' said Miss Hazelstone simply.

'And another thing,' the Kommandant continued hurriedly, 'some maniac shot down twenty-one of my men yesterday afternoon up at the gate to the Park. Now you're not going to try to tell me that you murdered them too, are you?'

'If the wish were father to the thought, yes,' said Miss Hazelstone.

Kommandant van Heerden smiled. 'It's not, I'm afraid. I wish I could hush this whole case up and if it were simply the death of your cook, I daresay it would be possible, but there is nothing I can do now. Justice must run its course.'

He swung his chair round and faced the bookshelves. He was feeling quite pleased with himself. Everything had sorted itself out in his own mind and he had no doubt that he would be able to convince the State Attorney. Kommandant van Heerden's career had been saved. Behind him Miss Hazelstone acted promptly. Seizing both

the opportunity provided by the back of the Kommandant's head, and the brass paperweight, she brought the
two together with as much strength as she could muster.
The Kommandant slumped to the floor.

Miss Hazelstone stepped nimbly across to the door.
'The Kommandant has had a stroke,' she said to the two
konstabels on duty there. 'Help me take him up to his
bedroom,' and she led the way upstairs. When the two
konstabels had deposited Kommandant van Heerden on
the bed in the blue bedroom, she sent them downstairs to
ring the hospital for an ambulance and the two men,
accustomed to obeying orders without question, dashed
down the corridor and told Sergeant de Kock. As soon
as they had gone Miss Hazelstone stepped to the door of
the bedroom and whistled. A Dobermann Pinscher that
had been asleep on the rug in the drawing-room heard the
whistle and left its sanctuary. Silently it climbed the stairs
and loped down the passage to its mistress.

By the time Sergeant de Kock had telephoned Piemburg Hospital and had arranged for an ambulance to be
sent up to the house, a call which necessitated explaining
to the telephonist that Kommandant van Heerden was
white and didn't need a Non-European Ambulance, it was
clear that van Heerden's condition had taken a turn for
the worse.

The Sergeant found Miss Hazelstone waiting for him at
the end of the passage. She stood demurely and with that
air of melancholy the Kommandant had so much admired
the day before, and in her hands she held something that
was decidedly melancholy and not in the least demure.
It was not the size of the elephant gun and it quite clearly
couldn't incapacitate a charging elephant at a thousand
yards, but in its own small way it was suited to the purpose Miss Hazelstone very clearly had in mind.

'That's right,' she said as the Sergeant stopped on the landing. 'Stand quite still and you won't get hurt. This is a scatter gun and if you want to find out how many cartridges the magazine holds I suggest you try to rush me. You'll need a lot of men.' Beside her the great Dobermann growled encouragingly. It had obviously had enough of policemen to last it a lifetime. On the landing Sergeant de Kock stood very still. It was obvious from the tone of Miss Hazelstone's voice that whatever the capabilities of the scatter gun, she was not in the habit of repeating herself.

'That's right,' she continued as the Sergeant stared at her. 'Have a good look and while you're about it have a good look at the weapons on the walls. They are all in working order and I have enough ammunition in my bedroom to last me quite some time.' She paused, and the Sergeant obediently looked at the guns. 'Now then, you trot off downstairs and don't attempt to come up again. Toby will tell me if you do.' The dog growled again knowingly. 'And when you get down there,' she went on, 'you are to release my brother. I shall give you ten minutes and then I shall expect to see him walk up the drive freely and without let or hindrance. If not I shall shoot Kommandant van Heerden. If you have any doubt about my ability to kill I suggest you look at the gum trees in the garden. I think you'll find the evidence you need there.' Sergeant de Kock needed no such evidence. He felt sure she could kill. 'Good, it seems you understand me. Now I will remain in intercourse with Kommandant van Heerden until I receive a telephone call from my brother in Barotseland. When I receive that call I will release the Kommandant. If I hear nothing from Jonathan within forty-eight hours I will release the Kommandant dead. Do you understand me?'

The Sergeant nodded.

'Now then, get out.'

Sergeant de Kock dashed downstairs and as he went Miss Hazelstone fired one shot by way of warning down the passage. Its results justified every expectation the Sergeant had entertained about the gun's lethal capacity. Sixty-four large holes appeared suddenly in the bathroom door.

Miss Hazelstone surveyed the holes with satisfaction and went back into the bedroom. Then having fastened the Kommandant by his wrists to the head of the bed with the handcuffs he had noted in the chest of drawers, she walked quietly along the corridor. Five minutes later she had collected a small arsenal from the walls and had erected two formidable barricades which would stop any attempt to rush her long enough for her to start using the scatter gun and other assorted weapons she had piled outside the bedroom door. Finally and for good measure she dragged several mattresses and a chaise-longue down the passage and built herself a bullet-proof barricade.

When she had finished, she surveyed her handiwork and smiled. 'I don't think we're likely to be disturbed just yet, Toby,' she said to the Dobermann which had climbed on to the chaise-longue, and patting the dog on the head she went into the bedroom and began to undress Kommandant van Heerden.

Chapter 11

Downstairs Konstabel Els was having a heated argument with Sergeant de Kock.

'I tell you,' he kept shouting, 'I'm no more like a flaming bishop than—'

'Than he is?' suggested the Sergeant, pointing at the manacled figure of Jonathan. 'He doesn't look like a bishop either.'

Konstabel Els had to admit that this was true. 'I don't care. I'm still not going to walk down the drive dressed up in his clothes. She'd spot me a mile off.'

'So what? She's only an old woman. She couldn't shoot straight if she tried,' said the Sergeant.

'Are you mad?' Els shouted. 'I've seen what that old bird can do with a gun. Why she blew that Zulu cook of hers to pieces without batting an eyelid. I should know. I had to pick the bugger up.'

'Listen to me, Els,' said the Sergeant, 'she won't have time to take a pot-shot at you. She'll go to the window to have a look and—'

'And the next moment I'll be scattered in little bits over half the fucking park. No thank you. If anyone has to pick the bits up afterwards, I'll pick up yours. I've had more experience.'

'If you would let me finish,' said the Sergeant. 'As soon as she goes to the window, we'll rush her down the passage. She won't have time to take a shot at you.'

In that case, why not make him walk down the drive?'
asked Els. 'I'll keep him covered, and as soon as you've got
his sister, we'll take him in again.'

Sergeant de Kock wasn't to be persuaded. 'That sod's
killed twenty-one men already. I wouldn't let him out of
those handcuffs if you paid me,' he said.

Konstabel Els had an answer to that one, but he decided
not to use it.

'What's going to be happening to the Kommandant
while all this is going on?' he asked. 'She'll kill him for
sure.'

'Good riddance,' said the Sergeant. 'He got himself into
her clutches, let him get himself out.'

'In that case, why don't we just sit tight and starve the
old bag out?'

Sergeant de Kock smiled. 'The Kommandant will be
pleased when he hears you wanted to let her knock him
off. Now then, stop messing about and get into his clothes.'

Konstabel Els realized his mistake. Without Kommandant van Heerden's incompetence he was likely to have to
answer a charge of killing twenty-one fellow officers. Els
decided he had better see to it that the old man didn't get
killed after all. He didn't want an efficient officer taking
his place. He started to put on the Bishop's clothes.

Upstairs Miss Hazelstone had been having almost as
much difficulty getting Kommandant van Heerden out of
his clothes as the Sergeant was in getting Els to put on the
Bishop's. It wasn't that he put up any resistance, but his
bulk and unconscious lack of cooperation hardly helped.
When he was finally naked, she went to the wardrobe
and picked out a pink rubber nightdress with a matching
hood and squeezed him into them. She was just putting

the finishing touches to her own ensemble when she heard a movement on the bed. Kommandant van Heerden was coming round.

In the days to come the Kommandant was wont to say that it was this fresh and horrifying experience which had led to the trouble with his heart. As he regained consciousness, the first thought to enter the disordered labyrinth of his mind was that he would never touch a drop again. Nothing less than a bottle of Old Rhino Skin could account for the pain in his head and the horrible sensation of something hot and sticky and tight adhering to his face. It was even worse when he opened his eyes. He had evidently gone down with the DTs or perhaps the fever he had suspected in the night had finally struck him down delirious. He shut his eyes and tried to work out what was wrong. His arms appeared to be tied to something above his head and his body dressed in something very tight and elastic. He tried to open his mouth to speak but some horrible stuff prevented a sound coming out. Unable to move or to speak he lifted his head and peered at the apparition that sat down on the bed beside him.

It appeared to be an elderly man with unspeakable feminine characteristics and it was dressed in a double-breasted suit of salmon-pink rubber with a yellow pin-stripe. As if that wasn't bad enough it had on a shirt of off-white latex and a mauve rubber tie complete with polka dots. For a moment the Kommandant gaped at the creature and was horrified to see it leer at him. The Kommandant shut his eyes and tried to conjure the apparition away by thinking about the pain in his head, but when he opened them again it was still there, leering for all it was worth. Kommandant van Heerden couldn't remember when last he had been leered at by an elderly gent but he

knew that it must have been a long time since and certainly when and if it had last happened, it had not pro-
duced anything like the degree of aversion he felt now.
He was shutting his eyes for the second time when he
opened them again hurriedly and in horror. A hand had
settled gently on his knee and was beginning to tickle his
thigh. In his revulsion from its touch the Kommandant
jerked his legs into the air and for the first time caught a
glimpse of what he was wearing and realized what he
was not. He was wearing a pink rubber nightdress with
frills along the bottom. The Kommandant shuddered and,
aware that he had left himself open by his seizure to
whatever depredations the ghastly old man had in mind, he
straightened his legs abruptly and vowed that no tempta-
tion would make him open them again. The apparition
continued to leer and to tickle, and the Kommandant
turned his head hurriedly away from the leer and faced
the wall.

Directly in front of his face was a small table and on
it lay something which made the leer seem preferable if
not actually alluring, and which forced the Kommandant
into an attempt to scream. He opened his mouth, but
nothing like a scream came out. Instead he sucked in a
mouthful of thin rubber which immediately popped out
again and left him gasping and he was just recovering
from the attempt when a growl from the passage attracted
the old man's attention. He rose from the bed, picked up a
gun and went to the door.

Kommandant van Heerden seized the opportunity to try
to break loose from the bed. He bounced and thrashed,
oblivious of the pain in his head, and as he thrashed he saw
the barrel of the gun point round the door at him. In the
face of its menace he lay still and tried to forget what he
had seen lying ready for use on the table by the bed. It

was a hypodermic syringe and an ampoule marked 'Novo-caine'.

The difficulties which from the word go had been atten-dant on getting Konstabel Els into the Bishop's clothes, had not been lessened by the discovery that they were not quite his size. The jacket was still the greatcoat it had been the night before, and the trousers made him look like a seal. They made his plan to run down the drive utterly impracticable. It was not a plan he had mentioned to the Sergeant who he felt, would take it amiss, but now that he had flippers where his boots should have been, running was definitely out. At this rate he would be lucky to waddle let alone run, and Els who had once been privileged to shoot a kaffir with a wooden leg knew that waddling targets were as good as dead ones. It was at this point that Els had his second attack of rabies.

It was as ineffectual as his first, and after he had got himself severely kicked for biting Sergeant de Kock in the ankle, and had loosened several teeth by champing on a wrought-iron table leg he had mistaken for wood, he gave up the attempt at deception and was shepherded outside to begin his imitation of a bishop.

'Do it half as well as you do a dog with rabies and they'll make you an Archbishop, Els,' said the Sergeant giving him a shove which sent him on his way. As the Sergeant and his men climbed stealthily to the top of the stairs, Els flapped off miserably on what he knew was to be his last walk. His hat was too large for him and made it difficult to see where he was going and when he did try to run he only succeeded in falling flat on his face. He gave up the attempt as more likely to lead to dire consequen-ces than the waddle. Behind him he heard a konstabel snigger. Els felt aggrieved. He knew that he must look like a large black duck. He was certain he would soon be a dead one.

Warned by the Dobermann's growl Miss Hazelstone peered down the corridor and listened to the boots creaking on the stairs. Behind her the Kommandant, evidently in ecstasy at the thought of the pleasures that lay ahead of him, thrashed wildly on the bed. She pointed the gun round the door at him and the anticipatory wriggles ceased abruptly. A voice from the stairs shouted, 'He's on his way. The Bishop is going down the drive now.'

'I'll just go and have a look,' Miss Hazelstone shouted back, and stayed where she was.

It was doubtful who was most astonished by what followed. Certainly Sergeant de Kock was amazed to find himself in the land of the living after Miss Hazelstone had fired her first volley as the assault force tried to breast her first barricade. He wasn't to know that she had fired high less to avoid casualties than to preserve her defences. This time sixty-four large holes appeared in the ceiling and the corridor was filled with a fine fog of powdered plaster. Under cover of this smokescreen the Sergeant and his men fell back thankfully and gathered among the potted plants in the hall.

Miss Hazelstone on the other hand surveyed her handiwork for a moment with satisfaction, and then went back to the bedroom window to watch whatever it was that was trying to run up the drive.

That it was nothing like her brother was obvious at first glance. With the enormous hat wedged down over his ears preventing him from seeing where he was heading and with the trouser bottoms splaying out behind him with each step he took, Els hopped across the Park. Miss Hazelstone burst out laughing and hearing the laughter

Konstabel Els redoubled his efforts to win the sack race. As Miss Hazelstone fired, he fell on his face involuntarily. He need not have bothered. Miss Hazelstone was laughing too much to aim straight. Her bullets crashed through the leaves of a tree some distance from him and merely wounded a large and well-fed vulture that had been digesting its breakfast there. As it fluttered to the ground near him and belched, Konstabel Els lying helpless on the grass looked at it speculatively. He could see nothing in the world to laugh at.

Kommandant van Heerden felt the same way about the laughter. It bore too many of the hallmarks of the expert in refined living to leave him in any doubt who the creature in the salmon-pink suit was. Nobody else of his acquaintance laughed like that, shot like that or had such a marked propensity for administering intramuscular injections of novocaine.

Miss Hazelstone returned to her seat on the bed and picked up the hypodermic. 'You won't feel anything,' she said inserting the ampoule. 'Not a thing.'

'I know I won't,' shouted the Kommandant inside the rubber hood. 'That's what's bothering me,' but Miss Hazelstone didn't hear him. The grunts and muffled screams that came out of the hood were quite indistinguishable as words.

'Just a little prick to begin with,' said Miss Hazelstone soothingly. She lifted the skirt of his nightdress and the Kommandant tried to make it even smaller. Eyeing the needle he found was the best way of maintaining his flaccidity, and he concentrated on it with grim determination.

'You'll have to do better than that,' said Miss Hazelstone after a moment's speculation and evidently thinking at cross-purposes to the Kommandant.

Inside the hood the Kommandant continued his attempt to explain that he wasn't afflicted with the same complaint as the Zulu cook.

'It's just the opposite with me,' he yelled. 'I take hours and hours.'

'You are a shy man,' said Miss Hazelstone, and thought for a moment. 'Perhaps you would find a little whipping helpful. Some men do, you know,' and she got up from the bed and rummaged in the wardrobe, emerging at last with a particularly horrid-looking riding crop.

'No I wouldn't,' yelled the Kommandant. 'I wouldn't find it helpful at all.'

'Yes or no?' said Miss Hazelstone as the muffled cries subsided. 'Nod for yes, shake your head for no.'

Kommandant van Heerden shook his head as hard as he could.

'Not your cup of tea, eh?' said Miss Hazelstone. 'Well then, how about some nasty pictures.' This time she fetched a folder from the wardrobe and the Kommandant found himself gazing fascinated at photographs that had evidently been taken by some lunatic with a taste for contortionists and dwarfs.

'Take the disgusting things away,' he yelled as she pressed an exceptionally perverse one on his attention.

'You like that one, do you?' Miss Hazelstone asked. 'It's a position Fivepence was particularly fond of. I'll see if I can get you in the right position.'

'No, I don't,' the Kommandant screamed. 'I loathe it. It's revolting.' But before he could shake his head to indicate his desire not to have his back broken, Miss Hazelstone had seized the hood with one hand and one of his legs with the other, and was trying to bring them together.

With a desperate heave he broke loose and sent her spinning across the room.

Out in the Park, Els had recovered his composure. Once he had established that he was not about to become part of the vulture's daily intake of protein, Els decided that his impersonation of the Bishop had gone on long enough. He got up and hobbled to a tree and rid himself of the ridiculous trousers. Then clad in his vest and pants he returned to the house, and found Sergeant de Kock covered in white dust and suffering from shock.

'I don't know what to do,' the Sergeant said. 'She's got barricades up and nothing will get past them.'

'I know something that will,' said Els. 'Where's that elephant gun?'

'You're not using that fucking thing,' Sergeant de Kock told him. 'You'll bring the whole building down round our ears, and besides it's evidence.'

'What does it matter, so long as we get the old bag?'

'Never mind about her, if you fire that gun inside the house, you'll blow the end wall out and probably kill the Kommandant as well.'

Els sat back and thought. 'All right,' he said at last, 'you let me have the machine-guns out of the Saracen turrets and I'll fix her for sure.'

Sergeant de Kock was doubtful. 'Go carefully, Els,' he said, 'and try not to shoot the Kommandant.'

'I'll try, but I can't promise anything,' said Els, and when the four Browning machine-guns had been taken out of the armoured cars, he silently stole up the stairs with them. He laid the four guns on a small coffee-table pointing down the corridor and tied them down. Konstabel Els had learnt the value of overwhelming firepower up at the blockhouse and he was putting his experience of it to good use. True, the Brownings hadn't anything like the power of the elephant gun, but what they lacked in calibre they made up for in rapid fire.

'Five thousand rounds a minute pumped down the passage will make matchwood of all that furniture and mincemeat of the old girl,' he thought happily, and went downstairs to collect more belts of ammunition. On his return he fastened a cord to the triggers of the guns and prepared his next move.

The Dobermann lying asleep on the chaise-longue and dreaming of his battle with Els smelt the Konstabel coming. It had long entertained the hope that it would be able to renew the challenge Els had thrown down to it on the lawn and now it sensed that the chance had come. It stretched lazily and dropped to the floor. With no warning growl and with a stealth and silence surpassing even that of the Konstabel it crept down the corridor and threaded its way through the barricades of furniture.

Miss Hazelstone had not been in the least put out by the Kommandant's rejection of her attempts to get him into an interesting position. The very violence and strength of his effort had increased her admiration for him.

'What a strong boy you are,' she said picking herself up off the floor. 'Quite the little judo expert,' and for the next few minutes the Kommandant had to resist the manual encouragement to virility Miss Hazelstone seemed determined to administer. By dint of concentrating on Konstabel Els as a sexual object, the Kommandant even managed to maintain his lack of interest and finally Miss Hazelstone had to admit herself defeated.

'One can see you're no great shakes as a ladies' man,' she said to the Kommandant, and before he could expostulate with so much as a meaningless grunt that if she must dress as a man she couldn't expect anything else, she had picked up the hypodermic again. 'Perhaps an injection of novocaine will put lead in your pencil,' she said. 'You'll probably feel like a new man afterwards.'

'I feel like a new man now,' the Kommandant shouted through the hood, squirming furiously, but Miss Hazelstone was too intent about her business to take any notice of his protests. As the needle approached the Kommandant shut his eyes and waited, already numb with terror for the jab and at that moment all hell broke loose on the landing. Miss Hazelstone dropped the syringe and seizing her gun made for the door. The sounds emanating from the passage indicated that some terrible and bestial encounter had just begun, and the Kommandant, stung into action by the hypodermic which Miss Hazelstone had dropped in her haste and which had landed like a dart in his groin and was leaking novocaine into some artery or other, made one last desperate attempt to escape. With a herculean effort he managed to reach the floor and dragging the bed behind him leapt out of the window.

If Kommandant van Heerden and Miss Hazelstone were astonished at the extraordinary turn events had taken, Konstabel Els was even more surprised. He had just finished putting the final touches to what he hoped was going to be Miss Hazelstone's execution when he was vaguely aware that something unforeseen was in the air. Like some dark premonition he glimpsed a black blur as the Dobermann leapt through the mist of powdered plaster that filled the corridor. The dog's mouth was already open and its eye was fastened prematurely on Els's jugular vein. Els dug his chin firmly into his chest and butted the beast's muzzle with the top of his head. The dog's teeth, missing the vein, fastened on Els's shoulder and a moment later the two animals were locked in their interrupted struggle for supremacy.

As they rolled across the landing, knocking chairs and tables over left, right and centre, as Miss Hazelstone opened up with the scatter gun and the barricades began to disintegrate above them, the Browning machine-guns, thrown off target and now pointing up at the ceiling began to pour tracer bullets at the rate of 5,000 rounds a minute out through the roof of Jacaranda House. A lame vulture which had only a few minutes before managed to take off after a long and painful run and was flying gamely above the house which had already provided supper, breakfast and very nearly lunch, evaporated in the hail of bullets with an explosion of feathers and odds and ends. It was the only casualty of the gun-battle that raged in Jacaranda House.

The only other person who nearly received a burst of gunfire in his vital parts was Kommandant van Heerden. The sudden eruption of violence on the landing which had allowed him the opportunity to eject himself with double bed attached, out of the window of the bedroom, had found Sergeant de Kock waiting in the garden in the hope of getting a chance to take a pot shot at Miss Hazelstone from below. The Sergeant had been regretting his decision to allow Konstabel Els to use the machine-guns and was fully expecting the plan to end in disaster. As the roar of gunfire erupted in the house, the Sergeant threw himself to the ground, and was lying there when there was a clatter of breaking glass followed by an awful thud just above his head. He got to his feet and stared up at the thing that hung dangling from the window above him.

The Sergeant was by no means a squeamish man and

not in the least averse to shooting women. Plenty of Zulu widowers could attest to that. And had he been able to imagine for one moment that the corpulent creature in the pink nightdress who squirmed and struggled against the wall of the house some twenty feet up was Miss Hazelstone, he would have shot her without a moment's thought. But it was all too apparent that what was dangling there was not the old lady. She wasn't fat like that, she wasn't hairy like that, and above all, he felt sure she didn't have reproductive organs like that. It was difficult enough for the Sergeant to believe that anything could look like that. Sergeant de Kock stood and wrestled with the problem of the thing's identity. He peered up at its face and saw that it was wearing a mask.

Of all the queer comings and goings Sergeant de Kock had seen since he arrived at the house, this was undoubtedly the queerest. And queer was the word that sprang most naturally to mind. Whatever was hanging hooded and partially dressed up there was exposing itself to him in a manner that was shameful and indecent beyond belief. The Sergeant didn't like pansies at the best of times and he certainly didn't relish being solicited by one in this disgusting fashion. He was just making up his mind to put an end to the obscene display by a burst from his sten gun when he was stunned by something that dropped out of the sky on to him. Enveloped in a cloud of feathers and draped with what appeared to be the half-digested contents of a stomach that had recently indulged in an enormous meal of raw meat, Sergeant de Kock staggered about the garden in a state of shock.

As he tried desperately to disentangle himself from the mess of entrails and feathers, he was temporarily put off his idea of ridding the world of the raving transvestite jerking spasmodically below the bedroom window. The discovery in the detritus that covered him of several brass buttons and a South African Police cap badge was making him wonder what the hell had hit him. He was still debating the point when a new burst of gunfire above his head told him that the gun-battle was by no means over. He glanced up and saw the mattress above the hooded figure erupt into an enormous cloud of feathers, and as they floated down and adhered to the blood and guts covering him, Sergeant de Kock turned and ran. Behind him a muffled voice yelled 'Chicken.'

Chapter 12

The failure of her rapid fire down the corridor to silence for an instant the roar of the machine-guns and the screams and snarls that were part and parcel of all Konstabel Els's encounters with the Dobermann forced Miss Hazelstone to the realization that her plans were not running true to form. As repeated volleys of shot smashed through her Louis Quinze barricades and riddled with new authenticity several pieces of mock-Jacobean furniture and an irreplaceable eighteenth-century escritoire previously inlaid with ivory, the din of battle on the landing increased. Above her head a fountain of tiles hurtled up into the air under the impact of the machine-gun bullets and crashed back on the roof like enormous hailstones. Miss Hazelstone gave up her attempt to peer through the fog of plaster and went back into the bedroom.

It was immediately apparent to her that here too something had gone astray. The room was pitch dark and some large object was completely obscuring the view of the Park she had previously enjoyed from the window. She switched on the light and stood gazing at the underside of the bed on which but a few minutes before she had sat encouraging Kommandant van Heerden to be a man. Looking at the enormous bed she realized for the first time what a tremendously powerful man the Kommandant was. It had taken ten men to manhandle that bed up the stairs and along the corridor, and now one man had lifted it by himself and had carried it to the window where he was evidently standing on the sill holding it at arm's length, a feat of strength she would never have believed possible. As she looked and wondered, a muffled yell came through the mattress.

'Let me down,' the Kommandant was shouting. 'Let me down. Let me down. That bloody woman will be the death of me.' Miss Hazelstone smiled to herself. 'Just as you say,' she murmured and aimed the scatter gun at the bedsprings. As she pulled the trigger she noted how appropriate it was that the Kommandant should meet his Maker strapped in a rubber nightdress to a mattress labelled Everrest and as the bed-springs twanged and the feathers flew, Miss Hazelstone turned and went out into the corridor with a sob.

It was in all likelihood the sound of that sob that led to the death of her beloved Toby. The Dobermann which had until then felt secure in the hold it had fastened on Konstabel Els's face relaxed for one fatal second. It raised its head and pricked its ears for the last faithful time and in that second, Els, half-asphyxiated by the dog's persistent hold on his nose, seized his opportunity and clamped his jaws on the dog's throat. With one hand he clasped the dog to him and with the other grabbed the dog's scrotum and squeezed. Squeezed was hardly adequate to describe the immense pressure he exerted.

Unable, thanks to Els's grip on its windpipe, to protest this infringement of the Queensberry rules, the dog hurled itself sideways and scrabbled furiously with all four feet in an attempt to free itself. Dragging the limpet-like Els with it, it accelerated from a standing start, hurtled towards the top of the stairs and a second later the two maddened animals were airborne several feet above the great staircase. As they avalanched into the hall, the por-

traits of Sir Theophilus and Judge Hazelstone gazed grimly
down on the sordid spectacle. Only the wild boar, itself
strapped to an unrelenting iron frame, can have appreciated what its modern counterpart was suffering.

Three minutes later Konstabel Els, lying on the marble
floor of the hall, knew that he had won. The Dobermann
lay still in death and Els relaxed his grip on its throat and
rose unsteadily to his feet. Around him the heads of
stuffed warthogs and buffaloes were his only audience in
the moment of triumph. Dragging the dog by the tail
Konstabel Els went out into the park to look for the vulture. It had looked at him ravenously enough, and he
thought it might like a change of diet. He had some difficulty in finding it, and when he did, even Konstabel Els
could see that it had not died of hunger.

The shots that had indirectly led to the death of Toby
had come very near to causing the death of Kommandant
van Heerden. Near but rather too high, for the Kommandant had had the good fortune to be hanging by his wrists
from what was now the bottom of the bed. He had chewed
through the hood and was staring down at Sergeant de
Kock who had from the look of him just emerged from a
nasty accident in a turkey abattoir. It didn't seem a likely
explanation of the Sergeant's condition but after his
recent experience of perversion the Kommandant
wouldn't have been at all surprised to learn that the Sergeant had been acting out some depraved obsession connected with his name.

He was just speculating on the matter when his
thoughts were drowned by the roar of a gun just above
his head and a cloud of feathers suddenly obscured his
view of the garden. 'Chicken,' he yelled as the Sergeant
disappeared round the corner of the house, and he was

still screaming abuse some minutes later when the Sergeant followed by several konstabels reappeared. It
seemed that his voice issuing through the hole he had
managed to chew in the rubber hood carried less than
its normal quota of authority. The little group of policemen gathered below him seemed more amused by his
orders than likely to obey them.

'Let me down,' yelled the Kommandant. 'Let me down.'
Against this background of ignored instructions, Sergeant
de Kock was explaining the nastier facts of life to the
young konstabels.

'What you see before you,' he said portentously, 'is a
transvestite.'

'What's that mean, Sergeant?' enquired a konstabel.

'It means a man who likes dressing up in women's
clothes. This transvestite is also a pervert.'

'Let me down, you sod,' yelled the Kommandant.

'It's a pervert,' continued the Sergeant, 'because it is a
homosexual and it's a pervert twice over because it's a
rubber fetishist.'

'I'll have you stripped of your stripes if you don't get
me down.'

'What's a rubber fetishist, Sergeant?'

'It's someone who dresses up in rubber nighties and
hangs out of other people's bedroom windows soliciting
people below,' continued the Sergeant plucking feathers
and lights off his uniform. 'It's also a product of the permissive society and as you all know South Africa is not a
permissive society. What this swine is doing is against the
law here, and what I suggest is that we shove a bullet or
two up his arse and give him the thrill to end all thrills.'

The suggestion was greeted with nods of approval from
the konstabels and a crescendo of screams from the

hooded dangling figure. Only one naïve konstabel objected.

'But wouldn't that be murder, Sergeant?' he enquired.

Sergeant de Kock looked at him sternly. 'Are you telling me,' he asked, 'that you think that blokes should be allowed to run around the country dressed in women's nighties?'

'No, Sergeant. It's against the law.'

'That's what I just said, so we'd be doing our duty if we put a bullet in him.'

'Couldn't we just arrest him?' the konstabel asked.

'This is your commanding officer, and I order you to let me down.'

'It's guilty of another crime now, Sergeant,' said another konstabel. 'It's impersonating a police officer.'

'You young konstabels know the procedure or you bloody well ought to,' continued the Sergeant. 'In the case of a criminal apprehended in the commission of a crime, what do you do?'

'Arrest him,' chorused the konstabels.

'And if you can't arrest him? If he tries to escape?'

'You give him a warning.'

'And what if he doesn't stop trying to escape?'

'You shoot him, Sergeant.'

'Right,' said the Sergeant. 'Now are you trying to tell me that that bastard isn't a criminal caught in the commission of a crime, and that he isn't trying to escape?'

The konstabels had to agree that the Sergeant was right, and they had just reached this point in their deliberations when Konstabel Els came limping triumphantly round the corner dragging the Dobermann after him.

'Look what I've got,' he said proudly.

Sergeant de Kock's little group were not impressed. 'Look what we've got,' they said, and Konstabel Els had to admit that what was hanging squirming from the window made his own trophy look pretty tame.

'Just doing a queer in,' said Sergeant de Kock. 'Want to join in, Els, should be just up your street?'

'Not my street,' said Els peering up at the figure. 'That's Kommandant van Heerden's street, that's what that is. I'd know it anywhere.'

As the firing party broke up in confusion at the news that it was the Kommandant who was hanging there, the woman largely responsible for his predicament was debating what to do next. She thought that she must have at last got it into the thick head of the Kommandant that she was capable of killing Fivepence and while she realized that Kommandant van Heerden's opinion no longer mattered, she hoped that his successor would have enough sense to arrest her promptly.

She went downstairs to look for a policeman to escort her to her cell in Piemburg Police Station, but the house appeared to be deserted.

'I must have scared them off,' she said to herself and went to fetch her car. Halfway to the garage she realized that Fivepence had the keys with him and instead she climbed into one of the police Land-rovers and started the engine.

As the konstabels on the other side of Jacaranda House assisted the Kommandant down the ladder, they gave no thought to the Land-rover that sailed unsteadily up the drive. At the gate the sentry signalled it out and the car disappeared round the corner and down the road into Piemburg.

Most of the events of the day had passed clean over the head of the Bishop of Barotseland. Manacled and naked, he lay in the cellar and tried to concentrate on spiritual questions as being less painful than the affairs of the flesh. He wasn't particularly successful in this effort; hunger and pain competed with fear to occupy his attention, and over them all there hung the awful dread that he was going mad. It was less in fact fear at the thought that he was going than that he had already gone. In twenty-four hours he had seen the accepted tenets of his world abused in a way which had, he had to admit, all the hallmarks of insanity.

'I am a bishop and my sister is a murderess,' he said to himself reassuringly. 'If my sister is not a murderess, it is possible that I am not a bishop.' This line of logic didn't seem very helpful and he gave it up as likely to disturb what little balance of mind he had left. 'Someone is mad,' he concluded, and began to wonder if the voices he had heard in the depths of the swimming bath were not after all symptoms of the insanity he seemed to be suffering from.

On the other hand his firm belief in the intervention of the Lord in the affairs of the world led him to wonder how he had transgressed so gravely as to warrant the punishment that had fallen on him. He came to the conclusion that he had been guilty of *hubris*. 'Pride comes before a fall,' he said, but he couldn't imagine what height of pride could justify the depths to which he had fallen. Certainly the little bit of self-congratulation he had allowed himself on his appointment to Barotseland hardly called for the appalling punishment he was now undergoing. He preferred to believe that his present sufferings were a preparation for better things to come, and a test of his faith. He consoled himself with the thought that there must be some people in the world in even worse plights, though he couldn't think who they were or what they were suffering.

'I shall bear my tribulations gladly and my soul will be renewed,' he said smugly and gave himself up to meditation.

Kommandant van Heerden had come to quite different conclusions. He had borne enough tribulations in the past twenty-four hours to last him a lifetime. He knew now that there were three things he never wanted to see again. Rubber nightdresses, Sergeant de Kock and Jacaranda House. All three had lost whatever charm they had once held for him, and in the case of the first two that was nil.

As for Jacaranda House, he had to admit he had once liked the place, but he could see now that his feelings were not reciprocated. The house evidently reserved its favours for those of impeccable social standing and British descent. For lesser mortals it held terrors. In decreasing order of social standing he placed himself, Els, the Dobermann, Fivepence and the Vulture. He himself had been trussed, terrified and threatened with death. Els had been savaged on two separate occasions. The Dobermann had been bitten to death. Fivepence had been deposited all over the garden and the Vulture all over Sergeant de Kock. All in all, these indignities had been too closely related to the class of the recipients for there to be any doubt that the reputation for snobbery the Hazelstones enjoyed was not without foundation in fact. On the whole he thought Els had come off pretty lightly, considering his origins and social standing.

On the other hand he had cause to suspect that Els's share of misfortune was yet to come. True, he had been instrumental in saving the Kommandant's life on two occasions. Kommandant van Heerden had to admit that the Konstabel's intervention on the landing had given him time to jump out of the window, and once there it had been Els who had stopped Sergeant de Kock exceeding his duty. But then again, there was the little matter of the fraças up at the gateway. It had too many of the trademarks of Els to be ignored entirely. Els had some explaining to do.

As he dressed in the study Kommandant van Heerden eyed Els warily. The Konstabel was dabbing antiseptic on his nose and playing with the paperweight. By the time he had put on his trousers, the Kommandant had come to some definite conclusions. Miss Hazelstone had made her point, and the Kommandant was convinced that in all probability she had killed Fivepence. Unfortunately, she could not, he knew, have butchered the policemen at the gate. Someone else was responsible for that, and while the evidence pointed to Jonathan Hazelstone, the Kommandant had seen him asleep on the bed just before the firing began. It followed that if Jonathan was innocent, the guilty person was Els. It was but a step from this conclusion to the question of responsibility. Who, it would be asked, had allowed a homicidal maniac like Els to have possession of a multi-barrelled elephant gun, and had given him permission to use it?

Weighing up the various debts he owed to Konstabel Els and the ugly possibilities that faced his career, the Kommandant came to a rapid decision.

'Els,' he said quietly, seating himself behind the desk, 'I want you to think carefully before you answer the next question. Very carefully indeed.'

Konstabel Els looked up nervously. He didn't like the tone of the Kommandant's voice.

'What time was it when you deserted your post at the gate yesterday afternoon?' the Kommandant continued.

'I didn't desert my post, sir,' said Els.

The Kommandant shivered. This was worse than he expected. The idiot was going to claim he stayed there all afternoon.

'I think you did desert your post, Els,' he said. 'In fact, I know you did. At half past three to be precise.'

'No, sir,' said Els, 'I was relieved.'

'Relieved?'

'Yes sir, by a large black-haired konstabel who had left his revolver at the station.'

'By a large black-haired konstabel who had left his revolver at the station?' the Kommandant repeated slowly, wondering where the trap was.

'That's right. That's what he told me, sir. That he had left his revolver at the station. He asked to borrow mine.'

'He asked to borrow yours?'

'Yes, sir.'

Kommandant van Heerden mulled this statement over in his mind before going on. He had to admit that it had the ring of utility about it.

'Would you be able to identify this large black-haired konstabel again if you saw him?' he asked.

'Oh yes sir,' Els said. 'He's sitting in the cellar.'

'Sitting in the cellar, is he?' Kommandant van Heerden glanced out of the window and pondered. Outside Sergeant de Kock was patrolling up and down on the path. Looking out at the Sergeant, the Kommandant began to think he might have a use for him after all. He went to the window and shouted.

'Sergeant de Kock,' he ordered, 'I want you in here at the double.'

A moment later the Sergeant was standing in front of the Judge's desk and regretting that he had ever mistaken the Kommandant for a transvestite.

'How many times have I told you, Sergeant,' the Kom-

mandant said sternly, 'that I will not have my men walking about in untidy uniforms. You're supposed to set an
example too. Look at your uniform, man. It's disgusting.
You're a disgrace to the South African Police.'

'Got dirty in the line of duty, sir,' said the Sergeant.
'Flipping vulture died on me, sir.'

'Birds of a feather, Sergeant de Kock, stick together,'
said the Kommandant.

'Very funny, I'm sure, sir,' said the Sergeant unpleasantly.

'Hm,' said the Kommandant. 'Well, as far as I'm concerned, it's inexcusable.'

'I didn't choose to be there.'

'Don't make excuses. I didn't choose to be where I was
just now, and I didn't notice any consideration on your
part for my state, so you needn't expect any from me. Get
out of that filthy uniform at once. Konstabel Els, fetch the
prisoner.'

As the Sergeant undressed, the Kommandant continued
to lecture him, and by the time he was out of his uniform,
he had learnt a great deal about himself that he would
have preferred to have remained ignorant about.

'And what do you think I'm going to wear back to
the barracks?' he asked.

Kommandant van Heerden tossed him the rubber nightdress. 'Try this for size,' he snarled.

'You don't expect me to go down into town wearing
this?' Sergeant de Kock asked incredulously. The Kommandant nodded.

'What's good for the goose. . . .' he said smugly.

'I'm not going to be made the laughing-stock of the
barracks,' the Sergeant insisted.

'Nobody will know who you are. You'll be wearing
this as well,' and the Kommandant gave him the hood.

Sergeant de Kock hesitated miserably. 'I don't know....' he said.

'I bloody well do,' yelled the Kommandant. 'Get into those clothes. That's an order,' and as the Sergeant, bowing before his wrath, squeezed himself into the revolting garments and wondered how he would explain his presence in them to his wife, the Kommandant continued, 'You're incognito now, Sergeant, and provided you keep your trap shut, you'll stay that way.'

'I sure as hell won't,' said the Sergeant. 'I'll be out of the fucking things as quick as I can. I don't know how the hell you expect me to keep discipline when you make me look bloody ridiculous.'

'Nonsense,' said the Kommandant. 'That hood is a perfect disguise. You ought to know that. And another thing, you keep quiet about what you've seen and I'll keep my mouth shut about you. Right?'

'I suppose it will have to be.'

In the next few minutes Sergeant de Kock learnt that he had never so much as seen a vulture and that he hadn't visited Jacaranda Park. He had, it seemed, been away on compassionate leave visiting his sick mother. The fact that his mother had died ten years before didn't seem worth mentioning. With the knowledge that he would be known for the rest of his life as Rubber Cock unless he did what he was told, the Sergeant didn't feel he was in any position to argue with the Kommandant.

The Bishop of Barotseland had reached much the same conclusion. The whole thing was a mistake, and the police would soon discover their error, he told himself as Konstabel Els frogmarched him up to the study. He was delighted to find the Kommandant in a much friendlier state of mind than he had been earlier in the day.

'You can take the handcuffs off him, Els,' said the Kommandant. 'Now then, Mr Hazelstone,' he continued when this had been done. 'We just want to make a little experiment. It concerns this uniform.' He held Sergeant de Kock's bloodstained tunic up. 'We have reason to believe that the man responsible for the murders yesterday was wearing this uniform. I just want you to try it on for size. If it doesn't fit you, and I don't for one moment suppose that it will, you will be free to leave here.'

The Bishop looked at the uniform doubtfully. It was clearly several sizes too small for him.

'I don't suppose I could get into it,' he said.

'Well, just put it on and we'll see,' said the Kommandant encouragingly and the Bishop climbed into the uniform. In the corner a grim figure in a nightdress and hood smiled to itself. Sergeant de Kock had begun to see daylight.

Finally, the Bishop was ready to prove his innocence. The trousers were too short by a foot. The fly wouldn't do up and the arms of the tunic just covered his elbows. It was obvious that he had never worn the uniform before. He could hardly move in the thing.

He turned cheerfully to the Kommandant. 'There you are,' he said. 'I told you it wouldn't fit.'

Kommandant van Heerden put the Sergeant's cap on his head where it perched precariously. Then he stood back and regarded him appreciatively.

'Just one more thing,' he said. 'We'll have to have an identity parade.'

Five minutes later the Bishop was standing in a row of twenty policemen while Konstabel Els walked slowly down the line. For the sake of verisimilitude, Els chose to hesitate in front of several other men before finally halting before the Bishop.

'This is the man who relieved me, sir,' he said emphatically. 'I'd know him anywhere. I never forget a face.'

'You're quite sure about it?' the Kommandant asked.

'Positive, sir,' said Els.

'Just as I thought,' said the Kommandant. 'Put the handcuffs on the swine.'

Before he knew what was happening the Bishop was manacled once more and being bundled into the back of a police car. Beside him, hooded and hot, sat the grim figure from the study.

'It's a lie. It's a mistake,' the Bishop shouted as the car began to move off. 'I've been framed.'

'You can say that again,' murmured the figure in the hood. The Bishop looked at it, 'Who are you?' he asked.

'I'm the executioner,' said the hooded man and chuckled. In the back of the police car the Bishop of Barotseland fainted.

On the front steps of Jacaranda House, Kommandant van Heerden was giving his orders. They were quite explicit. Find, restrain and transfer Miss Hazelstone to Fort Rapier Lunatic Asylum. Find, collect, and transfer every lethal weapon in Jacaranda House to the police armoury. Find, collect and transfer every piece of rubber including bathmats and raincoats to the Piemburg Police Station. In short, collect every piece of evidence and get the hell out. No, the Bubonic Plague and Rabies noticeboards could be left up. They were relevant, and if anything understated the dangers Jacaranda Park held for visitors. From now on Kommandant van Heerden was going to conduct the case from a more secure base. His Headquarters would be in Piemburg Prison itself where Jonathan Hazelstone couldn't get out, and more important, his sister couldn't get in. And get that damned hypodermic syringe out of his sight.

He'd seen enough hypodermics to last a lifetime.

As the men dispersed to carry out his orders, the Kommandant called Konstabel Els back.

'Very good, Els,' he said charitably. 'There was only one little mistake you made.'

'Mistake? What was that?'

The Kommandant smiled. 'It wasn't a konstabel who took over from you at the gate, it was a sergeant.'

'Oh yes, so it was. I remember now. A sergeant.'

Chapter 13

The Prison in Piemburg is situated on the edge of town. It is old and looks from the outside not altogether unattractive. An air of faded severity lingers about its stuccoed walls. Above the huge iron doorway are printed the words 'Piemburg Tronk and Gaol', and the door itself is painted a cheerful black. On either side the barred windows of the administrative block break the monotony of the walls whose heights are delicately topped with cast-iron cacti which give the whole building a faintly horticultural air. The visitor to Piemburg who passes the great rectangle of masonry might well imagine that he was in the neighbourhood of some enormous kitchen garden were it not for the frequent and persistent screams that float up over the ornamental ironwork and suggest that something more voracious than a Venus Flytrap has closed upon a victim.

Inside the impression is less deceptive. Opened by Sir Theophilus in 1897, the Viceroy had complimented the architect in his speech at the unveiling of the flogging post for 'creating in this building a sense of security it is hard to find in the world today', a remark which, coming as it did from a man in whom a sense of insecurity was so manifest, spoke for itself. Sir Theophilus's enthusiasm was not shared by most of the people who entered Piemburg Prison. Notorious throughout South Africa for the severity of its warden, Governor Schnapps, it had the

reputation for being escape-proof and having the fewest
recidivists.

If the Prison was escape-proof, the Maximum Security
Block was doubly so. Set near the execution shed which
was appropriately nicknamed Top, the Security block
huddling half-underground was known as Bottom.

The Bishop could find no fault with the name. 'I can
see it's the bottom,' he said to the warder who pushed him
into his tiny cell. 'I don't have to be told.'

'I could tell you a few other things,' said the warder
through the grille.

'I'm sure you could,' said the Bishop hastily. His experience with the hooded man in the car had taught him
not to ask unnecessary questions.

'I have always kept this cell for murderers,' the warder
continued. 'It's convenient for the door, you see.'

'I should have thought that was a disadvantage with
prisoners who have such strong motives to escape,' the
Bishop said, reconciling himself to the thought that he
was a captive audience.

'Oh, no. They didn't escape. It made it easy to take
them across to Top. We rushed them along the passage
and up the steps and they were gone before they knew
it.'

The Bishop was relieved to hear this. 'I am glad you
put so much emphasis on the past,' he said. 'I gather there
hasn't been a hanging for some time.'

'Not for twenty years. Not in Piemburg, that is. They
hang them all in Pretoria these days. Taken all the fun
out of life.'

The Bishop was just considering the dreariness of a life
that found hangings fun when the warder went on, 'Mind
you, it will be different in your case. You're a Hazelstone
and you're privileged,' the warder said enviously.

For once in his life the Bishop was thankful to be a Hazelstone. 'Why's that?' he asked hopefully.

'You've got the right to be hanged in Piemburg. It's something to do with your grandfather. Don't know what, but I'll see if I can find out for you,' and he went down the passage and left the Bishop cursing himself for asking yet another silly question. As he paced his cell he heard the sound of vehicles outside and peering out through the tiny barred window saw that the Kommandant had arrived.

The Kommandant had taken the precaution of driving down from Jacaranda House in an armoured-car and was busy explaining to Governor Schnapps that he was taking over his office.

'You can't do that,' the Governor protested.

'Can and will,' said the Kommandant. 'Got Emergency Powers. Now then if you'll be good enough to show me where your office is, I'll have my camp bed moved in and we can get down to business.'

And leaving the Governor to write a letter of complaint to Pretoria, the Kommandant installed himself in Schnapps's office and sent for Konstabel Els.

'Where's Luitenant Verkramp?' he asked. 'That's what I want to know.'

For once Konstabel Els was better informed. 'He's in hospital,' he said. 'Got himself wounded up at the gate.'

'That fellow shot him, did he? Deserves a medal.'

Els was surprised. What he had seen of Luitenant Verkramp's courage didn't seem to him to warrant a medal.

'Who? Verkramp?' he asked.

'No, of course not. The fellow who shot him.'

'He didn't get shot,' said Els. 'Threw himself into a ditch.'

'Typical,' said the Kommandant. 'Anyway, I want you to go and fetch him from the hospital. Tell him he's got to interrogate the prisoner. I want a full confession and quick.'

Konstabel Els hesitated. He was not anxious to renew his acquaintance with the Luitenant.

'He won't take orders from me,' he said. 'Besides he may have hurt himself seriously falling into that ditch.'

'I wish I had your optimism, Els,' said the Kommandant, 'but I doubt it. The swine's malingering.'

'Why not leave him where he is? I don't mind getting a confession out of the prisoner.'

The Kommandant shook his head. The case was too important to have Els botching it up with his dreadful methods.

'It's kind of you to offer,' he said, 'but I think we'll leave it to Luitenant Verkramp.'

'There's gratitude for you,' thought Els, as he went off to fetch Verkramp from the hospital.

He found the Luitenant lying on his stomach taking nourishment through a straw. Verkramp's back, it appeared, made it impossible to eat in any other position.

'Well?' he asked grumpily when Konstabel Els reported to him. 'What do you want?'

'Came to see how you were,' Els said tactfully.

'You can see how I am,' Verkramp answered, regarding Els's dirty boots with disapproval. 'I have been seriously wounded.'

'I can see that,' Els said, grateful that the Luitenant couldn't study his face. He regretted having peered down into the moat now. 'Got you in the back, did he?'

'Came at me from behind,' said the Luitenant who didn't like the imputation that he had been trying to escape.

'Nasty. Very nasty. Well, you'll be glad to know we've

got the bastard. The Kommandant wants you to start interrogating him straight away.'

Verkramp choked on his straw. 'He wants what?' he shouted at the Konstabel's boots.

'He says you're to come straight away.'

'Well, he can say what he likes, but I'm not budging. Besides,' he added, 'the doctors wouldn't let me.'

'Would you like to tell him yourself,' asked Els. 'He won't believe me.'

In the end a telephone was brought to the Luitenant's bedside and the Kommandant had a word with him. It was rather more than one word and in the end Luitenant Verkramp was persuaded to report for duty. Short of facing a court-martial for cowardice, desertion in the face of the enemy, and incompetence in that he allowed twenty-one policemen under his command to be slaughtered, there didn't seem much he could do to remain in hospital. Verkramp was in a very ugly mood and not altogether clearheaded when he arrived at the prison to question Jonathan Hazelstone.

It was hardly less ugly than the mood Kommandant van Heerden was in. After a momentary spasm of optimism that the case was as good as closed now that the prisoner was in Bottom, the Kommandant had succumbed to a state of extreme pessimism on learning that Miss Hazelstone was still at large. Since leaving the Park she had not been seen. The police Land-rover had been found abandoned but of Miss Hazelstone there was no trace, and while the Kommandant felt pretty sure she wouldn't break into the prison to renew their acquaintance, he had no doubt that what she might do outside was just as likely to jeopardize his future.

For one thing he couldn't afford to allow her to run

about the country telling all and sundry that she had had him trussed to a bed in a rubber nightdress and that he hadn't been man enough to take an injection. He was just consoling himself with the thought that Miss Hazelstone's circle of friends was pretty exclusive, when he remembered that among other assets like goldmines, the Hazelstone family owned the local newspaper, whose editor had never shown any great regard for the police. Kommandant van Heerden had no desire whatsoever to provide copy for the *Natal Chronicle* and the thought of headlines like: 'The Tiny Prick. Kommandant in Rubber Nightie says No to Needle,' made his blood run cold.

He gave orders that road blocks be set up on all roads leading out of Piemburg and that the homes of all Miss Hazelstone's friends were to be raided. Every hotel and guesthouse in the town was to be checked and plain-clothes men were to mingle with the crowds in the shops. Finally, the Kommandant ordered that notices be put up announcing a large reward for information leading to the capture of Miss Hazelstone, but just to make sure that Miss Hazelstone's confessions did not reach the public, he plucked up courage and left the safety of the prison to pay a personal call on the editor of the *Natal Chronicle*.

'I'm acting under Emergency Powers,' he told the man, 'and I am ordering you to publish nothing Miss Hazelstone may submit. In fact, if anything is submitted by her you're to forward it to me unread,' and the editor had gone off to cancel Miss Hazelstone's current contribution to the women's page which was called, 'How to Convert a Zulu Kraal into a Country Cottage'. He read it through to see if there was anything subversive in it, but apart from the recommendation to use latex for loose covers, he couldn't find anything unusual in it. In any case he had his hands full trying to find out how many victims there were in the bubonic plague and rabies epidemics that had apparently hit the community. As far as he had been able to ascertain, the only people exhibiting symptoms of rabies were the Piemburg police.

Throughout the night and the following day the search for Miss Hazelstone continued. Hundreds of plain-clothes men scoured the town or hung about indecisively in shops making life difficult for store detectives on the lookout for shoplifters. A number of elderly ladies suddenly found themselves in handcuffs and being driven at high speed in police cars to Fort Rapier Mental Hospital, where several had to be admitted with nervous breakdowns as a result of the experience.

On the roads out of Piemburg queues of cars and lorries waited for hours while policemen ransacked each vehicle. There were particularly tiresome delays on the Durban road where trucks carrying offal from the abattoir to the Jojo Dog and Servant Meat Cannery had to be searched. Since Kommandant van Heerden had impressed upon his men the need to search every square inch of every vehicle no matter how unlikely a hiding-place it seemed to be and since the Jojo trucks contained 25 tons of pig brains, ox guts and the inedible and doubtless nutritious entrails of every conceivable diseased animal that contributed its share to the liver and love Jojo promised the dogs and servants, the men at the Durban road search point had to go to considerable trouble to make absolutely sure that Miss Hazelstone was not hiding in the disgusting mess that greeted them every time they stopped one of the lorries. The occupants of the cars piling up behind were astonished to see policemen clad only in bathing-trunks and with face-masks and schnorkels clambering aboard the Jojo lorries and diving into piles of semi-liquid meat so enormous that even the late and unlamented vulture would have been put off its feed. The policemen who finally emerged from their prolonged and fruitless search were hardly a sight to reassure the citizens of Piemburg that the police were looking after their interests, and faced with the prospect of so thorough a search a good many motorists decided to cancel the trips they were making and go quietly home. Those that stayed had the upholstery of their cars irremediably stained by the half-naked and bloodsoaked cops who climbed in and poked under seats and inside glove compartments for the elusive Miss Hazelstone.

In the meantime the homes of Miss Hazelstone's friends were being searched with equal thoroughness, and a good many people, who had boasted of an acquaintanceship with her which they had never enjoyed, found that Miss Hazelstone's friendship carried with it some awesome consequences, not the least of which was the knowledge that they were suspected of harbouring a wanted criminal.

In spite of all these drastic measures, Miss Hazelstone remained at large and cheerfully unaware that she was the object of such a meticulous manhunt.

After driving the police Land-rover through the gates of Jacaranda Park she had followed the main road to town, had parked the car in the main street, and had walked into the Police Station to give herself up.

'I'm Miss Hazelstone of Jacaranda Park, and I've come here to be arrested,' she said to the elderly konstabel on duty at the desk, who was in fact one of the post-operative cases Kommandant van Heerden had insisted return to duty. Missing his gall bladder and the lower portion of his intestines, he had not lost his wits as well, and he had been in the police long enough to have got used to the queer customers who came in regularly to make false confessions. He looked the old gentleman in the salmon-pink suit up and down for a minute before replying.

'Oh yes,' he said sympathetically. 'So you're Miss Hazelstone are you, sir? And what do you want to be arrested for?'

'I've murdered my cook.'

'Lucky to have one to murder,' said the old konstabel. 'My old woman cooks for me and if the state of my insides or what remains of them is anything to go by, she's been trying to murder me for years, and it's only thanks to the miracles of modern surgery that she hasn't bloody well succeeded. Do you know,' he went on confidentially, 'it took the surgeons four hours to cut away all the rotten stuff there was in me. They took my gall bladder and then my. . . .'

'I have not come here to discuss the state of your health,' Miss Hazelstone snapped. 'It's not of the slightest interest to me.'

Konstabel Oosthuizen wasn't amused. 'If that's the way you want it,' he said, 'that's the way it's going to be. Now hop it.'

Miss Hazelstone wasn't going to be brushed off so easily. 'I have come here to be arrested for murder,' she insisted.

Konstabel Oosthuizen looked up from the medical dictionary he had been reading. 'Look,' he said, 'you've just told me you're not interested in my physical condition. Well, I'm bloody well not interested in your mental state either. So shove off.'

'Are you telling me you refuse to arrest me?'

Konstabel Oosthuizen sighed. 'I'll arrest you for loitering if you don't get out of here double quick,' he said.

'Good, that's what I've come for,' Miss Hazelstone sat down on a bench against the wall.

'You're making a bloody nuisance of yourself, that's

what you're doing. All right come on down to the cells,' and leading the way down to the basement he locked her in. 'Give me a shout when you want to come out,' he said, and went back to read about diseases of the intestinal tract. He was still so engrossed in his own pathology when he went off duty that he forgot to mention her presence in the cells to the konstabel who relieved him, and she was still sitting quietly in her rubber suit next morning when he came on duty once more.

It wasn't until mid-morning that he remembered that the old gent was still down in the cells, and he went down to let him out.

'Had enough?' he asked, unlocking the door.

'Have you come to question me?' Miss Hazelstone asked hopefully. She had been looking forward to third degree.

'I haven't come to bring you breakfast if that's what you think.'

'Good,' said Miss Hazelstone. 'Let's get on with it.'

Konstabel Oosthuizen looked bewildered. 'You're a weird old buzzard,' he said. 'Senile if you ask me.'

'What are you going to do?'

'Kick you out,' said the Konstabel. 'I can't have you cluttering up the station.'

'I'm Miss Hazelstone of Jacaranda Park, and I'm wanted for murder. It's your duty to arrest me.'

'And I'm the Queen of England,' said Konstabel Oosthuizen. 'Go on, clear out of here before you get me into trouble.'

'I tell you I'm wanted for murder,' Miss Hazelstone insisted.

'You're certainly not wanted for anything else,' and the Konstabel picked up his medical dictionary and began to read about gynecomastia.

Miss Hazelstone tried to make him see reason. 'What

do I have to do to get myself arrested if you won't arrest me for murder?' she asked.

'Try fucking a kaffir for a start,' suggested the Konstabel. 'That usually works wonders.'

'But that's what I've been doing for the last eight years,' Miss Hazelstone told him.

'Get along with you. I doubt if you've got the where-withal,' was all the answer she got, and with the final comment that she looked as though she might have gyne-comastia, which Konstabel Oosthuizen had just learnt was unusual development of the breasts of a male, the Konstabel went back to his book.

'If you won't arrest me, I demand to be taken home,' Miss Hazelstone said.

Konstabel Oosthuizen knew when to compromise. 'Where do you live?' he asked.

'Jacaranda Park of course,' said Miss Hazelstone.

'I might have known it,' said the Konstabel, and glad to be rid of her took her out into the station yard. 'Take the old gent up to Jacaranda Park,' he said to the driver of a police car that was just leaving, and with all the speed and social deference to which she was accustomed, Miss Hazelstone was driven to the gates of Jacaranda Park and deposited there. The car hadn't been stopped at the police checkpoints for obvious reasons.

Chapter 14

When Luitenant Verkramp arrived from hospital to begin his interrogation of the prisoner, he found the Kommandant waiting for him. He hobbled into the Governor's office to report for duty.

'I'm a sick man,' he said grumpily. 'The doctors didn't want me to leave the hospital.'

'Quite so, Luitenant,' said the Kommandant cheerfully. 'Quite so, but now that you're here, let's not waste time. I need your help.'

'What is it this time?' Verkramp asked. Kommandant van Heerden was always needing his help, but this was the first time he had known him acknowledge the fact.

'I have here the Hazelstone family file,' the Kommandant said. 'It includes the security report you submitted to the Bureau of State Security. I've read it through, and I must say, Luitenant, you showed more perspicacity than I gave you credit for.'

Luitenant Verkramp smiled. The Kommandant had never been so complimentary before.

'You say here,' continued the Kommandant, tapping the report, 'that the Hazelstones are noted for their left-wing and communistic leanings. I would like to know what made you say that.'

'Everybody knows they are Marxists,' said Verkramp.

'I don't,' said the Kommandant, 'and I would like to hear why you do.'

'Well, for one thing Miss Hazelstone's nephew is at the university.'

'Doesn't make him a commie.'

'He believes in evolution.'

'Hm,' said the Kommandant doubtfully. He knew it was a subversive doctrine, but with Els around it seemed irrefutable to him.

'What else?' he asked.

'I checked the library. It's full of Communist literature. They've got *The Red Badge of Courage, Black Beauty*, the collected works of Dostoyevsky, even Bertrand Russell's banned book, *Why I am not a Christian*. I tell you, they are all dangerous books.'

Kommandant van Heerden was impressed. Evidently Verkramp had gone more thoroughly into the matter than he had imagined. 'That seems conclusive enough,' he said. 'What about the brother, Jonathan Hazelstone. You say here he's got a criminal record.'

'That's right. He lives in Rhodesia and he's done time.'

'He says he's a bishop.'

'He can say what he bloody well pleases,' said Verkramp. 'It doesn't alter the facts. I checked them with the Rhodesian police. You'll find the telegram they sent back in the file.'

Kommandant van Heerden pulled out the telegram. 'I can't make head or tail of it,' he said. 'It's in code or something. You read it,' and he handed the telegram to Verkramp.

The Luitenant peered at the hieroglyphs. 'It's pretty obvious,' he said at last. 'Jonathan Hazelstone 2 yrs parson Bulawayo 3 yrs Barotse incumbent at present convocation 3 wks Umtali. Any fool can understand that,' he said.

'Well, this one can't,' snapped the Kommandant. 'You tell me what it means.'

Verkramp sighed. This was what came from having an

illiterate Kommandant.

'It's quite simple. He's done two years in Bulawayo prison for burning a building down. Three years for murdering a Barotse native who was having a nap and three weeks in Umtali for convoking.'

Kommandant van Heerden thought for a moment. 'What's convoking?' he asked.

'You've heard of con men, haven't you? It's fraud and swindling. It's convoking people into buying phoney shares and things.'

'Oh, is that what it is? You would think they'd have given him more than three weeks for a thing like that. After all he got three years for killing the coon boy which was a bit steep,' the Kommandant said, relieved to know that he had got the right man. There was no doubt now in his mind that he could make the case stick. A man who had killed a Barotse while the poor bastard was asleep was hardly likely to hesitate when it came to killing a Zulu cook.

'Well, all we need now is a nice tidy confession,' he said. 'I'll expect you to have it on my desk in the morning.'

Luitenant Verkramp shrugged. 'If you want it so quick you had better ask Els. My methods require that the prisoner be kept awake for at least three days and with a hardened professional like this fellow it will probably take more.'

'I can't ask Els. We can't have a Hazelstone hobbling into court with no toenails and his balls the size of pumpkins. Think what the defence attorney would make of that one. Use your head. No, the interrogation has got to be handled discreetly and I'm putting you in charge of it,' the Kommandant said, resorting to flattery. 'Do what you like with him, but see he's all in one piece when you've finished.'

With this *carte blanche*, the Kommandant ended the interview and ordered his supper.

In the Maximum Security Block, there was no supper for Jonathan Hazelstone, and if there had been it is doubtful if he would have had much appetite for it. He had just learnt from the old warder how it was he enjoyed the unusual privilege of being able to be hanged in Top.

'It's to do with something your grandfather said in his speech when he opened the prison,' the warder told him. 'He said he wanted the gallows to be kept in working order in case his family wanted to use them.'

'I'm sure he meant well,' the Bishop said sadly, wondering at the appalling legacy his grandfather had bequeathed the family.

'Your father, the late Judge, he was a great one for the gallows. Why some of the men who've had their last meal in that cell, where you're standing now, have told me that they were certain they were going to get off free as the air, and damn me if your old dad didn't go and put the black cap on and condemn them.'

'I have always regretted my father's reputation,' said the Bishop.

'I wouldn't worry about it now,' said the warder. 'It's the gallows would put me in a sweat if I were in your shoes.'

'I have every faith in the fairness of the court,' said the Bishop.

'They haven't been used for twenty years,' continued the warder. 'They're not safe.'

'No?' queried the Bishop. 'Is that unusual?'

'They've got the Death Watch Beetle. You'd be lucky

to get up the steps alive, if you ask me,' said the warder and shuffled off down the passage to let Luitenant Verkramp and Konstabel Els into Bottom. The interrogation was about to begin.

In spite of the fact that he was still feeling the effects of his injuries, Luitenant Verkramp was determined to apply the standard South African technique to the prisoner.

'I'll butter him up,' he told Konstabel Els, 'and make him feel I'm sympathetic and you can be the hard man and threaten him.'

'Can I use the Electric Shock machine?' Els asked eagerly.

'He's too important,' said Verkramp, 'and you're not to beat him up too much either.'

'What are we going to do then?' said Els, who couldn't imagine getting a confession out of an innocent man without some violence.

'Keep him awake until he's ready to drop. I've never known it to fail.'

Luitenant Verkramp seated himself behind the desk and ordering the prisoner to be brought in, assumed what he supposed to be an air of sympathetic understanding. To the Bishop, when he entered the room, the expression on the Luitenant's face suggested only a pained and vicious hostility. In the hours that followed, this first impression proved if anything to have been over-optimistic. Luitenant Verkramp's attempts at sympathetic understanding inspired in the Bishop the conviction that he was locked alone in a room with a sadistic homosexual suffering from an overdose of several powerful hallucinatory drugs. Certainly nothing else could explain the overtures the Luitenant was making nor the distorted version of his own life which Verkramp insisted he corroborate. Everything the Bishop imagined he had done took on an entirely contrary character as seen through the eyes of Verkramp.

He had not for instance been an undergraduate in Cambridge studying theology. He had, he learnt, been indoctrinated in Marxist-Leninist theory by a man whom he had previously imagined to be a leading Anglo-Catholic professor, but who had apparently been a Moscow-trained theoretician. As the hours dragged by the Bishop's faint hold on reality grew fainter. The illusions he had nourished for a lifetime slipped away and were replaced by the new certitudes his deranged interrogator insisted he subscribe to.

By the time they had arrived at the events of the previous day, the Bishop, who had eaten nothing for thirty-six hours, and who had been standing with his hands above his head for six, was prepared to admit to murdering the entire South African Police force, if doing so would allow him to sit down for five minutes.

'I shot them with a multi-barrelled rocket launcher supplied by the Chinese consul in Dar-es-Salaam,' he repeated slowly while Verkramp copied the admission down.

'Good,' said the Luitenant finally, 'that seems pretty conclusive.'

'I'm glad to hear it. Now if you don't mind I would like time to think about my future,' the Bishop said.

'I think you can safely leave that to us,' said the Luitenant. 'There's just one more matter I want to get straightened out. Why did you shoot your sister's cook?'

'I discovered he was a CIA agent,' said the Bishop, who by this time knew the lines along which Verkramp's mind was working. He had long since discovered that there was no point in arguing with the man, and since Verkramp's imagination had evidently been nurtured on spy-thrillers, this seemed the sort of explanation he would swallow.

'Oh, was he?' said Verkramp, and made a mental note to investigate the cooks of Piemburg to discover how many more were in the pay of the Americans.

By the time Verkramp had finished with him, the Bishop had decided that his only hope of escaping execution on the scaffold reserved for him by his grandfather lay in concocting a confession so absurd that it would either be thrown out of court by the judge, or allow him to plead insanity. 'I may as well be hanged for a sheep as a lamb,' he said to himself when Els came to take over the interrogation and wondered what new crimes he could add to the list he had already agreed to. Konstabel Els was glad to suggest some.

'I hear you want us to go around marrying kaffirs,' Els began. He knew he was supposed to be questioning a communist and the only thing he knew about communists was that they wanted white people to marry blacks.

'I can't remember having advocated it in public,' the Bishop said cautiously.

'I don't suppose you would in public,' said Els, whose own advocacy of sexual intercourse with blacks had always been undertaken in strictest privacy. 'You'd get arrested for it.'

The Bishop was puzzled. 'For what?' he asked.

'For advocating a black woman in public. What about in private?'

'It's true I have given the matter some thought.'

'Come on, admit it. You haven't just thought about it. You have done it too.'

The Bishop couldn't see much harm in admitting it. 'Well, once or twice I have raised the matter. I've brought it up at meetings of the parish council.'

'At meetings, eh?' said Els. 'Sort of group gropes?'

'I suppose you could put it that way,' said the Bishop who had never heard the expression before.

Els leered at him. 'I suppose you put it other ways too?'

'I put it to them straight, man to man,' said the Bishop, wondering what all this had to do with murdering policemen.

Konstabel Els had difficulty imagining how you could put it man to man and call it straight at the same time.

'I didn't beat about the bush.'

'I don't suppose you'd have to with men,' Els agreed.

'Oh, there were women present too,' said the Bishop. 'It's the sort of question where a woman's viewpoint often helps.'

'You can say that again.'

'Funnily enough, I found the women more receptive to the idea than the men.'

'I should think you would.'

'Of course, it's not something most people will accept at one go. I put it to them gradually, but on the whole they could see there was something to be said for it.'

'Hell,' said Els, 'you must have had some parties.'

'I hope I'm not boring you,' the Bishop said hopefully.

'I'm never bored by sex,' said Els.

'Do you mind if I take a seat?' the Bishop said on the spur of the moment, taking advantage of Els's evident interest.

'Help yourself.' Els couldn't get enough of the Bishop's tales of group gropes and similar perversions.

'Now then,' said the Bishop, when he was seated, 'where was I?'

'You were saying how the women liked it in the tail,' said Els.

'Was I really?' said the Bishop. 'How extraordinary. I had no idea.'

As the night wore on, Konstabel Els sat rapt in admiration for the prisoner. Here at last, was a man after his own heart, a man for whom there was no shame, no remorse, no regret, only a dedication to lust unequalled in Els's experience.

The difficulty for the Bishop was that his imagination was hardly adequate for the task Els set it. Faced with such rapacious curiosity, he stuck to his calling and Els listened fascinated to descriptions of midnight orgies involving chasubles and albs. Among the other invaluable pieces of information that the Konstabel picked up there were three facts which were particularly damning. The Bishop, he learned, wore a frock, possessed a rubric and owned a biretta.

'What the hell is a rubric?' Kommandant van Heerden asked him in the morning when he read the Bishop's signed confession.

'Short for rubber prick,' said Els. 'He uses it for genuflexion.'

'Does he really?' said the Kommandant and read the astonishing document through for the second time. If half of what the Bishop had confessed to was true, thought van Heerden, the sod should have been hanged years ago.

Chapter 15

While the case against Jonathan Hazelstone was being prepared, Kommandant van Heerden wrestled with the problem posed by the continuing disappearance of the
prisoner's sister. In spite of the most intensive manhunt
Miss Hazelstone continued to elude the police. Kommandant van Heerden increased the reward offered but still no
information worth the telling was telephoned into the
Piemburg police station. The only consolation the Kommandant could find was that Miss Hazelstone had not
added to his problems by communicating with her lawyer
or with newspapers outside his province.

'She's a cunning old devil,' he told Luitenant Verkramp,
and was alarmed to note in himself a return of the admiration he had previously felt for her.

'I wouldn't worry about the old bag, she'll probably
turn up at the trial,' Verkramp answered optimistically.
His fall had not, the Kommandant noted, deprived the
Luitenant of his capacity to say things calculated to upset
his commanding officer.

'If you're so bloody clever, where do you suggest we
start looking for her?' the Kommandant growled.

'Probably sitting in Jacaranda House laughing to herself,' and Verkramp took himself off to compile a list of
black cooks known to favour Chicken Maryland.

'Sarcastic bastard,' muttered the Kommandant. 'One of
these days somebody will fix him properly.'

*   *   *

It was in fact Konstabel Els whose initiative led to the capture of Miss Hazelstone. Ever since his battle with the Dobermann, Els had been regretting his decision to leave the body lying on the lawn of Jacaranda House.

'I should have had it stuffed. It would look nice in the hall,' he said to the Kommandant during an idle moment.

'I should have thought it had been stuffed enough already,' the Kommandant had replied. 'Besides, whoever heard of having a dog stuffed.'

'There are lots of stuffed lions and warthogs and things in the hall of Jacaranda House. Why shouldn't I have a stuffed dog in my hall?'

'You're getting ideas above your station,' the Kommandant said. Els had gone off to ask the warder in Bottom about getting dogs stuffed. The old man seemed to know about things like that.

'You want to take it to a taxidermist,' the warder told him. 'There's one in the Museum but I'd ask for a quote first. Stuffing's a costly business.'

'I don't mind spending a bit of money on it,' Els said and together they went to ask the Bishop about the dog.

'I believe it had a pedigree,' the Bishop told them.

'What's a pedigree?' Els asked.

'A family tree,' said the Bishop, wondering if killing the dog was going to be added to the list of crimes he was supposed to have committed.

'Fussy sort of dog, having a family tree,' Els said to the warder, 'you'd think it would pee against lamp-posts like any other dogs.'

'Spoilt if you ask me,' said the warder. 'Sounds more like a lapdog than a real Dobermann. I'm not surprised you could kill it so easily. Probably died of fright.'

'It bloody well didn't. It fought like mad. Fiercest dog I ever saw,' said Els, annoyed.

'I'll believe it when I see it,' said the warder and Els had promptly made up his mind to fetch the Dobermann to get rid of the slur on his honour.

'Permission to visit Jacaranda House,' he said to the Kommandant, later that day.

'Permission to do what?' the Kommandant asked incredulously.

'To go up to Jacaranda House. I want to get that dog's body.'

'You must be out of your mind, Els,' said the Kommandant, 'I should have thought you'd had enough of that bloody place by now.'

'It's not a bad place,' said Els whose own memories of the Park were quite different from those of the Kommandant.

'It's a bloody awful place, and you've done enough harm up there already,' said the Kommandant. 'You keep your nose out of it, do you hear me?' and Els had vented his anger by bullying some black convicts in the prison yard.

That evening Kommandant van Heerden decided to make a spot check on the road blocks around Piemburg. He was beginning to suspect that his enforced absence from the outside world was having a bad effect on the morale of his men, and since he thought it improbable that Miss Hazelstone would be out and about at eleven o'clock at night, and wouldn't be able to see him in the police car if she were, he decided to make his rounds when it seemed most likely his men would be asleep on the job.

'Drive slowly,' he told Els when he was seated in the back of the car. 'I just want to have a look around.' For an hour men on duty at street corners and at the road blocks were harassed by van Heerden's questions.

'How do you know she didn't come through here disguised as a coon?' he asked the sergeant on duty on the
Vlockfontein Road who had been complaining about the
numbers of cars he had had to search.

'We've checked them all, sir,' said the sergeant.

'Checked them? How have you checked them?'

'We give them the skin test, sir.'

'The skin test? Never heard of it.'

'We use a bit of sandpaper, sir. Rub their skin with it
and if the black comes off they're white. If it doesn't
they're not.'

Kommandant van Heerden was impressed. 'Shows initiative, Sergeant,' he said and they drove on.

It was shortly after this and as they were driving up
Town Hill to inspect the road block there that Konstabel
Els noticed that the Kommandant had fallen asleep.

'It's only the old man making his rounds,' Els told the
konstabel on duty, and was about to turn round and return to the prison when he realized that they were quite
close to Jacaranda Park. He looked over his shoulder and
regarded the sleeping figure in the back of the car.

'Permission to go up to Jacaranda House, sir,' he said
softly. In the back the Kommandant was snoring loudly.
'Thank you, sir,' said Els with a smile and the car moved
off past the road block and up the hill to Jacaranda House.
On either side of the road the headlights illuminated the
billboards which stood like advertisements for macabre
holiday resorts: Bubonic Plague, some sinister beach and
Rabies, a game reserve. Unaware of his destination, Kommandant van Heerden slept noisily in the back as the car
passed through the gates of Jacaranda House, and with a
crunch of tyres on gravel, moved slowly down the long
drive.

Els parked the car in front of the house and stepped quietly out into the night to collect his trophy. It was dark and clouds obscured the moon, and he had some difficulty finding the Dobermann's corpse.

'That's funny,' he said to himself, as he searched the lawn. 'I could have sworn I left the bugger here,' and continued to look for the beast.

In the back of the car Kommandant van Heerden snored more loudly than ever. He slipped sideways across the seat and bumped his head on the window. The next moment he was wide awake and staring out into the darkness.

'Els,' he said loudly, 'what have you stopped for and why are the headlights off?' From the driver's seat there came no comforting reply and as Kommandant van Heerden sat terrified in the back of the car and wondered where the hell Els had got to, the cloud slipped gently from the moon, and the Kommandant saw before him the front door of Jacaranda House. With a whimper the Kommandant crouched down in the cushions and cursed his own foolishness for leaving the prison. Above him the façade of the great house loomed threateningly, its unlighted windows dark with menace. Moaning with terror, the Kommandant opened the door and stepped on to the forecourt. A moment later he was in the driver's seat and searching for the keys. They had gone.

'I might have known the swine would do something like this,' the Kommandant gibbered and promising himself that more than the Dobermann would get himself stuffed, waited for Els to return. As the minutes passed and Els continued his search for the elusive Toby, the Kommandant's terror grew.

'I can't sit here all night,' he thought. 'I'll have to go and find him,' and he climbed out and moving stealthily stole into the garden. Around him bushes assumed strange and

terrifying shapes and the moon which had proved so
illuminating but a few minutes before discovered a convenient cloud to hide behind. In the darkness and not
daring to shout, Kommandant van Heerden stumbled on a
flower bed and fell flat on his face. 'Dog roses,' he thought
bitterly, clutching his face and as he clambered to his feet,
Kommandant van Heerden's ears and eyes caught sight
and sound of two things that sent his heart racing in his
breast. The car's engine had started on the forecourt. Els
had found the Dobermann and was departing. As the car's
headlights swung round floodlighting the front of Jacaranda House, the Kommandant stood rigid in the flower-
bed staring into the night sky at something far more
sinister than the house itself. A faint plume of smoke was
issuing slowly but steadily from one of the chimneys of
the deserted mansion. Kommandant van Heerden was not
alone.

Clutching his heart, the Kommandant fell back among
the roses and passed out. When he came round from
what he chose to call his first heart attack, it was to hear a
voice he had hoped never to hear again.

'Nights of wine and roses, Kommandant?' it enquired,
and as the Kommandant stared up he saw outlined against
the drifting clouds the elegant figure of Miss Hazelstone.
She was dressed as he had seen her first, and not, he
thanked Heaven, in the dreadful salmon-pink suit.

'You're not going to lie there all night, I hope,' Miss
Hazelstone continued. 'Come into the house and I'll make
you some coffee.'

'Don't want any coffee,' the Kommandant mumbled,
disengaging himself from the rose bushes.

'You may not want it, but that's what you obviously
need to sober you up. I'm not having drunken policemen
stumbling about my garden ruining the flowerbeds at this

time of night,' and bowing to that authority he could never resist, Kommandant van Heerden found himself once more in the drawing-room of Jacaranda House. The room was in darkness except for the lamp on a film projector which stood on a small table.

'I was just running through some old films I took, before I burn them,' Miss Hazelstone said, and the Kommandant understood the faint plume of smoke he had seen issuing from the chimney. 'I shan't be able to see them in prison, and besides I think it's better to forget the past, don't you, Kommandant?'

The Kommandant had to agree. The past was something he would have paid a fortune to forget. Unfortunately, it was all too present in his mind's eye. Trapped between his own terror and a sense of deference made all the more persuasive by the erratic beating of his heart, the Kommandant allowed himself to be seated in a low chair from which he expected never to rise, while Miss Hazelstone turned on a reading lamp.

'There's some coffee left over from supper,' Miss Hazelstone said. 'I'll have to heat it up, I'm afraid. In the normal way I would have some fresh made, but I'm rather short of home help at the moment.'

'I don't need any coffee,' the Kommandant said, and regretted his words immediately. He might have had a chance to escape if Miss Hazelstone had gone to the kitchen. Instead she looked at him doubtfully and sat down opposite him in the wing-backed armchair.

'Just as you like,' she said. 'You don't look unusually drunk. Just rather pale.'

'I'm not drunk. It's my heart,' said the Kommandant.

'In that case, coffee is the worst thing for you. It's a stimulant, you know. You should try to avoid any form of stimulation.'

'I know that,' said the Kommandant.

There was a pause, broken finally by Miss Hazelstone. 'I suppose you've finally come to arrest me,' she said. The Kommandant couldn't think of anything he would like to do more, but he didn't seem to have the energy. Mesmerized by the house and the air of gentle melancholy he found so fascinating in the old woman, he sat in his chair listening to his palpitations.

'I suppose Jonathan has confessed already,' Miss Hazelstone said by way of polite conversation. The Kommandant nodded.

'Such a waste,' Miss Hazelstone continued. 'The poor boy suffers from such a sense of guilt. I can't imagine why. I suspect it's because he had such a blameless childhood. Guilt is so often a substitute for good honest-to-goodness evil. You must find that in your profession, Kommandant.'

In his profession, the Kommandant had to agree it very often was, but he couldn't see the relevance in the case of a man who had several prison sentences behind him. He felt himself once more succumbing not only to deference but also to a sense of unease that Miss Hazelstone's conversation seemed to induce in him.

'I never suffered from the same weakness,' Miss Hazelstone continued primly. 'If anything, I had difficulty finding anything to do that wasn't depressingly good. Like the Devil, I too have felt how awful goodness is. So boring, but I daresay you don't have the same opportunity for being nauseated by it.'

'I daresay you're right,' said the Kommandant whose feeling of nausea sprang from quite different causes.

'As you must have gathered, I have done my best to bring a little gaiety into my life,' Miss Hazelstone went on. 'I write for the papers, you know.'

Kommandant van Heerden knew only too well.

'A little column every now and then on fashion and tasteful living.'

'I have read some of your articles,' said the Kommandant.

'I do hope you didn't follow my advice,' Miss Hazelstone went on. 'They were written with my tongue in my cheek, and I had great fun thinking up the most awful combinations of colours. Everybody took my recommendations seriously too. I think I can honestly say that I have made more homes unlivable in than all the termites in South Africa.'

Kommandant van Heerden gaped at her. 'Why on earth should you want to do that?' he asked.

'A sense of moral duty,' Miss Hazelstone murmured. 'My brother has given his life to spread light and goodness, I have merely sought to redress the balance. If people choose to follow my advice to put maroon wallpaper next to orange curtains, who am I to say them nay? People who believe that having a pink skin makes them civilized, while having a black one makes a man a savage, will believe anything.'

'You mean to say you don't believe in apartheid?' the Kommandant asked in astonishment.

'Really, Kommandant, what a silly question,' Miss Hazelstone replied. 'Do I behave as though I believed in it?'

Kommandant van Heerden had to admit that she didn't.

'You can't live with a Zulu for eight years and still believe in segregation,' Miss Hazelstone went on. 'As a matter of fact, the films I have just been looking at are ones I took of Fivepence. I wonder if you would care to see one.'

Kommandant van Heerden hesitated. What he had already seen of the cook didn't dispose him to want to see any more.

'I admire your delicacy of feeling,' Miss Hazelstone said, 'but you need not hesitate. I don't in the least mind sharing my memories with you,' and she started the projector.

A moment later the Kommandant saw on a screen at the far end of the room, the object of Miss Hazelstone's passion, moving about the garden of Jacaranda House as it had been in the summer some years before. The film had been shot from the same angle and in the same corner of the garden as had its actor nearly a decade later. At first sight the Kommandant had the illusion that there had been no murder and that he had dreamt the events of the preceding days. It was an illusion that did not last. As the image of Fivepence grew larger on the screen, the Kommandant decided that he preferred the reality he had known to the fantastic scene he was now witnessing. There had, he noted, been something almost healthy about the corpse of Fivepence. Living, the Zulu cook had quite clearly been diseased.

Tall and heavily built, he cavorted about the lawn like some appalling black nymph, and paused a moment to caress the bust of Sir Theophilus before kissing it passionately upon its unresponding mouth. Then he was off again, flitting about the garden and displaying his repulsive charms in a series of swirls and flounces designed to show off his garments to their very worst advantage. He was wearing a very short crimson frock trimmed with violet; as the Kommandant might have anticipated, it was made of rubber. As Fivepence executed his last pirouette and ended his performance with a curtsy, the Kommandant understood why Miss Hazelstone had murdered him. If the film was anything to go by, he had asked for it.

The film ended and Miss Hazelstone switched off the projector. 'Well?' she said.

'I can see why you shot him,' said the Kommandant.

'You can see nothing,' Miss Hazelstone snapped. 'What
you have just seen appears to your crude mind to be quite
horrible. To me it is beautiful.' She paused. 'That is life,
a black man pretending to be a white woman, dancing
steps of a ballet he has never seen, dressed in clothes made
of a material totally unsuited to a hot climate on a lawn
which was imported from England, and kissing the stone
face of a man who destroyed his nation, filmed by a
woman who is widely regarded as the arbiter of good
taste. Nothing could better express the quality of life in
South Africa.'

Kommandant van Heerden was about to say that he
didn't think she was very patriotic, when Miss Hazelstone
stood up.

'I'll get my suitcase. I have one packed ready,' she
said, and was moving towards the door when a dark shape
hurtled through the French windows and threw her to
the ground.

It had taken Konstabel Els some time to locate the body
of the Dobermann in the darkness, and in the end he had
been guided more by smell than sight to the rubbish
dump behind the house where Miss Hazelstone had deposited the dog. Carrying it carefully Els went back to the
car and put the body in the boot. He climbed in and started
the engine, and drove slowly off thankful that the Kommandant had not woken. It wasn't until he had got halfway down the hill into town that the absence of snores
from the back led him to realize that he had been mistaken.

With a curse he turned the car and headed back to the

Park. He stopped in the drive and looked about. Kommandant van Heerden was nowhere to be seen. Els left the car and walked round the house and found himself looking into the lighted drawing-room where the Kommandant and Miss Hazelstone were talking. In the darkness Els wondered what the hell was going on. 'The sly old devil,' he thought to himself at last. 'No wonder he wouldn't give me permission to come up here,' and Els began to think he understood how it was that the Kommandant should be sitting chatting in a very friendly way with a woman who had a reward on her head. He knew now why the Kommandant had been so eager to pin the murder of Fivepence on Jonathan Hazelstone.

'The old sod's courting her,' he thought, and a new respect for the Kommandant grew in Konstabel Els's mind. His own courtships were always accompanied by threats of violence or blackmail and it seemed obvious that the Kommandant, whose own lack of charm almost equalled that of Els, would have to employ pretty drastic methods to make himself at all attractive to a woman of Miss Hazelstone's wealth and social standing.

'He goes and arrests her brother for murder, and then puts a price on the old bag's head. What a way to get a dowry,' Els exclaimed, and immediately thought how he could forestall the plan. With a rush he was across the lawn and into the room. As he hurled himself on the Kommandant's fiancée he yelled. 'I claim the reward. I captured her,' and from the floor looked up and wondered why the Kommandant was looking so relieved.

Chapter 16

To Kommandant van Heerden the transition of Miss Hazelstone from the mistress of Jacaranda House to the inmate of Fort Rapier Mental Hospital was a sad affair. As he watched the stretcher on which the old lady lay carried for the last time past the portraits of her ancestors in the fern-infested hall, he knew that an epoch was ending. No longer would Jacaranda House stand supreme in the eyes of Zululand society, the symbol of all that was best in the British occupation of Africa and an emblem of an aristocratic way of life. No more garden parties, no more grand balls, no more of those dinner parties for which Miss Hazelstone had such a reputation, nothing of importance would happen within these walls. The house would stand empty and sepulchral until the white ants or the demolition men cleared it away to make room for a new suburb. As Kommandant van Heerden turned off the lights and the house stood dark under the moon, he was filled with a great sense of loss. The old arrogance on which he had relied to sharpen his servility was gone. He was a free man, and the architect of his own freedom. It was the last thing that he wanted.

It was a cortege which passed up the drive and out the contorted gates, a funeral cortege of motorcycles and police cars accompanying the ambulance in which Miss Hazelstone slept the sleep of the heavily sedated. In the driver's seat of the leading car sat Konstabel Els, happy in the knowledge that he had earned his just reward, and behind him in the darkness Kommandant van Heerden wondered at the strangeness of fate which had made a creature like Els the instrument of the fall of the house of Hazelstone.

It was not as if Els was clever, the Kommandant thought, as the procession wound its way through the unlighted streets of Piemburg, nor was there anything vaguely intentional about his activities which would explain their effect. Els was merely chance, random and trivial in its ways.

'Entropy made man,' the Kommandant said to himself, and opened the window. The car had begun to smell quite intolerable.

'Els,' said the Kommandant, 'you need a bath.'

'Me sir?' said Els.

'You, Els. You stink.'

'Not me, sir. That's Toby.'

'Who the hell's Toby?'

'The Dobermann, sir. He's a bit high.'

'You mean you've got the carcase of a rotting dog in the car?' shouted the Kommandant.

'Oh no, sir,' said Els. 'He's in the boot.'

The Kommandant was about to say that he wasn't going to share his car with a putrefying Dobermann, when they passed through the gates of Fort Rapier and drove up the drive to the hospital.

In the moonlight the buildings of Fort Rapier looked much as they had done when the garrison occupied the barracks. A few bars had been added here and there to convert an establishment which had been designed to keep people out into one that served to keep them in, but the atmosphere had not altered. Irrationality had kept its hold on the place.

'Old traditions die hard,' the Kommandant thought as the car stopped at the edge of the parade ground. He stepped out and patted a field gun that had once seen service at Paardeberg where his grandfather had slept through its bombardment and which now stood like an iron pensioner overlooking the lunacies of another generation.

While Miss Hazelstone was taken into a ward reserved for the criminally insane, Kommandant van Heerden explained her case to the Superintendent, Dr Herzog, who had been summoned from his bed to deal with the case.

'Couldn't you have waited till morning?' he asked grumpily. 'I didn't get to bed until one.'

'I haven't been to bed at all,' said the Kommandant, 'and in any case this is an emergency. Miss Hazelstone is something of a celebrity and her committal may arouse public comment.'

'She certainly is, and it certainly will,' said the doctor. 'She happens to be the chief benefactress of this hospital.'

'She has evidently been providing for her own future which will be to remain here until she decides to die,' said the Kommandant.

'Who has diagnosed her?' asked Dr Herzog.

'I have,' said the Kommandant.

'I wouldn't have thought you were qualified to.'

'I know a criminal lunatic when I see one. The police surgeon and her own doctor will be up in the morning, and committal papers will arrive in due course.'

'It seems rather irregular,' said the doctor.

'As a matter of fact, it is irregular,' said the Kommandant. 'But if you really want to know, we have pretty incontrovertible evidence that she has murdered someone. I won't go into details but I can assure you that we have enough evidence to have her tried for murder. I think you understand that the trial of such a prominent person would not be in the public interest.'

'Good God,' said the doctor, 'what is Zululand coming to? First her brother and now Miss Hazelstone.'

'Quite,' said the Kommandant. 'It's a reflection on our times.'

Having ensured that Miss Hazelstone would be allowed no visitors and that she would have no access to the press or to her lawyers, the Kommandant took his leave. Dawn had broken when he crossed the great parade ground, and a few grey figures had emerged from the wards and were shuffling about sadly in the early sunlight.

'To think it had to end like this,' the Kommandant thought and his mind dwelt not so much on Miss Hazelstone as on the Imperial splendour that had once marched red-coated and supreme across the square. He stood for a moment imagining the regiments that had passed the saluting base on which Miss Hazelstone's grandfather had stood before going to their deaths on Majuba Hill and Spion Kop and then he turned away and climbed into his reeking car.

When Miss Hazelstone woke to find herself in bed in a ward, she had difficulty understanding where she was. The decor and the row of beds brought back to her memories of her boarding school but her companions were hardly the gay carefree girls of her youth. Not that they were really gay, she thought lying back and studying the ceiling, merely expectant, which passed for gaiety. There was nothing remotely gay or expectant about the figures she could see now. Withdrawn into remote provinces of their own imaginations the patients wandered listlessly among the obstacles presented by reality. Miss Hazelstone looked at them and was tempted to follow their example. Only a sense of pride prevented her. 'Such lack of style,' she said to herself, and sitting on the edge of her bed looked round for her clothes.

In the days that followed she clung grimly to her arrogance, firmly rejecting the unreal worlds the other patients pressed on her.

'You may be,' she told a patient who introduced himself as Napoleon, 'though I doubt it. I am Miss Hazelstone of Jacaranda House,' and even the staff learnt that it was unwise to address her simply as Hazelstone.

'Miss Hazelstone to you,' she snapped at a sister who made the mistake.

'One must keep up appearances,' she told Dr von Blimenstein, the psychiatrist who had been assigned to deal with the new patient, and who was trying vainly to get Miss Hazelstone to recognize the sexual origins of her illness. Dr von Blimenstein was so wildly eclectic in her approach that it was difficult to tell which school of psychology she most favoured. She was known to prescribe Electric Shock Therapy in unlimited doses to the black patients, but with whites placed particular stress on sexual guilt as the cause of psychoses. She was so successful in this approach that she had once even managed to cure a keeper at the Durban Snake Park of his anxiety neurosis about snakes. His phobia had, he claimed, been brought on by his having been bitten on forty-eight separate occasions by snakes as venomous and varied as puff-adders, cobras, Gabon vipers, ringhals and asps, each of which had brought him to the verge of death. Dr von Blimenstein had convinced the poor man that his fears were purely sexual in origin and resulted from a feeling of inadequacy brought on by the realization that his penis was neither so long nor so potent as a mature python and had sent him back to work at the Snake Park where three weeks later he had been bitten, this time with fatal results, by a black mamba whose length he had been trying to measure by comparing it with his own erect member which he knew to be six inches long. 'Nine feet three inches,' he had just concluded, laying the mamba's head against his *glans penis*. It was practically the last thing he could conclude, as the mamba with a ferocity fully justified by the absurd comparison plunged its fangs into its symbolic counterpart. After that Dr von Blimenstein had turned away from psychoanalysis and had favoured a more behaviourist approach.

With Miss Hazelstone she decided there was no danger of such tragic results and she had encouraged the patient to record her dreams so that these could be examined for the symbolic meaning which would explain all her problems. The trouble was that Miss Hazelstone never dreamt and the concocted dreams that she supplied the doctor with were down-to-earth in the extreme. They were for one thing punctuated with phalluses and vaginas which no amount of symbolic interpretation could turn into anything else.

'How about snakes, or steeples?' Miss Hazelstone enquired when the doctor explained how difficult it was.

'I've never heard of people having dreams about penises before,' said the doctor.

'Probably wish-fulfilment dreams,' Miss Hazelstone said and went on to describe a dream in which a creature called Els had struggled with a black dog on a lawn.

'Extraordinary,' said von Blimenstein, 'absolutely archetypal,' and had begun to talk about the Shadow struggling with Instinctual Libido.

'Yes, it struck me like that at the time,' said Miss Hazelstone cryptically. After several weeks of these dreams the doctor had begun to think she would be able to write a monograph on 'The Policeman Archetype in South African Psychology' using this material.

For Miss Hazelstone these interviews provided a break from the boredom of life in Fort Rapier.

'Madness is so monotonous,' she told the doctor. 'You would think that fantasies would be more interesting, but really one has to conclude that insanity is a poor substitute for reality.'

Then again, when she looked around her, there didn't seem to be any significant difference between life in the mental hospital and life in South Africa as a whole. Black madmen did all the work, while white lunatics lounged about imagining they were God.

'I'm sure the Almighty has more dignity,' Miss Hazelstone said to herself, as she watched the shuffling figures moving aimlessly about the grounds. 'And I'm sure He hasn't delusions of grandeur.'

The news that his sister had finally been found and was now an inmate in Fort Rapier Mental Hospital came as no surprise to the Bishop of Barotseland.

'She was never very sane,' he told the Kommandant who came to see him personally to break the news, and demonstrated once more that lack of family loyalty the Kommandant found so deplorable in one who belonged to such an illustrious line, by adding, 'The best place for her. She should have been certified years ago.' The Bishop was shedding all his illusions, it seemed, and certainly he had ceased to feel kindly towards his sister and had stopped thinking she was merely mildly eccentric.

'I have a great admiration for Miss Hazelstone,' said the Kommandant coldly. 'She was a remarkable woman and Zululand will be the poorer for her passing.'

'You speak of her as though she were already dead,' said the Bishop, whose thoughts about mortality were markedly more frequent since he had moved into Bottom.

'I suppose in a way she has gone to a better life.'

'She won't be leaving there until she is dead,' said the Kommandant grimly. 'By the way, your trial starts next week so if you have anything to say in your defence you had better start thinking about it now,' and the Kommandant had gone away convinced that Jonathan Hazelstone deserved his fate.

The Bishop, left alone in his cell, decided that there was really nothing he could do to add to the confession he had made. It seemed to him a perfectly adequate defence in itself. Nobody on earth could possibly believe he had committed the crimes he had admitted to, and he doubted if any but an expert on high church ritual could disentangle criminal offences from ecclesiastical practices. No judge worth his salt could ever condemn him for latitudinarianism. The Bishop lay down on the mat on the floor of his cell which served as his bed and looked forward to the verdict he was sure would free him.

'It probably won't even come to that,' he thought cheerfully. 'The judge will throw the prosecution case out of court.'

As usual with the Bishop of Barotseland's prognostications events were to prove him entirely wrong. The Judge chosen to hear the case was Justice Schalkwyk, whose mother had died in a British concentration camp and who was noted both for his deafness and his loathing for all things British. The attorney for the defence, Mr Leopold Jackson, was likewise handicapped physically by a cleft palate which made his speeches almost inaudible, and who was in any case known for his tendency to defer to the authority of judges. He had been chosen to conduct the defence by the accused man's heirs, distant cousins who lived in a poor section of Capetown and who hoped by

speeding the course of justice to avoid any further un-
welcome publicity which would besmirch the family
name. Mr Jackson was only allowed to see his client a few
days before the trial began, and then only in the presence
of Konstabel Els.

The interview took place in Bottom and was marked by
an almost complete misunderstanding from the start.

'You thay you've thigned a confethion. Motht unfortunate,' said Mr Jackson.

'It was made under duress,' said the Bishop.

'It wasn't,' said Els. 'It was made in here.'

'Under dureth,' said Mr Jackson. 'Then it won't thtand
up.'

'I don't expect it to,' said the Bishop.

'It can't,' said Els. 'Confessions never do.'

'How wath it forthed out of you?'

'I was made to stand up.'

'You weren't,' said Els. 'I let you sit down.'

'So you did,' said the Bishop.

'Tho it wathn't made under dureth,' said Mr Jackson.

'I told you just now. It was made in here,' said Els.

'It was partly made under duress,' said the Bishop.

'Don't listen to him,' said Els. 'I know where it was
made. It was made in here.'

'Wath it made in here?' asked Mr Jackson.

'Yeth,' said the Bishop, lapsing into legal jargon.

'There you are, I told you it was,' said Els.

'There theemth to be thome confuthion,' said Mr Jackson. 'What did you confeth to?'

'Genuflexion with a rubber prick,' said Els hurriedly
forestalling lesser crimes.

'Genuflecthion with a what?' Mr Jackson asked.

'He means a rubric, I think,' said the Bishop.

'I don't. I mean a rubber prick,' said Els indignantly.

'Thoundth a thrange thort of offenth,' said Mr Jackson.

'You're telling me,' said Els.

'I thought thith wath a capital cathe,' said Mr Jackson.

'It is,' said Els, 'I'm enjoying it no end.'

'Genuflecthing ithn't a crime under Thouth African law.'

'It is with a rubber prick,' said Els.

'There were some other crimes in my confession,' said the Bishop.

'Thuthch ath?'

'Murder,' said the Bishop.

'Lesbianism,' said Els.

'Lethbianithm? Thatth impothible. A man can't commit lethbianithm. Are you thure you've got the right cathe?'

'Positive,' said Els.

'Would you mind allowing my client to thpeak for him-thelf?' Mr Jackson asked Els.

'I'm just trying to help,' said Els aggrieved.

'Now then,' Mr Jackson went on, 'ith it true that you have admitted to being a lethbian?'

'As a matter of fact, yes,' said the Bishop.

'And a murderer?'

'It does seem strange, doesn't it?' said the Bishop.

'It thoundth fantathtic. What elth did you confeth?'

The Bishop hesitated. He did not want Mr Jackson to object to his confession before it was read out in court. Everything depended on the absurdity of the document and Mr Jackson did not look like a lawyer who would under-stand that.

'I think I would prefer the case to go forward as it is,' he said, and excusing himself on the ground that he was tired, ushered the attorney out of the cell.

'Thee you on the day,' Mr Jackson said cheerily, and left Bottom.

*   *   *

It was not due to Mr Jackson however, that Jonathan Hazelstone's confession never reached the court in its unabridged version. It was thanks rather to the conscientiousness of Luitenant Verkramp who, eager for praise, had sent a copy of the confession to BOSS in Pretoria. The head of the Bureau of State Security found the document on his desk one morning and read the thing through with a growing sense of disbelief. It wasn't that he was unused to reading extravagant confessions. After all the Security Branch existed to manufacture them and he could boast that it had a reputation in this respect second to none. 180 days in solitary confinement and days of standing up without sleep while being questioned had the tendency to produce some pretty damning admissions from the suspects, but the confession that Verkramp had sent him made all previous ones look positively tame.

'The man's out of his mind,' he said after ploughing through a catalogue of crimes that included necrophilia, flagellation and liturgy, but it was not certain which man he was referring to. After a conference with leading members of the government, BOSS decided to intervene in the interests of Western Civilization incarnate in the Republic of South Africa and using the powers bestowed on it by Parliament, ordered the suppression of nine-tenths of the confession. Judge Schalkwyk was to try, convict, and condemn the prisoner, with no opportunity to appeal, on charges of murdering one Zulu cook and twenty-one policemen. No other charges were to be preferred and no evidence prejudicial to state security was to be presented in court. Grumbling furiously, the old Judge was forced in accordance with South African law to obey. Jonathan Hazelstone was to be hanged, there must be no miscarriage of justice, but he was after all to be hanged for a lamb.

* * *

The trial took place in Piemburg and in the very court-room in which the accused's father had made such a great reputation.

'The old order changeth,' Jonathan murmured to his lawyer as he took his seat in the dock. Mr Jackson was not amused.

'It hardly becometh you to make mockery of my defect,' he said. 'Bethideth from what I have heard you would do better to thay "The wortht ith yet to come."'

Mr Jackson for once was right. The discovery that his confession had been expurgated came as the real shock of the trial to the Bishop. In the adjournment that followed the announcement that he was only to be tried for murder, Jonathan consulted with his attorney.

'I thould plead inthanity. It theemth your only chanth,' was Mr Jackson's advice.

'But I'm entirely innocent. I had nothing to do with the murder of twenty-one policemen.'

'I darethay but it ith an unfortunate fact that you have confethed to killing them.'

'I was forced to. Why on earth should I want to murder them?'

'I have no idea,' said Mr Jackson. 'My clienth motiveth are alwayth a mythtery to me. The point ith that the evidenth againtht you theemth pretty concluthive. You had the opportunity and the weaponth were found in your pothethion. Furthermore you have admitted in a thigned confethion to having killed them. I thuggetht you change your plea from not guilty to guilty but inthane.'

'I'm not inthane,' shouted the Bishop.

'I haven't come here to be inthulted,' said Mr Jackson.

'I'm thorry,' said the Bishop. 'I mean I'm sorry.'

'I shall change the plea,' said Mr Jackson finally. 'Inthanity it ith.'

'I suppose so,' said the Bishop.

'It'th better than being hanged,' said Mr Jackson. They went back into the courtroom.

The trial proceeded rapidly. By the end of the afternoon the prosecution's case had been presented and Mr Jackson had made no attempt at a reasoned defence. He was relying on the leniency of the court in the face of the accused's obvious insanity.

In his summing-up to a jury handpicked from close relatives of the murdered policemen, Judge Schalkwyk spoke with a brevity and degree of impartiality quite unusual for him.

'You have heard it said,' he mumbled, though it was certain that thanks to his own deafness he hadn't, 'by the prosecuting counsel that the accused committed these crimes. You have seen the accused's confession with your own eyes, and you have heard the defence counsel's plea that his client is insane. Now you may think that there is something to be said for the hypothesis that a man who murders twenty-one policemen and then signs a confession saying that he has done so is manifestly not of his right mind. It is my duty however to point out to you that to plead insanity in the light of the overwhelming evidence against him is not the action of an insane person. It is a highly rational action and one that indicates a degree of perception only to be found in an intelligent and healthy mind. I think therefore that you can disregard the question of insanity altogether in your deliberations. You need only concern yourselves with the matter of guilt. There is in my mind no shadow of doubt that the defendant committed the murders of which he is accused. He possessed, as we have heard from the expert evidence presented by the prosecution, both the opportunity and the means. He was found in possession of the murder weapons and in the act of disposing of them. His wallet and handkerchief were found at the scene of the crime, and he has given no adequate explanation of how they got there. Finally, he has admitted in a signed confession that he was responsible for the murders. I think I need say no more. You and I both know that the defendant is guilty. Now go away and come back and say so.'

The jury filed out of the courtroom. Two minutes later they returned. Their verdict was unanimous. Jonathan Hazelstone was guilty of murder twenty-one and a quarter times over.

In passing sentence Judge Schalkwyk allowed himself to depart from the lack of bias he had shown in his summing-up. He took into account a previous conviction which concerned a motoring offence. The convicted man had failed to give adequate notice of intention to make a left-hand turn at an intersection and as the Judge pointed out, this threatened the very existence of the South African constitution which was based on a series of consistent moves to the right.

'You are a threat to the values of Western Civilization,' said the Judge, 'and it is the duty of this court to stamp communism out,' and he ordered the prisoner to be taken from the court and hanged by the neck until he was dead. He was about to leave the courtroom when Mr Jackson asked to have a word with him in private.

'I would like to draw your Honour'th attention to a privilege which belongth to the Hazelthtone family,' he gurgled.

'The Hazelstone family doesn't have any privileges any more, I'm glad to say,' said the Judge.

'It'th a prerogative of long thtanding. It dateth back to the dayth of Thir Theophiluth.'

'Long standing, what do you mean? There's no question of his standing long. He'll be hanged shortly.'

'I mean the privilege of being hanged in Piemburg Prithon. It wath conferred on the family for perpetuity,' Mr Jackson tried to explain.

'Mr Jackson,' the Judge shouted, 'you are wasting my time and that of this court, not to mention that of your client who has little enough left of it as it is. Perpetuity means the quality of preserving something from oblivion. The quality of the sentence I have just passed is in intent quite the opposite. I think I need say no more, and I should advise you to do the same.'

Mr Jackson made one last effort. 'Can my client be hanged in Piemburg Prithon?' he shouted.

'Of course he can,' the Judge yelled. 'He has to be. It's a long-standing privilege of the Hazelstone family.'

'Thank you,' said Mr Jackson. As the court was cleared Jonathan Hazelstone was taken back to his cell in a state of numbed shock.

Chapter 17

It was with something of the same sense of shock that Governor Schnapps learnt that it had fallen to him to preside over the first hanging Piemburg Prison had seen for twenty years. Not that he was in the least squeamish or upset at the thought of having to attend an execution. He had in his time as a prison officer attended any number of hangings, mostly unofficial ones carried out by black convicts anxious to escape once and for all from the regime he had prescribed for them, but none the less hangings and the prospect of having at least one official execution to his credit filled him with a feeling of satisfaction. The sense of shock stemmed from quite other considerations.

There was for instance the question of the gallows which had not been used for twenty years except as a convenient place in which to store odds and ends. Governor Schnapps inspected Top himself and, from the little of it he could see across the buckets and garden rollers that were packed inside, came to the conclusion that the scaffold was in no shape to hang anyone. The same might well be said of the prospective executioners. The old warder volunteered to advise whoever was chosen as hangman but adamantly refused to attend the execution in person on the grounds that the Death House was unsafe, and the Governor's attempts to persuade one of the other warders to accept the job of executioner met with no success. No one it seemed was anxious to join Jonathan Hazelstone on his last walk if this entailed climbing the rickety steps up to Top.

In desperation Governor Schnapps telephoned the official executioner in Pretoria to ask him if he could come down to Piemburg for the day but the executioner was far too busy.

'Out of the question,' he told Schnapps, 'I've got thirty-two customers that day and besides I never hang singles. I can't remember when I last did one man. I always do mine in batches of six at a time and in any case I have my reputation to think of. I hang more people every year than any other executioner in the world, more than all the other executioners in the free world put together as a matter of fact, and if it once got about that I had hanged a single man, people would think I was losing my touch.'

As a last resort Governor Schnapps raised the question of privilege with the State Attorney.

'I can't see why this man Hazelstone should be privileged,' he said. 'Everyone else is hanged in Pretoria. It seems wrong to me that a fellow who knocks off twenty-one policemen should be entitled to privileges which are denied to ordinary common-or-garden murderers.'

'I'm afraid there's nothing I can do about it,' the State Attorney told him, 'Judge Schalkwyk allowed the privilege to stand and I can't alter his decision.'

'But how did the Hazelstone family ever get the right to be hanged in Piemburg in the first place?'

The State Attorney looked up the records.

'It dates from the speech made by Sir Theophilus at the opening of the prison in 1888,' he told the Governor. 'In the course of that speech Sir Theophilus said, and I quote, "Capital punishment and flogging are essential to the peace and tranquillity of Zululand. They confer upon the native races a sense of the innate superiority of the white man and in declaring this prison open I should like to say that it is my considered opinion that the very future of

White civilization in this dark continent depends, one might almost say, hangs, on the frequent use of the scaffold we have been privileged to see here today. It will be a sad day for this country when the gallows traps falls for the last time and one that I trust no member of my family will live to see." Unquote.'

'All very commendable,' said the Governor, 'but I don't see that it necessarily means that we have to keep the gallows for the exclusive use of the Hazelstone family.'

The State Attorney picked up another document.

'Now here we have the statement of the late Judge Hazelstone made at the time all executions were transferred to Pretoria. The Judge was asked what he thought his father had meant in his speech. His answer was, I quote "It's perfectly obvious. The gallows and the Hazelstone family stand or fall together. My father believed and rightly believed that our family should set an example to Zululand. I can think of no finer example than that of having our own private scaffold in Piemburg Prison." Unquote. Pretty conclusive, don't you think?'

Governor Schnapps had to concede that it was and returned to the Prison still faced with the problem of finding an executioner.

In the end it was Konstabel Els who became the official hangman. The Konstabel was still happily contemplating how he was going to spend the reward money he had earned from the capture of Miss Hazelstone and was looking forward to the ceremony in the police drill hall when he would be presented with the cheque by the Commissioner of Police. He had decided it was worth the price asked by the taxidermist at the Piemburg Museum to have Toby stuffed.

'I'm having the Dobermann stuffed,' he announced to

Kommandant van Heerden one day.

'Then I expect you wouldn't mind earning some pocket money,' said the Kommandant.

'How?' said Els suspiciously.

'Nothing arduous,' said the Kommandant. 'It certainly doesn't require any effort on your part. In fact when I come to think of it I wonder you haven't tried your hand at it already. I can't think of a better man for the job.'

'Hm,' said Els who didn't like the Kommandant's beguiling tone.

'I'd say you've probably got a natural talent for it.'

Els tried to think what dirty jobs needed doing round the police station. 'What is it?' he asked shortly.

'It's the sort of job you'd really like,' said the Kommandant, 'and for once you would be doing it legally.'

Els tried to think of something he would really like which wasn't legal. Having it off with black women seemed the most obvious thing.

'Of course you'd get the usual fee,' continued the Kommandant.

'The usual fee?'

'Twenty-five rand, I think it is,' said the Kommandant, 'though it may have gone up.'

'Hm,' said Els who was beginning to think his ears were deceiving him.

'Not bad for a bit of fun,' said the Kommandant, who knew that Konstabel Els had shot at least fifteen people in the course of duty and twenty-one for pure pleasure. 'Of course the method would take some getting used to.'

Konstabel Els searched his memory to find some method he hadn't used. As far as he knew he'd used every position in the book and a few more besides.

'What method had you in mind?' he enquired.

The Kommandant was getting fed up with Els's diffi-

dence. 'With a rope round the neck and a ten foot drop,'
he snapped. 'That ought to do for a start.'

Els was appalled. If that was how it was going to start,
he hated to think what the finish would be like.

'Wouldn't that be a bit dangerous?' he asked.

'Of course not. Safe as houses.'

It was not as safe as any house Konstabel Els could
think of.

'Of course if you're scared,' began the Kommandant.

'I'm not scared,' said Els. 'If you really want me to do
it, I will, but I'm not taking any responsibility for what
will happen to the poor bitch. I mean you can't drop a
woman ten feet with a rope tied round her neck without
doing her some injury, not even a kaffir woman. And as
for stuffing—'

'What the hell are you talking about, Els?' the Kommandant asked. 'Who said anything about women? I'm
talking about hanging Jonathan Hazelstone. I'm offering
you the job of hangman and you keep going on like a
maniac about women. Are you feeling all right?'

'Yes sir. I am now,' said Els.

'Well, then will you do it or not?'

'Oh yes. I'll hang him all right. I don't mind doing that,'
and Els had gone off to practise on the gallows at Piemburg Prison.

'I'm Executioner Els,' he announced grandly to the
warder at the gate. 'I'm the official hangman.'

Left alone in his office Kommandant van Heerden
listened to his heart. Ever since the night he had found
himself alone in the garden of Jacaranda House, he had
known that there was something seriously wrong with it.

'It's all that running about and jumping out of windows,' he said to himself. 'Bound to be bad for a man of

my age.' He had visited his doctor several times only to be told that he needed to take more exercise.

'You must be mad,' the Kommandant told him. 'I've been running about all over the place.'

'You're overweight. That's the only thing wrong with you,' said the doctor.

'I've collapsed twice,' the Kommandant insisted. 'Once at Jacaranda House and the second time in court.'

'Probably bad conscience,' said the doctor cheerfully, and the Kommandant had gone away in a foul temper to take it out on Luitenant Verkramp.

Kommandant van Heerden's third seizure came during the ceremony in the Drill Hall at which the Commissioner of Police presented the reward to Konstabel Els. The Kommandant had regretted giving Els the reward as soon as he heard that it would be presented by the Commissioner before an audience of five hundred and seventy-nine policemen and their families. The prospect of Els standing up and making a speech of thanks was not one that Kommandant van Heerden could look forward to with any enthusiasm.

'Listen, Els,' he said before climbing on to the platform where the Commissoner was waiting. 'You don't have to say anything more than "Thank you very much." I don't want to listen to a long speech.'

Konstabel Els nodded. He wasn't given to making speeches, long or short. The two men entered the hall.

In the event, the evening was worse than even the Kommandant had anticipated. The Commissioner had just heard of the new honour conferred on Konstabel Els and he had decided to end his speech by announcing the news to the assembled men.

'And so I call on Konstabel Els to come up and receive

his reward,' he said finally, 'or should I say, Executioner Els.'

A wild burst of laughter and applause greeted the remark. 'That's right, call him Executioner Els,' someone shouted, and another voice yelled, 'Kaffir-Killer Els.'

The Commissioner held up his hand for silence as Els scrambled on to the platform.

'We all know what a vital contribution Konstabel Els has made to the solution of the racial problem in South Africa,' he continued amid laughter. 'I think I can honestly say that there can be few men in the South African Police force who have disposed of more obstacles to the establishment of a racially pure and truly white South Africa than Konstabel Els. But I am not referring now to Konstabel Els's excellence of aim nor to the sacrifices he has seen fit to make in pursuit of our common dream, a South Africa with no blacks in it. I speak now of his new duty. Konstabel Els has been chosen to carry out the duty of hanging the man whom we have to thank for our depleted ranks here tonight.' He paused and turned to Konstabel Els. 'I have great pleasure in presenting you with this cheque in reward for the capture of a dangerous criminal,' he said shaking Els by the hand. 'Hangman Els, you have done your fellow-policemen proud.'

A great round of applause greeted the news of Els's appointment. Els took the cheque and turned to go back to his seat.

'Thank God for that,' said the Kommandant out loud, but the next moment there were shouts of 'Speech. Speech. You've got to make a speech,' and 'Tell us how you're going to kill the bastard,' and Els standing awkwardly on the edge of the platform was finally persuaded to say something.

'Well,' he said hesitantly, when the shouting had died down, 'I expect you all want to know how I'm going to spend the money.' He paused and the Kommandant shut his eyes. 'Well, first of all I'm going to stuff a Dobermann.'

The audience roared its approval, and the Kommandant opened his eyes for a moment to see how the Commissioner of Police was taking it. The Commissioner was not laughing.

'It's a dog, sir,' whispered the Kommandant hurriedly.

'I know it's a dog. I know what a Dobermann is,' said the Commissioner icily, and before the Kommandant could explain the true nature of Els's intentions the Konstabel had started again.

'It's a big black one,' said Els, 'and it's been dead a few weeks now, so it's not going to be an easy job.'

The audience was delighted. Shouts and the stamping of boots greeted Els's news.

'Do your men make a habit of stuffing dogs?' asked the Commissioner.

'He's not using the word in its usual sense, sir,' said the Kommandant desperately.

'I'm fully aware of that,' said the Commissioner. 'I know exactly what he means.'

'I don't think you do, sir,' the Kommandant began, but Els had started to speak again and he had to keep quiet.

'It's sort of stiff,' said Els, 'and that's what makes it difficult to get at its insides.'

'You've got to stop him,' the Commissioner shouted at Kommandant van Heerden, as the hall erupted with hysterical laughter.

'You don't understand, sir,' the Kommandant shouted back. 'He killed the dog and—'

'I'm not at all surprised. It's a pity he didn't kill himself in the process.'

Around them in the hall pandemonium raged. Konstabel Els couldn't see anything in what he had said to laugh
at.

'You can laugh,' he shouted above the din, 'you can
bloody laugh, but I bet you haven't got a dog with a
family tree. My dog had a special tree...' The rest of his
sentence was drowned in the laughter.

'I'm not sitting here listening to any more of this filth,'
shouted the Commissioner.

'If you'd just wait for a moment, sir,' the Kommandant
screamed, 'I can explain what he means. He's going to
take the dog to a taxidermist.'

But the Commissioner had already risen from his seat
and had left the platform.

'Damned disgusting,' he said to his adjutant as he
entered his car. 'The fellow's a sexual maniac.'

Behind him in the hall Els had left the stage and was
telling a plain-clothes cop in the front row how he would
stuff him if he went on laughing. On the platform Kommandant van Heerden had had his third heart attack.

In Piemburg Prison Jonathan did not share his sister's
belief in the dignity of God. After a lifetime spent in the
service of the Lord and a month in Bottom he felt unable
any longer to believe that whatever had chosen to reveal
itself to him in the depths of the swimming-pool had been
even vaguely beneficent. As to its having been sane, his
view of the world and its ways led him to suppose that its
Maker must have been out of his mind.

'I should think He must have needed a rest on the
seventh day,' he told the old warder who insisted on bringing him consolation, 'and as for its being good, I think the
facts speak for themselves. Whatever was responsible for
the Creation cannot possibly have had anything good in

mind. Quite the opposite if you ask me.'

The old warder was shocked. 'You're the first man to occupy that cell,' he said, 'that didn't come round to being converted before he was hanged.'

'It may have something to do with the fact that I am innocent,' said the Bishop.

'Oh is that what it is,' said the old warder with a yawn. 'They all say that,' and shuffled off to give his advice to Konstabel Els who was practising in Top. Alone in his cell the Bishop lay on the floor and listened to the noises that reached him from the gallows. By the sound of things he was less likely to die from a broken neck than from some appalling form of hernia.

Executioner Els wasn't finding his new job at all easy. For one thing he was fed up with all the work it entailed. He had had to empty the Gallows Shed of all the junk that had accumulated there for the past twenty years. With the help of half a dozen black convicts, he had moved several tons of old furniture, garden rollers, disused cats-o'-nine-tails, and corroded lavatory buckets before he could begin to get the scaffold ready for its task, and when the shed was empty he was not sure what to do.

'Pull the lever,' the old warden told him when Els asked him how the thing worked, and the new hangman had returned to the shed and had pulled the lever. After falling twenty feet to the floor of the shed as the trap opened beneath him, Els began to think he was getting the hang of the contraption. He tried it out with several unsuspecting black convicts standing there, and they seemed to disappear quite satisfactorily. He was disappointed that he wasn't allowed to try it out properly.

'You can't do that,' the old warder told him, 'it's not

legal. The best thing I can suggest is a sack filled with sand.'

'Fussy old sod,' thought Els and sent the convicts off to fill some sacks with sand. They were quite satisfactory as stand-ins and didn't complain when the noose was fitted round their necks which was more than could be said for the black convicts. The trouble was that the bottom dropped out every time one was hanged. Els went back into Bottom to consult the old warder.

'He's not here any longer,' the Bishop told him.

'Where's he gone to?' Els asked.

'He's applied for sick leave,' the Bishop said. 'He's got stomach trouble.'

'It's the same with those sacks,' said Els and left the Bishop wondering which was worse, hanging or disembowelling.

'I don't suppose it makes a great deal of difference,' he thought finally. 'In any case there is nothing I can do about it.'

Kommandant van Heerden did not share the Bishop's fatalism. His third heart attack had convinced him that he too was under sentence of death, but he had decided that there was something he could do about it. He had been assisted in reaching this conclusion by Konstabel Oosthuizen whose experience of major surgery made him an unrivalled source of medical information.

'The most important thing is to have a healthy donor,' the Konstabel told him, 'after that it's a piece of cake, compared to my operation.' Kommandant van Heerden had hurried off to avoid having to listen to a description of the operation in which the greater portion of Konstabel Oosthuizen's digestive tract figured so memorably.

Sitting in his office he listened to Luitenant Verkramp

discussing very loudly the case of his uncle who had died of heart trouble. The Kommandant had noticed recently that an extraordinarily large proportion of the Verkramp family had succumbed to what was evidently an hereditary defect and the manner of their passing had been uniformly so atrocious that he could only hope that Verkramp would go the same way. The Luitenant's solicitude was getting on his nerves, and he was equally tired of enquiries about how he felt.

'I feel all right, damn it,' he told Verkramp a hundred times.

'Ah,' Verkramp said sadly, 'that's often the way it seems. Now my Uncle Piet said he was feeling fine the day he died but it came on all of a sudden.'

'I don't suppose it was quick,' the Kommandant said.

'Oh no. Very slow and agonizing.'

'I thought it would be,' said the Kommandant.

'A dreadful business,' said Verkramp. 'He—'

'I don't want to hear any more,' the Kommandant shouted.

'I just thought you'd like to know,' said Verkramp and went out to tell Konstabel Oosthuizen that irritability was a sure sign of incurable heart disease.

In the meantime the Kommandant had tried to occupy his mind by devising a suitably caustic reply to the Commissioner of Police, who had written ordering him to see that the men under his command got plenty of .outdoor exercise and had even hinted that it might be a good thing to organize a brothel for the police barracks in Piemburg. The Kommandant could see that Konstabel Els's confession was still preying on the mind of the Police Commissioner.

'How do you spell taxidermist?' he asked Konstabel Oosthuizen.

'Oh, I wouldn't go to one of them,' the Konstabel replied. 'You need a proper surgeon.'

'I wasn't thinking of going to a taxidermist,' the Kommandant shouted. 'I just want to know how to spell the word.'

'The first thing to do is to find a suitable donor,' the Konstabel went on, and the Kommandant had given up the attempt to finish the letter. 'Why don't you have a word with Els? He should be able to fix you up with one.'

'I'm not having a kaffir,' said the Kommandant firmly. 'I'd rather die.'

'That's what my cousin said the very day he passed on,' Verkramp began.

'Shut up,' snarled the Kommandant, and went into his office and shut the door. He sat down at his desk and began to think about Konstabel Els's capacity for supplying a donor. Half an hour later he picked up the phone.

It was with some surprise that Jonathan Hazelstone learnt that Kommandant van Heerden had put in a request to see him.

'Come to gloat, I suppose,' he said when the Governor brought him the note from the Kommandant. He was even more astonished at the way the request had been worded. Kommandant van Heerden did not actually beg an audience with the Bishop but his note spoke of 'a meeting perhaps in the privacy of the prison chapel, to discuss a matter of mutual interest to us both'. Jonathan racked his brains to think of some matter of mutual interest, and apart from his coming execution which Kommandant van Heerden must have had considerable interest in if his pains to achieve it were anything to go by, he couldn't think of any interests he might share with the Kommandant. At first he was inclined to refuse the request, but he was persuaded to go by the old warder, whose bowel trouble had stopped, now that Els had ceased rupturing the sacks.

'You never know. He might have some good news for you,' the warder said, and the Bishop had agreed to the meeting.

They met in the prison chapel one afternoon just a week before the execution was due to take place. The Bishop clanked over firmly chained and manacled to find the Kommandant sitting in a pew waiting for him. At the Kommandant's suggestion the two men made their way up the aisle and knelt side by side at the altar rail, out of hearing of the warders at the chapel door. Above them in the windows scenes of edifying horror done in late nineteenth-century stained glass filtered the sunlight that managed to penetrate the dense colours and the bars behind the glass, until the whole chapel was glowing with maroon gore.

While Kommandant van Heerden offered a short prayer the Bishop, having declined the Kommandant's invitation to say one, gazed up at the windows awestruck. He had never realized before how many ways there were of putting people to death. The windows provided a comprehensive catalogue of executions and ranged from simple crucifixion to burning at the stake. St Catherine on the wheel entirely merited her fame as a firework, the Bishop decided, while St Sebastian would have made an ideal trademark for pincushions. One after another the martyrs met their terrible ends with a degree of realism that seemed to mark the artist out as a genius and an insane one at that. The Bishop particularly liked the electric chair in one window. With a truly Victorian obsession for naturalism combined with high drama, the figure in the chair was portrayed encased in an aura of electric-blue sparks. Looking up at it, the Bishop was glad that he had agreed to the meeting. To have seen these windows was to know that his own end on the gallows, no matter how badly bungled by the incompetent Els, would be positively enjoyable by comparison with the sufferings portrayed here.

'I suppose I can be grateful for small mercies,' he said to himself as the Kommandant mumbled his final prayer which in the circumstances the Bishop thought was rather curiously worded.

'For what we are about to receive may the good Lord make us truly thankful, Amen,' said the Kommandant.

'Well?' said the Bishop after a short pause.

'You'll be glad to hear that your sister is doing very well at Fort Rapier,' the Kommandant whispered.

'It's nice to know.'

'Yes, she is in the best of health,' said the Kommandant.

'Hm,' said the Bishop.

'She has put on some weight,' said the Kommandant. 'But that is only to be expected with hospital food.' He paused, and the Bishop began to wonder when he was coming to the point.

'Overweight is something to be avoided,' said the Kommandant. 'Obesity is the cause of more premature deaths than cancer.'

'I daresay,' said the Bishop, who had lost two stone since he had been in prison.

'Particularly in middle age,' whispered the Kommandant. The Bishop turned his head and looked at him. He was beginning to suspect that the Kommandant was indulging in a rather tasteless joke.

'You haven't come here to lecture me on the dangers of being overweight I hope,' he said. 'I thought your note said that you wanted to discuss something of interest to us both, and frankly obesity isn't one of my problems.'

'I don't suppose it is,' said the Kommandant sadly.

'Well then?'

'I have trouble with it myself.'

'I don't see what that has to do with me,' said the Bishop.

'It can lead to all sorts of complications. It's one of the main causes of heart disease,' said the Kommandant.

'Anyone would think from the way you go on that I was in danger of having a coronary when in fact I don't think I am going to be allowed that particular luxury.'

'I wasn't really thinking of you,' said the Kommandant.

'I didn't suppose you were.'

'It's more my own obesity I'm thinking of,' continued van Heerden.

'Well, if that's the only thing you've come here to talk to me about, I think I'll go back to my cell, I have something better to think about in the hours left to me than the state of your health.'

'I was afraid you'd say that,' said the Kommandant mournfully.

'I can't think what else you supposed I would do. You surely didn't come here for sympathy. Have a heart.'

'Thank you,' said the Kommandant.

'What did you say?'

'Thank you,' said the Kommandant.

'Thank you for what?'

'For a heart.'

'For a what?'

'A heart.'

The Bishop looked at him incredulously. 'A heart?' he said finally. 'What the hell are you talking about?'

Kommandant van Heerden hesitated before continuing, 'I need a new heart,' he said finally.

'It hasn't escaped my notice,' said the Bishop, 'that a change of heart would do you a power of good, but to be frank I think you're too far gone for any prayers of mine to help you. In any case I am afraid that I have lost faith in the power of prayer.'

'I've tried prayer already,' said the Kommandant, 'but it hasn't done any good. I still get palpitations.'

'Perhaps if you truly repented,' the Bishop said.

'It's no good. I'm a doomed man,' said the Kommandant.

'Metaphorically I suppose we all are,' said the Bishop. 'It happens to be part of the condition of man, but if you don't mind my saying so I'm a damned sight more doomed than you are, and it's thanks to you that I'm going to be hanged next Friday.'

There was a long silence in the chapel while the two men considered their futures. It was broken by the Kommandant.

'I don't suppose you'd do something for me,' he said at last. 'A last bequest.'

'A last bequest?'

'A small thing really and nothing you'll have much use for.'

'You've got a nerve coming here and asking to be included in my will,' the Bishop said irritably.

'It's not in your will,' the Kommandant said desperately.

'No? Well where the hell is it?'

'In your chest.'

'What is?'

'Your heart.'

'You keep going on about my heart,' said the Bishop. 'I wish you would stop. It's bad enough knowing you're going to die without having someone harp on about your heart. Anyone would think you wanted the thing.'

'I do,' said the Kommandant simply.

'What?' screamed the Bishop, struggling to his feet with a clanking of chains. 'You want what?'

'Only your heart,' said the Kommandant. 'I need it for a transplant.'

'I'm going insane,' shouted the Bishop. 'I must be. It isn't possible. Do you mean to tell me that you've gone to all this trouble just so you could have my heart for a transplant operation?'

'It was no trouble,' said the Kommandant. 'I hadn't got anything to do this afternoon.'

'I'm not talking about this afternoon,' the Bishop screamed. 'I'm talking about the murders and the trial and having me condemned to death for crimes you knew I couldn't have committed. You did all that just so that you could hoik my heart out of my body to stick it in your own? It's incredible. You're a ghoul. You're....' the Bishop couldn't find words to express his horror.

Kommandant van Heerden was horrified too. He had never been accused of anything so disgraceful in his life.

'Good God,' he shouted back. 'What do you take me for?'

He could see it was the wrong thing to ask. It was perfectly obvious what the Bishop took him for. For one terrible moment it looked as if the manacled and chained prisoner was going to hurl himself on him. Then quite suddenly the Bishop's fury evaporated and the Kommandant saw that he was staring up at one of the stained-glass windows. Following the Bishop's gaze he found himself looking at the particularly grisly portrayal of a martyr in the process of being hanged, drawn and quartered. To Kommandant van Heerden the change in the prisoner's demeanour could only be explained by miracu-

lous intervention. In some strange way the stained-glass
window had communicated a sense of peace and tranquillity to his soul.

And this in its own way was true, for Jonathan Hazelstone had suddenly realized that the second verse of 'The
Forerunners' needed revising. It wasn't his brain they
wanted. It was his heart.

> 'Good men ye be, to leave me my best room,
> Ev'n all my heart, and what is lodged there.'

Turning back to the Kommandant, the Bishop was a
picture of truly Christian generosity.

'Yes,' he said quietly. 'If you want my heart, of course
you can have it,' and without another word he turned
from the altar rail and clanked down the aisle towards
the door. And as he went he composed the lines afresh,

> 'Bad men ye be, to pilfer my best room
> Ev'n all my heart. . . .'

The Bishop smiled happily to himself. It was extraordinarily appropriate, he thought, and he was still smiling beatifically when Kommandant van Heerden caught
up with him and overcome with emotion grabbed his
manacled hand and shook it as vigorously as the handcuffs would allow.

'You're a real gentleman,' he gasped, 'a real English
gentleman.'

'*Noblesse oblige*,' murmured the Bishop, whose heart
had been chronically weak since he had suffered from
rheumatic fever as a child.

Chapter 18

The Bishop was still in a cheerful frame of mind when Hangman Els visited him to weigh him for the drop.

'You can smile,' Els said as he dragged him out of the cell and shoved him on to the weighing machine. 'It's all right for you. You don't have to do anything. I'm the one who has to do all the work.'

'Each of us has his little part to play,' said the Bishop.

'Play?' said Els. 'I don't call what I'm doing playing. I'm having to work my guts out.'

'Just so long as you don't achieve the same result in my case,' said the Bishop uneasily. 'By the way, how are you getting on with those sacks?'

'I've practised with them till I'm fit to drop,' Els said, 'and I still don't seem to get it right. It's got to do with the weight how far you have to fall.' He tried to read the scales. 'I can't make these things out at all,' he said finally. 'What do you make your weight out to be?'

The Bishop came to his assistance.

'Three hundred and ninety-eight pounds,' he said.

Els consulted a little black book entitled, *The Hangman's Handbook*, which he had borrowed from the old warder.

'You're too heavy,' he said at last. 'It only goes up to three hundred pounds. Are you sure that's what the weighing machine said?'

The Bishop checked, 'Three hundred and ninety-eight pounds exactly.'

'Well I don't know what I'm going to do. It doesn't look as if you need any drop at all.'

'That's a nice thought,' Jonathan said, adding hopefully, 'Perhaps fat men don't commit murders.'

'Well, if they do, nobody seems to hang them,' said Els. 'Perhaps they shoot them.' On the whole he much preferred shooting. It was quicker and involved a lot less effort on his part.

'No, no,' said the Bishop hurriedly. 'They definitely have to be hanged.' He thought for a moment. 'What does it say is the drop for a man weighing two hundred pounds?' he asked.

Els consulted his little compendium. 'Six feet,' he said at last.

'Then three feet should be just about right,' said the Bishop.

'Why?' Els didn't like the sound of a shortened drop at all. It smacked too much of an attempt to avoid death.

'Double the weight and halve the drop,' the Bishop explained.

Els wasn't fool enough to fall into that trap. 'Double the weight and double the drop, you mean.'

The Bishop tried to explain. 'The heavier someone is the shorter the fall needed to break his neck. The light man needs a much longer drop to achieve the necessary momentum.'

Els tried to work it out. He found it very difficult.

'Why is a momentum necessary?' he asked. 'Nobody told me to get one.'

'Momentum is the product of a moving body's mass by its velocity.'

'I thought death was,' said Els.

'Yes, but you won't get death without momentum. It's not possible.'

'Oh, isn't it?' said Els. 'Well, I'll have a bloody good shot at it, don't you worry.'

Alarmed by the constant reference to shots, the Bishop tried again.

'When a man is hanged, how does he die?' he asked.

Els thought about it. 'By hanging,' he said finally.

'And hanging means doing what to him?'

'Dropping him down a hole with a rope round his neck.'

'And what happens then?'

'He dies.'

'Yes,' said the Bishop patiently, 'but what does the rope do?'

'Holds him up.'

'No, no. It breaks his neck.'

Els knew better than that. 'Oh no, it doesn't,' he said. 'I've been practising with sacks and it doesn't break their necks. Their bottoms drop out. It makes no end of a mess.'

The Bishop shuddered. 'I'm sure it must,' he said. 'Now we don't want that to happen to me, do we? That's why we've got to get the length of the drop right.'

'Oh, it wouldn't happen to you,' Els assured him. 'The old warder says it's the other way round with you. He says your head would....'

The Bishop didn't want to know what the old warder had said. He had had enough of his morbid interest in anatomy already.

'Look, if you're really so keen to get a permanent job as a hangman, you'll have to make a success of this execution. Nobody is going to employ you if you don't make a go of your first hanging.'

Els looked pathetically at the Bishop. 'I know that,' he said, 'but what can I do if your weight isn't in the handbook?'

'You could make me lighter,' the Bishop suggested

looking at his manacles and chains.

'Done,' said Els delighted. 'I'll have you put on a nil diet at once.'

'I didn't mean that,' said the Bishop who couldn't imagine anything niller than the diet he was already on. 'What I had in mind was taking all these chains off and weighing me without them. I think you might find me a lot lighter.'

'I doubt if I'd find you at all,' said Els.

'Well, if you won't take these chains off I don't see how I can help you,' said the Bishop wearily.

'If I were to take them off, I'm damned sure you would not help me either,' said Els.

'In that case I don't know what to suggest. You're not going to find my proper weight with the chains on and if you won't take them off. . . .' He paused as he remembered another scene in the chapel window. 'You don't surely intend to hang me in chains?' he asked.

'No,' said Els, 'there's a special set of leather straps and a cloth bag for your head.'

'Dear God what a way to go,' murmured the Bishop.

'I've put boot-polish on the straps and shone them up. They look quite smart,' Els went on. The Bishop wasn't listening to him. He had suddenly thought of a way round the problem of weight.

'I know what we can do,' he said. 'You go and get another set of chains and manacles and bring them here, and we'll weigh them by themselves.'

'I don't see how that's going to help,' said Els. 'I've just told you we won't be using chains on the day. You don't think I've been polishing those straps for nothing, do you?'

The Bishop was beginning to think that he would never be able to get Els to understand anything.

'Once we know how much the chains weigh by themselves we can subtract their weight from three hundred and ninety-eight pounds and then we'll know how much I weigh by myself.'

Els considered the proposal for a moment, but in the end he shook his head.

'It wouldn't work,' he said.

'Why on earth not?'

'I could never do subtraction at school,' Els confessed finally.

'Never mind,' said the Bishop. 'I was very good at it and I'll do the sum myself.'

'How do I know you won't cheat?'

'My dear Hangman Els,' said the Bishop. 'I can think of two good reasons why I am as anxious as you are that this hanging should go with a swing. Possibly three. One is that if you make the drop too short, I shall strangle to death and I really don't want to. Two is that if you make it too long you'll probably decapitate me.'

'I won't,' said Els. 'Your head will come off.'

'Quite,' said the Bishop hurriedly. 'Nothing like calling a spade a bloody shovel, is there?'

'What's three?' asked Els, who didn't care what a bloody shovel was called.

'Oh yes, three. I had almost forgotten three. Well three is that you are obviously a born executioner and while you've got a lot to learn about hanging, I like to see a man make use of the gifts he's been given. Yes, I know about the cloth bag,' the Bishop continued, as Els tried to interrupt with the news that he wouldn't see anything on the scaffold, 'but I am speaking metaphorically, and speaking metaphorically I hope you'll go on to greater things, one might almost say to the top of your profession.'

'You really think I'll make a good hangman?' Els asked eagerly.

'I'm sure of it,' said the Bishop. 'I can feel it in my bones that you will make a name for yourself among executioners the world over,' and having given the hangman the reassurance Els so desperately needed the Bishop went back to his cell while Els went off to fetch another set of chains and manacles. In the end they discovered that Jonathan Hazelstone weighed one hundred and eighty pounds and needed a seven-foot drop.

If the Bishop was having difficulty persuading Els to kill him properly, Kommandant van Heerden was finding it almost as difficult to persuade the surgeons at Piemburg Hospital to undertake the operation he needed to save his life. They seemed to insist on raising quite irrelevant objections, and the Kommandant found particularly irritating their insistence that there was nothing wrong with his heart. When he had disposed of that difficulty by threatening to charge them with attempted murder if they didn't agree with his diagnosis, they spent another hour discussing the ethical problems involved in transferring the heart of a murderer into the body of a man, who, as they pointed out, was so manifestly non-homicidal. The Kommandant soon set their minds at rest on that score, and it was only when they raised the technical problems of tissue typing and rejection and tried to explain how unlikely it was that the condemned man's tissues would match those of a purebred Afrikaaner, like Kommandant van Heerden, that he lost his temper.

'Are you telling me that I'm not a human being?' the Kommandant yelled at Dr Erasmus who led the transplant team. 'Are you telling me I'm a bloody baboon?'

'I'm not saying anything of the sort,' Dr Erasmus protested. 'You don't seem to understand. Each human being has a different type of tissue and yours may not be the same type as that of the donor.'

'You're telling me I've got coloured blood in me,' the Kommandant yelled. 'You're saying I can't have an Englishman's heart because I'm part-kaffir. Is that what you're saying?'

'I'm not saying anything of the sort. There's no reason at all why you shouldn't have a kaffir's heart,' Dr Erasmus said desperately. He found Kommandant van Heerden's violence positively unnerving.

'There you are. You said it. You said I could have a kaffir's heart,' shouted the Kommandant.

'I didn't mean that you had to have one. There's no reason why a black man's heart should not be put into a white man's body any more than there is any reason why a white man's organs shouldn't be transferred to a black man.'

Kommandant van Heerden had never heard such a flagrant violation of the basic concepts of apartheid in his life.

'There's every bloody reason,' he shouted, 'why a white man's organs shouldn't be put into a black man. No white man is allowed to put any portion of his body into a black man. It's against the fucking law.'

Dr Erasmus had never heard of the Fucking Law but he assumed it was police slang for the Immorality Act.

'You misunderstand me,' he said. 'I wasn't referring to sexual organs.'

'There you go again,' bellowed the Kommandant, 'I'll charge you with incitement to inter-racial homosexuality if you don't shut up.'

Dr Erasmus was silenced.

'Calm yourself, Kommandant,' he said soothingly. 'For goodness sake calm yourself. You'll do yourself an injury carrying on like this.'

'I'll do you an injury, you bastard,' yelled the Kommandant who wasn't going to be ordered about by any pig of a doctor who told him he had coloured blood. 'I know your sort. You're an enemy of South Africa, that's what you are. You're a bloody communist. I'll have you in under the Terrorist Act and we'll soon see how you like organ transplants.'

'For the sake of your health, please stop shouting,' the doctor pleaded.

'My health? You talk about my health? It's your health you should be worrying about if you don't do as I say,' the Kommandant screamed before he realized just what Dr Erasmus had meant. With a tremendous effort of will he calmed himself. Now he had not the slightest doubt that his heart needed changing. Dr Erasmus had admitted it in so many words.

In a quiet voice and with the authority he still possessed under Emergency Powers, Kommandant van Heerden gave his orders to the surgical team. They were to make all the necessary preparations for the transplant operation and were ordered not to divulge any information to the press, the public or their families. The whole operation was to be conducted in the utmost secrecy. It was the only welcome piece of news the doctors could glean from the Kommandant's brief.

The only other consolation was the knowledge that Kommandant van Heerden's body would almost certainly reject the new heart. As Dr Erasmus pointed out to him, he was probably committing suicide. The Kommandant knew better. He had been eating in the Police canteen for years and if his stomach could keep down the food they

served there, he couldn't imagine that his body would
reject a perfectly good heart.

Leaving the hospital still smarting at the affront to his
origins and the good name of his family, but pleased with
the way he had handled the situation, Kommandant van
Heerden decided the time had come to pay a visit to Fort
Rapier. His interest in the fortunes of Miss Hazelstone was
undimmed by the events of the past month and his respect had if anything been increased by the old lady's
remarkable resilience in the face of the misfortunes which
had overtaken the Hazelstone family. The reports that
had reached him from Fort Rapier indicated that Miss
Hazelstone had maintained her dignity and sense of social
prerogative in a situation which would have induced a
feeling of despondency if not of inferiority in a less vigor-
ous woman. Miss Hazelstone had succumbed to none of
the temptations of madness. She neither shuffled lost in
some interior wilderness nor imagined herself to be other
than she was.

'I am Miss Hazelstone of Jacaranda Park,' she insisted
in the face of attempts to turn her into a model patient
with problems amenable to psychotherapy, and instead
of conforming to the indolence that marked the lives of
the other patients, she had found plenty of interest to
occupy her time. The history of Fort Rapier and the part
played by her ancestors in the creation of the garrison
particularly fascinated her.

'My grandfather was C-in-C Zululand when this fort
was built,' she told Dr Herzog when she met him one
day crossing the parade-ground, and had astonished the
Superintendent by her grasp of military history.

'On this very parade ground in 1876 the Greys, the
Welch Regiment and the 12th Hussars marched past my

grandfather before leaving for the Zulu War,' she told the astonished doctor, and went on to give details of the uniforms of the various branches and the character of the officers in command.

'What a remarkable memory you have,' he said, 'to remember these things.'

'Part of the family history,' said Miss Hazelstone and had gone on to explain the mistakes made in the campaign, and in particular at the battle of Isandhlwana. Dr Herzog was so impressed with her interest, and especially by her knowledge of the Boer War and the part played in it by Dr Herzog's own grandfather, that he invited her to his house for tea and the discussion was continued until supper.

'Quite extraordinary,' he said to his wife when Miss Hazelstone went back to the ward. 'I had no idea my grandfather was responsible for our victory at Magersfontein.'

The following day he sent a memorandum to the staff, instructing them that Miss Hazelstone was to be given all the help and encouragement she needed to continue her study of military history and the part played in it by Fort Rapier.

'We have a duty to encourage patients to pursue their hobbies, particularly when they may well be of benefit to the hospital,' he told Dr von Blimenstein who complained that Miss Hazelstone had stopped attending her therapy classes.

'Miss Hazelstone hopes to publish the history of Fort Rapier and any publicity must surely rebound to our credit. It's not every day that lunatics publish military history.'

Dr von Blimenstein had reservations on that score, but she kept her thoughts to herself and Miss Hazelstone had continued her researches with growing enthusiasm. She had discovered regimental records in a trunk in the basement of what was now the staff canteen, but which had in earlier days been the officers' mess. These had led her to unearth even more interesting relics in the shape of discarded uniforms in the quartermaster's stores.

'We really ought to hold a pageant,' she told the Superintendent, 'the uniforms are there and while they do need patching up in places, because the cockroaches have got at them you see, there's no doubt they are authentic and it will give all the patients something to work for. It's so important for morale to create a common aim and something to look forward to.'

Dr Herzog had been impressed by the idea.

'A pageant of Fort Rapier's history,' he said, 'what a splendid idea,' and his mind toyed with the idea of an open day in which the public and the press could see the wonderful work being done on behalf of mental health in Zululand.

'I thought we might start with a march-past,' Miss Hazelstone continued, 'followed by several tableaux commemorating particularly memorable feats of courage in the history of South Africa.'

Dr Herzog was hesitant, 'I don't want any mock battles,' he said anxiously.

'Oh no, nothing like that,' Miss Hazelstone assured him, 'I was thinking more of purely stationary representations of the events.'

'We can't have the patients getting too excited.'

'Quite,' said Miss Hazelstone who had long since ceased to think of herself as a patient. 'I take your point. We shall have to see that the whole affair is conducted with truly military discipline. I was thinking of including as one of the set-pieces your great-grandfather's heroic defence of his homestead in the 6th Kaffir War.'

Dr Herzog was flattered. 'Were you really?' he said.
'I had no idea my family played such an important role
in the military history of the country.'

'The Herzogs were practically the Afrikaans counterpart of the Hazelstones,' Miss Hazelstone told him, and
with the knowledge that the pageant would enhance the
reputation of the Herzog family as well as that of the hospital, the Superintendent gave his permission for the event
to be held.

In the weeks that followed Miss Hazelstone threw herself into the preparations with an enthusiasm that communicated itself to the other inmates of Fort Rapier. She
took command of the organization with all the natural
authority of Sir Theophilus's granddaughter and with an
attention to detail made possible by her wealth. Bales of
red cloth were ordered from Durban on Miss Hazelstone's
account, and the patients in the sewing-rooms were kept
busy making new uniforms.

'It certainly brightens the place up,' Dr Herzog said to
Dr von Blimenstein as they watched Miss Hazelstone
drilling a squad of manic depressives on the parade-ground
one day.

'I can't help feeling uneasy,' Dr von Blimenstein said,
'Is it really necessary to include the Battle of Blood River
in the programme? I'm sure it will have an unfortunate
effect on the black patients.'

'Our chief responsibility is to the whites,' said Dr Herzog, 'and it can only help them to see the great events of
the past re-enacted here. I have every hope that by participating in them our patients will come to see that there
is still a place for the mentally sick in modern South Africa.
I like to think of this pageant as drama therapy on a vast
scale.'

'But surely, doctor, you don't consider insanity to be

simply a matter of morale?' Dr von Blimenstein said.

'Yes, I do, and if it isn't it ought to be. Besides,' said the Superintendent, 'the pageant will help to sublimate some of their aggression.'

On the parade ground Miss Hazelstone's squad marched past the saluting base which the carpenters had erected between the two field guns.

'Eyes right,' Miss Hazelstone shouted, and two hundred pairs of eyes fixed themselves manically on Dr Herzog. The Superintendent saluted.

'Eyes front,' and the squad marched on.

'Most impressive,' said Dr Herzog. 'What a pity we didn't think of this before.'

'I just hope we don't have cause to regret it,' said Dr von Blimenstein pessimistically.

As the day of the pageant approached, Miss Hazelstone had to deal with several problems. One was the question of assegais for the Zulu warriors. Dr Herzog was adamant.

'I'm not having hundreds of black patients running around brandishing spears. God alone knows what would happen.'

In the end the problem was solved by the purchase of one thousand rubber spears which had been used in the making of a film a year or two before.

Another problem centred round the question of the music and the sound effects to accompany the tableaux.

'I was thinking of the *1812 Overture*,' Miss Hazelstone explained to the conductor of the hospital band.

'We can't reach those heights,' the bandmaster objected, 'and in any case we haven't got a cannon.'

'We could use the field guns,' Miss Hazelstone said.

'We can't go round letting off loud bangs in the hospital grounds. It would have a terrible effect on the anxiety cases.'

In the end it was agreed that the band would restrict itself to simple marches like 'Colonel Bogey' and tunes like 'Goodbye Dolly Gray' and that a recording of the 1812 *Overture* should be played over loudspeakers to accompany the battle scenes.

A dress rehearsal was held the day before the pageant and Superintendent Herzog and the staff attended.

'Simply splendid,' Dr Herzog said afterwards. 'One has the feeling that one is actually present, it's so real.'

It was quite by chance that Kommandant van Heerden chose the afternoon of the pageant for his visit to the hospital. Unlike the Mayor of Piemburg and other notables, he had not been invited because it was felt that Miss Hazelstone might not like it.

'We don't want anything to put the old lady off her stride, and having the police here would only remind her of her brother's execution,' the Superintendent said.

As his car passed into the grounds of Fort Rapier Kommandant van Heerden noticed that a new air of festivity seemed to have come to the hospital.

'I hope it isn't too open,' he said to the driver who had replaced Konstabel Els, as the car passed under a banner which announced Open Day. They drove up to the parade ground which was decked with regimental flags and Kommandant van Heerden got out.

'Glad you could make it, Kommandant,' Dr Herzog said, and led the way to the saluting base, where the Mayor and his party were already seated. The Kommandant looked nervously around as he took his seat.

'What's going on?' he asked one of the aldermen.

'It's some sort of publicity stunt to foster public interest in mental health,' the alderman said.

'Funny place to hold it,' said the Kommandant. 'I

thought everyone up here was supposed to be barmy.
Good heavens, look at those kaffirs.'

A detachment of schïzophrenic Zulus marched across
the parade ground to take up their position for the tableaux.

'Who the hell gave them those spears?'

'Oh it's all right, they're only rubber,' said the councillor.

The Kommandant sank down in his chair in horror.
'Don't tell me,' he said, 'this whole thing has been organized by Miss Hazelstone.'

'Right first time,' said the councillor. 'Put up the money
herself. Just as well she did too. I hate to think what this
little lot cost.'

Kommandant van Heerden wasn't listening. He rose
from his chair and looked desperately round for some
way of escaping, but the crowd round the saluting base
was too dense to pass through, and in front the march-past
had already begun. He sank back into his chair in despair.

As the band played the regiments formed up and
marched towards the stand. Redcoated and surprisingly
well drilled for their mental health, they swung past the
Superintendent and at their head there marched the
familiar figure of Miss Hazelstone. For a moment the Kommandant thought he was back in the hall at Jacaranda House, and staring once more at the portrait of
Sir Theophilus. Miss Hazelstone's uniform was a replica of
the one the Viceroy had worn in the painting. Her face
was partially obscured by a plumed pith helmet but on
her chest were the stars and medals of her Grandfather's
disastrous campaigns. Behind the first regiment which
was the Welsh Guards, came the others, the county
regiments of England, appropriately less in step than the
Guards (it had been difficult to find enough compulsive

cases to be really smart) but shuffling along with determination all the same. After them came the Scots regiments recruited from women patients wearing kilts and
led by a chronic depressive playing the bagpipes. Last of
all was a small detachment of frogmen in rubber suits
with flippers who had difficulty keeping in step.

'A nice touch of modernity, don't you think?' Dr Herzog murmured to the Mayor as twenty crazed faces
turned their masks towards the stand.

'I hope those kaffirs aren't going to come too close,' said
the Mayor anxiously. There was no need to worry. The
black lunatics were not allowed the privilege of marching
past the stand. Miss Hazelstone was arranging them for
the first tableau.

In the interval Kommandant van Heerden left his seat
and spoke to the Superintendent.

'I thought I told you to keep Miss Hazelstone under
close surveillance,' he said angrily.

'She's made remarkable progress since she has been
here,' Dr Herzog answered. 'We like to see our patients
taking an interest in their hobbies.'

'You may,' said the Kommandant, 'but I don't. Miss
Hazelstone's hobbies happen to include murder and you
go and let her organize a military parade. You must be out
of your mind.'

'Nothing like allowing the patients to dramatize their
aggressive tendencies,' said the Superintendent.

'She's done that quite enough already,' said the Kommandant. 'My advice is to stop this thing before it's too
late.'

But already the first tableau had begun. A square of
cardboard ox wagons stood in the centre of the parade
ground and around them gathered the Zulu schizophrenics
brandishing their spears. After several minutes the Zulus

lay down on the tarmac in attitudes supposed to represent agonizing death.

'Blood River,' said the Superintendent.

'Very realistic,' said the Mayor.

'Bloody insane,' said Kommandant van Heerden.

A polite round of clapping greeted the end of the battle. For the next hour the history of South Africa unfurled before the spectators in a series of blood-curdling battles in which the blacks were invariably massacred by the whites.

'You would think they'd get tired of lying down and getting up and lying down again,' the Mayor said when the Zulus had gone through their death agonies for the umpteenth time. 'Must keep them physically fit, I suppose.'

'So long as the bastards don't win, I'm happy,' said the Kommandant.

'I think they do have a moment of triumph in the finale,' said Dr Herzog. 'It's the Battle of Isandhlwana. The British ran out of ammunition and were massacred.'

'Do you mean to tell me,' said the Kommandant, 'that you have allowed white men to be defeated by blacks? It's insane. What's more it's illegal. You are encouraging racial hatred.'

Dr Herzog was nonplussed. 'I hadn't thought of it like that,' he said.

'Well, you had better think of it now. You're breaking the law. You've got to put a stop to it. I'm not prepared to sit here and watch anything so outrageous.' the Kommandant said firmly.

'Nor am I,' said the Mayor. Several councillors nodded in agreement.

'I don't really see how I can,' Dr Herzog said. 'They're about to begin.'

In the middle of the parade-ground Miss Hazelstone had organized the British camp and was superintending the placement of the two old field guns. Several hundred yards away the Zulu army was gathered ready for its moment of triumph.

'I insist that you stop the battle,' said the Kommandant.

'So do I,' said the Mayor, who still didn't feel very comfortable about the rubber spears.

Dr Herzog hesitated. 'Oh dear, I do wish you had told me it was illegal before. I don't see what I can do now,' he said anxiously.

'Well, if you won't stop it, I will,' said the Kommandant.

'Good man,' said the Mayor, seconded by the councillors.

Before he could think about the likely consequences of his intervention, Kommandant van Heerden found himself being helped off the saluting base and on to the parade-ground. He marched slowly towards the two armies, and as he went the realization of his position slowly dawned on him. In the middle of the square halfway between the two opposing forces of lunatics, he began to regret his precipitate decision to intervene. On one side of him five hundred Zulu schizophrenics pawed the ground and waved their spears ferociously, while on the other, an equal number of white madmen awaited defeat with a determination made all the more awful by foreknowledge.

Kommandant van Heerden halted and raised his hand. Silence fell over the two armies.

'This is Kommandant van Heerden speaking,' he shouted. 'I am ordering you to disperse and return to your wards. This is an illegal gathering and contravenes the Riotous Assemblies Act.'

He stopped and waited for the armies to retire. There

was no sign of their doing anything of the sort. As his words echoed away, both sides stared insanely at their adversaries and there were murmurs in the ranks. Miss Hazelstone finished sighting the field guns and stepped forward. On the Zulu side an enormous warrior followed suit.

'What is the meaning of this nonsense?' Miss Hazelstone shouted.

'You heard me,' said the Kommandant. 'This battle constitutes a breach of the peace. I insist you disperse.'

In the space between the armies Kommandant van Heerden found his new role as keeper of the peace becoming more difficult.

'You've no right to come here and interfere with our pageant,' Miss Hazelstone insisted. 'And it's not a breach of the peace.'

'We won,' said the Zulu chief. 'We won the Battle of Isandhlwana and now we win it again.'

'Over my dead body,' said the Kommandant and regretted the words as soon as he had said them. The murmurs in the ranks of the two armies indicated all too clearly that the spirit of belligerency was spreading.

On the saluting base the spectators were growing as restless as the lunatics.

'Are those axes made of rubber too?' the Mayor asked as he watched several Zulus flourishing choppers in place of their spears.

'I certainly hope so,' said the Superintendent.

'The British appear to be loading those field guns,' said the Mayor.

'Impossible,' said the Superintendent. 'They've nothing to load them with.'

'They're putting something up the spout,' said the Mayor. 'And those Zulus seem to be putting something on the ends of their spears. They look like knitting needles to me. Either that or bicycle spokes.'

The alarm of the Mayor was as nothing to the panic that Kommandant van Heerden was beginning to feel. Miss Hazelstone and the Zulu chief were engaged in a fierce argument about who had won the battle of Isandhlwana.

'My grandfather was there,' said Miss Hazelstone.

'So was mine,' said the Zulu.

'Mine wasn't,' said the Kommandant, 'and in any case I don't care a stuff who won the battle, no one is going to win it here. I demand you withdraw your forces.'

'We're going to win,' said the Zulu. 'We've been losing all afternoon and we've a right to win.'

'Nonsense,' said Miss Hazelstone. 'My grandfather won the victory and that's all there is to be said.'

'My grandfather told my father and my father told me than your grandfather ran away,' the Zulu said.

'How dare you?' Miss Hazelstone shrieked. 'How dare you insult a Hazelstone?'

Kommandant van Heerden was horrified too. He knew from experience what was likely to be the result of any altercation between Miss Hazelstone and a Zulu. As the old lady wrestled with the sword that hung from her belt and the Zulu took refuge behind his enormous shield, Kommandant van Heerden made one last effort to restore harmony.

'I order you to leave this parade-ground,' he yelled, drawing his revolver from its holster, but it was already too late. With an upward sweep of her sword Miss Hazelstone knocked the Kommandant's arm into the air. The revolver fired harmlessly into the sky and with a great roar the two armies of the insane surged towards one another.

As Miss Hazelstone's sword swept through the air and the Zulu parried with his shield, Kommandant van Heerden turned to flee. One glance at the Zulu schizophrenics convinced him that if safety lay anywhere, it was with the British Army and he dashed towards the advancing lines of redcoats. A moment later he regretted his decision. Advancing at a run, a regiment of paranoid women in kilts still headed by the depressed piper playing 'The Road to the Isles', swept over the Kommandant and he had just time to turn and run with them before he was bowled over and thrown to the ground. He lay still and was trodden on several times before the regiment was past. Then raising his head, he surveyed the scene around him.

It was immediately clear that the Zulus had no intention of forgoing their victory. Nonplussed for a moment by the charge of the paranoid women, they had recovered their nerve and had counter-attacked to good effect. Using their short rubber spears now tipped with knitting needles, they were stabbing their way forward very successfully. On the left flank the Welsh Guards were making a desperate defence but their wooden rifles were no match for the assegais. As the Black Watch wavered and began to retreat Kommandant van Heerden scrambled to his feet and ran before them. Around him the parade-ground echoed to the war-cry of the Zulu hordes, the screams of the wounded women, and the weird noises coming from the bagpipes. To add to the din a tape recorder struck up the *1812 Overture* through the loudspeakers. In the middle of the battle, Miss Hazelstone's pith helmet could be seen bobbing about. Kommandant van Heerden made it to the British camp and collapsed inside one of the tents.

To the spectators on the stand the re-enactment of history appeared at first to be entirely convincing. The valiant charge of the British and their subsequent retreat had an air of authenticity about them which the previous tableaux had lacked.

'Amazing realism,' said the Mayor, who had just seen a Guardsman run through with a spear.

'I think the music helps too,' said the Superintendent.

The Mayor had to agree. 'People seem to be screaming rather a lot,' he said.

'I'm sure this sort of thing helps the patients,' Dr Herzog continued. 'Tends to take their minds off their problems.'

'I suppose it must,' said the Mayor. 'Certainly takes other things off. There's a fellow over there who seems to have lost a leg.'

On the square in front of them glimpses of a terrible reality were beginning to appear through the pageant of history. Increasingly it was becoming difficult to tell what was illusion from what was fact. History and present tragedy mingled inextricably. In some places death was being mimed with a series of violent contortions whose realism far surpassed the agonies of those whose deaths were in no way rehearsed. To the strains of Tchaikovsky a number of patients in the Black Watch found themselves being raped by Zulu warriors while a detachment of frogmen who had never been anywhere near Isandhlwana threw themselves into the fray with all the vigour their flippers would allow.

From the shelter of the tent into which he had crawled the Kommandant watched as the crew of a field gun aimed the weapon into the crowd of struggling combatants and was horrified to see Miss Hazelstone, minus her pith helmet and stained with blood, superintending the operation.

'More chlorate and less sugar,' he heard her say to a

man who was filling what appeared to be a pillow case with powder. The Kommandant waited no longer. He knew too well Miss Hazelstone's remarkable skill with large-calibre weapons to risk being in the line of fire. Disentangling himself from the canvas and refusing the passionate overtures of a private of the Black Watch who had crawled in beside him, the Kommandant dashed for shelter towards the saluting base. He had covered some twenty yards when he heard Miss Hazelstone give the order to fire, and a moment later a sheet of flame enveloped the British camp. As an enormous explosion threw him to the ground and the blast slid him across the tarmac the Kommandant shut his eyes and prayed. Above his head portions of field gun mingled with combatants interrupted in their struggles. Miss Hazelstone had not merely fired the gun, she had exploded it. As he slid to a halt under the saluting base Kommandant van Heerden raised his head and looked around at the subsiding chaos. The actors in the tableau had assumed a new and altogether convincing stillness and it was clear that nobody had won the battle of Isandhlwana.

The parade-ground was littered with black and white bodies while what survivors there were had lost all interest in history. With all the marks of an entirely sane instinct for self-preservation, they crawled towards the sick bay.

Only the staff seemed to have taken leave of their senses. On the stand above him the Kommandant could hear Dr Herzog still trying to reassure the late Mayor that the spears were made of rubber. To Kommandant van Heerden the assurance seemed quite unnecessary. Whatever had hit the Mayor had been made of something much more lethal.

The Kommandant waited until Dr Herzog had been taken away before crawling from his hiding place. He stood up and looked around. History had not merely been portrayed, he thought, it had been made. Not only the past but the present and future of South Africa was to be seen in the devastation that greeted his eyes. Picking his way over the bodies, the Kommandant made his way towards a large crater which had been blown in the middle of the parade ground. Beside it, there lay the remains of a plumed pith helmet and the Star Miss Hazelstone had been wearing.

'A last memento,' he murmured, and picked them up. Then still dazed and shaken he turned and made his way back to the car.

Chapter 19

On the morning of his execution Jonathan Hazelstone was denied the usual privilege of choosing a hearty breakfast on the grounds that before all major operations patients had to do with light refreshment. Instead of the bacon and eggs he had ordered, he was allowed a cup of coffee and a visit from an Anglican chaplain. Jonathan found it difficult to decide which was the more unpleasant. On the whole he thought he preferred the coffee.

His ties with the Church had been severed at the time of his trial and the Bishop had reached the conclusion that the refusal of the Church authorities to testify on his behalf had been due to the jealousy he knew to exist among his colleagues at the rapidity of his promotion to a Bishopric. He had no idea that parts of his confession, particularly those chosen by Konstabel Els, had been shown to the Archbishop.

'I knew the fellow was progressive,' the Archbishop muttered as he read the extraordinary document, 'but really this time he has gone too far,' and he recalled Jonathan's admission that he had used every possible method to attract people into the Church. 'High Church in ritual, Low Church in approach, that's my way,' Jonathan had said and the Archbishop could see that he had meant it. To combine sodomy with genuflexion was to be High Church and Low with a vengeance and it was hardly surprising his congregations had grown so quickly.

'I think the least said the soonest mended,' the Arch-

bishop had decided, and in short the Church had dis-
owned him.

The Chaplain who came to visit him in his last hours
was not a South African. It had been impossible to persuade any self-respecting parson to minister to the needs
of a man who had brought disgrace on his cloth and even
the Bishop of Piemburg had declined the invitation.

'There are moments when a man needs to be alone,' he
explained to Governor Schnapps over the telephone, 'and
this is surely one of them,' and had gone back to compose
a sermon on the Brotherhood of Man.

In the end it was the Chaplain of a Cambridge college
who was visiting Piemburg during the long vacation who
was inveigled into Piemburg Prison to attend to the
prisoner's spiritual needs.

'I understand there is a particularly fine display of
prickly pears in the prison garden,' the Vicar of Piemburg
explained to the Chaplain who was far more interested in
the physical needs of rock plants than in the spiritual
ones of his fellow men and the Chaplain had jumped at
the opportunity afforded by the hanging to see a riot of
prickly pears.

Standing in the cell, the Chaplain found it difficult to
know what to say.

'You weren't by any chance in the Navy?' he asked
finally.

Jonathan shook his head.

'I just wondered,' the Chaplain continued. 'There was
a middy on HMS *Clodius* in '43 I think it was, or it might
have been '44. His name was Hazelnut.'

'Mine's Hazelstone,' said the Bishop.

'So it is. How forgetful of me. One meets so many
people in my profession.'

'I suppose so,' said the Bishop.

The Chaplain paused, and looked at the manacles and chains. 'Do you wear those all the time?' he asked. 'They must be frightfully uncomfortable.'

'Only when I'm going to be hanged,' said the Bishop.

The Chaplain thought he detected a note of bitterness in the remark, and recollected the reason for his visit.

'Is there anything you would like to tell me?' he asked.

The Bishop could think of a great many things he would like to tell him, but there didn't seem much point.

'No,' he said, 'I have made my confession.'

The Chaplain sighed with relief. These occasions are so embarrassing, he thought.

'I've never actually attended an execution before,' he mumbled at last.

'Nor have I,' said the Bishop.

'Nasty things,' continued the Chaplain, 'nasty but necessary. Still they do say hanging is quick and painless. I dare say you'll be quite relieved when it is all over.'

The Bishop, whose hope of eternal life had vanished along with his faith, doubted if relieved was quite the right word. He tried to change the subject.

'Do you come here often?' he asked.

'To the prison?'

'To South Africa, though it's much the same thing.'

The Chaplain ignored the remark. He was a staunch supporter of the South African point of view at high table in his college, and had no time for liberals.

'I try to get away to sunnier climes at least once a year,' he said. 'Undergraduates are so irreligious these days and my real interest lies in gardening. South Africa is full of lovely gardens.'

'Then perhaps you'll appreciate this poem,' said the Bishop and began to recite 'The Forerunners'.

Lovely enchanting language, sugar cane,
Hony of roses, whither wilt thou flie?'

He was still reciting when Governor Schnapps and
Hangman Els arrived. As the chains were removed and he
was strapped into the harness that held his arms, the
Bishop continued:

'True beautie dwells on high: ours is a flame
But borrow'd thence to light us thither.
Beautie and beauteous words should go together.'

'Bugger these buckles,' said Els, who was having difficulty with the straps.

The solemn procession passed out of Bottom into the
bright sunshine of the prison courtyard. Stumbling between Els and the old warder, Jonathan looked round him
for the last time. Incongruous against the dead black paint
of the death house stood a white ambulance. To everyone's amazement, the condemned man laughed.

'Bleak paleness chalkes the doore,' he shouted,

'The harbingers are come. See, see their mark
White is their colour and behold my head.'

The two ambulance men stared in horror at the shouting figure whose corpse they had been sent to collect for
the transplant operation.

'But must they have my heart? Must they dispark
Those sparkling feelings which thereine were bred?'

The little group hurried on up the steps to the scaffold.
The old warder helped Els to get the Bishop on to the trap

and then rushed down the ladder and across the courtyard to his office. It wasn't that he was squeamish but he had no intention of being anywhere near the gallows when Els pulled the lever, and besides he had a good excuse for his absence. He had to phone the hospital the moment the ambulance left the prison.

Standing on the trap the Bishop continued his recitation. Governor Schnapps asked the Chaplain what a harbinger was. The Chaplain said he thought it was probably a member of the hydrangea family though he seemed to remember having served under a Captain Harbinger during the war. Els was trying to get the cloth bag over the Bishop's head. He was having some difficulty because the Bishop was so tall and the bag had evidently been made for a much smaller head. Els couldn't get the Bishop to bend his legs because the straps prevented any movement. In the end Governor Schnapps had to give Els a lift up before he could drag the hood down into position. He had to repeat the performance when it came to putting the noose round the condemned man's neck, and then Els pulled the rope so tight the Bishop was forced to stop his recitation,

'Must dulnesse turn me to a clo—' he ground to a halt.

'For goodness sake, Els, loosen the bloody thing,' Governor Schnapps shouted as the poem throttled to a stop, 'You're supposed to hang him down there, not strangle him up here.'

'They seem to grow best in sandy soil,' said the Chaplain.

'Is that loose enough for you?' Els asked after he had pulled the rope and loosened the noose so that it hung limply on the Bishop's shoulders. He was sick of people telling him how to do his job. If the Governor was so bloody knowledgeable about hangings, why didn't he do the job himself.

'What do?' Governor Schnapps said to the Chaplain.

'Hydrangeas.'

'Clod,' said the Bishop resuming his recital.

Els stepped over to the lever.

'Yet have they left me,' the Bishop's muffled voice came through the cloth bag. Els pulled the lever and the hooded figure disappeared through the trap into the well below, and his voice, already indistinct, was silenced by the dreadful thud that followed. As the trapdoor slammed and the scaffold rocked alarmingly under the impact, the Chaplain, recalled to the purpose of his visit by the intimations of mortality he had just witnessed, offered a prayer for the dead man.

'Let us pray for the soul of the departed wherever it may be,' he said, and lowered his head. Governor Schnapps and Els closed their eyes and listened with bowed heads as he prayed. For several minutes the Chaplain mumbled on before ending, 'And may Thy Servant depart in Peace, Amen.'

'Amen,' said Governor Schnapps and Els together. The men on the scaffold raised their heads and Els stepped forward to peer down into the well. The rope had stopped swinging and hung rather limply, Els thought, considering the weight of its burden. As his eyes became accustomed to the darkness below Els began to realize that something was missing. The noose on the rope hung loose and empty. The Chaplain's prayer had been answered. Wherever God's servant might be, he had certainly departed and evidently in one piece too. The well of the scaffold was absolutely empty.

As the Bishop dropped into eternity he thought how appropriate his last words had been and was glad he

hadn't reached the next line which went, 'Thou art still
my God,' because he no longer believed. He braced himself for the awful shock to his neck, but the pain came
from another extremity altogether. 'Corns,' he thought, as
he hit the ground with a tremendous crash and rolled
sideways, through the door and out into the sunlit courtyard. His cloth bag was ripped and his legs felt decidedly
painful, but it was evident that whatever else had been
broken, his neck had not. He lay still, waiting for Els to
fetch him for a second attempt and wasn't surprised when
he felt hands lifting his feet and shoulders.

A moment later he was lying on a stretcher and had been
lifted into the ambulance. As the doors were slammed the
ambulance moved off hurriedly, stopped for a moment
while the prison gates were opened, and hurtled out into
the street, its siren whirring.

Behind it the Death House had begun to fulfil the pre-
dictions of the old warder. Under the impact of the stam-
pede that followed on the scaffold when the distraught
hangman peering into the well slipped and grabbed Governor Schnapps' legs to prevent himself falling, the walls
of the gallows slowly toppled inwards and with a roar
of falling masonry, Governors, Hangmen and Chaplains,
disappeared from view in a dense cloud of black dust. The
old warder sat in his office and thanked his lucky stars. 'I
said it wasn't safe,' he murmured and picked up the phone
to dial the hospital.

As the ambulance sped through the streets of Piemburg,
Jonathan Hazelstone felt the attendant undoing the straps
that held his arms and legs. A hand slid inside his shirt
and felt his chest.

'It's all right. It's still beating,' he heard the attendant

tell the driver. Jonathan held his breath until the hand
went away. Then he relaxed slowly. Around him the
sounds of the city filtered through the canvas bag and as
he lay there Jonathan Hazelstone realized for the first
time that what lay in store for him might make death by
hanging seem infinitely preferable.

'I'll be hanged if anyone is going to cut my heart out
now,' he thought to himself as the ambulance swung
through the gates of Piemburg Hospital, and stopped outside the mortuary.

Inside the hospital the news of the execution had been
accompanied by the old warder's insistence that several
more ambulances be sent to the Prison to deal with the
victims of the disastrous collapse of the Death House. The
air of tension that was already present in the hospital developed into a state of wholesale panic. The Kommandant,
already prepared for the operation, was given a general
anaesthetic and wheeled unconscious into the operating
theatre. While the surgeons prepared for the transplant,
ambulance drivers rushed to their vehicles and preparations were made to receive the expected influx of victims
from the prison. Nurses already distraught at having to
deal with scores of lunatics injured in the massacre at Fort
Rapier tried to ready themselves for this fresh disaster.
When the ambulance carrying Jonathan Hazelstone
arrived at the mortuary it was caught up in the general
confusion.

'Get back to the prison,' yelled an orderly from a window when the two attendants carried the donor into the
mortuary and deposited him on a trolley. 'There's been
a major catastrophe there.' The two men dashed back to
their ambulance and drove off. Alone in the mortuary for
a moment the Bishop leapt off his trolley and snatched the

cloth bag from his head and looked around him. Under the sheets that covered still forms on their slabs he found what he was looking for, and by the time two orderlies arrived to fetch the donor for the transplant, the body lying snugly under its white sheet and with its head covered by a grey cloth bag contained a heart that was far too cold and still to be of much assistance to Kommandant van Heerden.

As the operation got under way, what remained of the late Bishop of Barotseland was strolling with the faint suggestion of a limp up the hill towards Jacaranda House, and as it strolled it was singing:

> 'Yet if you go, I passe not; take your way:
> For Thou art still my God, is all that ye
> Perhaps with more embellishment can say.
> Go birds of spring: let winter have his fee;
> Let a bleak paleness chalke the door,
> So all within be livelier than before.'

Jonathan Hazelstone had begun to think that there might, after all, be reasons for recovering his faith.

The state of panic that reigned at Piemburg Hospital when the ambulance containing the Bishop arrived was as nothing to the chaos and hysteria which began in the operating theatre when the body of the donor arrived on the trolley. An incision had already been made in Kommandant van Heerden's chest when it was discovered that whoever had been responsible for the execution had made an altogether too thorough job of it. The corpse on the trolley had multiple injuries of the most appalling sort. The only thing that didn't appear to be broken

on it was the neck. Not only was it fractured in a score
of places but it had been dead for at least 48 hours. And
when it was further revealed to be the corpse of a woman
of eighty-nine, the surgeons knew that what they had
considered stupid for the start, not to say criminal, had
degenerated now to the point of sheer lunacy.

Dr Erasmus was frantic. 'Who said this was beating?'
he yelled, slapping the withered object that hung out of
the old lady's chest. (She had in fact been run over by
a twenty-five ton truck while crossing the road.) 'This
hasn't beaten for days and, when it last worked, it didn't
bloody beat. It winced once in a while. I wouldn't feed
this heart to a starving dog let alone put it into that
maniac's body.' He sat down and wept.

After half an hour during which the mortuary was
searched again and again, and various possible donors in
the hospital wards had their deaths hastened by teams of
desperate surgeons who came masked and predatory to
stare at them and feel their pulses hopefully, Dr Erasmus
pulled himself together and taking a quick tot of ether
addressed the heart team.

'Gentlemen and ladies,' he said, 'what we have all been
witness to this afternoon is of such a regrettable and
dreadful nature that the sooner we forget about it the
better. As you know I never wanted to undertake this
transplant in the first place. We were forced to agree to it
by that bloody lunatic there.' He pointed to Kommandant
van Heerden's unconscious body. 'We acted under immense pressure and, thank heaven, in absolute secrecy.
And now owing to the prison authorities' delay in letting
us have the donor, and looking at her injuries I can fully
appreciate why there was this delay, we are quite unable
to proceed with the operation. I intend to stitch the
patient's chest up and leave his own heart beating

perfectly healthily in place.'

There were murmurs of protest from the other members of the transplant team.

'Yes, I know how you feel and given any further provocation I would agree to remove his heart and let the bastard rot. But I have decided against it. Thanks to the secrecy that surrounds this whole irregular business I have a better plan. I think it will be better to allow the Kommandant to remain in complete ignorance of the good fortune that has prevented him from getting this,' and Dr Erasmus slapped the old woman's heart again. 'We will simply maintain the fiction that the transplant has been completed successfully and I have every confidence that his stupidity is so colossal that it will never cross his mind to question our statement that he has a new heart.'

Amid congratulations and a few cheers, the eminent surgeon turned to Kommandant van Heerden and stitched him up.

An hour later the Kommandant woke up in his room. He felt rather sick and the wound in his chest hurt when he moved but otherwise he didn't seem to feel any ill effects from his operation. He took a deep tentative breath and listened to his new heart. It sounded perfect.

Chapter 20

As the great cloud of black dust swelled out in the centre of the prison courtyard and the last piece of rotten masonry fell with a final thud, an awestruck silence settled on the black convicts cowering in their cells. Konstabel Els, treading on Governor Schnapps's scrotum as a last tribute to the man who had ruined his career as a hangman, clambered painfully to the top of the pile of debris and stared into the murk. It was hardly a peak in Darien and the prospect ahead could hardly be called pacific but in his own way ex-Hangman Els was a proud man. At the very centre of a slowly expanding ball of black dust, Konstabel Els knew that he had once again put his great gifts of annihilation to good use. Below him lay the bodies of Governor Schnapps, the Chaplain and, he still hoped, the man he had attempted to hang. He, Hangman Els, had topped them all and no one would ever forget the day that Els had hanged a man in Piemburg Prison. He had made more than a reputation for himself, he had made a name, a great name. And as Els clambered down from the mound of debris and emerged dazed from the black cloud, he had no regrets.

Naked, bruised and black as the ace of spades, Els stepped forth to meet the world. He walked slowly and unsteadily up the great courtyard and as he walked men began to pour out of their prison cells where they had been waiting in silent fear, while the first hanging Piemburg Prison had known for twenty years took place. From every doorway overlooking the courtyard the convicts poured to gaze at the scene of disaster.

At first they stood and stared in silent wonder, and then a great cry went up, followed by shouts of joy and presently a man broke into song and a moment later the great courtyard was a mass of dancing and singing men who stamped their feet and clapped their hands in an ecstatic and triumphant dance. One thousand black convicts, Zulus to a man, danced as they had never danced before round the mound that had once been the dreaded Death House. Rank after rank they stamped and swayed and as the earth and sky reverberated to their dance they sang.

And their song was a great requiem of joy at the passing of Els, Kaffir-Killer Els, Hangman Els, the scourge of the Zulus. In their midst stamping and dancing and singing for dear life, naked and black as the best of them, was Els.

Someone threw a match on to the pile of masonry and rotten wood and a moment later the remains of the scaffold was ablaze. As the dust slowly subsided a plume of black smoke arose into the cloudless sky. Rising almost vertically in the still air the black plume signalled far and wide that something extraordinary and significant had occurred.

The swaying convicts, advancing with their knees raised high for the emphatic stamp of their feet and backing again for another triumphant surge, accompanied the flames and the roar of the fire with their endless chant.

> 'Els is dead, Kaffir-Killer Els,
> Gone to the devil where his soul belongs
> Raper of our women, killer of our men
> We won't see the swine again.'

The song was picked up by Zulus in the street outside

the prison and they took up the refrain. From house to house, from street to street, the chant spread like wild-fire as servants poured into the streets to watch the smoke of the funeral pyre rise over Piemburg Prison. Within an hour all Piemburg reverberated to the Zulus' chant. Lying in his bed in Piemburg Hospital Kommandant van Heer-den dozily caught the refrain and smiled. It seemed a good omen. He began to hum it cheerfully. It put him in good heart.

As dusk fell the convicts were still dancing and singing. In the administrative block the warders cowered in terror and peered fearfully through the bars at the black figures silhouetted against the flames. The old warder cursed Els and his bloody hanging but he knew better than to try to put a stop to the celebrations. He wasn't going to get him-self torn to bits by the mob by trying to intervene and when he rang the police station to ask for reinforcements he had been told by Luitenant Verkramp that the police station was itself under siege and he would have to pray and wait for the exuberance to die down of its own accord. Verkramp had not been exaggerating. The streets of Piemburg were filled with dancing crowds. Traffic ground to a halt and white drivers walked home or spent the night in their offices rather than risk trying to drive through the excited mobs. Not that there was any sign of anger among the crowds, only a great sense of liberation and joy.

As the plane for London passed low over Piemburg that night a large cheerful clergyman drew the attention of his companion to the fire and the crowds dancing in the streets.

'So all within is livelier than before,' he remarked enigmatically.

His companion put down the catalogue of rubber goods she had been reading. 'I'm sure you'll make a very good college chaplain,' she said and sighed, 'but I doubt if I'll find a Zulu cook in London.'

It was only a month before Kommandant van Heerden was well enough to leave hospital. His new heart had shown no signs of being rejected and the doctors were delighted with his progress. There had been a little trouble over the matter of injections and it had taken six male nurses all their strength to hold the Kommandant down, but apart from that he had been a model patient. After a fortnight he had been allowed out of bed and only then had he learnt the full story of the tragedy at Piemburg Prison.

'It was a miracle the ambulance men managed to get the body away in time,' he told Dr Erasmus. 'Another minute and I wouldn't be here today.'

Dr Erasmus had to agree. 'A genuine miracle,' he said.

'You're quite certain there won't be any rejection of the new heart?' the Kommandant asked, and was relieved that the doctor was so confident all would be well.

'I can honestly say,' said Dr Erasmus, 'that to all intents and purposes the heart that beats in your chest at this moment might well have been the one you were born with,' and with this assurance that there would be no rejection, the Kommandant smiled happily to himself.

When he finally left hospital, the Kommandant took a month's leave and spent it on the beach at Umhloti acquiring a healthy tan and reading books about the Hazelstone family. For a while he toyed with the idea of changing his name to van Heerden-Hazelstone. 'After all, I'm

practically one of the family,' he thought, but he gave up
the idea finally as being not in the best of taste. Instead
he cultivated an air of arrogance which irritated Luitenant
Verkramp and was ignored by everybody else. The doctors
had told him that his new heart needed plenty of exercise
and the Kommandant tried to get out of his office and
walk about the town as much as possible.

His favourite stroll took him up Town Hill to Jacaranda
Park where he would wander down the drive to the house.
It was still empty and there was talk of turning it into a
museum or even a National Park. In the meantime Kommandant van Heerden liked to go and sit on the stoep and
recall the events of the week that had changed his life
so momentously.

He often thought of Konstabel Els and now that Els was
dead he felt quite sorry. There had been a good side to
the Konstabel's nature, he supposed, and he had to admit
that Els had saved his life more than once.

'If it hadn't been for Els and that damned gun, I
wouldn't be here today,' he said to himself before remembering that it had been Els's lunacy that had caused his
heart trouble in the first place. Still he could afford to be
magnanimous now. Els had died as he had lived, killing
people. 'He went with a swing,' he thought, and recalled
nostalgically the Konstabel's epic struggle with the Dobermann. It reminded him of a case he had read about in
the paper recently. It concerned a coloured convict on a
prison farm in Northern Zululand who had bitten a guard
dog to death before hanging it. The fellow's name had been
Harbinger, which the Kommandant thought sounded
vaguely familiar. Anyway he had been given twenty
lashes for Indecent Assault and the Kommandant thought
he deserved them.

He settled himself comfortably in a wicker chair and

looked out over the lawn at the new bust of Sir Theophilus which he had had erected at his own expense—or rather at the expense of the reward money Els no longer had any use for. He had paid the taxidermist too for his trouble, and had taken the stuffed Toby and put it in his office at the police station where it gave him an opportunity to wax eloquent to the new konstabels on the virtues of Konstabel Els who had killed the dog to save his Kommandant's life.

All in all, the Kommandant reflected, he had good cause to be happy. The world was a good place to be in. South Africa was white still and would remain so. But above all he knew that he merited the high place he held in Piemburg and that his greatest ambition had finally been achieved. Within his chest there beat the heart of an English gentleman.

Tom Sharpe

Wilt

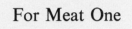

For Meat One

Chapter 1

Whenever Henry Wilt took the dog for a walk, or, to be more accurate, when the dog took him, or, to be exact, when Mrs Wilt told them both to go and take themselves out of the house so that she could do her yoga exercises, he always took the same route. In fact the dog followed the route and Wilt followed the dog. They went down past the Post Office, across the playground, under the railway bridge and out onto the footpath by the river. A mile along the river and then under the railway line again and back through streets where the houses were bigger than Wilt's semi and where there were large trees and gardens and the cars were all Rovers and Mercedes. It was here that Clem, a pedigree Labrador, evidently feeling more at home, did his business while Wilt stood looking around rather uneasily, conscious that this was not his sort of neighbourhood and wishing it was. It was about the only time during their walk that he was at all aware of his surroundings. For the rest of the way Wilt's walk was an interior one and followed an itinerary completely at variance with his own appearance and that of his route. It was in fact a journey of wishful thinking, a pilgrimage along trails of remote possibility involving the irrevocable disappearance of Mrs Wilt, the sudden acquisition of wealth, power, what he would do if he was appointed Minister of Education or, better still, Prime Minister. It was partly concocted of a series of desperate expedients and partly in an unspoken dialogue so that anyone noticing Wilt (and most people didn't) might have seen his lips move occasionally and his mouth curl into what he fondly imagined was a sardonic smile as he dealt with questions or parried arguments with devastating repartee. It was on one of these walks taken in the rain after a particularly trying day at the Tech that Wilt first conceived the notion that he would only be able to fulfil his latent promise and call his life his own if some not entirely fortuitous disaster overtook his wife.

Like everything else in Henry Wilt's life it was not a sudden

decision. He was not a decisive man. Ten years as an Assistant
Lecturer (Grade Two) at the Fenland College of Arts and Technology was proof of that. For ten years he had remained in the
Liberal Studies department teaching classes of Gasfitters, Plasterers, Bricklayers and Plumbers. Or keeping them quiet. And
for ten long years he had spent his days going from classroom
to classroom with two dozen copies of *Sons and Lovers* or
Orwell's *Essays* or *Candide* or *The Lord of the Flies* and had
done his damnedest to extend the sensibilities of Day-Release
Apprentices with notable lack of success.

'Exposure to Culture,' Mr Morris, the Head of Liberal
Studies, called it but from Wilt's point of view it looked more
like his own exposure to barbarism, and certainly the experience
had underminded the ideals and illusions which had sustained
him in his younger days. So had twelve years of marriage to
Eva.

If Gasfitters could go through life wholly impervious to
the emotional significance of the interpersonal relationships
portrayed in *Sons and Lovers*, and coarsely amused by
D. H. Lawrence's profound insight into the sexual nature of
existence, Eva Wilt was incapable of such detachment. She
hurled herself into cultural activities and self-improvement with
an enthusiasm that tormented Wilt. Worse still, her notion of
culture varied from week to week, sometimes embracing Barbara
Cartland and Anya Seton, sometimes Ouspensky, sometimes
Kenneth Clark, but more often the instructor at the Pottery
Class on Tuesdays or the lecturer on Transcendental Meditation
on Thursdays, so that Wilt never knew what he was coming
home to except a hastily cooked supper, some forcibly expressed
opinions about his lack of ambition, and a half-baked intellectual
eclecticism that left him disoriented.

To escape from the memory of Gasfitters as putative human
beings and of Eva in the lotus position, Wilt walked by the
river thinking dark thoughts, made darker still by the knowledge
that for the fifth year running his application to be promoted
to Senior Lecturer was almost certain to be turned down and
that unless he did something soon he would be doomed to
Gasfitters Three and Plasterers Two—and to Eva—for the rest
of his life. It was not a prospect to be borne. He would act
decisively. Above his head a train thundered by. Wilt stood

watching its dwindling lights and thought about accidents involving level crossings.

'He's in such a funny state these days,' said Eva Wilt, 'I don't know what to make of him.'

'I've given up trying with Patrick,' said Mavis Mottram studying Eva's vase critically. 'I think I'll put the lupin just a fraction of an inch to the left. Then it will help to emphasize the oratorical qualities of the rose. Now the iris over here. One must try to achieve an almost *audible* effect of contrasting colours. Contrapuntal, one might say.'

Eva nodded and sighed. 'He used to be so energetic,' she said, 'but now he just sits about the house watching telly. It's as much as I can do to get him to take the dog for a walk.'

'He probably misses the children,' said Mavis. 'I know Patrick does.'

'That's because he has some to miss,' said Eva Wilt bitterly. 'Henry can't even whip up the energy to have any.'

'I'm so sorry, Eva. I forgot,' said Mavis, adjusting the lupin so that it clashed more significantly with a geranium.

'There's no need to be sorry,' said Eva, who didn't number self-pity among her failings, 'I suppose I should be grateful. I mean, imagine having children like Henry. He's so uncreative, and besides children are so tiresome. They take up all one's creative energy.'

Mavis Mottram moved away to help someone else to achieve a contrapuntal effect, this time with nasturtiums and hollyhocks in a cerise bowl. Eva fiddled with her rose. Mavis was so lucky. She had Patrick, and Patrick Mottram was such an energetic man. Eva, in spite of her size, placed great emphasis on energy, energy and creativity, so that even quite sensible people who were not unduly impressionable found themselves exhausted after ten minutes in her company. In the lotus position at her yoga class she managed to exude energy, and her attempts at Transcendental Meditation had been likened to a pressure-cooker on simmer. And with creative energy there came enthusiasm, the febrile enthusiasms of the evidently unfulfilled woman for whom each new idea heralds the dawn of a new day and vice versa. Since the ideas she espoused were either trite or incomprehensible to her, her attachment to them was correspon-

dingly brief and did nothing to fill the gap left in her life by
Henry Wilt's lack of attainment. While he lived a violent life in
his imagination, Eva, lacking any imagination at all, lived
violently in fact. She threw herself into things, situations, new
friends, groups and happenings with a reckless abandon that
concealed the fact that she lacked the emotional stamina to stay
for more than a moment. Now, as she backed away from her
vase, she bumped into someone behind her.

'I beg your pardon,' she said and turned to find herself
looking into a pair of dark eyes.

'No need to apologize,' said the woman in an American
accent. She was slight and dressed with a simple scruffiness that
was beyond Eva Wilt's moderate income.

'I'm Eva Wilt,' said Eva, who had once attended a class on
Getting to Know People at the Oakrington Village College.
'My husband lectures at the Tech and we live at 34 Parkview
Avenue.'

'Sally Pringsheim,' said the woman with a smile. 'We're in
Rossiter Grove. We're over on a sabbatical. Gaskell's a biochemist.'

Eva Wilt accepted the distinctions and congratulated herself
on her perspicacity about the blue jeans and the sweater. People
who lived in Rossiter Grove were a cut above Parkview Avenue
and husbands who were biochemists on sabbatical were also
in the University. Eva Wilt's world was made up of such
nuances.

'You know, I'm not all that sure I could live with an oratorical
rose,' said Sally Pringsheim. 'Symphonies are OK in auditoriums
but I can do without them in vases.'

Eva stared at her with a mixture of astonishment and admiration. To be openly critical of Mavis Mottram's flower
arrangements was to utter blasphemy in Parkview Avenue. 'You
know, I've always wanted to say that,' she said with a sudden
surge of warmth, 'but I've never had the courage.'

Sally Pringsheim smiled. 'I think one should always say what
one thinks. Truth is so essential in any really meaningful
relationship. I always tell G baby exactly what I'm thinking.'

'Gee baby?' said Eva Wilt.

'Gaskell's my husband,' said Sally. 'Not that he's really a
husband. It's just that we've got this open-ended arrangement

for living together. Sure, we're legal and all that, but I think it's important sexually to keep one's options open, don't you?'

By the time Eva got home her vocabulary had come to include several new words. She found Wilt in bed pretending to be asleep and woke him up and told him about Sally Pringsheim. Wilt turned over and tried to go back to sleep wishing to God she had stuck to contrapuntal flower arrangements. Sexually open-ended freewheeling options were the last thing he wanted just now, and, coming from the wife of a biochemist who could afford to live in Rossiter Grove, didn't augur well for the future. Eva Wilt was too easily influenced by wealth, intellectual status and new acquaintances to be allowed out with a woman who believed that clitoral stimulation oralwise was a concomitant part of a fully emancipated relationship and that unisex was here to stay. Wilt had enough troubles with his own virility without having Eva demand that her conjugal rights be supplemented oralwise. He spent a restless night thinking dark thoughts about accidental deaths involving fast trains, level crossings, their Ford Escort and Eva's seat belt, and got up early and made himself breakfast. He was just going off to a nine o'clock lecture to Motor Mechanics Three when Eva came downstairs with a dreamy look on her face.

'I've just remembered something I wanted to ask you last night,' she said. 'What does "transexual diversification" mean?'

'Writing poems about queers,' said Wilt hastily and went out to the car. He drove down Parkview Avenue and got stuck in a traffic jam at the roundabout. He sat and cursed silently. He was thirty-four and his talents were being dissipated on MM 3 and a woman who was clearly educationally subnormal. Worst of all, he had to recognize the truth of Eva's constant criticism that he wasn't a man. 'If you were a proper man,' she was always saying, 'you would show more initiative. You've got to assert yourself.'

Wilt asserted himself at the roundabout and got into an altercation with a man in a mini-bus. As usual, he came off second best.

'The problem with Wilt as I see it is that he lacks drive,' said the Head of English, himself a nerveless man with a tendency to see and solve problems with a degree of equivocation that made good his natural lack of authority.

The Promotions Committee nodded its joint head for the fifth year running.

'He may lack drive but he *is* committed,' said Mr Morris, fighting his annual rearguard on Wilf's behalf.

'Committed?' said the Head of Catering with a snort. 'Committed to what? Abortion, Marxism or promiscuity? It's bound to be one of the three. I've yet to come across a Liberal Studies lecturer who wasn't a crank, a pervert or a red-hot revolutionary and a good many have been all three.'

'Hear, hear,' said the Head of Mechanical Engineering, on whose lathes a demented student had once turned out several pipe bombs.

Mr Morris bristled. 'I grant you that one or two lecturers have been . . . er . . . a little overzealous politically but I resent the imputation that . . .'

'Let's leave generalities aside and get back to Wilt,' said the Vice-Principal. 'You were saying that he is committed.'

'He needs encouragement,' said Mr Morris. 'Damn it, the man has been with us ten years and he's still only Grade Two.'

'That's precisely what I mean about his lacking drive,' said the Head of English. 'If he had been worth promoting he'd have been a Senior Lecturer by now.'

'I must say I agree,' said the Head of Geography. 'Any man who is content to spend ten years taking Gasfitters and Plumbers is clearly unfit to hold an administrative post.'

'Do we always have to promote solely for administrative reasons?' Mr Morris asked wearily. 'Wilt happens to be a good teacher.'

'If I may just make a point,' said Dr Mayfield, the Head of Sociology, 'at this moment in time it is vital we bear in mind that, in the light of the forthcoming introduction of the Joint Honours degree in Urban Studies and Medieval Poetry, provisional approval for which degree by the Council of National Academic Awards I am happy to announce at least in principle, that we maintain a viable staff position in regard to Senior Lectureships by allocating places for candidates with specialist knowledge in particular spheres of academic achievement rather than—'

'If I may just interrupt for a moment, in or out of time,' said Dr Board, Head of Modern Languages, 'are you saying we should save Senior Lectureships for highly qualified specialists who can't teach rather than promote Assistant Lecturers without doctorates who can?'

'If Dr Board had allowed me to continue,' said Dr Mayfield, 'he would have understood that I was saying . . .'

'I doubt it,' said Dr Board, 'quite apart from your syntax . . .'

And so for the fifth year running Wilt's promotion was forgotten. The Fenland College of Arts and Technology was expanding. New degree courses proliferated and more students with fewer qualifications poured in to be taught by more staff with higher qualifications until one day the Tech would cease to be a mere Tech and rise in status to become a Poly. It was the dream of every Head of Department and in the process Wilt's self-esteem and the hopes of Eva Wilt were ignored.

Wilt heard the news before lunch in the canteen.

'I'm sorry, Henry,' said Mr Morris as they lined up with their trays, 'it's this wretched economic squeeze. Even Modern Languages had to take a cut. They only got two promotions through.'

Wilt nodded. It was what he had come to expect. He was in the wrong department, in the wrong marriage and in the wrong life. He took his fish fingers across to a table in the corner and ate by himself. Around him other members of staff sat discussing A-level prospects and who was going to sit on the course board next term. They taught Maths or Economics or English, subjects that counted and where promotion was easy. Liberal Studies didn't count and promotion was out of the question. It was as simple as that. Wilt finished his lunch and went up to the reference library to look up Insulin in the Pharmacopoeia. He had an idea it was the one untraceable poison.

At five to two, none the wiser, he went down to Room 752 to extend the sensibilities of fifteen apprentice butchers, designated on the timetable as Meat One. As usual they were late and drunk.

'We've been drinking Bill's health,' they told him when they drifted in at ten past two.

'Really?' said Wilt, handing out copies of *The Lord of the Flies*. 'And how is he?'

'Bloody awful,' said a large youth with 'Stuff Off' painted across the back of his leather jacket. 'He's puking his guts out. It's his birthday and he had four vodkas and a Babycham . . .'

'We'd got to the part where Piggy is in the forest,' said Wilt, heading them off a discussion of what Bill had drunk for his birthday. He reached for a board duster and rubbed a drawing of a Dutch Cap off the blackboard.

'That's Mr Sedgwick's trademark,' said one of the butchers, 'he's always going on about contraceptives and things. He's got a thing about them.'

'A thing about them?' said Wilt loyally.

'You know, birth control. Well, he used to be a Catholic, didn't he? And now he's not, he's making up for lost time,' said a small pale-faced youth unwrapping a Mars Bar.

'Someone should tell him about the pill,' said another youth lifting his head somnolently from the desk. 'You can't feel a thing with a Frenchie. You get more thrill with the pill.'

'I suppose you do,' said Wilt, 'but I understood there were side-effects.'

'Depends which side you want it,' said a lad with sideburns.

Wilt turned back to *The Lord of the Flies* reluctantly. He had read the thing two hundred times already.

'Now Piggy goes into the forest . . .' he began, only to be stopped by another butcher, who evidently shared his distaste for the misfortunes of Piggy.

'You only get bad effects with the pill if you use ones that are high in oestrogen.'

'That's very interesting,' said Wilt. 'Oestrogen? You seem to know a lot about it.'

'Old girl down our street got a bloodclot in her leg . . .'

'Silly old clot,' said the Mars Bar.

'Listen,' said Wilt. 'Either we hear what Peter has to tell us about the effects of the pill or we get on and read about Piggy.'

'Fuck Piggy,' said the sideburns.

'Right,' said Wilt heartily, 'then keep quiet.'

'Well,' said Peter, 'this old girl, well she wasn't all that old, maybe thirty, she was on the pill and she got this bloodclot and the doctor told my auntie it was the oestrogen and she'd better take a different sort of pill just in case and the old girl down the street, her old man had to go and have a vasectomy so's she wouldn't have another bloodclot.'

'Buggered if anyone's going to get me to have a vasectomy,' said the Mars Bar, 'I want to know I'm all there.'

'We all have ambitions,' said Wilt.

'Nobody's going to hack away at my knackers with a bloody great knive,' said the sideburns.

'Nobody'd want to,' said someone else.

'What about the bloke whose missus you banged,' said the Mars Bar. 'I bet he wouldn't mind having a go.'

Wilt applied the sanction of Piggy again and got them back onto vasectomy.

'Anyway, it's not irreversible any more,' said Peter. 'They can put a tiny little gold tap in and you can turn it on when you want a nipper.'

'Go on! That's not true.'

'Well, not on the National Health you can't, but if you pay they can. I read about it in a magazine. They've been doing experiments in America.'

'What happens if the washer goes wrong?' asked the Mars Bar.

'I suppose they call a plumber in.'

Wilt sat and listened while Meat One ranged far and wide about vasectomy and the coil and Indians getting free transistors and the plane that landed at Audley End with a lot of illegal immigrants and what somebody's brother who was a policeman in Brixton said about blacks and how the Irish were just as bad and bombs and back to Catholics and birth control and who'd want to live in Ireland where you couldn't even buy French letters and so back to the Pill. And all the time his mind filled itself obsessively with ways and means of getting rid of Eva. A diet of birth-control pills high on oestrogen? If he ground them up and mixed them with the Ovaltine she took at bedtime there was a chance she'd develop bloodclots all over the place in no time at all. Wilt put the notion out of his head. Eva with bloodclots was too awful to stomach, and anyway it might not work. No, it would have to be something quick, certain and painless. Preferably an accident.

At the end of the hour Wilt collected the books and made his
way back to the Staff Room. He had a free period. On the way
he passed the site of the new Administration block. The ground
had been cleared and the builders had moved in and were
boring pile holes for the foundations. Wilt stopped and watched
as the drilling machine wound slowly down into the ground.
They were making wide holes. Very wide. Big enough for a body.

'How deep are you going?' he asked one of the workmen.

'Thirty feet.'

'Thirty feet?' said Wilt. 'When's the concrete going in?'

'Monday, with any luck,' said the man.

Wilt passed on. A new and quite horrible idea had just
occurred to him.

Chapter 2

It was one of Eva Wilt's better days. She had days, better days, and one of those days. Days were just days when nothing went wrong and she got the washing-up done and the front room vacuumed and the windows washed and the beds made and the bath Vimmed and the lavatory pan Harpicked and went round to the Harmony Community Centre and helped with Xeroxing or sorted old clothes for the Jumble Sale and generally made herself useful and came home for lunch and went to the library and had tea with Mavis or Susan or Jean and talked about life and how seldom Henry made love to her even perfunctorily nowadays and how she had missed her opportunity by refusing a bank clerk who was a manager now and came home and made Henry's supper and went out to Yoga or Flower Arrangement or Meditation or Pottery and finally climbed into bed with the feeling that she had got something done.

On one of those days nothing went right. The activities were exactly the same but each episode was tainted with some minor disaster like the fuse blowing on the vacuum-cleaner or the drain in the sink getting blocked with a piece of carrot so that by the time Henry came home he was either greeted by silence or subjected to a quite unwarranted exposé of all his faults and shortcomings. On one of those days Wilt usually took the dog for an extended walk via the Ferry Path Inn and spent a restless night getting up and going to the bathroom, thus nullifying the cleansing qualities of the Harpic Eva had puffed round the pan and providing her with a good excuse to point out his faults once again in the morning.

'What the hell am I supposed to do?' he had asked after one of those nights. 'If I pull the chain you grumble because I've woken you up and if I don't you say it looks nasty in the morning.'

'Well, it does, and in any case you don't have to wash all the Harpic off the sides. And don't say you don't. I've seen you. You aim it all the way round so that it all gets taken off. You do it quite deliberately.'

'If I pulled the chain it would all get flushed off anyway and you'd get woken up into the bargain,' Wilt told her, conscious that he did make a habit of aiming at the Harpic. He had a grudge against the stuff.

'Why can't you just wait until the morning? And anyway it serves you right,' she continued, forestalling his obvious answer, 'for drinking all that beer. You're supposed to be taking Clem for a walk, not swilling ale in that horrid pub.'

'To pee or not to pee, that is the question,' said Wilt helping himself to All-Bran. 'What do you expect me to do? Tie a knot in the damned thing?'

'It wouldn't make any difference to me if you did,' said Eva bitterly.

'It would make a hell of a lot of difference to me, thank you very much.'

'I was talking about our sex life and you know it.'

'Oh, that,' said Wilt.

But that was on one of those days.

On one of her better days something unexpected happened to inject the daily round with a new meaning and to awake in her those dormant expectations that somehow everything would suddenly change for the better and stay that way. It was on such expectations that her faith in life was based. They were the spiritual equivalent of the trivial activities that kept her busy and Henry subdued. On one of her better days the sun shone brighter, the floor in the hall gleamed brighter and Eva Wilt was brighter herself and hummed 'Some day my prince will come' while Hoovering the stairs. On one of her better days Eva went forth to meet the world with a disarming goodheartedness and awoke in others the very same expectations that so thrilled her in herself. And on one of her better days Henry had to get his own supper and if he was wise kept out of the house as long as possible. Eva Wilt's expectations demanded something a sight more invigorating than Henry Wilt after a day at the Tech. It was on the evenings of such days that he came nearest to genuinely deciding to murder her and to hell with the consequences.

On this particular day she was on her way to the Community Centre when she ran into Sally Pringsheim. It was one of those

entirely fortuitous meetings that resulted from Eva making her
way on foot instead of by bicycle and going through Rossiter
Grove instead of straight down Parkview Avenue which was
half a mile shorter. Sally was just driving out of the gate in a
Mercedes with a P registration which meant it was brand new.
Eva noted the fact and smiled accordingly.

'How funny me running into you like this,' she said brightly
as Sally stopped the car and unlocked the door.

'Can I give you a lift? I'm going into town to look for
something casual to wear tonight. Gaskell's got some Swedish
professor coming over from Heidelberg and we're taking him
to Ma Tante's.'

Eva Wilt climbed in happily, her mind computing the cost
of the car and the house and the significance of wearing something casual at Ma Tante's (where she had heard that starters
like Prawn Cocktails cost 95p) and the fact that Dr Pringsheim
entertained Swedish professors when they came to Ipford.

'I was going to walk to town,' she lied. 'Henry's taken the
car and it's such a lovely day.'

'Gaskell's bought a bicycle. He says it's quicker and it keeps
him fit,' said Sally, thus condemning Henry Wilt to yet another
misfortune. Eva made a note to see that he bought a bike at the
police auction and cycled to work in rain or snow. 'I was thinking of trying Felicity Fashions for a shantung poncho. I don't
know what they're like but I've been told they're good. Professor
Grant's wife goes there and she says they have the best selection.'

'I'm sure they must have,' said Eva Wilt, whose patronage
of Felicity Fashions had consisted of looking in the window and
wondering who on earth could afford dresses at forty pounds.
Now she knew. They drove into town and parked in the multi-
storey car park. By that time Eva had stored a lot more
information about the Pringsheims in her memory. They came
from California. Sally had met Gaskell while hitch-hiking
through Arizona. She had been to Kansas State but had dropped
out to live on a commune. There had been other men in her life.
Gaskell loathed cats. They gave him hay fever. Women's Lib
meant more than burning your bra. It meant total commitment
to the programme of women's superiority over men. Love was
great if you didn't let it get to you. Compost was in and colour
TV out. Gaskell's father had owned a chain of stores which

was sordid. Money was handy and Rossiter Grove was a bore. Above all, fucking had to be, just *had* to be fun whichever way you looked at it.

Eva Wilt received this information with a jolt. In her circle 'fuck' was a word husbands used when they hit their thumbs with hammers. When Eva used it she did so in the isolation of the bathroom and with a wistfulness that robbed it of its crudity and imbued it with a splendid virility so that a good fuck became the most distant and abstract of all her expectations and quite removed from Henry's occasional early morning fumblings. And if 'fuck' was reserved for the bathroom, fucking was even more remote. It suggested an almost continuous activity, a familiar occurrence that was both casual and satisfying and added a new dimension to life. Eva Wilt stumbled out of the car and followed Sally to Felicity Fashions in a state of shock.

If fucking was fun, shopping with Sally Pringsheim was a revelation. It was marked by a decisiveness that was truly breathtaking. Where Eva would have hummed and haaed, Sally selected and having selected moved on down the racks, discarded things she didn't like leaving them hanging over chairs, seized others, glanced at them and said she supposed they would do with a bored acceptance that was infectious, and left the shop with a pile of boxes containing two hundred pounds' worth of shantung ponchos, silk summer coats, scarves and blouses. Eva Wilt had spent seventy on a pair of yellow lounging pyjamas and a raincoat with lapels and a belt that Sally said was pure Gatsby.

'Now all you need is the hat and you'll be it,' she said as they loaded the boxes into the car. They bought the hat, a trilby, and then had coffee at the Mombasa Coffee House where Sally leant across the table intensely, smoking a long thin cigar, and talking about body contact in a loud voice so that Eva was conscious that the women at several nearby tables had stopped talking and were listening rather disapprovingly.

'Gaskell's nipples drive me wild,' Sally said. 'They drive him wild too when I suck them.'

Eva drank her coffee and wondered what Henry would do if she took it into her head to suck his nipples. Drive him wild was hardly the word and besides she was beginning to regret having spent seventy pounds. That would drive him wild too.

Henry didn't approve of credit cards. But she was enjoying herself too much to let the thought of his reaction spoil her day.

'I think teats are so important,' Sally went on. Two women at the next table paid their bill and walked out.

'I suppose they must be,' said Eva Wilt uneasily. 'I've never had much use for mine.'

'Haven't you?' said Sally. 'We'll have to do something about that.'

'I don't see that there is much anyone can do about it,' said Eva. 'Henry never even takes his pyjamas off and my nightie gets in the way.'

'Don't tell me you wear things in bed. Oh you poor thing. And nighties, God, how humiliating for you! I mean it's typical of a male-dominated society, all this costume differentiation. You must be suffering from touch deprivation. Gaskell says it's as bad as vitamin deficiency.'

'Well, Henry is always tired when he gets home,' Eva told her. 'And I go out a lot.'

'I'm not surprised,' said Sally, 'Gaskell says male fatigue is a symptom of penile insecurity. Is Henry's big or small?'

'Well it depends,' said Eva hoarsely. 'Sometimes it's big and sometimes it isn't.'

'I much prefer men with small ones,' said Sally, 'they try so much harder.'

They finished their coffee and went back to the car discussing Gaskell's penis and his theory that in a sexually undifferentiated society nipple stimulation would play an increasingly important role in developing the husband's sense of his hermaphroditic nature.

'He's written an article on it,' Sally said as they drove home. 'It's called "The Man As Mother." It was published in *Suck* last year.'

'Suck?' said Eva.

'Yes, it's a journal published by the Society for Undifferentiated Sexual Studies in Kansas. G's done a lot of work for them on animal behaviour. He did his thesis on Role Play in Rats there.'

'That sounds very interesting,' said Eva uncertainly. Roll or role? Whichever it was it was impressive and certainly Henry's occasional pieces on Day Release Apprentices and Literature in the *Liberal Studies Quarterly* hardly measured up to Dr Pringsheim's monographs.

'Oh I don't know. It's all so obvious really. If you put two male rats together in a cage long enough one of them is simply bound to develop active tendencies and the other passive ones,' said Sally wearily. 'But Gaskell was absolutely furious. He thought they ought to alternate. That's G all over. I told him how silly he was being. I said, "G honey, rats are practically undifferentiated anyway. I mean how can you expect them to be able to make an existential choice?" and you know what he said? He said, "Pubic baby, rats are the paradigm. Just remember that and you won't go far wrong. Rats are the paradigm." What do you think of that?'

'I think rats are rather horrid,' said Eva without thinking. Sally laughed and put her hand on her knee.

'Oh Eva, darling,' she murmured, 'you're so adorably down to earth. No, I'm not taking you back to Parkview Avenue. You're coming home with me for a drink and lunch. I'm simply dying to see you in those lemon loungers.'

They turned into Rossiter Grove.

If rats were a paradigm for Dr Pringsheim, Printers Three were a paradigm for Henry Wilt, though of a rather different sort. They represented all that was most difficult, insensitive and downright bloodyminded about Day Release classes and to make matters worse the sods thought they were literate because they could actually read and Voltaire was an idiot because he made everything go wrong for Candide. Coming after Nursery Nurses and during his Stand-In period, Printers Three brought out the worst in him. They had obviously brought out the worst in Cecil Williams who should have been taking them.

'It's the second week he's been off sick,' they told Wilt.

'I'm not at all surprised,' said Wilt. 'You lot are enough to make anyone sick.'

'We had one bloke went and gassed himself. Pinkerton his name was. He took us for a term and made us read this book *Jude the Obscure*. That wasn't half a depressing book. All about this twit Jude.'

'I had an idea it was,' said Wilt.

'Next term old Pinky didn't come back. He went down by

the river and stuck a pipe up the exhaust and gassed himself.'

'I can't say I blame him,' said Wilt.

'Well I like that. He was supposed to set us an example.'

Wilt looked at the class grimly.

'I'm sure he had that in mind when he gassed himself,' he said. 'And now if you'll just get on and read quietly, eat quietly and smoke so that no one can see you from the Admin block, I've got work to do.'

'Work? You lot don't know what work is. All you do is sit at a desk all day and read. Call that work? Buggered if I do and they pay you to do it . . .'

'Shut up,' said Wilt with startling violence. 'Shut your stupid trap.'

'Who's going to make me?' said the Printer.

Wilt tried to control his temper and for once found it impossible. There was something incredibly arrogant about Printers Three.

'I am,' he shouted.

'You and who else? You couldn't make a mouse shut its trap, not if you tried all day.'

Wilt stood up. 'You fucking little shit,' he shouted. 'You dirty snivelling . . .'

'I must say, Henry, I'd have expected you to show more restraint,' said the Head of Liberal Studies an hour later when Wilt's nose had stopped bleeding and the Tech Sister had put a Band-Aid on his eyebrow.

'Well it wasn't my class and they got my goat by gloating about Pinkerton's suicide. If Williams hadn't been off sick it wouldn't have happened,' Wilt explained. 'He's always sick when he has to take Printers Three.'

Mr Morris shook his head dispiritedly. 'I don't care who they were. You simply can't go around assaulting students . . .'

'Assaulting students? I never touched . . .'

'All right, but you did use offensive language. Bob Fenwick was in the next classroom and he heard you call this Allison fellow a fucking little shit and an evil-minded moron. Now, is it any wonder he took a poke at you?'

'I suppose not,' said Wilt. 'I shouldn't have lost my temper. I'm sorry.'

'In that case we'll just forget it happened,' said Mr Morris. 'But just remember if I'm to get you a Senior Lectureship I can't have you blotting your copybook having punch-ups with students.'

'I didn't have a punch-up,' said Wilt, 'he punched me.'

'Well, let's just hope he doesn't go to the police and charge you with assault. That's the last sort of publicity we want.'

'Just take me off Printers Three,' said Wilt, 'I've had my fill of the brutes.'

He went down the corridor and collected his coat and brief-case from the Staff Room. His nose felt twice its normal size and his eyebrow hurt abominably. On his way out to the car park he passed several other members of staff but no one stopped to ask him what had happened. Henry Wilt passed unnoticed out of the Tech and got into his car. He shut the door and sat for several minutes watching the piledrivers at work on the new block. Up, down, up, down. Nails in a coffin. And one day, one inevitable day he would be in his coffin, still unnoticed, still an Assistant Lecturer (Grade Two) and quite forgotten by everyone except some lout in Printers Three who would always remember the day he had punched a Liberal Studies lecturer on the nose and got away with it. He'd probably boast about it to his grandchildren.

Wilt started the car and drove out onto the main road filled with loathing for Printers Three, the Tech, life in general and himself in particular. He understood now why terrorists were prepared to sacrifice themselves for the good of some cause. Given a bomb and a cause he would cheerfully have blown himself and any innocent bystanders to Kingdom Come just to prove for one glorious if brief moment that he was an effective force. But he had neither bomb nor cause. Instead he drove home recklessly and parked outside 34 Parkview Avenue. Then he unlocked the front door and went inside.

There was a strange smell in the hall. Some sort of perfume. Musky and sweet. He put his brief-case down and looked into the living-room. Eva was evidently out. He went into the kitchen and put the kettle on and felt his nose. He would have a good look at it in the bathroom mirror. He was halfway upstairs and conscious that there was a positively miasmic quality about the perfume when he was brought to a halt. Eva Wilt stood in the bedroom doorway in a pair of astonishingly yellow pyjamas with enormously flared trousers. She looked quite hideous, and to make matters worse she was smoking a long thin cigarette in a long thin holder and her mouth was a brilliant red.

'Penis baby,' she murmured hoarsely and swayed. 'Come in here. I'm going to suck your nipples till you come me oral-wise.'

Wilt turned and fled downstairs. The bitch was drunk. It was one of her better days. Without waiting to turn the kettle off, Henry Wilt went out of the front door and got back into the car. He wasn't staying around to have her suck his nipples. He'd had all he could take for one day.

Chapter 3

Eva Wilt went downstairs and looked for penis baby half-heartedly. For one thing she didn't want to find him and for another she didn't feel like sucking his nipples and for a third she knew she shouldn't have spent seventy pounds on a raincoat and a pair of beach pyjamas she could have got for thirty at Blowdens. She didn't need them and she couldn't see herself walking down Parkview Avenue looking like The Great Gatsby. Besides, she felt a bit sick.

Still, he had left the kettle on so he must be somewhere. It wasn't like Henry to go out and leave the kettle on. She looked in the lounge. It had been the sitting-room until lunchtime when Sally called her sitting-room a lounge. She looked in the dining-room, now the diner, and even in the garden but Henry had vanished, taking with him the car and her hopes that nipple-sucking would bring new meaning to their marriage and put an end to her body contact deprivation. Finally she gave up the search and made herself a nice pot of tea and sat in the kitchen wondering what on earth had induced her to marry a male chauvinist pig like Henry Wilt who wouldn't have known a good fuck if he had been handed one on a plate and whose idea of a sophisticated evening was a boneless chicken curry at the New Delhi and a performance of *King Lear* at the Guildhall. Why couldn't she have married someone like Gaskell Pringsheim who entertained Swedish professors at Ma Tante and who understood the importance of clitoral stimulation as a necessary con-something-or-other of a truly satisfying interpersonal penetration? Other people still found her attractive. Patrick Mottram did and so did John Frost who taught her pottery, and Sally had said she was lovely. Eva sat staring into space, the space between the washing-up rack and the Kenwood mixer Henry had given her for Christmas, and thought about Sally and how she had looked at her so strangely when she was changing into her lemon loungers. Sally had stood in the doorway of the Pringsheims' bedroom, smoking a cigar and watching her movements with a sensual calculation that had made Eva blush.

'Darling, you have such a lovely body,' she had said as Eva turned hurriedly and scrambled into the trousers to avoid revealing the hole in her panties. 'You mustn't let it go to waste.'

'Do you really think they suit me?'

But Sally had been staring at her breasts intently. 'Booby baby,' she murmured. Eva Wilt's breasts were prominent and Henry, in one of his many off moments, had once said something about the dugs of hell going dingalingaling for you but not for me. Sally was more appreciative, and had insisted that Eva remove her bra and burn it. They had gone down to the kitchen and had drunk Tequila and had put the bra on a dish with a sprig of holly on it and Sally had poured brandy over it and had set it alight. They had had to carry the dish out into the garden because it smelt so horrible and smoked so much and they had lain on the grass laughing as it smouldered. Looking back on the episode Eva regretted her action. It had been a good bra with double-stretch panels designed to give confidence where a woman needs it, as the TV adverts put it. Still, Sally had said she owed it to herself as a free woman and with two drinks inside her Eva was in no mood to argue.

'You've got to feel free,' Sally had said. 'Free to be. Free to be.'

'Free to be what?' said Eva.

'Yourself, darling,' Sally whispered, 'your secret self,' and had touched her tenderly where Eva Wilt, had she been sober and less elated, would staunchly have denied having a self. They had gone back into the house and had lunch, a mixture of more Tequila, salad and Ryvita and cottage cheese which Eva, whose appetite for food was almost as omnivorous as her enthusiasm for new experiences, found unsatisfying. She had hinted as much but Sally had poohpoohed the idea of three good meals a day.

'It's not good caloriewise to have a high starch intake,' she said, 'and besides it's not how much you put into yourself but what. Sex and food, honey, are much the same. A little a lot is better than a lot a little.' She had poured Eva another Tequila, insisted she take a bite of lemon before knocking it back and had helped her upstairs to the big bedroom with the big bed and the big mirror in the ceiling.

'It's time for TT,' she said adjusting the slats of the Venetian blinds.

'Tea tea,' Eva mumbled, 'but we've just had din din.'

'Touch Therapy, darling,' said Sally and pushed her gently back onto the bed. Eva Wilt stared up at her reflection in the mirror; a large woman, two large women in yellow pyjamas lying on a large bed, a large crimson bed; two large women without yellow pyjamas on a large crimson bed; four women naked on a large crimson bed.

'Oh Sally, no Sally.'

'Darling,' said Sally and silenced her protests oralwise. It had been a startlingly new experience though only partly remembered. Eva had fallen asleep before the Touch Therapy had got well under way and had woken an hour later to find Sally fully dressed standing by the bed with a cup of black coffee.

'Oh I do feel bad,' Eva said, referring as much to her moral condition as to her physical.

'Drink this and you'll feel better.'

Eva had drunk the coffee and got dressed while Sally explained that post-contact inhibitory depression was a perfectly natural reaction to Touch Therapy at first.

'You'll find it comes naturally after the first few sessions. You'll probably break down and cry and scream and then feel tremendously liberated and relieved.'

'Do you think so? I'm sure I don't know.'

Sally had driven her home. 'You and Henry must come to our barbecue Thursday night,' she said. 'I know G baby will want to meet you. You'll like him. He's a breast baby. He'll go crazy about you.'

'I tell you she was pissed,' said Wilt as he sat in the Braintrees' kitchen while Peter Braintree opened a bottle of beer for him. 'Pissed and wearing some Godawful yellow pyjamas and smoking a cigarette in a long bloody holder.'

'What did she say?'

'Well if you must know, she said, "Come here . . ." No, it's too much. I have a perfectly foul day at the Tech. Morris tells me I haven't got my senior lectureship. Williams is off sick again so I lose a free period. I get punched in the face by a great lout in Printers Three and I come home to a drunk wife who calls me penis baby.'

'She called you what?' said Peter Braintree, staring at him.

'You heard me.'

'Eva called you penis baby? I don't believe it.'

'Well you go round there and see what she calls you,' said Wilt bitterly, 'and don't blame me if she sucks your nipples off oralwise while she's about it.'

'Good Lord. Is that what she threatened to do?'

'That and more,' said Wilt.

'It doesn't sound like Eva. It really doesn't.'

'It didn't fucking look like her either, come to that. She was all dolled up in yellow beach pyjamas. You should have seen the colour. It would have made a buttercup look drab. And she'd got some ghastly scarlet lipstick smeared round her mouth and she was smoking . . . She hasn't smoked for six years and then all this penis baby nipple-sucking stuff. And oralwise.'

Peter Braintree shook his head. 'That's a filthy word,' he said.

'It's a perfectly filthy act too, if you ask me,' said Wilt.

'Well, I must say it all sounds pretty peculiar,' said Braintree, 'God knows what I'd do if Susan came home and started insisting on sucking my teats.'

'Do what I did. Get out of the house,' said Wilt. 'And anyway it isn't just nipples either. Damn it, we've been married twelve long years. It's a bit late in the day to start arsing about oralwise. The thing is she's on this sexual liberation kick. She came home last night from Mavis Mottram's flower arrangement do jabbering about clitoral stimulation and open-ended freewheeling sexual options.'

'Freewheeling what?'

'Sexual options. Perhaps I've got it wrong. I know sexual options came into it somewhere. I was half asleep at the time.'

'Where the hell did she get all this from?' asked Braintree.

'Some bloody Yank called Sally Pringsheim,' said Wilt. 'You know what Eva's like. I mean she can smell intellectual claptrap a mile off and homes in on it like a bloody dung-beetle heading for an open sewer. You've no idea how many phoney "latest ideas" I've had to put up with. Well, most of them I can manage to live with. I just let her get on with it and go my own quiet way, but when it comes to participating oralwise while she blathers on about Women's Lib, well you can count me out.'

'What I don't understand about Sexual Freedom and Women's Lib is why you have to go back to the nursery to be liberated,' said Braintree. 'There seems to be this loony idea that you have to be passionately in love all the time.'

'Apes,' said Wilt morosely.

'Apes? What about apes?'

'It's all this business about the animal model. If animals do it then humans must. Territorial Imperative and the Naked Ape. You stand everything on its head and instead of aspiring you retrogress a million years. Hitch your wagon to an orang-outang. The egalitarianism of the lowest common denominator.'

'I don't quite see what that has to do with sex,' said Braintree.

'Nor do I,' said Wilt. They went down to the Pig In A Poke and got drunk.

It was midnight before Wilt got home and Eva was asleep. Wilt climbed surreptitiously into bed and lay in the darkness thinking about high levels of oestrogen.

In Rossiter Grove the Pringsheims came back from Ma Tante's tired and bored.

'Swedes are the bottom,' said Sally as she undressed.

Gaskell sat down and took off his shoes. 'Ungstrom's all right. His wife has just left him for a low-temperature physicist at Cambridge. He's not usually so depressed.'

'You could have fooled me. And talking about wives, I've met the most unliberated woman you've ever set eyes on. Name of Eva Wilt. She's got boobs like cantaloupes.'

'Don't,' said Dr Pringsheim, 'if there's one thing I don't need right now it's unliberated wives with breasts.' He climbed into bed and took his glasses off.

'I had her round here today.'

'Had her?'

Sally smiled, 'Gaskell, honey, you've got a toadsome mind.'

Gaskell Pringsheim smiled myopically at himself in the mirror above. He was proud of his mind. 'I just know you, lover,' he said, 'I know your funny little habits. And while we're on the subject of habits what are all those boxes in the guest room?

You haven't been spending money again? You know our budget this month . . .'

Sally flounced into bed. 'Budget fudget,' she said, 'I'm sending them all back tomorrow.'

'All?'

'Well, not all, but most. I had to impress booby baby somehow.'

'You didn't have to buy half a shop just to . . .'

'Gaskell, honey, if you would just let me finish,' said Sally, 'she's a manic, a lovely, beautiful, obsessive compulsive manic. She can't sit still for half a minute without tidying and cleaning and polishing and washing up.'

'That's all we need, a manic compulsive woman around the house all the time. Who needs two?'

'Two? I'm not manic.'

'You're manic enough for me,' said Gaskell.

'But this one's got boobs, baby, boobs. Anyway I've invited them over on Thursday for the barbecue.'

'What the hell for?'

'Well, if you won't buy me a dishwasher like I've asked you a hundred times, I'm going out to get me one. A nice manic compulsive dishwasher with boobs on.'

'Jesus,' sighed Gaskell, 'are you a bitch.'

'Henry Wilt, you are a sod,' Eva said next morning. Wilt sat up in bed. He felt terrible. His nose was even more painful than the day before, his head ached and he had spent much of the night expunging the Harpic from the bowl in the bathroom. He was in no mood to be woken and told he was a sod. He looked at the clock. It was eight o'clock and he had Bricklayers Two at nine. He got out of bed and made for the bathroom.

'Did you hear what I said?' Eva demanded, getting out of bed herself.

'I heard,' said Wilt, and saw that she was naked. Eva Wilt naked at eight o'clock in the morning was almost as startling a sight as Eva Wilt drunk, smoking and dressed in lemon yellow pyjamas at six o'clock at night. And even less enticing. 'What the hell are you going about like that for?'

'If it comes to that, what's wrong with your nose? I suppose you got drunk and fell down. It looks all red and swollen.'

'It *is* all red and swollen. And if you must know I didn't fall down. Now for goodness sake get out of the way. I've got a lecture at nine.'

He pushed past her and went into the bathroom and looked at his nose. It looked awful. Eva followed him in. 'If you didn't fall on it what did happen?' she demanded.

Wilt squeezed foam from an aerosol and patted it gingerly on his chin.

'Well?' said Eva.

Wilt picked up his razor and put it under the hot tap. 'I had an accident,' he muttered.

'With a lamp-post, I suppose. I knew you'd been drinking.'

'With a Printer,' said Wilt indistinctly and started to shave.

'With a Printer?'

'To be precise, I got punched in the face by a particularly pugnacious apprentice printer.'

Eva stared at him in the mirror. 'You mean to say a student hit you in the classroom?'

Wilt nodded.

'I hope you hit him back.'

Wilt cut himself.

'No I bloody didn't,' he said, dabbing his chin with a finger. 'Now look what you've made me do.'

Eva ignored his complaint. 'Well you should have. You're not a man. You should have hit him back.'

Wilt put down the razor. 'And got the sack. Got hauled up in court for assaulting a student. Now that's what I call a brilliant idea.' He reached for the sponge and washed his face.

Eva retreated to the bedroom satisfied. There would be no mention of her lemon loungers now. She had taken his mind off her own little extravagance and given him a sense of grievance that would keep him occupied for the time being. By the time she had finished dressing, Wilt had eaten a bowl of All-Bran, drunk half a cup of coffee and was snarled up in a traffic jam at the roundabout. Eva went downstairs and had her own breakfast and began the daily round of washing up and Hoovering and cleaning the bath and . . .

'Commitment,' said Dr Mayfield, 'to an integrated approach is an essential element in . . .'

The Joint Committee for the Further Development of Liberal Studies was in session. Wilt squirmed in his chair and wished to hell it wasn't. Dr Mayfield's paper 'Cerebral Content and the Non-Academic Syllabus' held no interest for him, and besides, it was delivered in such convoluted sentences and with so much monotonous fervour that Wilt found it difficult to stay awake. He stared out of the window at the machines boring away on the site of the new Admin block. There was a reality about the work going on down there that was in marked contrast to the impractical theories Dr Mayfield was expounding. If the man really thought he could instil Cerebral Content, whatever that was, into Gasfitters Three he was out of his mind. Worse still, his blasted paper was bound to provoke an argument at question time. Wilt looked round the room. The various factions were all there, the New Left, the Left, the Old Left, the Indifferent Centre, the Cultural Right and the Reactionary Right.

Wilt classed himself with the Indifferents. In earlier years he had belonged to the Left politically and to the Right culturally. In other words he had banned the bomb, supported abortion and the abolition of private education and had been against capital punishment, thus earning himself something of a reputation as a radical while at the same time advocating a return to the craft of the wheelwright, the blacksmith and the handloom weaver which had done much to undermine the efforts of the Technical staff to instil in their students an appreciation of the opportunities provided by modern technology. Time and the intransigent coarseness of Plasterers had changed all that. Wilt's ideals had vanished, to be replaced by the conviction that the man who said the pen was mightier than the sword ought to have tried reading *The Mill on the Floss* to Motor Mechanics Three before he opened his big mouth. In Wilt's view, the sword had much to recommend it.

As Dr Mayfield droned on, as question time with its ideological arguments followed, Wilt studied the pile hole on the building site. It would make an ideal depository for a body and there would be something immensely satisfying in knowing that Eva, who in her lifetime had been so unbearable, was in death supporting the weight of a multi-storey concrete building. Besides it would make her discovery an extremely remote possibility and her identification out of the question. Not even

Eva, who boasted a strong constitution and a stronger will, could maintain an identity at the bottom of a pile shaft. The difficulty would be in getting her to go down the hole in the first place. Sleeping pills seemed a sensible preliminary but Eva was a sound sleeper and didn't believe in pills of any sort. 'I can't imagine why not,' Wilt thought grimly, 'she's prepared to believe in just about everything else.'

His reverie was interrupted by Mr Morris who was bringing the meeting to a close. 'Before you all go,' he said, 'there is one more subject I want to mention. We have been asked by the Head of Engineering to conduct a series of one-hour lectures to Sandwich-Course Trainee Firemen. The theme this year will be Problems of Contemporary Society. I have drawn up a list of topics and the lecturers who will give them.'

Mr Morris handed out subjects at random. Major Millfield got Media, Communications and Participatory Democracy about which he knew nothing and cared less. Peter Braintree was given The New Brutalism in Architecture, Its Origins and Social Attributes, and Wilt ended up with Violence and the Break-Up of Family Life. On the whole he thought he had done rather well. The subject fitted in with his present preoccupations. Mr Morris evidently agreed.

'I thought you might like to have a go at it after yesterday's little episode with Printers Three,' he said, as they went out. Wilt smiled wanly and went off to take Fitters and Turners Two. He gave them *Shane* to read and spent the hour jotting down notes for his lecture. In the distance he could hear the pile-boring machines grinding away. Wilt could imagine Eva lying at the bottom as they poured the concrete in. In her lemon pyjamas. It was a nice thought, and helped him with his notes. He wrote down a heading, Crime in the family, subheading (A) Murder of Spouse, decline in since divorce laws.

Yes, he should be able to talk about that to Trainee Firemen.

Chapter 4

'I loathe parties,' said Wilt on Thursday night, 'and if there's one thing worse than parties it's university parties and bottle parties are worst of all. You take along a bottle of decent burgundy and end up drinking someone else's rotgut.'

'It isn't a party,' said Eva, 'it's a barbecue.'

'It says here "Come and Touch and Come with Sally and Gaskell 9PM Thursday. Bring your own ambrosia or take pot luck with the Pringsheim punch." If ambrosia doesn't mean Algerian bilgewater I'd like to know what it does mean.'

'I thought it was that stuff people take to get a hard-on,' said Eva.

Wilt looked at her with disgust. 'You've picked up some choice phrases since you've met these bloody people. A hard-on. I don't know what's got into you.'

'You haven't. That's for sure,' said Eva, and went through to the bathroom. Wilt sat on the bed and looked at the card. The beastly thing was shaped like a . . . What the hell was it shaped like? Anyway it was pink and opened out and inside were all these ambiguous words. Come and Touch and Come. Anyone touched him and they'd get an earful. And what about pot luck? A lot of trendy dons smoking joints and talking about set-theoretic data-manipulation systems or the significance of pre-Popper Hegelianism in the contemporary dialectical scene, or something equally unintelligible, and using fuck and cunt every now and then to show that they were still human.

'And what do you do?' they would ask him.

'Well, actually I teach at the Tech.'

'At the Tech? How frightfully interesting,' looking over his shoulder towards more stimulating horizons, and he would end the evening with some ghastly woman who felt strongly that Techs fulfilled a real function and that intellectual achievement was vastly overrated and that people should be oriented in a way that would make them community coordinated and that's what Techs were doing, weren't they? Wilt knew what Techs were doing. Paying people like him £3500 a year to keep Gasfitters quiet for an hour.

And Pringsheim Punch. Planters Punch. Printers Punch. He'd had enough punches recently.

'What the hell am I to wear?' he asked.

'There's that Mexican shirt you bought on the Costa del Sol last year,' Eva called from the bathroom. 'You haven't had a chance to wear it since.'

'And I don't intend to now,' muttered Wilt, rummaging through a drawer in search of something nondescript that would demonstrate his independence. In the end he put on a striped shirt with blue jeans.

'You're surely not going like that?' Eva told him emerging from the bathroom largely naked. Her face was plastered with white powder and her lips were carmine.

'Jesus wept,' said Wilt, 'Mardi Gras with pernicious anaemia.'

Eva pushed past him. 'I'm going as The Great Gatsby,' she announced, 'and if you had any imagination you'd think of something better than a business shirt with blue jeans.'

'The Great Gatsby happened to be a man,' said Wilt.

'Bully for him,' said Eva, and put on her lemon loungers.

Wilt shut his eyes and took off his shirt. By the time they left the house he was wearing a red shirt with jeans while Eva, in spite of the hot night, insisted on putting on her new raincoat and trilby.

'We might as well walk,' said Wilt.

They took the car. Eva wasn't yet prepared to walk down Parkview Avenue in a trilby, a belted raincoat and lemon loungers. On the way they stopped at an off-licence where Wilt bought a bottle of Cyprus red.

'Don't think I'm going to touch the muck,' he said, 'and you had better take the car keys now. If it's as bad as I think it will be, I'm walking home early.'

It was. Worse. In his red shirt and blue jeans Wilt looked out of place.

'Darling Eva,' said Sally, when they finally found her talking to a man in a loincloth made out of a kitchen towel advertising Irish cheeses, 'you look great. The twenties suit you. And so this is Henry.' Henry didn't feel Henry at all. 'In period costume too. Henry meet Raphael.'

The man in the loincloth studied Wilt's jeans. 'The fifties are back,' he said languidly, 'I suppose it was bound to happen.'

Wilt looked pointedly at a Connemara Cheddar and tried to smile.

'Help yourself, Henry,' said Sally, and took Eva off to meet the freest but the most liberated woman who was simply dying to meet booby baby. Wilt went into the garden and put his bottle on the table and looked for a corkscrew. There wasn't one. In the end he looked into a large bucket with a ladle in it. Half an orange and segments of bruised peach floated in a purple liquid. He poured himself a paper cup and tried it. As he had anticipated, it tasted like cider with wood alcohol and orange squash. Wilt looked round the garden. In one corner a man in a chef's hat and a jockstrap was cooking, was *burning* sausages over a charcoal grill. In another corner a dozen people were lying in a circle listening to the Watergate tapes. There was a sprinkling of couples talking earnestly and a number of individuals standing by themselves looking supercilious and remote. Wilt recognized himself among them and selected the least attractive girl on the theory that he might just as well jump in the deep end and get it over with. He'd end up with her anyway.

'Hi,' he said, conscious that already he was slipping into the Americanese that Eva had succumbed to. The girl looked at him blankly and moved away.

'Charming,' said Wilt, and finished his drink. Ten minutes and two drinks later he was discussing Rapid Reading with a small round man who seemed deeply interested in the subject.

In the kitchen Eva was cutting up French bread while Sally stood with a drink and talked about Lévi-Strauss with an Ethiopian who had just got back from New Guinea.

'I've always felt that L-S was all wrong on the woman's front,' she said, languidly studying Eva's rear, 'I mean he disregards the essential similarity . . .' She stopped and stared out of the window. 'Excuse me a moment,' she said, and went out to rescue Dr Scheimacher from the clutches of Henry Wilt.

'Ernst is such a sweetie,' she said, when she came back, 'you'd never guess he got the Nobel prize for spermatology.'

Wilt stood in the middle of the garden and finished his third drink. He poured himself a fourth and went to listen to the Watergate tapes. He got there in time to hear the end.

'You get a much clearer insight into Tricky Dick's character quadraphonically,' someone said as the group broke up.

'With the highly gifted child one has to develop a special relationship. Roger and I find that Tonio responds best to a constructional approach.'

'It's a load of bull. Take what he says about quasars for example . . .'

'I can't honestly see what's wrong with buggery . . .'

'I don't care what Marcuse thinks about tolerance. What I'm saying is . . .'

'At minus two-fifty nitrogen . . .'

'Bach does have his moments I suppose but he has his limitations . . .'

'We've got this place at St Trop . . .'

'I still think Kaldor had the answer . . .'

Wilt finished his fourth drink and went to look for Eva. He'd had enough. He was halted by a yell from the man in the chef's hat.

'Burgers up. Come and get it.'

Wilt staggered off and got it. Two sausages, a burnt beefburger and a slosh of coleslaw on a paper plate. There didn't seem to be any knives or forks.

'Poor Henry's looking so forlorn,' said Sally, 'I'll go and transfuse him.'

She went out and took Wilt's arm.

'You're so lucky to have Eva. She's the babiest baby.'

'She's thirty-five,' said Wilt drunkenly, 'thirty-five if she's a day.'

'It's marvellous to meet a man who says what he means,' said Sally, and took a piece of beefburger from his plate. 'Gaskell just never says anything straightforwardly. I love down-to-earth people.' She sat down on the grass and pulled Wilt down with her. 'I think it's terribly important for two people to tell one another the truth,' she went on, breaking off another piece of beefburger and popping it into Wilt's mouth.

She licked her fingers slowly and looked at him with wide eyes. Wilt chewed the bit uneasily and finally swallowed it. It tasted like burnt mincemeat with a soupçon of Lancôme. Or a bouquet.

'Why two?' he asked, rinsing his mouth out with coleslaw.

'Why two what?'

'Why two people,' said Wilt. 'Why is it so important for two people to tell the truth?'

'Well, I mean . . .'

'Why not three? Or four? Or a hundred?'

'A hundred people can't have a relationship. Not an intimate one,' said Sally, 'not a meaningful one.'

'I don't know many twos who can either,' said Wilt. Sally dabbed her finger in his coleslaw.

'Oh but you do. You and Eva have this real thing going between you.'

'Not very often,' said Wilt. Sally laughed.

'Oh baby, you're a truth baby,' she said, and got up and fetched two more drinks. Wilt looked down into his paper cup doubtfully. He was getting very drunk.

'If I'm a truth baby, what sort of baby are you, baby?' he asked, endeavouring to instil the last baby with more than a soupçon of contempt. Sally snuggled up to him and whispered in his ear.

'I'm a body baby,' she said.

'I can see that,' said Wilt. 'You've got a very nice body.'

'That's the nicest thing anybody has ever said to me,' said Sally.

'In that case,' said Wilt, picking up a blackened sausage, 'you must have had a deprived childhood.'

'As a matter of fact I did,' Sally said and plucked the sausage from his fingers. 'That's why I need so much loving now.' She put most of the sausage in her mouth, drew it slowly out and nibbled the end. Wilt finished off the coleslaw and washed it down with Pringsheim Punch.

'Aren't they all awful?' said Sally, as shouts and laughter came from the corner of the garden by the grill.

Wilt looked up.

'As a matter of fact they are,' he said, 'who's the clown in the jockstrap?'

'That's Gaskell. He's so arrested. He loves playing at things.

In the States he just loves to ride footplate on a locomotive and he goes to rodeos and last Christmas he insisted on dressing up as Santa Claus and going down to Watts and giving out presents to the black kids at an orphanage. Of course they wouldn't let him.'

'If he went in a jockstrap I'm not in the least surprised,' said Wilt. Sally laughed.

'You must be an Aries,' she said, 'you don't mind what you say.' She got to her feet and pulled Wilt up. 'I'm going to show you his toy room. It's ever so droll.'

Wilt put his plate down and they went into the house. In the kitchen Eva was peeling oranges for a fruit salad and talking about circumcision rites with the Ethiopian, who was slicing bananas for her. In the lounge several couples were dancing back to back very vigorously to an LP of Beethoven's Fifth played at 78.

'Christ,' said Wilt, as Sally collected a bottle of Vodka from a cupboard. They went upstairs and down a passage to a small bedroom filled with toys. There was a model train set on the floor, a punchbag, an enormous Teddy Bear, a rocking horse, a fireman's helmet and a lifesize inflated doll that looked like a real woman.

'That's Judy,' said Sally, 'she's got a real cunt. Gaskell is a plastic freak.' Wilt winced. 'And here are Gaskell's toys. Puberty baby.'

Wilt looked round the room at the mess and shook his head. 'Looks as though he's making up for a lost childhood,' he said.

'Oh, Henry, you're so perceptive,' said Sally, and unscrewed the top of the Vodka bottle.

'I'm not. It's just bloody obvious.'

'Oh you are. You're just terribly modest, is all. Modest and shy and manly.' She swigged from the bottle and gave it to Wilt. He took a mouthful inadvisedly and had trouble swallowing it. Sally locked the door and sat down on the bed. She reached up a hand and pulled Wilt towards her.

'Screw me, Henry baby,' she said and lifted her skirt, 'fuck me, honey. Screw the pants off me.'

'That,' said Wilt, 'would be a bit difficult.'

'Oh. Why?'

'Well for one thing you don't appear to be wearing any and anyway why should I?'

'You want a reason? A reason for screwing?'

'Yes,' said Wilt. 'Yes I do.'

'Reason's treason. Feel free.' She pulled him down and kissed him. Wilt didn't feel at all free. 'Don't be shy, baby.'

'Shy?' said Wilt lurching to one side. 'Me shy?'

'Sure you're shy. OK, you're small. Eva told me . . .'

'Small? What do you mean I'm small?' shouted Wilt furiously.

Sally smiled up at him. 'It doesn't matter. It doesn't matter. Nothing matters. Just you and me and . . .'

'It bloody well does matter,' snarled Wilt. 'My wife said I was small. I'll soon show the silly bitch who's small. I'll show . . .'

'Show me, Henry baby, show me. I like them small. Prick me to the quick.'

'It's not true,' Wilt mumbled.

'Prove it, lover,' said Sally squirming against him.

'I won't,' said Wilt, and stood up.

Sally stopped squirming and looked at him. 'You're just afraid,' she said. 'You're afraid to be free.'

'Free? Free?' shouted Wilt, trying to open the door. 'Locked in a room with another man's wife is freedom? You've got to be joking.'

Sally pulled down her skirt and sat up.

'You won't?'

'No,' said Wilt.

'Are you a bondage baby? You can tell me. I'm used to bondage babies. Gaskell is real . . .'

'Certainly not,' said Wilt. 'I don't care what Gaskell is.'

'You want a blow job, is that it? You want for me to give you a blow job?' She got off the bed and came towards him. Wilt looked at her wildly.

'Don't you touch me,' he shouted, his mind alive with images of burning paint. 'I don't want anything from you.'

Sally stopped and stared at him. She wasn't smiling any more.

'Why not? Because you're small? Is that why?'

Wilt backed against the door.

'No, it isn't.'

'Because you haven't the courage of your instincts? Because you're a psychic virgin? Because you're not a man? Because you can't take a woman who thinks?'

'Thinks?' yelled Wilt, stung into action by the accusation that he wasn't a man. 'Thinks? You think? You know something? I'd rather have it off with that plastic mechanical doll than you. It's got more sex appeal in its little finger than you have in your whole rotten body. When I want a whore I'll buy one.'

'Why you little shit,' said Sally, and lunged at him. Wilt scuttled sideways and collided with the punchbag. The next moment he had stepped on a model engine and was hurtling across the room. As he slumped down the wall onto the floor Sally picked up the doll and leant over him.

In the kitchen Eva had finished the fruit salad and had made coffee. It was a lovely party. Mr Osewa had told her all about his job as underdevelopment officer in Cultural Affairs to UNESCO and how rewarding he found it. She had been kissed twice on the back of the neck by Dr Scheimacher in passing and the man in the Irish Cheese loincloth had pressed himself against her rather more firmly than was absolutely necessary to reach the tomato ketchup. And all around her terribly clever people were being so outspoken. It was all so sophisticated. She helped herself to another drink and looked around for Henry. He was nowhere to be seen.

'Have you seen Henry?' she asked when Sally came into the kitchen holding a bottle of Vodka and looking rather flushed.

'The last I saw of him he was sitting with some dolly bird,' said Sally, helping herself to a spoonful of fruit salad. 'Oh, Eva darling, you're absolutely Cordon Bleu baby.' Eva blushed.

'I do hope he's enjoying himself. Henry's not awfully good at parties.'

'Eva baby, be honest. Henry's not awfully good period.'

'It's just that he . . .' Eva began but Sally kissed her.

'You're far too good for him,' she said, 'we've got to find you someone really beautiful.' While Eva sipped her drink, Sally found a young man with a frond of hair falling across his forehead who was lying on a couch with a girl, smoking and staring at the ceiling.

'Christopher precious,' she said, 'I'm going to steal you for a moment. I want you to do someone for me. Go into the kitchen and sweeten the woman with the boobies and the awful yellow pyjamas.'

'Oh God. Why me?'

'My sweet, you know you're utterly irresistible. But the sexiest. For me, baby, for me.'

Christopher got off the couch and went into the kitchen and Sally stretched out beside the girl.

'Christopher is a dreamboy,' she said.

'He's a gigolo,' said the girl. 'A male prostitute.'

'Darling,' said Sally, 'it's about time we women had them.'

In the kitchen Eva stopped pouring coffee. She was feeling delightfully tipsy.

'You mustn't,' she said hastily.

'Why not?'

'I'm married.'

'I like it. I like it.'

'Yes but . . .'

'No buts, lover.'

'Oh.'

Upstairs in the toyroom Wilt, recovering slowly from the combined assaults on his system of Pringsheim punch, Vodka, his nymphomaniac hostess and the corner of the cupboard against which he had fallen, had the feeling that something was terribly wrong. It wasn't simply that the room was oscillating, that he had a lump on the back of his head or that he was naked. It was rather the sensation that something with all the less attractive qualities of a mousetrap, or a vice, or a starving clam, had attached itself implacably to what he had up till now always considered to be the most private of his parts. Wilt opened his eyes and found himself staring into a smiling if slightly swollen face. He shut his eyes again, hoped against hope, opened them again, found the face still there and made an effort to sit np.

It was an uuwise move. Judy, the plastic doll, inflated beyond her normal pressure, resisted. With a squawk Wilt fell back onto the floor. Judy followed. Her nose bounced on his face and her breasts on his chest. With a curse Wilt rolled onto his side and considered the problem. Sitting up was out of the question. That way led to castration. He would have to try something else. He rolled the doll over further and climbed on top only to decide that his weight on it was increasing the pressure on what remained of his penis and that if he wanted to get gangrene that was the way to go about getting it. Wilt rolled off precipitately and groped for a valve. There must be one somewhere if he could only find it. But if there was a valve it was well hidden and by the feel of things he hadn't got time to waste finding it. He felt round on the floor for something to use as a dagger, something sharp, and finally broke off a piece of railway track and plunged it into his assailant's back. There was a squeak of plastic but Judy's swollen smile remained unchanged and her unwanted attentions as implacable as ever. Again and again he stabbed her but to no avail. Wilt dropped his makeshift dagger and considered other means. He was getting frantic, conscious of a new threat. It was no longer that he was the subject of her high airpressure. His own internal pressures were mounting. The Pringsheim Punch and the Vodka were making their presence felt. With a desperate thought that if he didn't get out of her soon he would burst, Wilt seized Judy's head, bent it sideways and sank his teeth into her neck. Or would have had her pounds per square inch permitted. Instead he bounced off and spent the next two minutes trying to find his false tooth which had been dislodged in the exchange.

By the time he had got it back in place, panic had set in. He had to get out of the doll. He just had to. There would be a razor in the bathroom or a pair of scissors. But where on earth was the bathroom? Never mind about that. He'd find the damned thing. Carefully, very carefully he rolled the doll onto her back and followed her over. Then he inched his knees up until he was straddling the thing. All he needed now was something to hold on to while he got to his feet. Wilt leant over and grasped the edge of a chair with one hand while lifting Judy's head off the floor with the other. A moment later he was on his feet. Holding the doll to him he shuffled towards the door and opened it. He peered out into the passage. What if someone saw him? To hell with that. Wilt no longer cared what people thought about him. But which way was the bathroom? Wilt turned right, and peering frantically over Judy's shoulder, shuffled off down the passage.

Downstairs, Eva was having a wonderful time. First Christopher, then the man in the Irish Cheese loincloth and finally Dr Scheimacher, had all made advances to her and been rebuffed. It was such a change from Henry's lack of interest. It showed she was still attractive. Dr Scheimacher had said that she was an interesting example of latent steatopygia, Christopher tried to kiss her breasts and the man in the loincloth had made the most extraordinary suggestion to her. And through it all, Eva had remained entirely virtuous. Her massive skittishness, her insistence on dancing and, most effective of all, her habit of saying in a loud and not wholly cultivated voice, 'Oh, you are awful' at moments of their greatest ardour, had had a markedly deterrent effect. Now she sat on the floor in the living-room, while Sally and Gaskell and the bearded man from the Institute of Ecological Research argued about sexually interchangeable role-playing in a population-restrictive society. She felt strangely elated. Parkview Avenue and Mavis Mottram and her work at the Harmony Community Centre seemed to belong to another world. She had been accepted by people who flew to California or Tokyo to conferences and Think Tanks as casually as she took the bus to town. Dr Scheimacher had mentioned that he was flying to New Delhi in the morning, and Christopher had just come back from a photographic assignment in Trinidad. Above all, there was an aura of importance about what they were doing, a glamour that was wholly lacking in Henry's job at the Tech. If only she could get him to do something interesting and adventurous. But Henry was such a stick-in-the-mud. She had made a mistake in marrying him. She really had. All he was interested in was books, but life wasn't to be found in books. Like Sally said, life was for living. Life was people and experiences and fun. Henry would never see that.

In the bathroom Wilt could see very little. He certainly couldn't see any way of getting out of the doll. His attempt to slit the beastly thing's throat with a razor had failed, thanks largely to the fact that the razor in question was a Wilkinson bonded blade. Having failed with the razor he had tried shampoo as a lubricant but apart from working up a lather which even to his jaundiced eye looked as though he had aroused the doll to positively frenzied heights of sexual expectation the shampoo had achieved nothing. Finally he had reverted to a quest for the valve. The damned thing had one somewhere if only he could find it. In this endeavour he peered into the mirror on the door of the medicine cabinet but the mirror was too small. There was a large one over the washbasin. Wilt pulled down the lid of the toilet and climbed onto it. This way he would be able to get a clear view of the doll's back. He was just inching his way round when there were footsteps in the passage. Wilt stopped inching and stood rigid on the toilet lid. Someone tried the door and found it locked. The footsteps retreated and Wilt breathed a sigh of relief. Now then, just let him find that valve.

And at that moment disaster struck. Wilt's left foot stepped in the shampoo that had dripped onto the toilet seat, slid sideways off the edge and Wilt, the doll and the door of the medicine cabinet with which he had attempted to save himself were momentarily airborne. As they hurtled into the bath, as the shower curtain and fitting followed, as the contents of the medicine cabinet cascaded onto the washbasin, Wilt gave a last despairing scream. There was a pop reminiscent of champagne corks and Judy, finally responding to the pressure of Wilt's eleven stone dropping from several feet into the bath, ejected him. But Wilt no longer cared. He had in every sense passed out. He was only dimly aware of shouts in the corridor, of someone breaking the door down, of faces peering at him and of hysterical laughter. When he came to he was lying on the bed in the toy room. He got up and put on his clothes and crept downstairs and out of the front door. It was 3AM.

Chapter 5

Eva sat on the edge of the bed crying.

'How could he? How could he do a thing like that?' she said, 'in front of all these people.'

'Eva baby, men are like that. Believe me,' said Sally.

'But with a doll. . . .'

'That's symbolic of the male chauvinist pig attitude to women. We're just fuck artefacts to them. Objectification. So now you know how Henry feels about you.'

'It's horrible,' said Eva.

'Sure it's horrible. Male domination debases us to the level of objects.'

'But Henry's never done anything like that before,' Eva wailed.

'Well, he's done it now.'

'I'm not going back to him. I couldn't face it. I feel so ashamed.'

'Honey, you just forget about it. You don't have to go anywhere. Sally will look after you. You just lie down and get some sleep.'

Eva lay back, but sleep was impossible. The image of Henry lying naked in the bath on top of that horrible doll was fixed in her mind. They had had to break the door down and Dr Scheimacher had cut his hand on a broken bottle trying to get Henry out of the bath . . . Oh, it was all too awful. She would never be able to look people in the face again. The story was bound to get about and she would be known as the woman whose husband went around . . . With a fresh paroxysm of embarrassment Eva buried her head in the pillow and wept.

'Well that sure made the party go with a bang,' said Gaskell. 'Guy screws a doll in the bathroom and everyone goes berserk.' He looked round the living-room at the mess. 'If anyone thinks I'm going to start clearing this lot up now they'd better think again. I'm going to bed.'

'Just don't wake Eva up. She's hysterical,' said Sally.

'Oh great. Now we've got a manic obsessive compulsive woman with hysteria in the house.'

'And tomorrow she's coming with us on the boat.'

'She's what?'

'You heard me. She's coming with us on the boat.'

'Now wait a bit . . .'

'I'm not arguing with you, G. I'm telling you. She's coming with us.'

'Why, for Chrissake?'

'Because I'm not having her go back to that creep of a husband of hers. Because you won't get me a cleaning-woman and because I like her.'

'Because I won't get you a cleaning-woman. Now I've heard it all.'

'Oh no you haven't,' said Sally, 'you haven't heard the half of it. You may not know it but you married a liberated woman. No male pig is going to put one over on me . . .'

'I'm not trying to put one over on you,' said Gaskell. 'All I'm saying is that I don't want to have to . . .'

'I'm not talking about you. I'm talking about that creep Wilt. You think he got into that doll by himself? Think again, G baby, think again.'

Gaskell sat down on the sofa and stared at her.

'You must be out of your mind. What the hell did you want to do a thing like that for?'

'Because when I liberate someone I liberate them. No mistake.'

'Liberate someone by . . .' he shook his head. 'It doesn't make sense.'

Sally poured herself a drink. 'The trouble with you, G, is that you talk big but you don't do. It's yakkity yak with you. "My wife is a liberated woman. My wife's free." Nice-sounding talk but come the time your liberated wife takes it into her head to do something, you don't want to know.'

'Yeah, and when you take it into your goddam head to do something who takes the can back? I do. Where's petticoats then? Who got you out of that mess in Omaha? Who paid the fuzz in Houston that time . . .'

'So you did. So why did you marry me? Just why?'

Gaskell polished his glasses with the edge of the chef's hat. 'I don't know,' he said, 'so help me I don't know.'

'For kicks, baby, for kicks. Without me you'd have died of boredom. With me you get excitement. With me you get kicks.'

'In the teeth.'

Gaskell got up wearily and headed for the stairs. It was at times like these that he wondered what he had married.

Wilt walked home in agony. His pain was no longer physical. It was the agony of humiliation, hatred and self-contempt. He had been made to look a fool, a pervert and an idiot in front of people he despised. The Pringsheims and their set were everything he loathed, false, phoney, pretentious, a circus of intellectual clowns whose antics had not even the merit of his own, which had at least been real. Theirs were merely a parody of enjoyment. They laughed to hear themselves laughing and paraded a sensuality that had nothing to do with feelings or even instincts but was dredged up from shallow imaginations to mimic lust. *Copulo ergo sum.* And that bitch, Sally, had taunted him with not having the courage of his instincts as if instinct consisted of ejaculating into the chemically sterilized body of a woman he had first met twenty minutes before. And Wilt had reacted instinctively, shying away from a concupiscence that had to do with power and arrogance and an intolerable contempt for him which presupposed that what he was, what little he was, was a mere extension of his penis and that the ultimate expression of his thoughts, feelings, hopes and ambitions was to be attained between the legs of a trendy slut. And *that* was being liberated.

'Feel free,' she had said and had knotted him into that fucking doll. Wilt ground his teeth underneath a streetlamp.

And what about Eva? What sort of hell was she going to make for him now? If life had been intolerable with her before this, it was going to be unadulterated misery now. She wouldn't believe that he hadn't been screwing that doll, that he hadn't got into it of his own accord, that he had been put into it by Sally. Not in a month of Sundays. And even if by some miracle she accepted his story, a fat lot of difference that would make.

'What sort of man do you think you are, letting a woman do a thing like that to you?' she would ask. There was absolutely no reply to the question. What sort of man was he? Wilt had no idea. An insignificant little man to whom things happened and for whom life was a chapter of indignities. Printers punched him in the face and he was blamed for it. His wife bullied him and other people's wives made a laughing-stock out of him. Wilt wandered on along suburban streets past semi-detached houses and little gardens with a mounting sense of determination. He had had enough of being the butt of circumstance. From now on things would happen because he wanted them to. He would change from being the recipient of misfortune. He would be the instigator. Just let Eva try anything now. He would knock the bitch down.

Wilt stopped. It was all very well to talk. The bloody woman had a weapon she wouldn't hesitate to use. Knock her down, my eye. If anyone went down it would be Wilt, and in addition she would parade his affair with the doll to everyone they knew. It wouldn't be long before the story reached the Tech. In the darkness of Parkview Avenue Wilt shuddered at the thought. It would be the end of his career. He went through the gate of Number 34 and unlocked the front door with the feeling that unless he took some drastic action in the immediate future he was doomed.

In bed an hour later he was still awake, wide awake and wrestling with the problem of Eva, his own character and how to change it into something he could respect. And what did he respect? Under the blankets Wilt clenched his fist.

'Decisiveness,' he murmured. 'The ability to act without hesitation. Courage.' A strange litany of ancient virtues. But how to acquire them now? How had they turned men like him into Commandos and professional killers during the war? By training them. Wilt lay in the darkness and considered ways in which he could train himself to become what he was clearly not. By the time he fell asleep he had determined to attempt the impossible.

At seven the alarm went. Wilt got up and went into the bathroom and stared at himself in the mirror. He was a hard man, a man without feelings. Hard, methodical, cold-blooded and logical. A man who made no mistakes. He went downstairs and ate his All-Bran and drank his cup of coffee. So Eva wasn't home. She had stayed the night at the Pringsheims. Well that was something. It made things easier for him. Except that she still had the car and the keys. He certainly wasn't going to go round and get the car. He walked down to the roundabout and caught the bus to the Tech. He had Bricklayers One in Room 456. When he arrived they were talking about gradbashing.

'There was this student all dressed up like a waiter see. "Do you mind?" he says, "Do you mind getting out of my way." Just like that and all I was doing was looking in the window at the books . . .'

'At the books?' said Wilt sceptically. 'At eleven o'clock at night you were looking at books? I don't believe it.'

'Magazines and cowboy books,' said the bricklayer. 'They're in a junk shop in Finch Street.'

'They've got girlie mags,' someone else explained. Wilt nodded. That sounded more like it.

'So I says "Mind what?"' continued the bricklayer, 'and he says, "Mind out of my way." His way. Like he owned the bloody street.'

'So what did you say?' asked Wilt.

'Say? I didn't say anything. I wasn't wasting words on him.'

'What did you do then?'

'Well, I put the boot in and duffed him up. Gave him a good going-over and no mistake. Then I pushed off. There's one bloody grad who won't be telling people to get out of his way for a bit.'

The class nodded approvingly.

'They're all the bloody same, students,' said another bricklayer. 'Think because they've got money and go to college they can order you about. They could all do with a going-over. Do them a power of good.'

Wilt considered the implications of mugging as part of an intellectual's education. After his experience the previous night he was inclined to think there was something to be said for it. He would have liked to have duffed up half the people at the Pringsheims' party.

'So none of you feel there's anything wrong with beating a student up if he gets in your way?' he asked.

'Wrong?' said the bricklayers in unison. 'What's wrong with

a good punch-up? It's not as if a grad is an old woman or something. He can always hit back, can't he?'

They spent the rest of the hour discussing violence in the modern world. On the whole, the bricklayers seemed to think it was a good thing.

'I mean what's the point of going out on a Saturday night and getting pissed if you can't have a bit of a barney at the same time? Got to get rid of your aggression somehow,' said an unusually articulate bricklayer, 'I mean it's natural isn't it?'

'So you think man is a naturally aggressive animal,' said Wilt.

'Course he is. That's history for you, all them wars and things. It's only bloody poofters don't like violence.'

Wilt took this view of things along to the Staff Room for his free period and collected a cup of coffee from the vending machine. He was joined by Peter Braintree.

'How did the party go?' Braintree asked.

'It didn't,' said Wilt morosely.

'Eva enjoy it?'

'I wouldn't know. She hadn't come home by the time I got up this morning.'

'Hadn't come home?'

'That's what I said,' said Wilt.

'Well did you ring up and find out what had happened to her?'

'No,' said Wilt.

'Why not?'

'Because I'd look a bit of a twit ringing up and being told she was shacked up with the Abyssinian ambassador, wouldn't I?'

'The Abyssinian ambassador? Was he there?'

'I don't know and I don't want to know. The last I saw of her she was being chatted up by this big black bloke from Ethiopia. Something to do with the United Nations. She was making fruit salad and he was chopping bananas for her.'

'Doesn't sound a very compromising sort of activity to me,' said Braintree.

'No, I daresay it doesn't. Only you weren't there and don't know what sort of party it was,' said Wilt rapidly coming to the conclusion that an edited version of the night's events was called for. 'A whole lot of middle-aged with-it kids doing their withered thing.'

'It sounds bloody awful. And you think Eva . . .'

'I think Eva got pissed and somebody gave her a joint and she passed out,' said Wilt, 'that's what I think. She's probably sleeping it off in the downstairs loo.'

'Doesn't sound like Eva to me,' said Braintree. Wilt drank his coffee and considered his strategy. If the story of his involvement with that fucking doll was going to come out, perhaps it would be better if he told it his way first. On the other hand . . .

'What were you doing while all this was going on?' Braintree asked.

'Well,' said Wilt, 'as a matter of fact . . .' He hesitated. On second thoughts it might be better not to mention the doll at all. If Eva kept her trap shut . . . 'I got a bit slewed myself.'

'That sounds more like it,' said Braintree, 'I suppose you made a pass at another woman too.'

'If you must know,' said Wilt, 'another woman made a pass at me. Mrs Pringsheim.'

'Mrs Pringsheim made a pass at you?'

'Well, we went upstairs to look at her husband's toys. . . .'

'His toys? I thought you told me he was a biochemist.'

'He is a biochemist. He just happens to like playing with toys. Model trains and Teddy Bears and things. She says he's a case of arrested development. She would, though. She's that sort of loyal wife.'

'What happened then?'

'Apart from her locking the door and lying on the bed with her legs wide open and asking me to screw her and threatening me with a blow job, nothing happened,' said Wilt.

Peter Braintree looked at him sceptically. 'Nothing?' he said finally. 'Nothing? I mean what did you do?'

'Equivocated,' said Wilt.

'That's a new word for it,' said Braintree. 'You go upstairs with Mrs Pringsheim and equivocate while she lies on a bed with her legs open and you want to know why Eva hasn't come home? She's probably round at some lawyer's office filing a petition for divorce right now.'

'But I tell you I didn't screw the bitch,' said Wilt, 'I told her to hawk her pearly somewhere else.'

'And you call that equivocating? Hawk her pearly? Where the hell did you get that expression from?'

'Meat One,' said Wilt and got up and fetched himself another cup of coffee.

By the time he came back to his seat he had decided on his version.

'I don't know what happened after that,' he said when Braintree insisted on hearing the next episode. 'I passed out. It must have been the vodka.'

'You just passed out in a locked room with a naked woman? Is that what happened?' said Braintree. He didn't sound as if he believed a word of the story.

'Precisely,' said Wilt.

'And when you came to?'

'I was walking home,' said Wilt. 'I've no idea what happened in between.'

'Oh well, I daresay we'll hear about that from Eva,' said Braintree. 'She's bound to know.'

He got up and went off and Wilt was left alone to consider his next move. The first thing to do was to make sure that Eva didn't say anything. He went through to the telephone in the corridor and dialled his home number. There was no reply. Wilt went along to Room 187 and spent an hour with Turners and Fitters. Several times during the day he tried to telephone Eva but there was no answer.

'She's probably spent the day round at Mavis Mottram's weeping on her shoulder and telling all and sundry what a pig I am,' he thought. 'She's bound to be waiting for me when I get home tonight.'

But she wasn't. Instead there was a note on the kitchen table and a package. Wilt opened the note.

'I'm going away with Sally and Gaskell to think things over. What you did last night was horrible. I won't ever forgive you. Don't forget to buy some dogfood. Eva. P.S. Sally says next time you want a blow job get Judy to give you one.'

Wilt looked at the package. He knew without opening it what it contained. That infernal doll. In a sudden paroxysm of rage Wilt picked it up and hurled it across the kitchen at the sink. Two plates and a saucer bounced off the washing-up rack and broke on the floor.

'Bugger the bitch,' said Wilt inclusively, Eva, Judy and Sally Pringsheim all coming within the ambit of his fury. Then he sat down at the table and looked at the note again. 'Going away to think things over.' Like hell she was. Think? The stupid cow wasn't capable of thought. She'd emote, drool over his deficiencies and work herself into an ecstasy of self-pity. Wilt could hear her now blathering on about that blasted bank manager and how she should have married him instead of saddling herself with a man who couldn't even get promotion at the Tech and who went around fucking inflatable dolls in other people's bathrooms. And there was that filthy slut, Sally Pringsheim, egging her on. Wilt looked at the postscript. 'Sally says next time you want a blow job . . .' Christ. As if he'd wanted a blow job the last time. But there it was, a new myth in the making, like the business of his being in love with Betty Crabtree when all he had done was give her a lift home one night after an Evening Class. Wilt's home life was punctuated by such myths, weapons in Eva's armoury to be brought out when the occasion demanded and brandished above his head. And now Eva had the ultimate deterrent at her disposal, the doll and Sally Pringsheim and a blow job. The balance of recrimination which had been the sustaining factor in their relationship had shifted dramatically. It would take an act of desperate invention on Wilt's part to restore it.

'Don't forget to buy some dogfood.' Well at least she had left him the car. It was standing in the carport. Wilt went out and drove round to the supermarket and bought three tins of dogfood, a boil-in-the-bag curry and a bottle of gin. He was going to get pissed. Then he went home and sat in the kitchen watching Clem gulp his Bonzo while the bag boiled. He poured himself a stiff gin, topped it up with lime and wandered about. And all the time he was conscious of the package lying there on the draining board waiting for him to open it. And inevitably he would open it. Out of sheer curiosity. He knew it and they knew it wherever they were, and on Sunday night Eva would come home and the first thing she would do would be to ask about the doll and if he had had a nice time with it. Wilt helped himself to some more gin and considered the doll's utility. There must be some way of using the thing to turn the tables on Eva.

By the time he had finished his second gin he had begun to formulate a plan. It involved the doll, a pile hole and a nice test of his own strength of character. It was one thing to have fantasies about murdering your wife. It was quite another to put them into effect and between the two there lay an area of uncertainty. By the end of his third gin Wilt was determined to put the plan into effect. If it did nothing else it would prove he was capable of executing a murder.

Wilt got up and unwrapped the doll. In his interior dialogue Eva was telling him what would happen if Mavis Mottram got to hear about his disgusting behaviour at the Pringsheim's. 'You'd be the laughing stock of the neighbourhood,' she said, 'you'd never live it down.'

Wouldn't he though? Wilt smiled drunkenly to himself and went upstairs. For once Eva was mistaken. He might not live it down but Mrs Eva Wilt wouldn't be around to gloat. She wouldn't live at all.

Upstairs in the bedroom he closed the curtains and laid the doll on the bed and looked for the valve which had eluded him the previous night. He found it and fetched a footpump from the garage. Five minutes later Judy was in good shape. She lay on the bed and smiled up at him. Wilt half closed his eyes and squinted at her. In the half darkness he had to admit that she was hideously lifelike. Plastic Eva with the mastic boobs. All that remained was to dress it up. He rummaged around in several drawers in search of a bra and blouse, decided she didn't need a bra, and picked out an old skirt and a pair of tights. In a cardboard box in the wardrobe he found one of Eva's wigs. She had had a phase of wigs. Finally a pair of shoes. By the time he had finished, Eva Wilt's replica lay on the bed smiling fixedly at the ceiling.

'That's my girl,' said Wilt and went down to the kitchen to see how the boil-in-the-bag was coming along. It was burnt-in-the-bag. Wilt turned the stove off and went into the lavatory under the stairs and sat thinking about his next move. He would use the doll for dummy runs so that if and when it came to the day he would be accustomed to the whole process of murder and would act without feeling like an automaton. Killing by conditioned reflex. Murder by habit. Then again he would know how to time the whole affair. And Eva's going off with the

Pringsheims for the weekend would help too. It would establish
a pattern of sudden disappearances. He would provoke her
somehow to do it again and again and again. And then the visit
to the doctor.

'It's just that I can't sleep, doctor. My wife keeps on going
off and leaving me and I just can't get used to sleeping on my
own.' A prescription for sleeping tablets. Then on the night.
'I'll make the Ovaltine tonight, dear. You're looking tired. I'll
bring it up to you in bed.' Gratitude followed by snores. Down
to the car . . . fairly early would be best . . . around ten thirty
. . . over to the Tech and down the hole. Perhaps inside a plastic
bag . . . no, not a plastic bag. 'I understand you bought a large
plastic bag recently, sir. I wonder if you would mind showing
it to us.' No, better just to leave her down the hole they were
going to fill with concrete next morning. And finally a bewildered
Wilt. He would go round to the Pringsheims'. 'Where's Eva?
Yes, you do.' 'No, we don't.' 'Don't lie to me. She's always
coming round here.' 'We're not lying. We haven't seen her.'
After that he would go to the police.

Motiveless, clueless and indiscoverable. And proof that he
was a man who could act. Or wasn't. What if he broke down
under the strain and confessed? That would be some sort of
vindication too. He would know what sort of man he was one
way or another and at least he would have acted for once in his
life. And fifteen years in prison would be almost identical to
fifteen, more, twenty years at the Tech confronting louts who
despised him and talking about Piggy and the Lord of the
Flies. Besides he could always plead the book as a mitigating
circumstance at his trial.

'Me lud, members of the Jury, I ask you to put yourself in
the defendant's place. For twelve years he has been confronted
by the appalling prospect of reading this dreadful book to
classes of bored and hostile youths. He has had to endure
agonies of repetition, of nausea and disgust at Mr Golding's
revoltingly romantic view of human nature. Ah, but I hear you
say that Mr Golding is not a romantic, that his view of human
nature as expressed in his portrait of a group of young boys
marooned on a desert island is the very opposite of romanticism
and that the sentimentality of which I accuse him and to which
my client's appearance in this court attests is to be found not in

The Lord of the Flies but in its predecessor, *Coral Island*. But me lud, gentlemen of the Jury, there is such a thing as inverted romanticism, the romanticism of disillusionment, of pessimism and of nihilism. Let us suppose for one moment that my client had spent twelve years reading not Mr Golding's work but *Coral Island* to groups of apprentices; is it reasonable to imagine that he would have been driven to the desperate remedy of murdering his wife? No. A hundred times no. Mr Ballantyne's book would have given him the inspiration, the self-discipline, the optimism and the belief in man's ability to rescue himself from the most desperate situation by his own ingenuity . . .'

It might not be such a good idea to pursue that line of argument too far. The defendant Wilt had after all exercised a good deal of ingenuity in rescuing himself from a desperate situation. Still, it was a nice thought. Wilt finished his business in the lavatory and looked around for the toilet paper. There wasn't any. The bloody roll had run out. He reached in his pocket and found Eva's note and put it to good use. Then he flushed it down the U-bend, puffed some Harpic after it to express his opinion of it and her and went out to the kitchen and helped himself to another gin.

He spent the rest of the evening sitting in front of the TV with a piece of bread and cheese and a tin of peaches until it was time to try his first dummy run. He went out to the front door and looked up and down the street. It was almost dark now and there was no one in sight. Leaving the front door open he went upstairs and fetched the doll and put it in the back seat of the car. He had to push and squeeze a bit to get it in but finally the door shut. Wilt climbed in and backed the car out into Parkview Avenue and drove down to the roundabout. By the time he reached the car park at the back of the Tech it was half past ten exactly. He stopped and sat in the car looking around. Not a soul in sight and no lights on. There wouldn't be. The Tech closed at nine.

Chapter 6

Sally lay naked on the deck of the cabin cruiser, her tight breasts pointing to the sky and her legs apart. Beside her Eva lay on her stomach and looked downriver.

'Oh God, this is divine,' Sally murmured, 'I have this deep thing about the countryside.'

'You've got this deep thing period,' said Gaskell steering the cruiser erratically towards a lock. He was wearing a Captain's cap and sunglasses.

'Cliché baby,' said Sally.

'We're coming to a lock,' said Eva anxiously. 'There are some men there.'

'Men? Forget men, darling. There's just you and me and G and G's not a man, are you G baby?'

'I have my moments,' said Gaskell.

'But so seldom, so awfully seldom,' Sally said. 'Anyway what does it matter? We're here idyllicstyle, cruising down the river in the good old summertime.'

'Shouldn't we have cleared the house up before we left?' Eva asked.

'The secret of parties is not to clear up afterward but to clear off. We can do all that when we get back.'

Eva got up and went below. They were quite near the lock and she wasn't going to be stared at in the nude by the two old men sitting on the bench beside it.

'Jesus, Sally, can't you do something about soulmate? She's getting on my teats,' said Gaskell.

'Oh G baby, she's never. If she did you'd Cheshire cat.'

'Cheshire cat?'

'Disappear with a smile, honey chil', foetus first. She's but positively gargantuanly uterine.'

'She's but positively gargantuanly boring.'

'Time, lover, time. You've got to accentuate the liberated, eliminate the negative and not mess with Mister-in-between.'

'Not mess with Missus-in-between. Operative word missus,' said Gaskell bumping the boat into the lock.

'But that's the whole point.'

'What is?' said Gaskell.

'Messing with Missus-in-between. I mean it's all ways with Eva and us. She does the housework. Gaskell baby can play ship's captain and teatfeast on boobs and Sally sweetie can minotaur her labyrinthine mind.'

'Mind?' said Gaskell. 'Polyunsaturated hasn't got a mind. And talking of cretins, what about Mister-in-between?'

'He's got Judy to mess with. He's probably screwing her now and tomorrow night he'll sit up and watch *Kojak* with her. Who knows, he may even send her off to Mavis Contracuntal Mottram's Flower Arrangement evening. I mean they're suited. You can't say he wasn't hooked on her last night.'

'You can say that again,' said Gaskell and closed the lock gates.

As the cruiser floated downwards the two old men sitting on the bench stared at Sally. She took off her sunglasses and glared at them.

'Don't blow your prostates, senior citizens,' she said rudely. 'Haven't you seen a fanny before?'

'You talking to me?' said one of the men.

'I wouldn't be talking to myself.'

'Then I'll tell you,' said the man, 'I've seen one like yours before. Once.'

'Once is about right,' said Sally. 'Where?'

'On an old cow as had just dropped her calf,' said the man and spat into a neat bed of geraniums.

In the cabin Eva sat and wondered what they were talking about. She listened to the lapping of the water and the throb of the engine and thought about Henry. It wasn't like him to do a thing like that. It really wasn't. And in front of all those people. He must have been drunk. It was so humiliating. Well, he could suffer. Sally said men ought to be made to suffer. It was part of the process of liberating yourself from them. You had to show them that you didn't need them and violence was the only thing the male psyche understood. That was why she was so harsh with Gaskell. Men were like animals. You had to show them who was master.

Eva went through to the galley and polished the stainless-steel sink. Henry would have to learn how important she was by missing her and doing the housework and cooking for himself and when she got back she would give him such a telling-off about that doll. I mean, it wasn't natural. Perhaps Henry ought to go and see a psychiatrist. Sally said that he had made the most horrible suggestion to her too. It only went to show that you couldn't trust anyone. And Henry of all people. She would never have imagined Henry would think of doing anything like that. But Sally had been so sweet and understanding. She knew how women felt and she hadn't even been angry with Henry.

'It's just that he's a sphincter baby,' she had said, 'it's symptomatic of a male-dominated chauvinist pig society. I've never known an MCP who didn't say "Bugger you" and mean it.'

'Henry's always saying "Bugger",' Eva had admitted. 'It's bugger this, and bugger that.'

'There you are, Eva baby. What did I tell you? It's semantic degradation analwise.'

'It's bloody disgusting,' said Eva, and so it was.

She went on polishing and cleaning until they were clear of the lock and steering downriver towards the open water of the Broads. Then she went up on deck and sat looking out over the flat empty landscape at the sunset. It was all so romantic and exciting, so different from everything she had known before. This was life as she had always dreamt it might be, rich and gay and fulfilling. Eva Wilt sighed. In spite of everything she was at peace with the world.

In the car park at the back of the Tech Henry Wilt wasn't at peace with anything. On the contrary, he was at war with Eva's replica. As he stumbled drunkenly round the car and struggled with Judy he was conscious that even an inflatable doll had a will of its own when it came to being dragged out of small cars. Judy's arms and legs got caught in things. If Eva behaved in the same way on the night of her disposal he would have the devil's own job getting her out of the car. He would have to tie her up in a neat bundle. That would be the best thing to do. Finally, by tugging at the doll's legs, he hauled her out and laid her on the ground. Then he got back into the car to look for her wig. He found it under the seat and after rearranging Judy's skirt so that it wasn't quite so revealing, he put the wig on her head. He looked round the car park at the terrapin huts and the main building but there was no one to be seen. All clear. He picked the doll up and carrying it under his arm set off towards the building site. Halfway there he realized that he wasn't doing it properly. Eva drugged and sleeping would be far too heavy to carry under his arm. He would have to use a fireman's lift. Wilt stopped and hoisted the doll onto his back, and set off again weaving erratically, partly because, thanks to the gin, he couldn't help it, and partly because it added verisimilitude to the undertaking. With Eva over his shoulder he would be bound to weave a bit. He reached the fence and dropped the doll over. In the process the wig fell off again. Wilt groped around in the mud and found it. Then he went round to the gate. It was locked. It would be. He would have to remember that. Details like that were important. He tried to climb over but couldn't. He needed something to give him a leg up. A bicycle. There were usually some in the racks by the main gate. Stuffing the wig into his pocket Wilt made his way round the terrapin huts and past the canteen and was just crossing the grass by the Language Lab when a figure appeared out of the darkness and a torch shone in his face. It was the caretaker.

'Here, where do you think you're going?' the caretaker asked. Wilt halted.

'I've . . . I've just come back to get some notes from the Staff Room.'

'Oh it's you, Mr Wilt,' said the caretaker. 'You should know by now that you can't get in at this time of night. We lock up at nine thirty.'

'I'm sorry. I forgot,' said Wilt.

The caretaker sighed. 'Well, since it's you and it's just this once . . .' he said, and unlocked the door to the General Studies building. 'You'll have to walk up. The lifts don't work at this time of night. I'll wait for you down here.'

Wilt staggered slowly up five flights of stairs to the Staff Room and went to his locker. He took out a handful of papers and a copy of *Bleak House* he'd been meaning to take home for some months and hadn't. He stuffed the notes into his pocket and found the wig. While he was about it he might as well pick up an elastic band. That would keep the wig on Judy's head. He found some in a box in the stationery cupboard, stuffed the notes into his other pocket and went downstairs.

'Thanks very much,' he told the caretaker, 'sorry to have bothered you.' He wove off round the corner to the bike sheds.

'Pissed as a newt,' said the caretaker, and went back into his office.

Wilt watched him light his pipe and then turned his attention to the bicycles. The bloody things were all locked. He would just have to carry one round. He put *Bleak House* in the basket, picked the bike up and carried it all the way round to the fence. Then he climbed up and over and groped around in the darkness for the doll. In the end he found it and spent five minutes trying to keep the wig on while he fastened the elastic band under her chin. It kept on jumping off. 'Well, at least that's one problem I won't have with Eva,' he muttered to himself when the wig was secured. Having satisfied himself that it wouldn't come off he moved cautiously forward skirting mounds of gravel, machines, sacks and reinforcing rods when it suddenly occurred to him that he was running considerable risk of disappearing down one of the pile holes himself. He put the doll down and fumbled in his pocket for the torch and shone it on the ground. Some yards ahead there was a large square of thick plywood. Wilt moved forward and lifted it. Underneath was the hole, a nice big hole. Just the right size. She would fit in there perfectly. He shone the torch down. Must be thirty feet deep. He pushed the plywood to one side and went back for the doll. The wig had fallen off again.

'Fuck,' said Wilt, and reached in his pocket for another elastic band. Five minutes later Judy's wig was firmly in place with four elastic bands fastened under her chin. That should do it. Now all he had to do was to drag the replica to the hole and make sure it fitted. At this point Wilt hesitated. He was beginning to have doubts about the soundness of the scheme. Too many unexpected contingencies had arisen for his liking. On the other hand there was a sense of exhilaration about being alone on the building site in the middle of the night. Perhaps it would be better if he went home now. No, he had to see the thing through. He would put the doll into the hole to make quite sure that it fitted. Then he would deflate it and go home and repeat the process until he had trained himself to kill by proxy. He would keep the doll in the boot of the car. Eva never looked there. And in future he would only blow her up when he reached the car park. That way Eva would have no idea what was going on. Definitely not. Wilt smiled to himself at the simplicity of the scheme. Then he picked Judy up and pushed her towards the hole feet first. She slid in easily while Wilt leant forward. Perfect. And at that moment he slipped on the muddy ground. With a desperate effort which necessitated letting go of the doll he hurled himself to one side and grabbed at the plywood. He got to his feet cautiously and cursed. His trousers were covered with mud and his hands were shaking.

'Damned near went down myself,' he muttered, and looked around for Judy. But Judy had disappeared. Wilt reached for his torch and shone it down the hole. Halfway down the doll was wedged lightly against the sides and for once the wig was still on. Wilt stared desperately down at the thing and wondered what the hell to do. It—or she—must be at least twenty feet down. Fifteen. Anyway a long way down and certainly too far for him to reach. But still too near the top not to be clearly visible to the workmen in the morning. Wilt switched off the torch and pulled the plywood square so that it covered half the hole. That way he wouldn't be in danger of joining the doll. Then he stood up and tried to think of ways of getting it out.

Rope with a hook on the end of it? He hadn't a rope or a hook. He might be able to find a rope but hooks were another matter. Get a rope and tie it to something and climb down it and bring the doll up? Certainly not. It would be bad enough climbing down the rope with two hands but to think of climbing back up with one hand holding the doll in the other was sheer lunacy. That way he would end up at the bottom of the hole himself and if one thing was clear in his mind it was that he didn't intend to be discovered at the bottom of a thirty-foot pile hole on Monday morning clutching a plastic fucking doll with a cunt dressed in his wife's clothes. That way lay disaster. Wilt visualized the scene in the Principal's office as he tried to explain how he came to be . . . And anyway they might not find him or hear his yells. Those damned cement lorries made a hell of a din and he bloody well wasn't going to risk being buried under . . . Shit. Talk about poetic justice. No the only thing to do was to get that fucking doll down to the bottom of the hole and hope to hell that no one spotted it before they poured the concrete in. Well, at least that way he would learn if it was a sensible method of getting rid of Eva. There was that to be said for it. Every cloud had . . .

Wilt left the hole and looked around for something to move Judy down to the bottom. He tried a handful of gravel but she merely wobbled a bit and stayed put. Something weightier was needed. He went across to a pile of sand and scooped some into a plastic sack and poured it down the hole, but apart from adding an extra dimension of macabre realism to Mrs Wilt's wig the sand did nothing. Perhaps if he dropped a brick on the doll it would burst. Wilt looked around for a brick and ended up with a large lump of clay. That would have to do. He dropped it down the hole. There was a thump, a rattle of gravel and another thump. Wilt shone his torch down. Judy had reached the bottom of the hole and had settled into a grotesque position with her legs crumpled up in front of her and one arm outstretched towards him as if in supplication. Wilt fetched another lump of clay and hurled it down. This time the wig slid sideways and her head lolled. Wilt gave up. There was nothing more he could do. He pulled the plywood back over the hole and went back to the fence.

Here he ran into more trouble. The bicycle was on the other side. He fetched a plank, leant it against the fence and climbed over. Now to carry the bike back to the shed. Oh bugger the bicycle. It could stay where it was. He was fed up with the whole business. He couldn't even dispose of a plastic doll properly. It was ludicrous to think that he could plan, commit and carry through a real murder with any hope of success. He must have been mad to think of it. It was all that blasted gin.

'That's right, blame the gin,' Wilt muttered to himself, as he trudged back to his car. 'You had this idea months ago.' He climbed into the car and sat there in the darkness wondering what on earth had ever possessed him to have fantasies of murdering Eva. It was insane, utterly insane, and just as mad as to imagine that he could train himself to become a cold-blooded killer. Where had the idea originated from? What was it all about? All right, Eva was a stupid cow who made his life a misery by nagging at him and by indulging a taste for Eastern mysticism with a frenetic enthusiasm calculated to derange the soberest of husbands, but why his obsession with murder? Why the need to prove his manliness by violence? Where had he got that from? In the middle of the car park, Henry Wilt, suddenly sober and clear-headed, realized the extraordinary effect that ten years of Liberal Studies had had upon him. For ten long years Plasterers Two and Meat One had been exposed to culture in the shape of Wilt and *The Lord of the Flies*, and for as many years Wilt himself had been exposed to the barbarity, the unhesitating readiness to commit violence of Plasterers Two and Meat One. That was the genesis of it all. That and the unreality of the literature he had been forced to absorb. For ten years Wilt had been the duct along which travelled creatures of imagination, Nostromo, Jack and Piggy, Shane, creatures who acted and whose actions effected something. And all the time he saw himself, mirrored in their eyes, an ineffectual passive person responding solely to the dictates of circumstance. Wilt shook his head. And out of all that and the traumas of the past two days had been born this *acte gratuit*, this semi-crime, the symbolic murder of Eva Wilt.

He started the car and drove out of the car park. He would go and see the Braintrees. They would still be up and glad to see him and besides he needed to talk to someone. Behind him on the building site his notes on Violence and the Break-Up of Family Life drifted about in the night wind and stuck in the mud.

Chapter 7

'Nature is so libidinous,' said Sally, shining a torch through the porthole at the reeds. 'I mean take bullrushes. I mean they're positively archetypally phallus. Don't you think so, G?'

'Bullrushes?' said Gaskell, gazing helplessly at a chart. 'Bullrushes do nothing for me.'

'Maps neither, by the look of it.'

'Charts, baby, charts.'

'What's in a name?'

'Right now, a hell of a lot. We're either in Frogwater Reach or Fen Broad. No telling which.'

'Give me Fen Broad every time. I just adore broads. Eva sweetheart, how's about another pot of coffee? I want to stay awake all night and watch the dawn come up over the bullrushes.'

'Yes, well I don't,' said Gaskell. 'Last night was enough for me. That crazy guy with the doll in the bath and Schei cutting himself. That's enough for one day. I'm going to hit the sack.'

'The deck,' said Sally, 'hit the deck, G. Eva and I are sleeping down here. Three's a crowd.'

'Three? With boobs around it's five at the least. OK, so I sleep on deck. We've got to be up early if we're to get off this damned sandbank.'

'Has Captain Pringsheim stranded us, baby?'

'It's these charts. If only they would give an exact indication of depth.'

'If you knew where we were, you'd probably find they do. It's no use knowing it's three feet—'

'Fathoms, honey, fathoms.'

'Three fathoms in Frogwater Reach if we're really in Fen Broad.'

'Well, wherever we are, you'd better start hoping there's a tide that will rise and float us off,' said Gaskell.

'And if there isn't?'

'Then we'll have to think of something else. Maybe someone will come along and tow us off.'

'Oh God, G, you're the skilfullest,' said Sally. 'I mean why couldn't we have just stayed out in the middle? But no, you had to come steaming up this creek wham into a mudbank and all because of what? Ducks, goddamned ducks.'

'Waders, baby, waders. Not just ducks.'

'OK, so they're waders. You want to photograph them so now we're stuck where no one in their right minds would come in a boat. Who do you think is going to come up here? Jonathan Seagull?'

In the galley Eva made coffee. She was wearing the bright red plastic bikini Sally had lent her. It was rather too small for her so that she bulged round it uncomfortably and it was revealingly tight but at least it was better than going around naked even though Sally said nudity was being liberated and look at the Amazonian Indians. She should have brought her own things but Sally had insisted on hurrying and now all she had were the lemon loungers and the bikini. Honestly Sally was so authora . . . authorasomething . . . well, bossy then.

'Dual-purpose plastic, baby, apronwise,' she had said, 'and G has this thing about plastic, haven't you, G?'

'Bio-degradably yes.'

'Bio-degradably?' asked Eva, hoping to be initiated into some new aspect of women's liberation.

'Plastic bottles that disintegrate instead of lying around making an ecological swamp,' said Sally, opening a porthole and dropping an empty cigar packet over the side, 'that's G's lifework. That and recyclability. Infinite recyclability.'

'Right,' said Gaskell. 'We've got in-built obsolescence in the automotive field where it's outmoded. So what we need now is in-built bio-degradable deliquescence in ephemera.'

Eva listened incomprehendingly but with the feeling that she was somehow at the centre of an intellectual world far surpassing that of Henry and his friends who talked about new degree courses and their students so boringly.

'We've got a compost heap at the bottom of the garden,' she said when she finally understood what they were talking about. 'I put the potato peelings and odds and ends on it.'

Gaskell raised his eyes to the cabin roof. Correction. Deckhead.

'Talking of odds and ends,' said Sally, running a fond hand over Eva's bottom, 'I wonder how Henry is getting along with Judy.'

Eva shuddered. The thought of Henry and the doll lying in the bath still haunted her.

'I can't think what had got into him,' she said, and looked disapprovingly at Gaskell when he sniggered. 'I mean it's not as if he has ever been unfaithful or anything like that. And lots of husbands are. Patrick Mottram is always going off and having affairs with other women but Henry's been very good in that respect. He may be quiet and not very pushing but no one could call him a gadabout.'

'Oh sure,' said Gaskell, 'so he's got a hang-up about sex. My heart bleeds for him.'

'I don't see why you should say he's got something wrong with him because he's faithful,' said Eva.

'G didn't mean that, did you, G?' said Sally. 'He meant that there has to be true freedom in a marriage. No dominance, no jealousy, no possession. Right, G?'

'Right,' said Gaskell.

'The test of true love is when you can watch your wife having it off with someone else and still love her,' Sally went on.

'I could never watch Henry . . .' said Eva. 'Never.'

'So you don't love him. You're insecure. You don't trust him.'

'Trust him?' said Eva. 'If Henry went to bed with another woman I don't see how I could trust him. I mean if that's what he wants to do why did he marry me?'

'That,' said Gaskell, 'is the sixty-four-thousand dollar question.' He picked up his sleeping bag and went out on deck. Behind him Eva had begun to cry.

'There, there,' said Sally, putting her arm round her. 'G was just kidding. He didn't mean anything.'

'It's not that,' said Eva, 'it's just that I don't understand anything any more. It's all so complicated.'

'Christ, you look bloody awful,' said Peter Braintree as Wilt stood on the doorstep.

'I feel bloody awful,' said Wilt. 'It's all this gin.'

'You mean Eva's not back?' said Braintree, leading the way down the passage to the kitchen.

'She wasn't there when I got home. Just a note saying she was going away with the Pringsheims to think things over.'

'To think things over? Eva? What things?'

'Well . . .' Wilt began and thought better of it, 'that business with Sally I suppose. She says she won't ever forgive me.'

'But you didn't do anything with Sally. That's what you told me.'

'I know I didn't. That's the whole point. If I had done what that nymphomaniac bitch wanted there wouldn't have been all this bloody trouble.'

'I don't see that, Henry. I mean if you had done what she wanted Eva would have had something to grumble about. I don't see why she should be up in the air because you didn't.'

'Sally must have told her that I did do something,' said Wilt, determined not to mention the incident in the bathroom with the doll.

'You mean the blow job?'

'I don't know what I mean. What is a blow job anyway?'

Peter Braintree looked puzzled.

'I'm not too sure,' he said, 'but it's obviously something you don't want your husband to do. If I came home and told Betty I'd done a blow job she'd think I'd been robbing a bank.'

'I wasn't going to do it anyway,' said Wilt. 'She was going to do it to me.'

'Perhaps it's a suck off,' said Braintree, putting a kettle on the stove. 'That's what it sounds like to me.'

'Well it didn't sound like that to me,' said Wilt with a shudder. 'She made it sound like a paint-peeling exercise with a blow lamp. You should have seen the look on her face.'

He sat down at the kitchen table despondently.

Braintree eyed him curiously. 'You certainly seem to have been in the wars,' he said.

Wilt looked down at his trousers. They were covered with mud and there were round patches caked to his knees. 'Yes . . . well . . . well I had a puncture on the way here,' he explained with lack of conviction, 'I had to change a tyre and I knelt down. I was a bit pissed.'

Peter Braintree grunted doubtfully. It didn't sound very convincing to him. Poor old Henry was obviously a bit under the weather. 'You can wash up in the sink,' he said.

Presently Betty Braintree came downstairs. 'I couldn't help hearing what you said about Eva,' she said, 'I'm so sorry, Henry. I wouldn't worry. She's bound to come back.'

'I wouldn't be too sure,' said Wilt, gloomily, 'and anyway I'm not so sure I want her back.'

'Oh, Eva's all right,' Betty said. 'She gets these sudden urges and enthusiasms but they don't last long. It's just the way she's made. It's easy come and easy go with Eva.'

'I think that's what's worrying Henry,' said Braintree, 'the easy come bit.'

'Oh surely not. Eva isn't that sort at all.'

Wilt sat at the kitchen table and sipped his coffee. 'I wouldn't put anything past her in the company she's keeping now,' he muttered lugubriously. 'Remember what happened when she went through that macrobiotic diet phase? Dr Mannix told me I was the nearest thing to a case of scurvy he'd seen since the Burma railway. And then there was that episode with the trampoline. She went to a Keep Fit Class at Bulham Village College and bought herself a fucking trampoline. You know she put old Mrs Portway in hospital with that contraption.'

'I knew there was some sort of accident but Eva never told me what actually happened,' said Betty.

'She wouldn't. It was a ruddy miracle we didn't get sued,' said Wilt. 'It threw Mrs Portway clean through the greenhouse roof. There was glass all over the lawn and it wasn't even as though Mrs Portway was a healthy woman at the best of times.'

'Wasn't she the woman with the rheumatoid arthritis?'

Wilt nodded dismally. 'And the duelling scars on her face,' he said, 'that was our greenhouse, that was.'

'I must say I can think of better places for trampolines than greenhouses,' said Braintree. 'It wasn't a very big greenhouse was it?'

'It wasn't a very big trampoline either, thank God,' said Wilt, 'she'd have been in orbit otherwise.'

'Well it all goes to prove one thing,' said Betty, looking on the bright side, 'Eva may do crazy things but she soon gets over them.'

'Mrs Portway didn't,' said Wilt, not to be comforted, 'she was in hospital for six weeks and the skin grafts didn't take. She hasn't been near our house since.'

'You'll see. Eva will get fed up with these Pringsheim people in a week or two. They're just another fad.'

'A fad with a lot of advantages if you ask me,' said Wilt. 'Money, status and sexual promiscuity. All the things I couldn't give her and all dressed up in a lot of intellectual claptrap about Women's Lib and violence and the intolerance of tolerance and the revolution of the sexes and you're not fully mature unless you're ambisextrous. It's enough to make you vomit and it's just the sort of crap Eva would fall for. I mean she'd buy rotten herrings if some clown up the social scale told her they were the sophisticated things to eat. Talk about being gullible!'

'The thing is that Eva's got too much energy,' said Betty. 'You should try and persuade her to get a full-time job.'

'Full-time job?' said Wilt. 'She's had more full-time jobs than I've had hot dinners. Mind you, that's not saying much these days. All I ever get is a cold supper and a note saying she's gone to Pottery or Transcendental Meditation or something equally half-baked. And anyway Eva's idea of a job is to take over the factory. Remember Potters, that engineering firm that went broke after a strike a couple of years ago? Well, if you ask me that was Eva's fault. She got this job with a consultancy firm doing time and motion study and they sent her out to the factory and the next thing anyone knew they had a strike on their hands . . .'

They went on talking for another hour until the Braintrees asked him to stay the night. But Wilt wouldn't. 'I've got things to do tomorrow.'

'Such as?'

'Feed the dog for one thing.'

'You can always drive over and do that. Clem won't starve overnight.'

But Wilt was too immersed in self-pity to be persuaded and besides he was still worried about that doll. He might have another go at getting the thing out of that hole. He drove home and went to bed in a tangle of sheets and blankets. He hadn't made it in the morning.

'Poor old Henry,' said Betty as she and Peter went upstairs.
'He did look pretty awful.'

'He said he'd had a puncture and had to change the wheel.'

'I wasn't thinking of his clothes. It was the look on his face
that worried me. You don't think he's on the verge of a breakdown?'

Peter Braintree shook his head. 'You'd look like that if you
had Gasfitters Three and Plasterers Two every day of your life
for ten years and then your wife ran away,' he told her.

'Why don't they give him something better to teach?'

'Why? Because the Tech wants to become a Poly and they
keep starting new degree courses and hiring people with PhDs
to teach them and then the students don't enrol and they're
lumbered with specialists like Dr Fitzpatrick who knows all
there is to know about child labour in four cotton mills in
Manchester in 1837 and damn all about anything else. Put him
in front of a class of Day Release Apprentices and all hell
would break loose. As it is I have to go into his A-level classes
once a week and tell them to shut up. On the other hand Henry
looks meek but he can cope with rowdies. He's too good at his
job. That's his trouble and besides he's not a bumsucker and
that's the kiss of death at the Tech. If you don't lick arses you
get nowhere.'

'You know,' said Betty, 'teaching at that place has done
horrible things to your language.'

'It's done horrible things to my outlook on life, never mind my
language,' said Braintree. 'It's enough to drive a man to drink.'

'It certainly seems to have done that to Henry. His breath
reeked of gin.'

'He'll get over it.'

But Wilt didn't. He woke in the morning with the feeling that
something was missing quite apart from Eva. That bloody doll.
He lay in bed trying to think of some way of retrieving the thing
before the workmen arrived on the site on Monday morning
but apart from pouring a can of petrol down the hole and
lighting it, which seemed on reflection the best way of drawing
attention to the fact that he had stuffed a plastic doll dressed in
his wife's clothes down there, he could think of nothing practical. He would just have to trust to luck.

When the Sunday papers came he got out of bed and went
down to read them over his All-Bran. Then he fed the dog and
mooched about the house in his pyjamas, walked down to the
Ferry Path Inn for lunch, slept in the afternoon and watched
the box all evening. Then he made the bed and got into it and
spent a restless night wondering where Eva was, what she was
doing, and why, since he had occupied so many fruitless hours
speculating on ways of getting rid of her homicidally, he should
be in the least concerned now that she had gone of her own
accord.

'I mean if I didn't want this to happen why did I keep thinking
up ways of killing her,' he thought at two o'clock. 'Sane people
don't go for walks with a Labrador and devise schemes for
murdering their wives when they can just as easily divorce
them.' There was probably some foul psychological reason for
it. Wilt could think of several himself, rather too many in fact to
be able to decide which was the most likely one. In any case a
psychological explanation demanded a degree of self-knowledge
which Wilt, who wasn't at all sure he had a self to know, felt
was denied him. Ten years of Plasterers Two and Exposure
to Barbarism had at least given him the insight to know that
there was an answer for every question and it didn't much
matter what answer you gave so long as you gave it convin-
cingly. In the 14th century they would have said the devil
put such thoughts into his head, now in a post-Freudian world
it had to be a complex or, to be really up-to-date, a chemical
imbalance. In a hundred years they would have come up with
some completely different explanation. With the comforting
thought that the truths of one age were the absurdities of
another and that it didn't much matter what you thought so
long as you did the right thing, and in his view he did, Wilt
finally fell asleep.

At seven he was woken by the alarm clock and by half past
eight had parked his car in the parking lot behind the Tech.
He walked past the building site where the workmen were
already at work. Then he went up to the Staff Room and looked
out of the window. The square of plywood was still in place
covering the hole but the pile-boring machine had been backed
away. They had evidently finished with it.

At five to nine he collected twenty-five copies of *Shane* from the cupboard and took them across to Motor Mechanics Three. *Shane* was the ideal soporific. It would keep the brutes quiet while he sat and watched what happened down below. Room 593 in the Engineering block gave him a grandstand view. Wilt filled in the register and handed out copies of *Shane* and told the class to get on with it. He said it with a good deal more vigour than was usual even for a Monday morning and the class settled down to consider the plight of the homesteaders while Wilt stared out of the window, absorbed in a more immediate drama.

A lorry with a revolving drum filled with liquid concrete had arrived on the site and was backing slowly towards the plywood square. It stopped and there was an agonizing wait while the driver climbed down from the cab and lit a cigarette. Another man, evidently the foreman, came out of a wooden hut and wandered across to the lorry and presently a little group was gathered round the hole. Wilt got up from his desk and went over to the window. Why the hell didn't they get a move on? Finally the driver got back into his cab and two men removed the plywood. The foreman signalled to the driver. The chute for the concrete was swung into position. Another signal. The drum began to tilt. The concrete was coming. Wilt watched as it began to pour down the chute and just at that moment the foreman looked down the hole. So did one of the workmen. The next instant all hell had broken loose. There were frantic signals and shouts from the foreman. Through the window Wilt watched the open mouths and the gesticulations but still the concrete came. Wilt shut his eyes and shuddered. They had found that fucking doll.

Outside on the building site the air was thick with misunderstanding.

'What's that? I'm pouring as fast as I can,' shouted the driver, misconstruing the frenzied signals of the foreman. He pulled the lever still further and the concrete flood increased. The next moment he was aware that he had made some sort of mistake. The foreman was wrenching at the door of the cab and screaming blue murder.

'Stop, for God's sake stop,' he shouted. 'There's a woman down that hole!'

'A what?' said the driver, and switched off the engine.

'A fucking woman and look what you've been and fucking done. I told you to stop. I told you to stop pouring and you went on. You've been and poured twenty tons of liquid concrete on her.'

The driver climbed down from his cab and went round to the chute where the last trickles of cement were still sliding hesitantly into the hole.

'A woman?' he said. 'What? Down that hole? What's she doing down there?'

The foreman stared at him demonically. 'Doing?' he bellowed, 'what do you think she's doing? What would you be doing if you'd just had twenty tons of liquid concrete dumped on top of you? Fucking drowning, that's what.'

The driver scratched his head. 'Well I didn't know she was down there. How was I to know? You should have told me.'

'Told you?' shrieked the foreman. 'I told you. I told you to stop. You weren't listening.'

'I thought you wanted me to pour faster. I couldn't hear what you were saying.'

'Well, every other bugger could,' yelled the foreman. Certainly Wilt in Room 593 could. He stared wild-eyed out of the window as the panic spread. Beside him Motor Mechanics Three had lost all interest in *Shane*. They clustered at the window and watched.

'Are you quite sure?' asked the driver.

'Sure? Course I'm sure,' yelled the foreman. 'Ask Barney.'

The other workman, evidently Barney, nodded. 'She was down there all right. I'll vouch for that. All crumpled up she was. She had one hand up in the air and her legs was . . .'

'Jesus,' said the driver, visibly shaken. 'What the hell are we going to do now?'

It was a question that had been bothering Wilt. Call the police, presumably. The foreman confirmed his opinion. 'Get the cops. Get an ambulance. Get the Fire Brigade and get a pump. For God's sake get a pump.'

'Pump's no good,' said the driver, 'you'll never pump that concrete out of there, not in a month of Sundays. Anyway it wouldn't do any good. She'll be dead by now. Crushed to death.

Wouldn't drown with twenty tons on her. Why didn't she say something?'

'Would it have made any difference if she had?' asked the foreman hoarsely. 'You'd have still gone on pouring.'

'Well, how did she get down there in the first place?' said the driver, to change the subject.

'How the fuck would I know. She must have fallen . . .'

'And pulled that plywood sheet over her, I suppose,' said Barney, who clearly had a practical turn of mind. 'She was bloody murdered.'

'We all know that,' squawked the foreman. 'By Chris here. I told him to stop pouring. You heard me. Everyone for half a mile must have heard me but not Chris. Oh, no, he has to go on—'

'She was murdered before she was put down the hole,' said Barney. 'That wooden cover wouldn't have been there if she had fallen down herself.'

The foreman wiped his face with a handkerchief and looked at the square of plywood. 'There is that to it,' he muttered. 'No one can say we didn't take proper safety precautions. You're right. She must have been murdered. Oh, my God!'

'Sex crime, like as not,' said Barney. 'Raped and strangled her. That or someone's missus. You mark my words. She was all crumpled up and that hand . . . I'll never forget that hand, not if I live to be a hundred.'

The foreman stared at him lividly. He seemed incapable of expressing his feelings. So was Wilt. He went back to his desk and sat with his head in his hands while the class gaped out of the window and tried to catch what was being said. Presently sirens sounded in the distance and grew louder. A police car arrived, four fire engines hurtled into the car park and an ambulance followed. As more and more uniformed men gathered around what had once been a hole in the ground it became apparent that getting the doll down there had been a damned sight easier than getting it out.

'That concrete starts setting in twenty minutes,' the driver explained when a pump was suggested for the umpteenth time. An Inspector of Police and the Fire Chief stared down at the hole.

'Are you sure you saw a woman's body down there?' the Inspector asked. 'You're positive about it?'

'Positive?' squeaked the foreman, 'course I'm positive. You don't think . . . Tell them, Barney. He saw her too.'

Barney told the Inspector even more graphically than before. 'She had this hair see and her hand was reaching up like it was asking for help and there were these fingers . . . I tell you it was horrible. It didn't look natural.'

'No, well, it wouldn't,' said the Inspector sympathetically. 'And you say there was a board on top of the hole when you arrived this morning.'

The foreman gesticulated silently and Barney showed them the board. 'I was standing on it at one time,' he said. 'It was here all right so help me God.'

'The thing is, how are we to get her out?' said the Fire Chief. It was a point that was put to the manager of the construction company when he finally arrived on the scene. 'God alone knows,' he said. 'There's no easy way of getting that concrete out now. We'd have to use drills to get down thirty feet.'

At the end of the hour they were no nearer a solution to the problem. As the Motor Mechanics dragged themselves away from this fascinating situation to go to Technical Drawing, Wilt collected the unread copies of *Shane* and walked across to the Staff Room in a state of shock. The only consolation he could think of was that it would take them at least two or three days to dig down and discover that what had all the appearances of being the body of a murdered woman was in fact an inflatable doll. Or had been once. Wilt rather doubted if it would be inflated now. There had been something horribly intractable about that liquid concrete.

Chapter 8

There was something horribly intractable about the mudbank on which the cabin cruiser had grounded. To add to their troubles the engine had gone wrong. Gaskell said it was a broken con rod.

'Is that serious?' asked Sally.

'It just means we'll have to be towed to a boatyard.'

'By what?'

'By a passing cruiser I guess,' said Gaskell.

Sally looked over the side at the bullrushes.

'Passing?' she said. 'We've been here all night and half the morning and nothing has passed so far and if it did we wouldn't be able to see it for all these fucking bullrushes.'

'I thought bullrushes did something for you.'

'That was yesterday,' snapped Sally, 'today they just mean we're invisible to anyone more than fifty feet away. And now you've screwed the motor. I told you not to rev it like that.'

'So how was I to know it would bust a con rod,' said Gaskell. 'I was just trying to get us off this mudbank. You just tell me how I'm supposed to do it without revving the goddamned motor.'

'You could get out and push.'

Gaskell peered over the side. 'I could get out and drown,' he said.

'So the boat would be lighter,' said Sally. 'We've all got to make sacrifices and you said the tide would float us off.'

'Well I was mistaken. That's fresh water down there and means the tide doesn't reach this far.'

'Now he tells me. First we're in Frogwater Beach . . .'

'Reach,' said Gaskell.

'Frogwater wherever. Then we're in Fen Broad. Now where are we for God's sake?'

'On a mudbank,' said Gaskell.

In the cabin Eva bustled about. There wasn't much space for bustling but what there was she put to good use. She made the bunks and put the bedding away in the lockers underneath and she plumped the cushions and emptied the ashtrays. She swept the floor and polished the table and wiped the windows and dusted the shelves and generally made everything as neat and tidy as it was possible to make it. And all the time her thoughts got untidier and more muddled so that by the time she was finished and every object in sight was in its right place and the whole cabin properly arranged she was quite confused and in two minds about nearly every thing.

The Pringsheims were ever so sophisticated and rich and intellectual and said clever things all the time but they were always quarrelling and getting at one another about something and to be honest they were quite impractical and didn't know the first thing about hygiene. Gaskell went to the lavatory and didn't wash his hands afterwards and goodness only knew when he had last had a shave. And look at the way they had walked out of the house in Rossiter Grove without clearing up after the party and the living-room all over cups and things. Eva had been quite shocked. She would never have left her house in that sort of mess. She had said as much to Sally but Sally had said how nonspontaneous could you get and anyway they were only renting the house for the summer and that it was typical of a male-oriented social system to expect a woman to enter a contractual relationship based upon female domestic servitude. Eva tried to follow her and was left feeling guilty because she couldn't and because it was evidently infra dig to be houseproud and she was.

And then there was what Henry had been doing with that doll. It was so unlike Henry to do anything like that and the more she thought about it the more unlike Henry it became. He must have been drunk but even so . . . without his clothes on ? And where had he found the doll? She had asked Sally and had been horrified to learn that Gaskell was mad about plastic and just adored playing games with Judy and men were like that and so to the only meaningful relationships being between women because women didn't need to prove their virility by any overt act of extrasexual violence did they? By which time Eva was lost in a maze of words she didn't understand but which sounded important and they had had another session of Touch Therapy.

And that was another thing she was in two minds about.

WILT 341

Touch Therapy. Sally had said she was still inhibited and being inhibited was a sign of emotional and sensational immaturity. Eva battled with her mixed feelings about the matter. On the one hand she didn't want to be emotionally and sensationally immature and if the revulsion she felt lying naked in the arms of another woman was anything to go by and in Eva's view the nastier a medicine tasted the more likely it was to do you good, then she was certainly improving her psycho-sexual behaviour pattern by leaps and bounds. On the other hand she wasn't altogether convinced that Touch Therapy was quite nice. It was only by the application of considerable will-power that she overcame her objections to it and even so there was an undertow of doubt about the propriety of being touched quite so sensationally. It was all very puzzling and to cap it all she was on The Pill. Eva had objected very strongly and had pointed out that Henry and she had always wanted babies and she'd never had any but Sally had insisted.

'Eva baby,' she had said, 'with Gaskell one just never knows. Sometimes he goes for months without so much as a twitch and then, bam, he comes all over the place. He's totally undiscriminating.'

'But I thought you said you had this big thing between you,' Eva said.

'Oh, sure. In a blue moon. Scientists sublimate and G just lives for plastic. And we wouldn't want you to go back to Henry with G's genes in your ovum, now would we?'

'Certainly not,' said Eva horrified at the thought and had taken the pill after breakfast before going through to the tiny galley to wash up. It was all so different from Transcendental Meditation and Pottery.

On deck Sally and Gaskell were still wrangling.

'What the hell are you giving brainless boobs?' Gaskell asked.

'TT, Body Contact, Tactile Liberation,' said Sally. 'She's sensually deprived.'

'She's mentally deprived too. I've met some dummies in my time but this one is the dimwittiest. Anyway, I meant those pills she takes at breakfast.'

Sally smiled. 'Oh those,' she said.

'Yes those. You blowing what little mind she's got or something?' said Gaskell. 'We've got enough troubles without Moby Dick taking a trip.'

'Oral contraceptives, baby, just the plain old Pill.'

'Oral contraceptives? What the hell for? I wouldn't touch her with a sterilized stirring rod.'

'Gaskell, honey, you're so naïve. For authenticity, pure authenticity. It makes my relationship with her so much more real, don't you think. Like wearing a rubber on a dildo.'

Gaskell gaped at her. 'Jesus, you don't mean you've . . .'

'Not yet. Long John Silver is still in his bag but one of these days when she's a little more emancipated. . . .' She smiled wistfully over the bullrushes. 'Perhaps it doesn't matter all that much us being stuck here. It gives us time, so much lovely time and you can look at your ducks . . .'

'Waders,' said Gaskell, 'and we're going to run up one hell of a bill at the Marina if we don't get this boat back in time.'

'Bill?' said Sally. 'You're crazy. You don't think we're paying for this hulk?'

'But you hired her from the boatyard. I mean you're not going to tell me you just took the boat,' said Gaskell. 'For Chrissake, that's theft!'

Sally laughed. 'Honestly, G, you're so moral. I mean you're inconsistent. You steal books from the library and chemicals from the lab but when it comes to boats you're all up in the air.'

'Books are different,' said Gaskell hotly.

'Yes,' said Sally, 'books you don't go to jail for. That's what's different. So you want to think I stole the boat, you go on thinking that.'

Gaskell took out a handkerchief and wiped his glasses. 'Are you telling me you didn't?' he asked finally.

'I borrowed it.'

'Borrowed it? Who from?'

'Schei.'

'Scheimacher?'

'That's right. He said we could have it whenever we wanted it so we've got it.'

'Does he know we've got it?'

Sally sighed. 'Look, he's in India isn't he, currying sperm? So what does it matter what he knows? By the time he gets back we'll be in the Land of the Free.'

'Shit,' said Gaskell wearily, 'one of these days you're going to land us in it up to the eyeballs.'

'Gaskell honey, sometimes you bore me with your worrying so.'

'Let me tell you something. You worry me with your god-damned attitude to other people's property.'

'Property is theft.'

'Oh sure. You just get the cops to see it that way when they catch up with you. The fuzz don't go a ball on stealing in this country.'

The fuzz weren't going much of a ball on the well-nourished body of a woman apparently murdered and buried under thirty feet and twenty tons of rapidly setting concrete. Barney had supplied the well-nourished bit. 'She had big breasts too,' he explained, in the seventh version of what he had seen. 'And this hand reaching up—'

'Yes, well we know all about the hand,' said Inspector Flint. 'We've been into all that before but this is the first time you've mentioned breasts.'

'It was the hand that got me,' said Barney. 'I mean you don't think of breasts in a situation like that.'

The Inspector turned to the foreman. 'Did you notice the deceased's breasts?' he enquired. But the foreman just shook his head. He was past speech.

'So we've got a well-nourished woman . . . What age would you say?'

Barney scratched his chin reflectively. 'Not old,' he said finally. 'Definitely not old.'

'In her twenties?'

'Could have been.'

'In her thirties?'

Barney shrugged. There was something he was trying to recall. Something that had seemed odd at the time.

'But definitely not in her forties?'

'No,' said Barney. 'Younger than that.' He said it rather hesitantly.

'You're not being very specific,' said Inspector Flint.

'I can't help it,' said Barney plaintively. 'You see a woman down a dirty great hole with concrete sloshing down on top of her you don't ask her her age.'

'Quite. I realize that but if you could just think. Was there anything peculiar about her . . .'

'Peculiar? Well, there was this hand see . . .'

Inspector Flint sighed. 'I mean anything out of the ordinary about her appearance. Her hair for instance. What colour was it?'

Barney got it. 'I knew there was something,' he said, triumphantly. 'Her hair. It was crooked.'

'Well, it would be, wouldn't it. You don't dump a woman down a thirty-foot pile shaft without mussing up her hair in the process.'

'No, it wasn't like that. It was on sideways and flattened. Like she'd been hit.'

'She probably had been hit. If what you say about the wooden cover being in place is true, she didn't go down there of her own volition. But you still can't give any precise indication of her age?'

'Well,' said Barney, 'bits of her looked young and bits didn't. That's all I know.'

'Which bits?' asked the Inspector, hoping to hell Barney wasn't going to start on that hand again.

'Well, her legs didn't look right for her teats if you see what I mean.' Inspector Flint didn't. 'They were all thin and crumpled-up like.'

'Which were? Her legs or her teats?'

'Her legs, of course,' said Barney. 'I've told you she had these lovely great . . .'

'We're treating this as a case of murder,' Inspector Flint told the Principal ten minutes later. The Principal sat behind his desk and thought despairingly about adverse publicity.

'You're quite convinced it couldn't have been an accident?'

'The evidence to date certainly doesn't suggest accidental death,' said the Inspector, 'however, we'll only be absolutely certain on that point when we manage to reach the body and I'm afraid that is going to take some time.'

'Time?' said the Principal. 'Do you mean to say you can't get her out this morning?'

Inspector Flint shook his head. 'Out of the question, sir,' he said. 'We are considering two methods of reaching the body and they'll both take several days. One is to drill down through the concrete and the other is to sink another shaft next to the original hole and try and get at her from the side.'

'Good Lord,' said the Principal, looking at his calendar, 'but that means you're going to be digging away out there for several days.'

'I'm afraid it can't be helped. Whoever put her down there made a good job of it. Still, we'll try to be as unobtrusive as possible.'

Out of the window the Principal could see four police cars, a fire engine and a big blue van. 'This is really most unfortunate,' he murmured.

'Murder always is,' said the Inspector, and got to his feet. 'It's in the nature of the thing. In the meantime we are sealing off the site and we'd be grateful for your cooperation.'

'Anything you require,' said the Principal, with a sigh.

In the Staff Room the presence of so many uniformed men peering down a pile hole provoked mixed reactions. So did the dozen policemen scouring the building site, stopping now and then to put things carefully into envelopes, but it was the arrival of the dark blue caravan that finally clinched matters.

'That's a Mobile Murder Headquarters,' Peter Fenwick explained. 'Apparently some maniac has buried a woman at the bottom of one of the piles.'

The New Left, who had been clustered in a corner discussing the likely implications of so many paramilitary Fascist pigs, heaved a sigh of unmartyred regret but continued to express doubts.

'No, seriously,' said Fenwick, 'I asked one of them what they were doing. I thought it was some sort of bomb scare.'

Dr Cox, Head of Science, confirmed it. His office looked directly onto the hole. 'It's too dreadful to contemplate,' he murmured, 'every time I look up I think what she must have suffered.'

'What do you suppose they are putting into those envelopes,' asked Dr Mayfield.

'Clues,' said Dr Board, with evident satisfaction. 'Hairs. Bits of skin and bloodstains. The usual trivial detritus of violent crime.'

Dr Cox hurried from the room and Dr Mayfield looked

disgusted. 'How revolting,' he said, 'isn't it possible that there
has been some mistake? I mean why should anyone want to
murder a woman here?'

Dr Board sipped his coffee and looked wistfully at him. 'I
can think of any number of reasons,' he said happily. 'There are
at least a dozen women in my evening class whom I would
cheerfully beat to death and drop down holes. Sylvia Swansbeck
for one.'

'Whoever did it must have known they were going to pour
concrete down today,' said Fenwick. 'It looks like an inside job
to me.'

'One of our less community-conscious students perhaps,'
suggested Dr Board, 'I don't suppose they've had time to check
if any of the staff are missing.'

'You'll probably find it had nothing to do with the Tech,'
said Dr Mayfield. 'Some maniac . . .'

'Come now, give credit where credit is due,' interrupted Dr
Board. 'There was obviously an element of premeditation
involved. Whoever the murderer was . . . is, he planned it pretty
carefully. What puzzles me is why he didn't shovel earth down
on top of the wretched woman so that she couldn't be seen.
Probably intended to but was disturbed before he could get
around to it. One of those little accidents of fate.'

In the corner of the Staff Room Wilt sat and drank his
coffee, conscious that he was the only person not staring out of
the window. What the hell was he to do? The sensible thing
would be to go to the police and explain that he had been trying
to get rid of an inflatable doll that someone had given him. But
would they believe him? If that was all that had happened why
had he dressed it up in a wig and clothes? And why had he left
it inflated? Why hadn't he just thrown the thing away? He was
just rehearsing the pros and cons of the argument when the
Head of Engineering came in and announced that the police
intended boring another hole next to the first one instead of
digging down through the concrete.

'They'll probably be able to see bits of her sticking out the side,'
he explained. 'Apparently she had one arm up in the air and with
all that concrete coming down on top of her there's a chance
that arm will have been pressed against the side of the hole.
Much quicker that way.'

'I must say I can't see the need for haste,' said Dr Board, 'I should have thought she'd be pretty well preserved in all that concrete. Mummified I daresay.'

In his corner Wilt rather doubted it. With twenty tons of concrete on top of her even Judy who had been an extremely resilient doll was hardly likely to have withstood the pressure. She would have burst as sure as eggs were eggs in which case all the police would find was the empty plastic arm of a doll. They would hardly bother to dig a burst plastic doll out.

'And another thing,' continued the Head of Engineering, 'if the arm is sticking out they'll be able to take fingerprints straight away.'

Wilt smiled to himself. That was one thing they weren't going to find on Judy, fingerprints. He finished his coffee more cheerfully and went off to a class of Senior Secretaries. He found them agog with news of the murder.

'Do you think it was a sex killing?' a small blonde girl in the front row asked as Wilt handed out copies of *This Island Now*. He had always found the chapter on the Vicissitudes of Adolescence appealed to Senior Secs. It dealt with sex and violence and was twelve years out of date but then so were the Senior Secretaries. Today there was no need for the book.

'I don't think it was any sort of killing,' said Wilt taking his place behind the desk.

'Oh but it was. They saw a woman's body down there,' the small blonde insisted.

'They thought they saw something down there that looked like a body,' said Wilt, 'that doesn't mean it was one. People's imaginations play tricks with them.'

'The police don't think so,' said a large girl whose father was something in the City. 'They must be certain to go to all that trouble. We had a murder on our golf course and all they found were bits of body cut up and put in the water hazard on the fifteenth. They'd been there six months. Someone sliced a ball on the dogleg twelfth and it went into the pond. They fished out a foot first. It was all puffy and green and . . .' A pale girl from Wilstanton fainted in the third row. By the time Wilt had revived her and taken her to the Sick Room, the class had got onto Crippen, Haigh and Christie. Wilt returned to find them discussing acid baths.

'. . . and all they found were her false teeth and gallstones.'

'You seem to know a lot about murder,' Wilt said to the large girl.

'Daddy plays bridge with the Chief Constable,' she explained. 'He comes to dinner and tells super stories. He says they ought to bring back hanging.'

'I'm sure he does,' said Wilt grimly. It was typical of Senior Secs that they knew Chief Constables who wanted to bring back hanging. It was all mummy and daddy and horses with Senior Secretaries.

'Anyway, hanging doesn't hurt,' said the large girl. 'Sir Frank says a good hangman can have a man out of the condemned cell and onto the trap with a noose around his neck and pull the lever in twenty seconds.'

'Why confine the privilege to men?' asked Wilt bitterly. The class looked at him with reproachful eyes.

'The last woman they hanged was Ruth Ellis,' said the blonde in the front row.

'Anyway with women it's different,' said the large girl.

'Why?' said Wilt inadvisedly.

'Well it's slower.'

'Slower?'

'They had to tie Mrs Thomson to a chair,' volunteered the blonde. 'She behaved disgracefully.'

'I must say I find your judgements peculiar,' said Wilt. 'A woman murdering her husband is doubtless disgraceful. The fact that she puts up a fight when they come to execute her doesn't strike me as disgraceful at all. I find that . . .'

'It's not just that,' interrupted the large girl, who wasn't to be diverted.

'What isn't?' said Wilt.

'It's being slower with women. They have to make them wear waterproof pants.'

Wilt gaped at her in disgust. 'Waterproof what?' he asked without thinking.

'Waterproof pants,' said the large girl.

'Dear God,' said Wilt.

'You see, when they get to the bottom of the rope their insides drop out,' continued the large girl, administering the *coup de grâce*. Wilt stared at her wildly and stumbled from the room.

'What's the matter with him?' said the girl. 'Anyone would think I had said something beastly.'

In the corridor Wilt leant against the wall and felt sick. Those fucking girls were worse than Gasfitters. At least Gasfitters didn't go in for such disgusting anatomical details and besides Senior Secs all came from so-called respectable families. By the time he felt strong enough to face them again the hour had ended. Wilt went back into the classroom sheepishly and collected the books.

'Name of Wilt mean anything to you? Henry Wilt?' asked the Inspector.

'Wilt?' said the Vice-Principal, who had been left to cope with the police while the Principal spent his time more profitably trying to offset the adverse publicity caused by the whole appalling business. 'Well, yes it does. He's one of our Liberal Studies lecturers. Why? Is there . . .'

'If you don't mind, sir, I'd just like a word with him. In private.'

'But Wilt's a most inoffensive man,' said the Vice-Principal, 'I'm sure he couldn't help you at all.'

'Possibly not but all the same . . .'

'You're not suggesting for one moment that Henry Wilt had anything to do with . . .' the Vice-Principal stopped and studied the expression on the Inspector's face. It was ominously neutral.

'I'd rather not go into details,' said Inspector Flint, 'and it's best if we don't jump to conclusions.'

The Vice-Principal picked up the phone. 'Do you want him to come across to that . . . er . . . caravan?' he asked.

Inspector Flint shook his head. 'We like to be as inconspicuous as possible. If I could just have the use of an empty office.'

'There's an office next door. You can use that.'

Wilt was in the canteen having lunch with Peter Braintree when the Vice-Principal's secretary came down with a message.

'Can't it wait?' asked Wilt.

'He said it was most urgent.'

'It's probably your senior lectureship come through at last,' said Braintree brightly. Wilt swallowed the rest of his Scotch egg and got up.

'I doubt that,' he said and went wanly out of the canteen and up the stairs. He had a horrid suspicion that promotion was the last thing the Vice-Principal wanted to see him about.

'Now, sir,' said the Inspector when they were seated in the office, 'my name is Flint, Inspector Flint, CID, and you're Mr Wilt? Mr Henry Wilt?'

'Yes,' said Wilt.

'Now, Mr Wilt, as you may have gathered we are investigating the suspected murder of a woman whose body is believed to have been deposited at the bottom of one of the foundation holes for the new building. I daresay you know about it.' Wilt nodded. 'And naturally we are interested in anything that might be of assistance. I wonder if you would mind having a look at these notes.'

He handed Wilt a piece of paper. It was headed 'Notes on Violence and the Break-Up of Family Life', and underneath were a number of sub-headings.

1. Increasing use of violence in public life to attain political ends. A) Bombings. B) Hijacking. C) Kidnapping. D) Assassination.

2. Ineffectuality of Police Methods in combating Violence.
    A) Negative approach. Police able only to react to crime after it has taken place.
    B) Use of violence by police themselves.
    C) Low level of intelligence of average policeman.
    D) Increasing use of sophisticated methods such as diversionary tactics by criminals.

3. Influence of media. TV brings crime techniques into the home.

There was more. Much more. Wilt looked down the list with a sense of doom.

'You recognize the handwriting?' asked the Inspector.

'I do,' said Wilt, adopting rather prematurely the elliptical language of the witness box.

'You admit that you wrote those notes?' The Inspector reached out a hand and took the notes back.

'Yes.'

'They express your opinion of police methods?'

Wilt pulled himself together. 'They were jottings I was making for a lecture to Sandwich-Course Trainee Firemen,' he explained. 'They were simply rough ideas. They need amplifying of course . . .'

'But you don't deny you wrote them?'

'Of course I don't. I've just said I did, haven't I?'

The Inspector nodded and picked up a book. 'And this is yours too?'

Wilt looked at *Bleak House*. 'It says so, doesn't it?'

Inspector Flint opened the cover. 'So it does,' he said with a show of astonishment, 'so it does.'

Wilt stared at him. There was no point in maintaining the pretence any longer. The best thing to do was to get it over quickly. They had found that bloody book in the basket of the bicycle and the notes must have fallen out of his pocket on the building site.

'Look, Inspector,' he said, 'I can explain everything. It's really quite simple. I did go into that building site . . .'

The Inspector stood up. 'Mr Wilt, if you're prepared to make a statement I think I should warn you . . .'

Wilt went down to the Murder Headquarters and made a statement in the presence of a police stenographer. His progress to the blue caravan and his failure to come out again were noted with interest by members of the staff teaching in the Science block, by students in the canteen and by twenty-five fellow lecturers gaping through the windows of the Staff Room.

Chapter 9

'Goddamn the thing,' said Gaskell as he knelt greasily beside the engine of the cruiser, 'you'd think that even in this pre-technological monarchy they'd fit a decent motor. This contraption must have been made for the Ark.'

'Ark Ark the Lark,' said Sally, 'and cut the crowned heads foolery. Eva's a reginaphile.'

'A what?'

'Reginaphile. Monarchist. Get it. She's the Queen's Bee so don't be anti-British. We don't want her to stop working as well as the motor. Maybe it isn't the con rod.'

'If I could only get the head off I could tell,' said Gaskell.

'And what good would that do? Buy you another?' said Sally and went into the cabin where Eva was wondering what they were going to have for supper. 'Tarbaby is still tinkering with the motor. He says it's the con rod.'

'Con rod?' said Eva.

'Only connect, baby, only connect.'

'With what?'

'The thigh bone's connected to the knee bone. The con rod's connected to the piston and as everyone knows pistons are penis symbols. The mechanized male's substitute for sex. The Outboard Motor Syndrome. Only this happens to be inboard like his balls never dropped. Honestly, Gaskell is so regressive.'

'I'm sure I don't know,' said Eva.

Sally lay back on the bunk and lit a cigar. 'That's what I love about you, Eva. You don't know. Ignorance is blissful, baby. I lost mine when I was fourteen.'

Eva shook her head. 'Men,' she said disapprovingly.

'He was old enough to be my grandfather,' said Sally. 'He *was* my grandfather.'

'Oh no. How awful.'

'Not really,' said Sally laughing, 'he was an artist. With a beard. And the smell of paint on his smock and there was this studio and he wanted to paint me in the nude. I was so pure in those days. He made me lie on this couch and he arranged my legs. He was always arranging my legs and then standing back to look at me and painting. And then one day when I was lying there he came over and bent my legs back and kissed me and then he was on top of me and his smock was up and . . .'

Eva sat and listened, fascinated. She could visualize it all so clearly, even the smell of the paint in the studio and the brushes. Sally had had such an exciting life, so full of incident and so romantic in a dreadful sort of way. Eva tried to remember what she had been like at fourteen and not even going out with boys and there was Sally lying on a couch with a famous artist in his studio.

'But he raped you,' she said finally. 'Why didn't you tell the police?'

'The police? You don't understand. I was at this terribly exclusive school. They would have sent me home. It was progressive and all that but I shouldn't have been out being painted by this artist and my parents would never have forgiven me. They were so strict.' Sally sighed, overcome by the rigours of her wholly fictitious childhood. 'And now you can see why I'm so afraid of being hurt by men. When you've been raped you know what penile aggression means.'

'I suppose you do,' said Eva, in some doubt as to what penile aggression was.

'You see the world differently too. Like G says, nothing's good and nothing's bad. It just is.'

'I went to a lecture on Buddhism once,' said Eva, 'and that's what Mr Podgett said. He said—'

'Zen's all wrong. Like you just sit around waiting. That's passive. You've got to make things happen. You sit around waiting long enough, you're dead. Someone's trampled all over you. You've got to see things happen your way and no one else's.'

'That doesn't sound very sociable,' said Eva. 'I mean if we all did just what we wanted all the time it wouldn't be very nice for other people.'

'Other people are hell,' said Sally. 'That's Sartre and he should know. You do what you want is good and no moral kickback. Like G says, rats are the paradigm. You think rats go around thinking what's good for other people?'

'Well no, I don't suppose they do,' said Eva.

'Right. Rats aren't ethical. No way. They just do. They don't get screwed up thinking.'

'Do you think rats can think?' asked Eva, now thoroughly engaged in the problems of rodent psychology.

'Of course they can't. Rats just are. No *Schadenfreude* with rats.'

'What's *Schadenfreude*?'

'Second cousin to *Weltschmerz*,' said Sally, stubbing her cigar out in the ashtray. 'So we can all do what we want whenever we want to. That's the message. It's only people like G who've got the know bug who get balled up.'

'No bug?' said Eva.

'They've got to know how everything works. Scientists. Lawrence was right. It's all head and no body with G.'

'Henry's a bit like that,' said Eva. 'He's always reading or talking about books. I've told him he doesn't know what the real world is like.'

In the Mobile Murder Headquarters Wilt was learning. He sat opposite Inspector Flint whose face was registering increasing incredulity.

'Now, we'll just go over that again,' said the Inspector. 'You say that what those men saw down that hole was in actual fact an inflatable plastic doll with a vagina.'

'The vagina is incidental,' said Wilt, calling forth reserves of inconsequence.

'That's as maybe,' said the Inspector. 'Most dolls don't have them but . . all right, we'll let that pass. The point I'm trying to get at is that you're quite positive there isn't a real live human being down there.'

'Positive,' said Wilt, 'and if there were it is doubtful if it would still be alive now.'

The Inspector studied him unpleasantly. 'I don't need you to point that out to me,' he said. 'If there was the faintest possibility of whatever it is down there being alive I wouldn't be sitting here, would I?'

'No,' said Wilt.

'Right. So now we come to the next point. How is it that what those men saw, they say a woman and you say a doll . . . that this thing was wearing clothes, had hair and even more remarkably had its head bashed in and one hand stretched up in the air?'

'That was the way it fell,' said Wilt. 'I suppose the arm got caught up on the side and lifted up.'

'And its head was bashed in?'

'Well, I did drop a lump of mud on it,' Wilt admitted, 'that would account for that.'

'You dropped a lump of mud on its head?'

'That's what I said,' Wilt agreed.

'I know that's what you said. What I want to know is why you felt obliged to drop a lump of mud on the head of an inflatable doll that had, as far as I can gather, never done you any harm.'

Wilt hesitated. That damned doll had done him a great deal of harm one way and another but this didn't seem an opportune moment to go into that. 'I don't know really,' he said finally, 'I just thought it might help.'

'Help what?'

'Help . . . I don't know. I just did it, that's all. I was drunk at the time.'

'All right, we'll come back to that in a minute. There's still one question you haven't answered. If it was a doll, why was it wearing clothes?'

Wilt looked desperately round the caravan and met the eyes of the police stenographer. There was a look in them that didn't inspire confidence. Talk about lack of suspension of disbelief.

'You're not going to believe this,' Wilt said. The Inspector looked at him and lit a cigarette.

'Well?'

'As a matter of fact I had dressed it up,' Wilt said, squirming with embarrassment.

'You had dressed it up?'

'Yes,' said Wilt.

'And may one enquire what purpose you had in mind when you dressed it up?'

'I don't know exactly.'

The Inspector sighed significantly. 'Right. We go back to the beginning. We have a doll with a vagina which you dress up and bring down here in the dead of night and deposit at the bottom of a thirty-foot hole and drop lumps of mud on its head. Is that what you're saying?'

'Yes,' said Wilt.

'You wouldn't prefer to save everyone concerned a lot of time and bother by admitting here and now that what is at present resting, hopefully at peace, under twenty tons of concrete at the bottom of that pile hole is the body of a murdered woman?'

'No,' said Wilt, 'I most definitely wouldn't.'

Inspector Flint sighed again. 'You know, we're going to get to the bottom of this thing,' he said. 'It may take time and it may take expense and God knows it's taking patience but when we do get down there—'

'You're going to find an inflatable doll,' said Wilt.

'With a vagina?'

'With a vagina.'

In the Staff Room Peter Braintree staunchly defended Wilt's innocence. 'I tell you I've known Henry well for the past seven years and whatever has happened he had nothing to do with it.'

Mr Morris, the Head of Liberal Studies, looked out of the window sceptically. 'They've had him in there since ten past two. That's four hours,' he said. 'They wouldn't do that unless they thought he had some connection with the dead woman.'

'They can think what they like. I know Henry and even if the poor sod wanted to he's incapable of murdering anyone.'

'He did punch that printer on Tuesday. That shows he's capable of irrational violence.'

'Wrong again. The printer punched him,' said Braintree.

'Only after Wilt had called him a snivelling fucking moron,' Mr Morris pointed out. 'Anyone who goes into Printers Three and calls one of them that needs his head examined. They killed poor old Pinkerton, you know. He gassed himself in his car.'

'They had a damned good try at killing old Henry come to that.'

'Of course, that blow might have affected his brain,' said Mr Morris, with morose satisfaction. 'Concussion can do funny things to a man's character. Change him overnight from a nice quiet inoffensive little fellow like Wilt into a homicidal maniac who suddenly goes berserk. Stranger things have happened.'

'I daresay Henry would be the first to agree with you,' said Braintree. 'It can't be very pleasant sitting in that caravan being questioned by detectives. I wonder what they're doing to him.'

'Just asking questions. Things like "How have you been getting on with your wife?" and "Can you account for your movements on Saturday night?" They start off gently and then work up to the heavy stuff later on.'

Peter Braintree sat in silent horror. Eva. He'd forgotten all about her and as for Saturday night he knew exactly what Henry had said he had been doing before he turned up on the doorstep covered with mud and looking like death . . .

'All I'm saying,' said Mr Morris, 'is that it seems very strange to me that they find a dead body at the bottom of a shaft filled with concrete and the next thing you know they've got Wilt in that Murder HQ for questioning. Very strange indeed. I wouldn't like to be in his shoes.' He got up and left the room and Peter Braintree sat on wondering if there was anything he should do like phone a lawyer and ask him to come round and speak to Henry. It seemed a bit premature and presumably Henry could ask to see a lawyer himself if he wanted one.

Inspector Flint lit another cigarette with an air of insouciant menace. 'How well do you get on with your wife?' he asked.

Wilt hesitated. 'Well enough,' he said.

'Just well enough? No more than that?'

'We get along just fine,' said Wilt, conscious that he had made an error.

'I see. And I suppose she can substantiate your story about this inflatable doll.'

'Substantiate it?'

'The fact that you made a habit of dressing it up and carrying on with it.'

'I didn't make a habit of anything of the sort,' said Wilt indignantly.

'I'm only asking. You were the one who first raised the fact that it had a vagina. I didn't. You volunteered the information and naturally I assumed . . .'

'What did you assume?' said Wilt. 'You've got no right . . .'

'Mr Wilt,' said the Inspector, 'put yourself in my position. I am investigating a case of suspected murder and a man comes along and tells me that what two eye-witnesses describe as the body of a well-nourished woman in her early thirties . . .'

'In her early thirties? Dolls don't have ages. If that bloody doll was more than six months old. . . .'

'Please, Mr Wilt, if you'll just let me continue. As I was saying we have a prima facie case of murder and you admit yourself to having put a doll with a vagina down that hole. Now if you were in my shoes what sort of inference would you draw from that?'

Wilt tried to think of some totally innocent interpretation and couldn't.

'Wouldn't you be the first to agree that it does look a bit peculiar?'

Wilt nodded. It looked horribly peculiar.

'Right,' continued the Inspector. 'Now if we put the nicest possible interpretation on your actions and particularly on your emphasis that this doll had a vagina—'

'I didn't emphasize it. I only mentioned the damned thing to indicate that it was extremely lifelike. I wasn't suggesting I made a habit of . . .' He stopped and looked miserably at the floor.

'Go on, Mr Wilt, don't stop now. It often helps to talk.'

Wilt stared at him frantically. Talking to Inspector Flint wasn't helping him one iota. 'If you're implying that my sex life was confined to copulating with an inflatable fucking doll dressed in my wife's clothes. . . .'

'Hold it there,' said the Inspector, stubbing out his cigarette significantly. 'Ah, so we've taken another step forward. You admit then that whatever is down that hole is dressed in your wife's clothes? Yes or no.'

'Yes,' said Wilt miserably.

Inspector Flint stood up. 'I think it's about time we all went and had a little chat with Mrs Wilt,' he said, 'I want to hear what she has to say about your funny little habits.'

'I'm afraid that's going to be a little difficult,' said Wilt.

'Difficult?'

'Well you see the thing is she's gone away.'

'Gone away?' said the Inspector. 'Did I hear you say that Mrs Wilt has gone away?'

'Yes.'

'And where has Mrs Wilt gone to?'

'That's the trouble. I don't know.'

'You don't know?'

'No, I honestly don't,' said Wilt.

'She didn't tell you where she was going?'

'No. She just wasn't there when I got home.'

'She didn't leave a note or anything like that?'

'Yes,' said Wilt, 'as a matter of fact she did.'

'Right, well let's just go up to your house and have a look at that note.'

'I'm afraid that's not possible,' said Wilt. 'I got rid of it.'

'You got rid of it?' said the Inspector. 'You got rid of it? How?'

Wilt looked pathetically across at the police stenographer. 'To tell the truth I wiped my bottom with it,' he said.

Inspector Flint gazed at him demonically. 'You did what?'

'Well, there was no toilet paper in the lavatory so I . . .' he stopped. The Inspector was lighting yet another cigarette. His hands were shaking and he had a distant look in his eyes that suggested he had just peered over some appalling abyss. 'Mr Wilt,' he said when he had managed to compose himself, 'I trust I am a reasonably tolerant man, a patient man and a humane man, but if you seriously expect me to believe one word of your utterly preposterous story you must be insane. First you tell me you put a doll down that hole. Then you admit that it was dressed in your wife's clothes. Now you say that she went away without telling you where she was going and finally to cap it all you have the temerity to sit there and tell me that you wiped your arse with the one piece of solid evidence that could substantiate your statement.'

'But I did,' said Wilt.

'Balls,' shouted the Inspector. 'You and I both know where Mrs Wilt has gone and there's no use pretending we don't. She's down at the bottom of that fucking hole and you put her there.'

'Are you arresting me?' Wilt asked as they walked in a tight group across the road to the police car.

'No,' said Inspector Flint, 'you're just helping the police with their enquiries. It will be on the news tonight.'

'My dear Braintree, of course we'll do all we can,' said the Vice-Principal. 'Wilt has always been a loyal member of staff and there has obviously been some dreadful mistake. I'm sure you needn't worry. The whole thing will right itself before long.'

'I hope you're right,' said Braintree, 'but there are complicating factors. For one thing there's Eva . . .'

'Eva? Mrs Wilt? You're not suggesting . . .'

'I'm not suggesting anything. All I'm saying is . . . well, she's missing from home. She walked out on Henry last Friday.'

'Mrs Wilt walked . . . well I hardly knew her, except by reputation of course. Wasn't she the woman who broke Mr Lockyer's collar-bone during a part-time Evening Class in Judo some years back?'

'That was Eva,' said Braintree.

'She hardly sounds the sort of woman who would allow Wilt to put her down . . .'

'She isn't,' said Braintree hastily. 'If anyone was liable to be murdered in the Wilt household it was Henry. I think the police should be informed of that.'

They were interrupted by the Principal who came in with a copy of the evening paper. 'You've seen this I suppose,' he said, waving it distraughtly. 'It's absolutely appalling.' He put the paper down on the desk and indicated the headlines. MURDERED WOMAN BURIED IN CONCRETE AT TECH. LECTURER HELPING POLICE.

'Oh dear,' said the Vice-Principal. 'Oh dear. How very unfortunate. It couldn't have come at a worse moment.'

'It shouldn't have come at all,' snapped the Principal. 'And that's not all. I've already had half a dozen phone calls from parents wanting to know if we make a habit of employing murderers on the full-time staff. Who is this fellow Wilt anyway?'

'He's in Liberal Studies,' said the Vice-Principal. 'He's been with us ten years.'

'Liberal Studies. I might have guessed it. If they're not poets manqué they're Maoists or . . . I don't know where the hell Morris gets them from. And now we've got a blasted murderer. God knows what I'm going to tell the Education Committee tonight. They've called an emergency meeting for eight.'

'I must say I resent Wilt being called a murderer,' said

Braintree loyally. 'There is nothing to suggest that he has murdered anyone.'

The Principal studied him for a moment and then looked back at the headlines. 'Mr Braintree, when someone is helping the police with their enquiries into a murder it may not be proven that he is a murderer but the suggestion is there.'

'This certainly isn't going to help us to get the new CNAA degree off the ground,' intervened the Vice-Principal tactfully. 'We've got a visit from the Inspection Committee scheduled for Friday.'

'From what the police tell me it isn't going to help get the new Administration block off the ground either,' said the Principal. 'They say it's going to take at least three days to bore down to the bottom of that pile and then they'll have to drill through the concrete to get the body out. That means they'll have to put a new pile down and we're already well behind schedule and our building budget has been halved. Why on earth couldn't he have chosen somewhere else to dispose of his damned wife?'

'I don't think . . .' Braintree began.

'I don't care what you think,' said the Principal, 'I'm merely telling you what the police think.'

Braintree left them still wrangling and trying to figure out ways and means of counteracting the adverse publicity the case had already brought the Tech. He went down to the Liberal Studies office and found Mr Morris in a state of despair. He was trying to arrange stand-in lecturers for all Wilt's classes.

'But he'll probably be back in the morning,' Braintree said.

'Like hell he will,' said Mr Morris 'When they take them in like that they keep them. Mark my words. The police may make mistakes, I'm not saying they don't, but when they act this swiftly they're onto a sure thing. Mind you, I always thought Wilt was a bit odd.'

'Odd? I've just come from the VP's office. You want to hear what the Principal's got to say about Liberal Studies staff.'

'Christ,' said Mr Morris, 'don't tell me.'

'Anyway what's so odd about Henry?'

'Too meek and mild for my liking. Look at the way he accepted remaining a Lecturer Grade Two all these years.'

'That was hardly his fault.'

'Of course it was his fault. All he had to do was threaten to resign and go somewhere else and he'd have got promotion like a shot. That's the only way to get on in this place. Make your presence felt.'

'He seems to have done that now,' said Braintree. 'The Principal is already blaming him for throwing the building programme off schedule and if we don't get the Joint Honours degree past the CNAA, Henry's going to be made the scapegoat. It's too bad. Eva should have had more sense than to walk out on him like that.'

Mr Morris took a more sombre view. 'She'd have shown a damned sight more sense if she'd walked out on him before the sod took it into his head to beat her to death and dump her down that bloody shaft. Now who the hell can I get to take Gasfitters One tomorrow?'

Chapter 10

At 34 Parkview Avenue Wilt sat in the kitchen with Clem while the detectives ransacked the house. 'You're not going to find anything incriminating here,' he told Inspector Flint.

'Never you mind what we're going to find. We're just having a look.'

He sent one detective upstairs to examine Mrs Wilt's clothes or what remained of them.

'If she went away she'd have taken half her wardrobe,' he said. 'I know women. On the other hand if she's pushing up twenty tons of premix she wouldn't need more than what she's got on.'

Eva's wardrobe was found to be well stocked. Even Wilt had to admit that she hadn't taken much with her.

'What was she wearing when you last saw her?' the Inspector asked.

'Lemon loungers,' said Wilt.

'Lemon what?'

'Pyjamas,' said Wilt, adding to the list of incriminating evidence against him. The Inspector made a note of the fact in his pocketbook.

'In bed, was she?'

'No,' said Wilt. 'Round at the Pringsheims.'

'The Pringsheims? And who might they be?'

'The Americans I told you about who live in Rossiter Grove.'

'You haven't mentioned any Americans to me,' said the Inspector.

'I'm sorry. I thought I had. I'm getting muddled. She went away with them.'

'Oh did she? And I suppose we'll find they're missing too?'

'Almost certainly,' said Wilt. 'I mean if she was going away with them they must have gone too and if she isn't with them I can't imagine where she has got to.'

'I can,' said the Inspector looking with distasteful interest at a stain on a sheet one of the detectives had found in the dirty linen basket. By the time they left the house the incriminating evidence consisted of the sheet, an old dressing-gown cord that had found its way mysteriously into the attic, a chopper that Wilt had once used to open a tin of red lead, and a hypodermic syringe which Eva had got from the vet for watering cacti very precisely during her Indoor Plant phase. There was also a bottle of tablets with no label on it.

'How the hell would I know what they are?' Wilt asked when confronted with the bottle. 'Probably aspirins. And anyway it's full.'

'Put it with the other exhibits,' said the Inspector. Wilt looked at the box.

'For God's sake, what do you think I did with her? Poisoned her, strangled her, hacked her to bits with a chopper and injected her with Biofood?'

'What's Biofood?' asked Inspector Flint with sudden interest.

'It's stuff you feed plants with,' said Wilt. 'The bottle's on the windowsill.'

The Inspector added the bottle of Biofood to the box. 'We know what you did with her, Mr Wilt,' he said. 'It's how that interests us now.'

They went out to the police car and drove round to the Pringsheims' house in Rossiter Grove. 'You just sit in the car with the constable here while I go and see if they're in,' said Inspector Flint and went to the front door. Wilt sat and watched while he rang the bell. He rang again. He hammered on the doorknocker and finally he walked round through the gate marked Tradesman's Entrance to the kitchen door. A minute later he was back and fumbling with the car radio.

'You've hit the nail on the head all right, Wilt,' he snapped. 'They've gone away. The place is a bloody shambles. Looks like they've had an orgy. Take him out.'

The two detectives bundled Wilt, no longer Mr Wilt but plain Wilt and conscious of the fact, out of the car while the Inspector called Fenland Constabulary and spoke with sinister urgency about warrants and sending something that sounded like the D brigade up. Wilt stood in the driveway of 12 Rossiter Grove and wondered what the hell was happening to him. The order of things on which he had come to depend was disintegrating around him.

'We're going in the back way,' said the Inspector. 'This doesn't look good.'

They went down the path to the kitchen door and round to the back garden. Wilt could see what the Inspector had meant by a shambles. The garden didn't look at all good. Paper plates lay about the lawn or, blown by the wind, had wheeled across the garden into honeysuckle or climbing rose while paper cups, some squashed and some still filled with Pringsheim punch and rainwater, littered the ground. But it was the beefburgers that gave the place its air of macabre filth. They were all over the lawn, stained with coleslaw so that Wilt was put in mind of Clem.

'The dog returns to his vomit,' said Inspector Flint evidently reading his mind. They crossed the terrace to the lounge windows and peered through. If the garden was bad the interior was awful.

'Smash a pane in the kitchen window and let us in,' said the Inspector to the taller of the two detectives. A moment later the lounge window slid back and they went inside.

'No need for forcible entry,' said the detective. 'The back door was unlocked and so was this window. They must have cleared out in a hell of a hurry.'

The Inspector looked round the room and wrinkled his nose. The smell of stale pot, sour punch and candle smoke still hung heavily in the house.

'If they went away,' he said ominously and glanced at Wilt.

'They must have gone away,' said Wilt who felt called upon to make some comment on the scene, 'no one would live in all this mess for a whole weekend without . . .'

'Live? You did say "live" didn't you?' said Flint stepping on a piece of burnt beefburger.

'What I meant . . .'

'Never mind what you meant, Wilt. Let's see what's happened here.'

They went into the kitchen where the same chaos reigned and then into another room. Everywhere it was the same. Dead cigarette ends doused in cups of coffee or ground out on the carpet. Pieces of broken record behind the sofa marked the end of Beethoven's Fifth. Cushions lay crumpled against the wall. Burnt-out candles hung limply post-coital from bottles. To add a final touch to the squalor someone had drawn a portrait of Princess Anne on the wall with a red felt pen. She was surrounded by helmeted policemen and underneath was written. THE FUZZ AROUND OUR ANNY THE ROYAL FAMLYS FANNY THE PRICK IS DEAD LONG LIVE THE CUNT. Sentiments that were doubtless perfectly acceptable in Women's Lib circles but were hardly calculated to establish the Pringsheims very highly in Inspector Flint's regard.

'You've got some nice friends, Wilt,' he said.

'No friends of mine,' said Wilt, with feeling. 'The sods can't even spell.'

They went upstairs and looked in the big bedroom. The bed was unmade, clothes, mostly underclothes, were all over the floor or hung out of drawers and an unstoppered bottle of Joy lay on its side on the dressing-table. The room stank of perfume.

'Jesus wept,' said the Inspector, eyeing a pair of jockstraps belligerently. 'All that's missing is some blood.'

They found it in the bathroom. Dr Scheimacher's cut hand had rained bloodstains in the bath and splattered the tiles with dark blotches. The bathroom door with its broken frame was hanging from the bottom hinge and there were spots of blood on the paintwork.

'I knew it,' said the Inspector, studying their message and that written in lipstick on the mirror above the washbasin. Wilt looked at it too. It seemed unduly personal.

WHERE WILT FAGGED AND EVA RAN WHO WAS THEN THE MALE CHAUVINIST PIG?

'Charming,' said Inspector Flint. He turned to look at Wilt whose face was now the colour of the tiles. 'I don't suppose you'd know anything about that. Not your handiwork?'

'Certainly not,' said Wilt.

'Nor this?' said the Inspector, pointing to the bloodstains in the bath. Wilt shook his head. 'And I suppose this has nothing to do with you either?' He indicated a diaphragm that had been nailed to the wall above the lavatory seat. WHERE THE B SUCKS THERE SUCK I UNDERNEATH A DUTCH CAP NICE AND DRY. Wilt stared at the thing in utter disgust.

'I don't know what to say,' he muttered. 'It's all so awful.'

'You can say that again,' the Inspector agreed, and turned to more practical matters. 'Well, she didn't die in here.'

'How can you tell?' asked the younger of the two detectives.
'Not enough blood.' The Inspector looked round uncertainly. 'On the other hand one hard bash . . .' They followed the bloodstains down the passage to the room where Wilt had been dollknotted.

'For God's sake don't touch anything,' said the Inspector, easing the door open with his sleeve, 'the fingerprint boys are going to have a field day here.' He looked inside at the toys.

'I suppose you butchered the children too,' he said grimly.

'Children?' said Wilt, 'I didn't know they had any.'

'Well if you didn't,' said the Inspector, who was a family man, 'the poor little buggers have got something to be thankful for. Not much by the look of things but something.'

Wilt poked his head round the door and looked at the Teddy Bear and the rocking horse. 'Those are Gaskell's,' he said, 'he likes to play with them.'

'I thought you said you didn't know they had any children?'

'They haven't. Gaskell is Dr Pringsheim. He's a biochemist and a case of arrested development according to his wife.' The Inspector studied him thoughtfully. The question of arrest had become one that needed careful consideration.

'I don't suppose you're prepared to make a full confession now?' he asked without much hope.

'No I am not,' said Wilt.

'I didn't think you would be, Wilt,' said the Inspector. 'All right, take him down to the Station. I'll be along later.'

The detectives took Wilt by the arms. It was the last straw.

'Leave me alone,' he yelled. 'You've got no right to do this. You've got—'

'Wilt,' shouted Inspector Flint, 'I'm going to give you one last chance. If you don't go quietly I'm going to charge you here and now with the murder of your wife.'

Wilt went quietly. There was nothing else to do.

'The screw?' said Sally. 'But you said it was the con rod.'

'So I was wrong,' said Gaskell. 'She cranks over.'

'It, G, it. It cranks over.'

'OK, It cranks over so it can't be a con rod. It could be something got tangled with the propshaft.'

'Like what?'

WILT

'Like weeds.'

'Why don't you go down and have a look yourself?'

'With these glasses?' said Gaskell, 'I wouldn't be able to see anything.'

'You know I can't swim,' said Sally. 'I have this leg.'

'I can swim,' said Eva.

'We'll tie a rope round you. That way you won't drown,' said Gaskell, 'all you've got to do is go under and feel if there's anything down there.'

'We know what's down there,' said Sally. 'Mud is.'

'Round the propshaft,' said Gaskell. 'Then if there is you can take it off.'

Eva went into the cabin and put on the bikini.

'Honestly, Gaskell, sometimes I think you're doing this on purpose. First it's the con rod and now it's the screw.'

'Well, we've got to try everything. We can't just sit here,' said Gaskell, 'I'm supposed to be back in the lab tomorrow.'

'You should have thought of that before,' said Sally. 'Now all we need is a goddam Albatross.'

'If you ask me we've got one,' said Gaskell, as Eva came out of the cabin and put on a bathing cap.

'Now where's the rope?' she asked. Gaskell looked in a locker and found some. He tied it round her waist and Eva clambered over the side into the water.

'It's ever so cold,' she giggled.

'That's because of the Gulf stream,' said Gaskell, 'it doesn't come this far round.'

Eva swam out and put her feet down.

'It's terribly shallow and full of mud.'

She waded round hanging onto the rope and groped under the stern of the cruiser.

'I can't feel anything,' she called.

'It will be further under,' said Gaskell, peering down at her. Eva put her head under water and felt the rudder.

'That's the rudder,' said Gaskell.

'Of course it is,' said Eva, 'I know that, silly. I'm not stupid.'

She disappeared under the boat. This time she found the propeller but there was nothing wrapped round it.

'It's just muddy, that's all,' she said, when she resurfaced. 'There's mud all along the bottom.'

'Well there would be wouldn't there,' said Gaskell. Eva waded round to the side. 'We just happen to be stuck on a mudbank.'

Eva went down again but the propshaft was clear too. 'I told you so,' said Sally, as they hauled Eva back on board. 'You just made her do it so you could see her in her plastic kini all covered with mud. Come, Botticelli baby, let Sally wash you off.'

'Oh Jesus,' said Gaskell. 'Penis arising from the waves.' He went back to the engine and looked at it uncertainly. Perhaps there was a blockage in the fuel line. It didn't seem very likely but he had to try something. They couldn't stay stuck on the mudbank forever.

On the foredeck Sally was sponging Eva down.

'Now the bottom half, darling,' she said untying the string.

'Oh, Sally. No, Sally.'

'Labia babia.'

'Oh, Sally, you are awful.'

Gaskell struggled with the adjustable wrench. All this Touch Therapy was getting to him. And the plastic.

At the County Hall the Principal was doing his best to pacify the members of the Education Committee who were demanding a full Enquiry into the recruitment policy of the Liberal Studies Department.

'Let me explain,' he said patiently, looking round at the Committee, which was a nice balance of business interests and social commitment. 'The 1944 Education Act laid down that all apprentices should be released from their places of employment to attend Day Release Classes at Technical Colleges . . .'

'We know all that,' said a building contractor, 'and we all know it's a bloody waste of time and public money. This country would be a sight better off if they were left to get on with their jobs.'

'The courses they attend,' continued the Principal before anyone with a social conscience could intervene, 'are craft-oriented with the exception of one hour, one obligatory hour of Liberal Studies. Now the difficulty with Liberal Studies is that no one knows what it means.'

'Liberal Studies means,' said Mrs Chatterway, who prided

herself on being an advocate of progressive education, in which role she had made a substantial contribution to the illiteracy rate in several previously good primary schools, 'providing socially deprived adolescents with a firm grounding in liberal attitudes and culturally extending topics . . .'

'It means teaching them to read and write,' said a company director. 'It's no good having workers who can't read instructions.'

'It means whatever anyone chooses it to mean,' said the Principal hastily. 'Now if you are faced with the problem of having to find lecturers who are prepared to spend their lives going into classrooms filled with Gasfitters or Plasterers or Printers who see no good reason for being there, and keeping them occupied with a subject that does not, strictly speaking, exist, you cannot afford to pick and choose the sort of staff you employ. That is the crux of the problem.'

The Committee looked at him doubtfully.

'Am I to understand that you are suggesting that Liberal Studies teachers are not devoted and truly creative individuals imbued with a strong sense of vocation?' asked Mrs Chatterway belligerently.

'No,' said the Principal, 'I am not saying that at all. I am merely trying to make the point that Liberal Studies lecturers are not as other men are. They either start out odd or they end up odd. It's in the nature of their occupation.'

'But they are all highly qualified,' said Mrs Chatterway, 'they all have degrees.'

'Quite. As you say they all hold degrees. They are all qualified teachers but the stresses to which they are subject leave their mark. Let me put it this way. If you were to take a heart transplant surgeon and ask him to spend his working life docking dogs' tails you would hardly expect him to emerge unscathed after ten years' work. The analogy is exact, believe me, exact.'

'Well, all I can say,' protested the building contractor, 'is that not all Liberal Studies lecturers end up burying their murdered wives at the bottom of pile shafts.'

'And all I can say,' said the Principal, 'is that I am extremely surprised more don't.'

The meeting broke up undecided.

Chapter 11

As dawn broke glaucously over East Anglia Wilt sat in the Interview Room at the central Police Station isolated from the natural world and in a wholly artificial environment that included a table, four chairs, a detective sergeant and a fluorescent light on the ceiling that buzzed slightly. There were no windows, just pale green walls and a door through which people came and went occasionally and Wilt went twice to relieve himself in the company of a constable. Inspector Flint had gone to bed at midnight and his place had been taken by Detective Sergeant Yates who had started again at the beginning.

'What beginning?' said Wilt.

'At the very beginning.'

'God made heaven and earth and all . . .'

'Forget the wisecracks,' said Sergeant Yates.

'Now that,' said Wilt, appreciatively, 'is a more orthodox use of wise.'

'What is?'

'Wisecrack. It's slang but it's good slang wisewise if you get my meaning.'

Detective Sergeant Yates studied him closely. 'This is a sound-proof room,' he said finally.

'So I've noticed,' said Wilt.

'A man could scream his guts out in here and no one outside would be any the wiser.'

'Wiser?' said Wilt doubtfully. 'Wisdom and knowledge are not the same thing. Someone outside might not be aware that . . .'

'Shut up,' said Sergeant Yates.

Wilt sighed. 'If you would just let me get some sleep . . .'

'You'll get some sleep when you tell us why you murdered your wife, where you murdered her and how you murdered her.'

'I don't suppose it will do any good if I tell you I didn't murder her.'

Sergeant Yates shook his head.

'No,' he said. 'We know you did. You know you did. We know where she is. We're going to get her out. We know you put her there. You've at least admitted that much.'

'I keep telling you I put an inflatable . . .'

'Was Mrs Wilt inflatable?'

'Was she fuck,' said Wilt.

'Right, so we'll forget the inflatable doll crap . . .'

'I wish to God I could,' said Wilt. 'I'll be only too glad when you get down there and dig it out. It will have burst of course with all that concrete on it but it will still be recognizably an inflatable plastic doll.'

Sergeant Yates leant across the table. 'Let me tell you something. When we do get Mrs Wilt out of there, don't imagine she'll be unrecognizable.' He stopped and stared intently at Wilt. 'Not unless you've disfigured her.'

'Disfigured her?' said Wilt with a hollow laugh. 'She didn't need disfiguring the last time I saw her. She was looking bloody awful. She had on these lemon pyjamas and her face was all covered with . . .' He hesitated. There was a curious expression on the Sergeant's face.

'Blood?' he suggested. 'Were you going to say "blood"?'

'No,' said Wilt, 'I most certainly wasn't. I was going to say powder. White powder and scarlet lipstick. I told her she looked fucking awful.'

'You must have had a very happy relationship with her,' said the Sergeant. 'I don't make a habit of telling my wife she looks fucking awful.'

'You probably don't have a fucking awful-looking wife,' said Wilt making an attempt to conciliate the man.

'What I have or don't have by way of a wife is my business. She lies outside the domain of this discussion.'

'Lucky old her,' said Wilt, 'I wish to God mine did.' By two o'clock they had left Mrs Wilt's appearance and got onto teeth and the question of identifying dead bodies by dental chart.

'Look,' said Wilt wearily, 'I daresay teeth fascinate you but at this time of night I can do without them.'

'You wear dentures or something?'

'No. No, I don't,' said Wilt, rejecting the plural.

'Did Mrs Wilt?'

'No,' said Wilt, 'she was always very . . .'

'I thank you,' said Sergeant Yates, 'I knew it would come out in the end.'

'What would?' said Wilt, his mind still on teeth.

'That "was". The past tense. That's the giveaway. Right, so you admit she's dead. Let's go on from there.'

'I didn't say anything of the sort. You said "Did she wear dentures?" and I said she didn't . . .'

'You said "She was." It's that "was" that interests me. If you had said "is" it would have been different.'

'It might have sounded different,' said Wilt, rallying his defences, 'but it wouldn't have made the slightest difference to the facts.'

'Which are?'

'That my wife is probably still around somewhere alive and kicking . . .'

'You don't half give yourself away, Wilt,' said the Sergeant. 'Now it's "probably" and as for "kicking" I just hope for your sake we don't find she was still alive when they poured that concrete down on top of her. The Court wouldn't take kindly to that.'

'I doubt if anyone would,' said Wilt. 'Now when I said "probably" what I meant was that if you had been held in custody for a day and half the night being questioned on the trot by detectives you'd begin to wonder what had happened to your wife. It might even cross your mind that, all evidence to the contrary, she might not be alive. You want to try sitting on this side of the table before you start criticizing me for using terms like "probable". Anything more improbable than being accused of murdering your wife when you know for a fact that you haven't you can't imagine.'

'Listen, Wilt,' said the Sergeant, 'I'm not criticizing you for your language. Believe me I'm not. I'm merely trying as patiently as I can to establish the facts.'

'The facts are these,' said Wilt. 'Like a complete idiot I made the mistake of dumping an inflatable doll down the bottom of a pile shaft and someone poured concrete in and my wife is away from home and . . .'

'I'll tell you one thing,' Sergeant Yates told Inspector Flint when he came on duty at seven in the morning. 'This one is a

hard nut to crack. If you hadn't told me he hadn't a record I'd
have sworn he was an old hand and a good one at that. Are you
sure Central Records have got nothing on him?' Inspector
Flint shook his head.

'He hasn't started squealing for a lawyer yet?'

'Not a whimper. I tell you he's either as nutty as a fruit cake
or he's been through this lot before.'

And Wilt had. Day after day, year in year out. With Gasfitters
One and Printers Three, with Day Release Motor Mechanics
and Meat Two. For ten years he had sat in front of classes
answering irrelevant questions, discussing why Piggy's rational
approach to life was preferable to Jack's brutishness, why
Pangloss' optimism was so unsatisfactory, why Orwell hadn't
wanted to shoot that blasted elephant or hang that man, and all
the time fending off verbal attempts to rattle him and reduce
him to the state poor old Pinkerton was in when he gassed
himself. By comparison with Bricklayers Four, Sergeant Yates
and Inspector Flint were child's play. If only they would let him
get some sleep he would go on running inconsequential rings
round them.

'I thought I had him once,' the Sergeant told Flint as they
conferred in the corridor. 'I had got him onto teeth.'

'Teeth?' said the Inspector.

'I was just explaining we can always identify bodies from their
dental charts and he almost admitted she was dead. Then he got
away again.'

'Teeth, eh? That's interesting. I'll have to pursue that line of
questioning. It may be his weak link.'

'Good luck on you,' said the Sergeant. 'I'm off to bed.'

'Teeth?' said Wilt. 'We're not going through that again
are we? I thought we'd exhausted that topic. The last bloke
wanted to know if Eva had them in the past tense. I told him
she did and . . .'

'Wilt,' said Inspector Flint, 'I am not interested in whether or
not Mrs Wilt had teeth. I presume she must have done. What I
want to know is if she still has them. Present tense.'

'I imagine she must have,' said Wilt patiently. 'You'd better
ask her when you find her.'

'And when we find her will she be in a position to tell us?'

'How the hell should I know? All I can say is that if for some quite inexplicable reason she's lost all her teeth there'll be the devil to pay. I'll never hear the end of it. She's got a mania for cleaning the things and sticking bits of dental floss down the loo. You've no idea the number of times I've thought I'd got worms.'

Inspector Flint sighed. Whatever success Sergeant Yates had had with teeth, it was certainly eluding him. He switched to other matters.

'Let's go over what happened at the Pringsheims' party again,' he said.

'Let's not,' said Wilt who had so far managed to avoid mentioning his contretemps with the doll in the bathroom. 'I've told you five times already and it's wearing a bit thin. Besides it was a filthy party. A lot of trendy intellectuals boosting their paltry egos.'

'Would you say you were an introverted sort of man, Wilt? A solitary type of person?'

Wilt considered the question seriously. It was certainly more to the point than teeth.

'I wouldn't go that far,' he said finally. 'I'm fairly quiet but I'm gregarious too. You have to be to cope with the classes I teach.'

'But you don't like parties?'

'I don't like parties like the Pringsheims', no.'

'Their sexual behaviour outrages you? Fills you with disgust?'

'Their sexual behaviour? I don't know why you pick on that. Everything about them disgusts me. All that crap about Women's Lib for one thing when all it means to someone like Mrs Pringsheim is that she can go around behaving like a bitch on heat while her husband spends the day slaving over a hot test tube and comes home to cook supper, wash up and is lucky if he's got enough energy to wank himself off before going to sleep. Now if we're talking about real Women's Lib that's another matter. I've got nothing against . . .'

'Let's just hold it there,' said the Inspector. 'Now two things you said interest me. One, wives behaving like bitches on heat. Two, this business of you wanking yourself off.'

'Me?' said Wilt indignantly. 'I wasn't talking about myself.'

'Weren't you?'

'No, I wasn't.'

'So you don't masturbate?'

'Now look here, Inspector. You're prying into areas of my private life which don't concern you. If you want to know about masturbation read the Kinsey Report. Don't ask me.'

Inspector Flint restrained himself with difficulty. He tried another tack. 'So when Mrs Pringsheim lay on the bed and asked you to have intercourse with her . . .'

'Fuck is what she said,' Wilt corrected him.

'You said no?'

'Precisely,' said Wilt.

'Isn't that a bit odd?'

'What, her lying there or me saying no?'

'You saying no.'

Wilt looked at him incredulously.

'Odd?' he said. 'Odd? A woman comes in here and throws herself flat on her back on this table, pulls up her skirt and says "Fuck me, honey, prick me to the quick." Are you going to leap onto her with a "Whoopee, let's roll baby"? Is that what you mean by not odd?'

'Jesus wept, Wilt,' snarled the Inspector, 'you're walking a fucking tightrope with my patience.'

'You could have fooled me,' said Wilt. 'All I do know is that your notion of what is odd behaviour and what isn't doesn't begin to make sense with me.'

Inspector Flint got up and left the room. 'I'll murder the bastard, so help me God I'll murder him,' he shouted at the Duty Sergeant. Behind him in the Interview Room Wilt put his head on the table and fell asleep.

At the Tech Wilt's absence was making itself felt in more ways than one. Mr Morris had had to take Gasfitters One at nine o'clock and had come out an hour later feeling that he had gained fresh insight into Wilt's sudden excursion into homicide. The Vice-Principal was fighting off waves of crime reporters anxious to find out more about the man who was helping the police with their enquiries into a particularly macabre and newsworthy crime. And the Principal had begun to regret his criticisms of Liberal Studies to the Education Committee. Mrs Chatterway had phoned to say that she had found his remarks in the worst of taste and had hinted that she might well ask for an enquiry into the running of the Liberal Studies Department. But it was at the meeting of the Course Board that there was most alarm.

'The visitation of the Council for National Academic Awards takes place on Friday,' Dr Mayfield, head of Sociology, told the committee. 'They are hardly likely to approve the Joint Honours degree in the present circumstances.'

'If they had any sense they wouldn't approve it in any circumstances,' said Dr Board. 'Urban Studies and Medieval Poetry indeed. I know academic eclecticism is the vogue these days but Helen Waddell and Lewis Mumford aren't even remotely natural bedfellows. Besides the degree lacks academic content.'

Dr Mayfield bristled. Academic content was his strong point. 'I don't see how you can say that,' he said. 'The course has been structured to meet the needs of students looking for a thematic approach.'

'The poor benighted creatures we manage to lure away from universities to take this course wouldn't know a thematic approach if they saw one,' said Dr Board. 'Come to think of it I wouldn't either.'

'We all have our limitations,' said Dr Mayfield suavely.

'Precisely,' said Dr Board, 'and in the circumstances we should recognize them instead of concocting Joint Honours degrees which don't make sense for students who, if their A-level results are anything to go by, haven't any in the first place. Heaven knows I'm all for educational opportunity but—'

'The point is,' interjected Dr Cox, Head of Science, 'that it is not the degree course as such that is the purpose of the visitation. As I understand it they have given their approval to the degree in principle. They are coming to look at the facilities the College provides and they are hardly likely to be impressed by the presence of so many murder squad detectives. That blue caravan is most off-putting.'

'In any case with the late Mrs Wilt structured into the foundations . . .' began Dr Board.

'I am doing my best to get the police to remove her from . . .'

'The syllabus?' asked Dr Board.

'The premises,' said Dr Mayfield. 'Unfortunately they seem to have hit a snag.'

'A snag?'

'They have hit bedrock at eleven feet.'

Dr Board smiled. 'One wonders why there was any need for thirty-foot piles in the first instance if there is bedrock at eleven,' he murmured.

'I can only tell you what the police have told me,' said Dr Mayfield. 'However they have promised to do all they can to be off the site by Friday. Now I would just like to run over the arrangements again with you. The Visitation will start at eleven with an inspection of the library. We will then break up into groups to discuss Faculty libraries and teaching facilities with particular reference to our ability to provide individual tuition . . .'

'I shouldn't have thought that was a point that needed emphasizing,' said Dr Board. 'With the few students we're likely to get we're almost certain to have the highest teacher to student ratio in the country.'

'If we adopt that approach the Committee will gain the impression that we are not committed to the degree. We must provide a united front,' said Dr Mayfield, 'we can't afford at this stage to have divisions among ourselves. This degree could mean our getting Polytechnic status.'

There were divisions too among the men boring down on the building site. The foreman was still at home under sedation suffering nervous exhaustion brought on by his part in the cementation of a murdered woman and it was left to Barney to superintend operations. 'There was this hand, see . . .' he told the Sergeant in charge.

'On which side?'

'On the right,' said Barney.

'Then we'll go down on the left. That way if the hand is sticking out we won't cut it off.'

They went down on the left and cut off the main electricity cable to the canteen.

'Forget that bleeding hand,' said the Sergeant, 'we go down on the right and trust to luck. Just so long as we don't cut the bitch in half.'

They went down on the right and hit bedrock at eleven feet. 'This is going to slow us up no end,' said Barney, 'who would have thought there'd be rock down there.'

'Who would have thought some nut would incorporate his missus in the foundation of a college of further education where he worked,' said the Sergeant.

'Gruesome,' said Barney.

In the meantime the staff had as usual divided into factions. Peter Braintree led those who thought Wilt was innocent and was joined by the New Left on the grounds that anyone in conflict with the fuzz must be in the right. Major Millfield reacted accordingly and led the Right against Wilt on the automatic assumption that anyone who incurred the support of the Left must be in the wrong and that anyway the police knew what they were doing. The issue was raised at the meeting of the Union called to discuss the annual pay demand. Major Millfield proposed a motion calling on the union to support the campaign for the reintroduction of capital punishment. Bill Trent countered with a motion expressing solidarity with Brother Wilt. Peter Braintree proposed that a fund be set up to help Wilt with his legal fees. Dr Lomax, Head of Commerce, argued against this and pointed out that Wilt had, by dismembering his wife, brought the profession into disrepute. Braintree said Wilt hadn't dismembered anyone and that even the police hadn't suggested he had, and there was such a thing as a law against slander. Dr Lomax withdrew his remark. Major Millfield insisted that there were good grounds for thinking Wilt had murdered his wife and that anyway Habeas Corpus didn't exist in Russia. Bill Trent said that capital punishment didn't either. Major Millfield said, 'Bosh.' In the end, after prolonged argument, Major Millfield's motion on hanging was passed by a block vote of the Catering Department while Braintree's proposal and the motion of the New Left were defeated, and the meeting went on to discuss a pay increase of forty-five per cent to keep Teachers in Technical Institutes in line with comparably qualified professions. Afterwards Peter Braintree went down to the Police Station to see if there was anything Henry wanted.

'I wonder if I might see him,' he asked the Sergeant at the desk.

'I'm afraid not, sir,' said the Sergeant, 'Mr Wilt is still helping us with our enquiries.'

'But isn't there anything I can get him? Doesn't he need anything?'

'Mr Wilt is well provided for,' said the Sergeant, with the private reservation that what Wilt needed was his head read.

'But shouldn't he have a solicitor?'

'When Mr Wilt asks for a solicitor he will be allowed to see one,' said the Sergeant, 'I can assure you that so far he hasn't asked.'

And Wilt hadn't. Having finally been allowed three hours sleep he had emerged from his cell at twelve o'clock and had eaten a hearty breakfast in the police canteen. He returned to the Interview Room, haggard and unshaven, and with his sense of the improbable markedly increased.

'Now then, Henry,' said Inspector Flint, dropping an official octave nomenclaturewise in the hope that Wilt would respond, 'about this blood.'

'What blood?' said Wilt, looking round the aseptic room.

'The blood on the walls of the bathroom at the Pringsheims' house. The blood on the landing. Have you any idea how it got there? Any idea at all?'

'None,' said Wilt, 'I can only assume that someone was bleeding.'

'Right,' said the Inspector, 'who?'

'Search me,' said Wilt.

'Quite, and you know what we've found?'

Wilt shook his head.

'No idea?'

'None,' said Wilt.

'Bloodspots on a pair of grey trousers in your wardrobe,' said the Inspector. 'Bloodspots, Henry, bloodspots.'

'Hardly surprising,' said Wilt, 'I mean if you looked hard enough you'd be bound to find some bloodspots in anyone's wardrobe. The thing is I wasn't wearing grey trousers at that party. I was wearing blue jeans.'

'You were wearing blue jeans? You're quite sure about that?'

'Yes.'

'So the bloodspots on the bathroom wall and the bloodspots

on your grey trousers have nothing to do with one another?'

'Inspector,' said Wilt, 'far be it from me to teach you your own business but you have a technical branch that specializes in matching bloodstains. Now may I suggest that you make use of their skills to establish . . .'

'Wilt,' said the Inspector, 'Wilt, when I need your advice on how to conduct a murder investigation I'll not only ask for it but I'll resign from the force.'

'Well?' said Wilt.

'Well what?'

'Do they match? Do the bloodstains match?'

The Inspector studied him grimly. 'If I told you they did?' he asked.

Wilt shrugged. 'I'm not in any position to argue,' he said. 'If you say they do, I take it they do.'

'They don't,' said Inspector Flint, 'but that proves nothing,' he continued before Wilt could savour his satisfaction. 'Nothing at all. We've got three people missing. There's Mrs Wilt at the bottom of that shaft . . . No, don't say it, Wilt, don't say it. There's Dr Pringsheim and there's Mrs Fucking Pringsheim.'

'I like it,' said Wilt appreciatively, 'I definitely like it.'

'Like what?'

'Mrs Fucking Pringsheim. It's apposite.'

'One of these days, Wilt,' said the Inspector softly, 'you'll go too far.'

'Patiencewise? To use a filthy expression,' asked Wilt.

The Inspector nodded and lit a cigarette.

'You know something, Inspector,' said Wilt, beginning to feel on top of the situation, 'you smoke too much. Those things are bad for you. You should try . . .'

'Wilt,' said the Inspector, 'in twenty-five years in the service I have never once resorted to physical violence while interrogating a suspect but there comes a time, a time and a place and a suspect when with the best will in the world . . .' He got up and went out. Wilt sat back in his chair and looked up at the fluorescent light. He wished it would stop buzzing. It was getting on his nerves.

Chapter 12

On Eel Stretch—Gaskell's map-reading had misled him and they were nowhere near Frogwater Reach or Fen Broad—the situation was getting on everyone's nerves. Gaskell's attempts to mend the engine had had the opposite effect. The cockpit was flooded with fuel oil and it was difficult to walk on deck without slipping.

'Jesus, G, anyone would think to look at you that this was a goddam oil rig,' said Sally.

'It was that fucking fuel line,' said Gaskell, 'I couldn't get it back on.'

'So why try starting the motor with it off?'

'To see if it was blocked.'

'So now you know. What you going to do about it? Sit here till the food runs out? You've gotta think of something.'

'Why me? Why don't you come up with something?'

'If you were any sort of a man . . .'

'Shit,' said Gaskell. 'The voice of the liberated woman. Comes the crunch and all of a sudden I've got to be a man. What's up with you, man–woman? You want us off of here, you do it. Don't ask me to be a man, uppercase M, in an emergency. I've forgotten how.'

'There must be some way of getting help,' said Sally.

'Oh sure. You just go up top and take a crowsnest at the scenery. All you'll get is a beanfeast of bullrushes.' Sally climbed on top of the cabin and scanned the horizon. It was thirty feet away and consisted of an expanse of reeds.

'There's something over there looks like a church tower,' she said. Gaskell climbed up beside her.

'It is a church tower. So what?'

'So if we flashed a light or something someone might see it.'

'Brilliant. A highly populated place like the top of a church tower there's bound to be people just waiting for us to flash a light.'

'Couldn't we burn something?' said Sally, 'somebody would see the smoke and . . .'

'You crazy? You start burning anything with all that fuel oil floating around they'll see something all right. Like an exploding cruiser with bodies.'

'We could fill a can with oil and put it over the side and float it away before lighting it.'

'And set the reedbeds on fire? What the hell do you want? A fucking holocaust?'

'G baby, you're just being unhelpful.'

'I'm using my brains is all,' said Gaskell. 'You keep coming up with bright ideas like that you're going to land us in a worse mess than we're in already.'

'I don't see why,' said Sally.

'I'll tell you why,' said Gaskell, 'because you went and stole this fucking *Hesperus*. That's why.'

'I didn't steal it. I . . .'

'You tell the fuzz that. Just tell them. You start setting fire to reedbeds and they'll be all over us asking questions. Like whose boat this is and how come you're sailing someone else's cruiser . . . So we got to get out of here without publicity.'

It started to rain.

'That's all we need. Rain,' said Gaskell. Sally went down into the cabin where Eva was tidying up after lunch. 'God, G's hopeless. First he lands us on a mudbank in the middle of nowhere, then he gefucks the motor but good and now he says he doesn't know what to do.'

'Why doesn't he go and get help?' asked Eva.

'How? Swimming? G couldn't swim that far to save his life.'

'He could take the airbed and paddle down to the open water,' said Eva. 'He wouldn't have to swim.'

'Airbed? Did I hear you say airbed? What airbed?'

'The one in the locker with the lifejackets. All you've got to do is blow it up and . . .'

'Honey you're the practicallest,' said Sally, and rushed outside. 'G, Eva's found a way for you to go and get help. There's an airbed in the locker with the lifejackets.' She rummaged in the locker and took out the airbed.

'You think I'm going anywhere on that damned thing you've got another think coming,' said Gaskell.

'What's wrong with it?'

'In this weather? You ever tried to steer one of those things? It's bad enough on a sunny day with no wind. Right now I'd end up in the reeds and anyhow the rain's getting on my glasses.'

'All right, so we wait till the storm blows over. At least we know how to get off here.'

She went back into the cabin and shut the door. Outside Gaskell squatted by the engine and toyed with the wrench. If only he could get the thing to go again.

'Men,' said Sally contemptuously, 'claim to be the stronger sex but when the chips are down it's us women who have to bail them out.'

'Henry's impractical too,' said Eva. 'It's all he can do to mend a fuse. I do hope he isn't worried about me.'

'He's having himself a ball,' said Sally.

'Not Henry. He wouldn't know how.'

'He's probably having it off with Judy.'

Eva shook her head. 'He was just drunk, that's all. He's never done anything like that before.'

'How would you know?'

'Well he is my husband.'

'Husband hell. He just uses you to wash the dishes and cook and clean up for him. What does he give you? Just tell me that.'

Eva struggled with her thoughts inarticulately. Henry didn't give her anything very much. Not anything she could put into words. 'He needs me,' she said finally.

'So he needs you. Who needs needing? That's the rhetoric of female feudalism. So you save someone's life, you've got to be grateful to them for letting you? Forget Henry. He's a jerk.'

Eva bristled. Henry might not be very much but she didn't like him insulted.

'Gaskell's nothing much to write home about,' she said and went into the kitchen. Behind her Sally lay back on the bunk and opened the centre spread of *Playboy*. 'Gaskell's got bread,' she said.

'Bread?'

'Money, honey. Greenstuff. The stuff that makes the world go round Cabaretwise. You think I married him for his looks? Oh no. I can smell a cool million when it comes by me and I do mean buy me.'

'I could never marry a man for his money,' said Eva primly. 'I'd have to be in love with him. I really would.'

'So you've seen too many movies. Do you really think Gaskell was in love with me?'

'I don't know. I suppose he must have been.'

Sally laughed. 'Eva baby you are naïve. Let me tell you about G. G's a plastic freak. He'd fuck a goddam chimpanzee if you dressed it up in plastic.'

'Oh honestly. He wouldn't,' said Eva. 'I don't believe it.'

'You think I put you on the Pill for nothing? You go around in that bikini and Gaskell's drooling over you all the time—if I wasn't here he'd have raped you.'

'He'd have a hard time,' said Eva, 'I took Judo classes.'

'Well he'd try. Anything in plastic drives him crazy. Why do you think he had that doll?'

'I wondered about that.'

'Right. You can stop wondering,' said Sally.

'I still don't see what that has to do with you marrying him,' said Eva.

'Then let me tell you a little secret. Gaskell was referred to me . . .'

'Referred?'

'By Dr Freeborn. Gaskell had this little problem and he consulted Dr Freeborn and Dr Freeborn sent him to me.'

Eva looked puzzled. 'But what were you supposed to do?'

'I was a surrogate,' said Sally.

'A surrogate?'

'Like a sex counsellor,' said Sally. 'Dr Freeborn used to send me clients and I would help them.'

'I wouldn't like that sort of job,' said Eva, 'I couldn't bear to talk to men about sex. Weren't you embarrassed?'

'You get used to it and there are worse ways of earning a living. So G comes along with his little problem and I straightened him out but literally and we got married. A business arrangement. Cash on the tail.'

'You mean you . . .'

'I mean I have Gaskell and Gaskell has plastic. It's an elastic relationship. The marriage with the two-way stretch.'

Eva digested this information with difficulty. It didn't seem right somehow. 'Didn't his parents have anything to say about it?' she asked. 'I mean did he tell them about you helping him and all that?'

'Say? What could they say? G told them he'd met me at summer school and Pringsy's greedy little eyes popped out of his greasy little head. Baby, did that fat little man have penis projection. Sell? He could sell anything. The Rockefeller Centre to Rockefeller. So he accepted me. Old Ma Pringsheim didn't. She huffed and she puffed and she blew but this little piggy stayed right where the bank was. G and me went back to California and G graduated in plastic and we've been bio-degradable ever since.'

'I'm glad Henry isn't like that,' said Eva. 'I couldn't live with a man who was queer.'

'G's not queer, honey. Like I said he's a plastic freak.'

'If that's not queer I don't know what is,' said Eva.

Sally lit a cigarillo.

'All men get turned on by something,' she said. 'They're manipulable. All you've got to do is find the kink. I should know.'

'Henry's not like that. I'd know if he was.'

'So he makes with the doll. That's how much you know about Henry. You telling me he's the great lover?'

'We've been married twelve years. It's only natural we don't do it as often as we used to. We're so busy.'

'Busy lizzie. And while you're housebound what's Henry doing?'

'He's taking classes at the Tech. He's there all day and he comes home tired.'

'Takes classes takes asses. You'll be telling me next he's not a sidewinder.'

'I don't know what you mean,' said Eva.

'He has his piece on the side. His secretary knees up on the desk.'

'He doesn't have a secretary.'

'Then students prudence. Screws their grades up. I know. I've seen it. I've been around colleges too long to be fooled.'

'I'm sure Henry would never . . .'

'That's what they all say and then bingo, it's divorce and bobbysex and all you're left to look forward to is menopause and peeking through the blinds at the man next door and waiting for the Fuller Brush man.'

'You make it all sound so awful,' said Eva. 'You really do.'
'It is, Eva teats. It is. You've got to do something about it
before it's too late. You've got to liberate yourself from Henry.
Make the break and share the cake. Otherwise it's male
domination doomside.'

Eva sat on the bunk and thought about the future. It didn't
seem to hold much for her. They would never have any children
now and they wouldn't ever have much money. They would go
on living in Parkview Avenue and paying off the mortgage and
maybe Henry would find someone else and then what would
she do? And even if he didn't, life was passing her by.

'I wish I knew what to do,' she said presently. Sally sat up
and put her arm round her.

'Why don't you come to the States with us in November?'
she said. 'We could have such fun.'

'Oh I couldn't do that,' said Eva. 'It wouldn't be fair to
Henry.'

No such qualms bothered Inspector Flint. Wilt's intransi-
gence under intense questioning merely indicated that he was
harder than he looked.

'We've had him under interrogation for thirty-six hours
now,' he told the conference of the Murder Squad in the
briefing room at the Police Station, 'and we've got nothing out
of him. So this is going to be a long hard job and quite frankly
I have my doubts about breaking him.'

'I told you he was going to be a hard nut to crack,' said
Sergeant Yates.

'Nut being the operative word,' said Flint. 'So it's got to be
concrete evidence.'

There was a snigger which died away quickly. Inspector Flint
was not in a humorous mood.

'Evidence, hard evidence is the only thing that is going to
break him. Evidence is the only thing that is going to bring him
to trial.'

'But we've got that,' said Yates. 'It's at the bott . . .'

'I know exactly where it is, thank you Sergeant. What I am
talking about is evidence of multiple murder. Mrs Wilt is
accounted for. Dr and Mrs Pringsheim aren't. Now my guess is
that he murdered all three and that the other two bodies

are . . .' He stopped and opened the file in front of him and hunted through it for Notes on Violence and the Break-Up of Family Life. He studied them for a moment and shook his head. 'No,' he muttered, 'it's not possible.'

'What isn't, sir?' asked Sergeant Yates. 'Anything is possible with this bastard.'

But Inspector Flint was not to be drawn. The notion was too awful.

'As I was saying,' he continued, 'what we need now is hard evidence. What we have got is purely circumstantial. I want more evidence on the Pringsheims. I want to know what happened at that party, who was there and why it happened and at the rate we're going with Wilt we aren't going to get anything out of him. Snell, you go down to the department of Biochemistry at the University and get what you can on Dr Pringsheim. Find out if any of his colleagues were at that party. Interview them. Get a list of his friends, his hobbies, his girl friends if he had any. Find out if there is any link between him and Mrs Wilt that would suggest a motive. Jackson, you go up to Rossiter Grove and see what you can get on Mrs Pringsheim . . .'

By the time the conference broke up detectives had been despatched all over town to build up a dossier on the Pringsheims. Even the American Embassy had been contacted to find out what was known about the couple in the States. The murder investigation had begun in earnest.

Inspector Flint walked back to his office with Sergeant Yates and shut the door. 'Yates,' he said, 'this is confidential. I wasn't going to mention it in there but I've a nasty feeling that I know why that sod is so bloody cocky. Have you ever known a murderer sit through thirty-six hours of questioning as cool as a cucumber when he knows we've got the body of his victim pinpointed to the nearest inch?'

Sergeant Yates shook his head. 'I've known some pretty cool customers in my time and particularly since they stopped hanging but this one takes the biscuit. If you ask me he's a raving psychopath.'

Flint dismissed the idea. 'Psychopaths crack easy,' he said. 'They confess to murders they haven't committed or they confess to murders they have committed, but they confess. This

Wilt doesn't. He sits there and tells me how to run the investigation. Now take a look at this.' He opened the file and took out
Wilt's notes. 'Notice anything peculiar?'

Sergeant Yates read the notes through twice.

'Well, he doesn't seem to think much of our methods,' he
said finally. 'And I don't much like this bit about low level of
intelligence of average policeman.'

'What about Point Two D?' said the Inspector, 'Increasing
use of sophisticated methods such as diversionary tactics by
criminals. Diversionary tactics. Doesn't that suggest anything
to you?'

'You mean he's trying to divert our attention away from the
real crime to something else?'

Inspector Flint nodded. 'What I mean is this. I wouldn't mind
betting that when we do get down to the bottom of that fucking
pile we're going to find an inflatable doll dressed up in Mrs
Wilt's clothes and with a vagina. That's what I think.'

'But that's insane.'

'Insane? It's fucking diabolical,' said the Inspector. 'He's
sitting in there like a goddamn dummy giving as good as he gets
because he knows he's got us chasing a red herring.'

Sergeant Yates sat down mystified. 'But why? Why draw
attention to the murder in the first place? Why didn't he just
lie low and act normally?'

'What, and report Mrs Wilt as missing? You're forgetting the
Pringsheims. A wife goes missing, so what? Two of her friends
go missing and leave their house in a hell of a mess and covered
with bloodstains. That needs explaining, that does. So he puts
out a false trail . . .'

'But that still doesn't help him,' objected the Sergeant. 'We
dig up a plastic doll. Doesn't mean we're going to halt the
investigation.'

'Maybe not but it gives him a week while the other bodies
disintegrate.'

'You think he used an acid bath like Haigh?' asked the
Sergeant. 'That's horrible.'

'Of course it's horrible. You think murder's nice or something? Anyway the only reason they got Haigh was that stupid
bugger told them where to look for the sludge. If he'd kept his
trap shut for another week they wouldn't have found anything.

The whole lot would have been washed away. Besides I don't know what Wilt's used. All I do know is he's an intellectual, a clever sod and he thinks he's got it wrapped up. First we take him in for questioning, maybe even get him remanded and when we've done that, we go and dig up a plastic inflatable doll. We're going to look right Charlies going into court with a plastic doll as evidence of murder. We'll be the laughing stock of the world. So the case gets thrown out of court and what happens when we pick him up a second time for questioning on the real murders? We'd have the Civil Liberties brigade sinking their teeth into our throats like bleeding vampire bats.'

'I suppose that explains why he doesn't start shouting for a lawyer,' said Yates.

'Of course it does. What does he want with a lawyer now? But pull him in a second time and he'll have lawyers falling over themselves to help him. They'll be squawking about police brutality and victimization. You won't be able to hear yourself speak. His bloody lawyers will have a field day. First plastic dolls and then no bodies at all. He'll get clean away.'

'Anyone who can think that little lot up must be a madman,' said the Sergeant.

'Or a fucking genius,' said Flint bitterly. 'Christ what a case.' He stubbed out a cigarette resentfully.

'What do you want me to do? Have another go at him.'

'No, I'll do that. You go up to the Tech and chivvy his boss there into saying what he really thinks of Wilt. Get any little bit of dirt on the blighter you can. There's got to be something in his past we can use.'

He went down the corridor and into the Interview Room. Wilt was sitting at the table making notes on the back of a statement form. Now that he was beginning to feel, if not at home in the Police Station, at least more at ease with his surroundings, his mind had turned to the problem of Eva's disappearance. He had to admit that he had been worried by the bloodstains in the Pringsheims' bathroom. To while away the time he had tried to formulate his thoughts on paper and he was still at it when Inspector Flint came into the room and banged the door.

'Right, so you're a clever fellow, Wilt,' he said, sitting down and pulling the paper towards him. 'You can read and write and you've got a nice logical and inventive mind so let's just see what you've written here. Who's Ethel?'

'Eva's sister,' said Wilt. 'She's married to a market gardener in Luton. Eva sometimes goes over there for a week.'

'And "Blood in the bath"?'

'Just wondering how it got there.'

'And "Evidence of hurried departure".'

'I was simply putting down my thoughts about the state of the Pringsheims' house,' said Wilt.

'You're trying to be helpful?'

'I'm here helping you with your enquiries. That's the official term isn't it?'

'It may be the official term, Wilt, but in this case it doesn't correspond with the facts.'

'I don't suppose it does very often,' said Wilt. 'It's one of those expressions that covers a multitude of sins.'

'And crimes.'

'It also happens to ruin a man's reputation,' said Wilt. 'I hope you realize what you're doing to mine by holding me here like this. It's bad enough knowing I'm going to spend the rest of my life being pointed out as the man who dressed a plastic doll with a cunt up in his wife's clothes and dropped it down a pile hole without everyone thinking I'm a bloody murderer as well.'

'Where you're going to spend the rest of your life nobody is going to care what you did with that plastic doll,' said the Inspector.

Wilt seized on the admission.

'Ah, so you've found it at last,' he said eagerly. 'That's fine. So now I'm free to go.'

'Sit down and shut up,' snarled the Inspector. 'You're not going anywhere and when you do it will be in a large black van. I haven't finished with you yet. In fact I'm only just beginning.'

'Here we go again,' said Wilt. 'I just knew you'd want to start at the beginning again. You fellows have primary causes on the brain. Cause and effect, cause and effect. Which came first, the chicken or the egg, protoplasm or demiurge? I suppose this time it's going to be what Eva said when we were dressing to go to the party.'

'This time,' said the Inspector, 'I want you to tell me precisely why you stuck that damned doll down that hole.'

'Now that is an interesting question,' said Wilt, and stopped. It didn't seem a good idea to try to explain to Inspector Flint in the present circumstances just what he had had in mind when he dropped the doll down the shaft. The Inspector didn't look the sort of person who would understand at all readily that a husband could have fantasies of murdering his wife without actually putting them into effect. It would be better to wait for Eva to put in an appearance in the flesh before venturing into that uncharted territory of the wholly irrational. With Eva present Flint might sympathize with him. Without her he most certainly wouldn't.

'Let's just say I wanted to get rid of the beastly thing,' he said.

'Let's not say anything of the sort,' said Flint. 'Let's just say you had an ulterior motive for putting it there.'

Wilt nodded. 'I'll go along with that,' he said.

Inspector Flint nodded encouragingly. 'I thought you might. Well, what was it?'

Wilt considered his words carefully. He was getting into deep waters.

'Let's just say it was by way of being a rehearsal.'

'A rehearsal? What sort of rehearsal?'

Wilt thought for a moment.

'Interesting word "rehearsal",' he said. 'It comes from the old French, *rehercer*, meaning . . .'

'To hell with where it comes from,' said the Inspector, 'I want to know where it ends up.'

'Sounds a bit like a funeral too when you come to think of it,' said Wilt, continuing his campaign of semantic attrition.

Inspector Flint hurled himself into the trap. 'Funeral? Whose funeral?'

'Anyone's,' said Wilt blithely. 'Hearse, rehearse. You could say that's what happens when you exhume a body. You rehearse it though I don't suppose you fellows use hearses.'

'For God's sake,' shouted the Inspector. 'Can't you ever stick to the point? You said you were rehearsing something and I want to know what that something was.'

'An idea, a mere idea,' said Wilt, 'one of those ephemera of mental fancy that flit like butterflies across the summer landscape of the mind blown by the breezes of association that come like sudden showers . . . I rather like that.'

'I don't,' said the Inspector, looking at him bitterly. 'What I want to know is what you were rehearsing. That's what I'd like to know.'

'I've told you. An idea.'

'What sort of idea?'

'Just an idea,' said Wilt. 'A mere . . .'

'So help me God, Wilt,' shouted the Inspector, 'if you start on these fucking butterflies again I'll break the unbroken habit of a lifetime and wring your bloody neck.'

'I wasn't going to mention butterflies this time,' said Wilt reproachfully, 'I was going to say that I had this idea for a book . . .'

'A book?' snarled Inspector Flint. 'What sort of book? A book of poetry or a crime story?'

'A crime story,' said Wilt, grateful for the suggestion.

'I see,' said the Inspector. 'So you were going to write a thriller. Well now, just let me guess the outline of the plot. There's this lecturer at the Tech and he has this wife he hates and he decides to murder her . . .'

'Go on,' said Wilt, 'you're doing very well so far.'

'I thought I might be,' said Flint delightedly. 'Well, this lecturer thinks he's a clever fellow who can hoodwink the police. He doesn't think much of the police. So he dumps a plastic doll down a hole that's going to be filled with concrete in the hope that the police will waste their time digging it out and in the meantime he's buried his wife somewhere else. By the way, where did you bury Mrs Wilt, Henry? Let's get this over once and for all. Where did you put her? Just tell me that. You'll feel better when it's out.'

'I didn't put her anywhere. If I've told you that once I've told you a thousand times. How many more times have I got to tell you I don't know where she is.'

'I'll say this for you, Wilt,' said the Inspector, when he could bring himself to speak. 'I've known some cool customers in my time but I have to take my hat off to you. You're the coolest bastard it's ever been my unfortunate experience to come across.'

Wilt shook his head. 'You know,' he said, 'I feel sorry for you,

Inspector, I really do. You can't recognize the truth when it's staring you in the face.'

Inspector Flint got up and left the room. 'You there,' he said to the first detective he could find. 'Go into that Interview Room and ask that bastard questions and don't stop till I tell you.'

'What sort of questions?'

'Any sort. Just any. Keep asking him why he stuffed an inflatable plastic doll down a pile hole. That's all. Just ask it over and over and over again. I'm going to break that sod.'

He went down to his office and slumped into his chair and tried to think.

Chapter 13

At the Tech Sergeant Yates sat in Mr Morris' office. 'I'm sorry to disturb you again,' he said, 'but we need some more details on this fellow Wilt.'

The Head of Liberal Studies looked up with a haggard expression from the timetable. He had been having a desperate struggle trying to find someone to take Bricklayers Four. Price wouldn't do because he had Mechanics Two and Williams wouldn't anyway. He had already gone home the day before with a nervous stomach and was threatening to repeat the performance if anyone so much as mentioned Bricklayers Four to him again. That left Mr Morris himself and he was prepared to be disturbed by Sergeant Yates for as long as he liked if it meant he didn't have to take those bloody bricklayers.

'Anything to help,' he said, with an affability that was in curious contrast to the haunted look in his eyes. 'What details would you like to know?'

'Just a general impression of the man, sir,' said the Sergeant. 'Was there anything unusual about him?'

'Unusual?' Mr Morris thought for a moment. Apart from a preparedness to teach the most awful Day Release Classes year in and year out without complaint he could think of nothing unusual about Wilt. 'I suppose you could call what amounted to a phobic reaction to *The Lord of the Flies* a bit unusual but then I've never much cared for . . .'

'If you'd just wait a moment, sir,' said the Sergeant busying himself with his notebook. 'You did say "phobic reaction" didn't you?'

'Well what I meant was . . .'

'To flies, sir?'

'To *The Lord of the Flies*. It's a book,' said Mr Morris, now uncertain that he had been wise to mention the fact. Policemen were not noticeably sensitive to those niceties of literary taste that constituted his own definition of intelligence. 'I do hope I haven't said the wrong thing.'

'Not at all, sir. It's these little details that help us to build up a picture of the criminal's mind.'

Mr Morris sighed. 'I'm sure I never thought when Mr Wilt came to us from the University that he would turn out like this.'

'Quite so, sir. Now did Mr Wilt ever say anything disparaging about his wife?'

'Disparaging? Dear me no. Mind you he didn't have to. Eva spoke for herself.' He looked miserably out of the window at the pile-boring machine.

'Then in your opinion Mrs Wilt was not a very likable woman?'

Mr Morris shook his head. 'She was a ghastly woman,' he said.

Sergeant Yates licked the end of his ballpen.

'You did say "ghastly" sir?'

'I'm afraid so. I once had her in an evening class for Elementary Drama.'

'Elementary?' said the Sergeant, and wrote it down.

'Yes, though elemental would have been more appropriate in Mrs Wilt's case. She threw herself into the parts rather too vigorously to be wholly convincing. Her Desdemona to my Othello is something I am never likely to forget.'

'An impetuous woman, would you say?'

'Let me put it this way,' said Mr Morris, 'had Shakespeare written the play as Mrs Wilt interpreted it, Othello would have been the one to be strangled.'

'I see, sir,' said the Sergeant, 'then I take it she didn't like black men.'

'I have no idea what she thought about the racial issue,' said Mr Morris, 'I am talking of her physical strength.'

'A powerful woman, sir?'

'Very,' said Mr Morris with feeling.

Sergeant Yates looked puzzled. 'It seems strange a woman like that allowing herself to be murdered by Mr Wilt without putting up more of a struggle,' he said thoughtfully.

'It seems incredible to me,' Mr Morris agreed, 'and what is more it indicates a degree of fanatical courage in Henry that his behaviour in this department never led me to suspect. I can only suppose he was insane at the time.'

Sergeant Yates seized on the point. 'Then it is your considered opinion that he was not in his right mind when he killed his wife?'

'Right mind? I can think of nothing rightminded about killing your wife and dumping her body . . .'

'I meant sir,' said the Sergeant, 'that you think Mr Wilt is a lunatic.'

Mr Morris hesitated. There were a good many members of his department whom he would have classified as mentally unbalanced but he hardly liked to advertise the fact. On the other hand it might help poor Wilt.

'Yes, I suppose so,' he said finally for at heart he was a kindly man. 'Quite mad. Between ourselves, Sergeant, anyone who is prepared to teach the sort of bloodyminded young thugs we get can't be entirely sane. And only last week Wilt got into an altercation with one of the Printers and was punched in the face. I think that may have had something to do with his subsequent behaviour. I trust you will treat what I say in the strictest confidence. I wouldn't want . . .'

'Quite so, sir,' said Sergeant Yates. 'Well, I needn't detain you any longer.'

He returned to the Police Station and reported his findings to Inspector Flint.

'Nutty as a fruitcake,' he announced. 'That's his opinion. He's quite positive about it.'

'In that case he had no right to employ the sod,' said Flint. 'He should have sacked the brute.'

'Sacked him? From the Tech? You know they can't sack teachers. You've got to do something really drastic before they give you the boot.'

'Like murdering three people, I suppose. Well as far as I'm concerned they can have the little bastard back.'

'You mean he's still holding out?'

'Holding out? He's counterattacking. He's reduced me to a nervous wreck and now Bolton says he wants to be relieved. Can't stand the strain any longer.'

Sergeant Yates scratched his head. 'Beats me how he does it,' he said. 'Anyone would think he was innocent. I wonder when he'll start asking for a lawyer.'

'Never,' said Flint. 'What does he need a lawyer for? If I had

a lawyer in there handing out advice I'd have got the truth out
of Wilt hours ago.'

As night fell over Eel Stretch the wind increased to Gale
Force Eight. Rain hammered on the cabin roof, waves slapped
against the hull and the cabin cruiser, listing to starboard,
settled more firmly into the mud. Inside the cabin the air was
thick with smoke and bad feelings. Gaskell had opened a bottle
of vodka and was getting drunk. To pass the time they played
Scrabble.

'My idea of hell,' said Gaskell, 'is to be huis closed with a
couple of dykes.'

'What's a dyke?' said Eva.

Gaskell stared at her. 'You don't know?'

'I know the sort they have in Holland . . .'

'Yoga bear,' said Gaskell, 'you are the naïvest. A dyke is—'

'Forget it, G,' said Sally. 'Whose turn to play?'

'It's mine,' said Eva. 'I . . . M . . . P spells Imp.'

'O . . . T . . . E . . . N . . . T spells Gaskell,' said Sally.

Gaskell drank some more vodka. 'What the hell sort of game
we supposed to be playing? Scrabble or some sort of Truth
group?'

'Your turn,' said Sally.

Gaskell put D . . . I . . . L . . . D on the O. 'Try that for size.'

Eva looked at it critically.

'You can't use proper names,' she said. 'You wouldn't let me
use Squezy.'

'Eva teats, dildo is not a proper name. It's an improper thing.
A surrogate penis.'

'A what?'

'Never mind what it is,' said Sally. 'Your turn to play.' Eva
studied her letters. She didn't like being told what to do so often
and besides she still wanted to know what a dyke was. And a
surrogate penis. In the end she put L . . . O . . . V on the E.

'Is a many-splendoured thing,' said Gaskell and put D . . .
I . . . D on the L and O.

'You can't have two of them,' said Eva. 'You've got one
Dildo already.'

'This one's different,' said Gaskell, 'it's got whiskers.'

'What difference does that make?'

'Ask Sally. She's the one with penis envy.'

'You asshole,' said Sally and put F . . . A . . . G . . . G . . . O on the T. 'Meaning you.'

'Like I said. Truth Scrabble,' said Gaskell. 'Trubble for short. So why don't we just have an encounter group instead. Let the truth hang out like it is.'

Eva used the F to make Faithful. Gaskell followed with Hooker and Sally went Insane.

'Great,' said Gaskell, 'Alphabetical I Ching.'

'Wunderkind, you slay me,' said Sally.

'Go Zelda yourself,' said Gaskell and slid his hand up Eva's thigh.

'Keep your hands to yourself,' said Eva and pushed him away. She put S and N on the I. Gaskell made Butch with the B.

'And don't tell me it's a proper name.'

'Well it's certainly not a word I've heard,' said Eva.

Gaskell stared at her and then roared with laughter.

'Now I've heard it all,' he said. 'Like cunnilingus is a cough medicine. How dumb can you get?'

'Go look in the mirror,' said Sally.

'Oh sure. So I married a goddam lesbian whore who goes round stealing other people's wives and boats and things. I'm dumb. But boobs here beats me. She's so fucking hypocritical she pretends she's not a dyke . . .'

'I don't know what a dyke is,' said Eva.

'Well let me inform you, fatso. A dyke is a lesbian.'

'Are you calling me a lesbian?' said Eva.

'Yes,' said Gaskell.

Eva slapped him across the face hard. Gaskell's glasses came off and he sat down on the floor.

'Now G . . .' Sally began but Gaskell had scrambled to his feet.

'Right you fat bitch,' he said. 'You want the truth you're going to get it. First off, you think husband Henry got into that doll off his own bat, well let me tell you . . .'

'Gaskell, you just shut up,' shouted Sally.

'Like hell I will. I've had about enough of you and your rotten little ways. I picked you out of a cathouse . . .'

'That's not true. It was a clinic,' screamed Sally, 'a clinic for sick perverts like you.'

Eva wasn't listening. She was staring at Gaskell. He had

called her a lesbian and had said Henry hadn't got into that
doll of his own accord.

'Tell me about Henry,' she shouted. 'How did he get into
that doll?'

Gaskell pointed at Sally. 'She put him there. That poor goof
wouldn't know . . .'

'You put him there?' Eva said to Sally. 'You did?'

'He tried to make me, Eva. He tried to—'

'I don't believe it,' Eva shouted. 'Henry isn't like that.'

'I tell you he did. He . . .'

'And you put him in that doll?' Eva screamed and launched
herself across the table at Sally. There was a splintering sound
and the table collapsed. Gaskell scudded sideways onto the bunk
and Sally shot out of the cabin. Eva got to her feet and moved
forward towards the door. She had been tricked, cheated and
lied to. And Henry had been humiliated. She was going to kill
that bitch Sally. She stepped out into the cockpit. On the far side
Sally was a dark shadow. Eva went round the engine and lunged
at her. The next moment she had slipped on the oily deck and
Sally had darted across the cockpit and through the door into
the cabin. She slammed the door behind her and locked it.
Eva Wilt got to her feet and stood with the rain running down
her face and as she stood there the illusions that had sustained
her through the week disappeared. She saw herself as a fat, silly
woman who had left her husband in pursuit of a glamour that
was false and shoddy and founded on brittle talk and money.
And Gaskell had said she was a lesbian. The full nausea of
knowing what Touch Therapy had meant dawned on Eva.
She staggered to the side of the boat and sat down on a locker.

And slowly her self-disgust turned back to anger, and a cold
hatred of the Pringsheims. She would get her own back on
them. They would be sorry they had ever met her. She got up
and opened the locker and took out the lifejackets and threw
them over the side. Then she blew up the airbed, dropped it into
the water and climbed over herself. She let herself down into
the water and lay on the airbed. It rocked alarmingly but Eva
was not afraid. She was getting her revenge on the Pringsheims
and she no longer cared what happened to her. She paddled off
through the little waves pushing the lifejackets in front of her.
The wind was behind her and the airbed moved easily. In five

minutes she had turned the corner of the reeds and was out of sight of the cruiser. Somewhere in the darkness ahead there was the open water where they had seen the dinghies and beyond it land.

Presently she found herself being blown sideways into the reeds. The rain stopped and Eva lay panting on the airbed. It would be easier if she got rid of the lifejackets. She was far enough from the boat for them to be well hidden. She pushed them into the reeds and then hesitated. Perhaps she should keep one for herself. She disentangled a jacket from the bunch and managed to put it on. Then she lay face down on the airbed again and paddled forward down the widening channel.

Sally leant against the cabin door and looked at Gaskell with loathing.

'You stupid jerk,' she said. 'You had to open your big mouth. So what the hell are you going to do now?'

'Divorce you for a start,' said Gaskell.

'I'll alimony you for all the money you've got.'

'Fat chance. You won't get a red cent,' Gaskell said and drank some more vodka.

'I'll see you dead first,' said Sally.

Gaskell grinned. 'Me dead? Anyone's going to die round here, it's you. Booby baby is out for blood.'

'She'll cool off.'

'You think so? Try opening that door if you're so sure. Go on, unlock it.'

Sally moved away from the door and sat down.

'This time you've really bought yourself some trouble,' said Gaskell. 'You had to pick a goddam prizefighter.'

'You go out and pacify her,' said Sally.

'No way. I'd as soon play blind man's bluff with a fucking rhinoceros.' He lay back on the bunk and smiled happily. 'You know there's something really ironical about all this. You had to go and liberate a Neanderthal. Women's Lib for paleolithics. She Tarzan, you Jane. You've bought yourself a piece of zoo.'

'Very funny,' said Sally. 'And what's your role?'

'Me Noah. Just be thankful she hasn't got a gun.' He pulled a pillow up under his head and went to sleep.

Sally sat on staring at his back venomously. She was frightened.

Eva's reaction had been so violent that it had destroyed her confidence in herself. Gaskell was right. There had been something primeval in Eva Wilt's behaviour. She shuddered at the thought of that dark shape moving towards her in the cockpit. Sally got up and went into the galley and found a long sharp knife. Then she went back into the cabin and checked the lock on the door and lay down on her bunk and tried to sleep. But sleep wouldn't come. There were noises outside. Waves lapped against the side of the boat. The wind blew. God, what a mess it all was! Sally clutched her knife and thought about Gaskell and what he had said about divorce.

Peter Braintree sat in the office of Mr Gosdyke, Solicitor, and discussed the problem. 'He's been in there since Monday and it's Thursday now. Surely they've no right to keep him there so long without his seeing a solicitor.'

'If he doesn't ask for one and if the police want to question him and he is prepared to answer their questions and refuses to demand his legal rights I don't really see that there is anything I can do about it,' said Mr Gosdyke.

'But are you sure that that is the situation?' asked Braintree.

'As far as I can ascertain that is indeed the situation. Mr Wilt has not asked to see me. I spoke to the Inspector in charge, you heard me, and it seems quite clear that Mr Wilt appears, for some extraordinary reason, to be prepared to help the police with their enquiries just as long as they feel his presence at the Police Station is necessary. Now if a man refuses to assert his own legal rights then he has only himself to blame for his predicament.'

'But are you absolutely certain that Henry has refused to see you? I mean the police could be lying to you.'

Mr Gosdyke shook his head. 'I have known Inspector Flint for many years,' he said, 'and he is not the sort of man to deny a suspect his rights. No, I'm sorry, Mr Braintree. I would like to be of more assistance but frankly, in the circumstances, I can do nothing. Mr Wilt's predilection for the company of police officers is quite incomprehensible to me, but it disqualifies me from interfering.'

'You don't think they're giving him third degree or anything of that sort?'

'My dear fellow, third degree? You've been watching too many old movies on the TV. The police don't use strong-arm methods in this country.'

'They've been pretty brutal with some of our students who have been on demos,' Braintree pointed out.

'Ah, but students are quite another matter and demonstrating students get what they deserve. Political provocation is one thing but domestic murders of the sort your friend Mr Wilt seems to have indulged in come into a different category altogether. I can honestly say that in all my years in the legal profession I have yet to come across a case in which the police did not treat a domestic murderer with great care and not a little sympathy. After all, they are nearly all married men themselves, and in any case Mr Wilt has a degree and that always helps. If you are a professional man, and in spite of what some people may say lecturers in Technical Colleges are members of a profession if only marginally, then you can rest assured that the police will do nothing in the least untoward. Mr Wilt is perfectly safe.'

And Wilt felt safe. He sat in the Interview Room and contemplated Inspector Flint with interest.

'Motivation? Now there's an interesting question,' he said. 'If you had asked me why I married Eva in the first place I'd have some trouble trying to explain myself. I was young at the time and . . .'

'Wilt,' said the Inspector, 'I didn't ask you why you married your wife. I asked you why you decided to murder her.'

'I didn't decide to murder her,' said Wilt.

'It was a spontaneous action? A momentary impulse you couldn't resist? An act of madness you now regret?'

'It was none of those things. In the first place it was not an act. It was mere fantasy.'

'But you do admit that the thought crossed your mind?'

'Inspector,' said Wilt, 'if I acted upon every impulse that crossed my mind I would have been convicted of child rape, buggery, burglary, assault with intent to commit grievous bodily harm and mass murder long ago.'

'All those impulses crossed your mind?'

'At some time or other, yes,' said Wilt.

'You've got a bloody odd mind.'

'Which is something I share with the vast majority of mankind. I daresay that even you in your odd contemplative moments have . . .'

'Wilt,' said the Inspector, 'I don't have odd contemplative moments. Not until I met you anyhow. Now then, you admit you thought of killing your wife . . .'

'I said the notion had crossed my mind, particularly when I have to take the dog for a walk. It is a game I play with myself. No more than that.'

'A game? You take the dog for a walk and think of ways and means of killing Mrs Wilt? I don't call that a game. I call it premeditation.'

'Not badly put,' said Wilt with a smile, 'the meditation bit. Eva curls up in the lotus position on the living-room rug and thinks beautiful thoughts. I take the bloody dog for a walk and think dreadful ones while Clem defecates on the grass verge in Grenville Gardens. And in each case the end result is just the same. Eva gets up and cooks supper and washes up and I come home and watch the box or read and go to bed. Nothing has altered one way or another.'

'It has now,' said the Inspector. 'Your wife has disappeared off the face of the earth together with a brilliant young scientist and his wife, and you are sitting here waiting to be charged with their murder.'

'Which I don't happen to have committed,' said Wilt. 'Ah well, these things happen. The moving finger writes and having writ . . .'

'Fuck the moving finger. Where are they? Where did you put them? You're going to tell me.'

Wilt sighed. 'I wish I could,' he said, 'I really do. Now you've got that plastic doll . . .'

'No we haven't. Not by a long chalk. We're still going down through solid rock. We won't get whatever is down there until tomorrow at the earliest.'

'Something to look forward to,' said Wilt. 'Then I suppose you'll let me go.'

'Like hell I will. I'll have you up for remand on Monday.'

'Without any evidence of murder? Without a body? You can't do that.'

Inspector Flint smiled. 'Wilt,' he said, 'I've got news for you. We don't need a body. We can hold you on suspicion, we can bring you up for trial and we can find you guilty without a body. You may be clever but you don't know your law.'

'Well I must say you fellows have an easy job of it. You mean you can go out in the street and pick up some perfectly innocent passer-by and lug him in here and charge him with murder without any evidence at all?'

'Evidence? We've got evidence all right. We've got a blood-spattered bathroom with a busted-down door. We've got an empty house in a filthy mess and we've got some bloody thing or other down that pile hole and you think we haven't got evidence. You've got it wrong.'

'Makes two of us,' said Wilt.

'And I'll tell you another thing, Wilt. The trouble with bastards like you is that you're too clever by half. You overdo things and you give yourselves away. Now if I'd been in your shoes, I'd have done two things. Know what they are?'

'No,' said Wilt, 'I don't.'

'I'd have washed that bathroom down, number one, and number two I'd have stayed away from that hole. I wouldn't have tried to lay a false trail with notes and making sure the caretaker saw you and turning up at Mr Braintree's house at midnight covered in mud. I'd have sat tight and said nothing.'

'But I didn't know about those bloodstains in the bathroom and if it hadn't been for that filthy doll I wouldn't have dumped the thing down the hole. I'd have gone to bed. Instead of which I got pissed and acted like an idiot.'

'Let me tell you something else, Wilt,' said the Inspector. 'You *are* an idiot, a fucking cunning idiot but an idiot all the same. You need your head read.'

'It would make a change from this lot,' said Wilt.

'What would?'

'Having my head read instead of sitting here and being insulted.'

Inspector Flint studied him thoughtfully. 'You mean that?' he asked.

'Mean what?'

'About having your head read? Would you be prepared to undergo an examination by a qualified psychiatrist?'

'Why not?' said Wilt. 'Anything to help pass the time.'

'Quite voluntarily, you understand. Nobody is forcing you to, but if you want . . .'

'Listen, Inspector, if seeing a psychiatrist will help to convince you that I have not murdered my wife I'll be only too happy to. You can put me on a lie detector. You can pump me full of truth drugs. You can . . .'

'There's no need for any of that other stuff,' said Flint, and stood up. 'A good shrink will do very nicely. And if you think you can get away with guilty but insane, forget it. These blokes know when you're malingering madness.' He went to the door and paused. Then he came back and leant across the table.

'Tell me, Wilt,' he said. 'Tell me just one thing. How come you sit there so coolly? Your wife is missing, we have evidence of murder, we have a replica of her, if you are to be believed, under thirty feet of concrete and you don't turn a hair. How do you do it?'

'Inspector,' said Wilt. 'If you had taught Gasfitters for ten years and been asked as many damnfool questions in that time as I have, you'd know. Besides you haven't met Eva. When you do you'll see why I'm not worried. Eva is perfectly capable of taking care of herself. She may not be bright but she's got a built-in survival kit.'

'Jesus, Wilt, with you around for twelve years she must have had something.'

'Oh she has. You'll like Eva when you meet her. You'll get along like a house on fire. You've both got literal minds and an obsession with trivia. You can take a wormcast and turn it into Mount Everest.'

'Wormcast? Wilt, you sicken me,' said the Inspector, and left the room.

Wilt got up and walked up and down. He was tired of sitting down. On the other hand he was well satisfied with his performance. He had surpassed himself and he took pride in the fact that he was reacting so well to what most people would consider an appalling predicament. But to Wilt it was something else, a challenge, the first real challenge he had had to meet for a long time. Gasfitters and Plasterers had challenged him once but he had learnt to cope with them. You jollied them along. Let them talk, ask questions, divert them, get them going, accept their red herrings and hand out a few of your own, but above all you had to refuse to accept their preconceptions. Whenever they asserted something with absolute conviction as a self-evident truth like all wogs began at Calais, all you had to do was agree and then point out that half the great men in English history had been foreigners like Marconi or Lord Beaverbrook and that even Churchill's mother had been a Yank or talk about the Welsh being the original Englishmen and the Vikings and the Danes and from that lead them off through Indian doctors to the National Health Service and birth control and any other topic under the sun that would keep them quiet and puzzled and desperately trying to think of some ultimate argument that would prove you wrong.

Inspector Flint was no different. He was more obsessive but his tactics were just the same. And besides he had got hold of the wrong end of the stick with a vengeance and it amused Wilt to watch him trying to pin a crime on him he hadn't committed. It made him feel almost important and certainly more of a man than he had done for a long, long time. He was innocent and there was no question about it. In a world where everything else was doubtful and uncertain and open to scepticism the fact of his innocence was sure. For the first time in his adult life Wilt knew himself to be absolutely right, and the knowledge gave him a strength he had never supposed he possessed. And besides there was no question in his mind that Eva would turn up eventually, safe and sound, and more than a little subdued when she realized what her impulsiveness had led to. Serve her right for giving him that disgusting doll. She'd regret that to the end of her days. Yes, if anybody was going to come off badly in this affair it was dear old Eva with her bossyness and her busyness. She'd have a job explaining it to Mavis Mottram and the neighbours. Wilt smiled to himself at the thought. And even the Tech would have to treat him differently in future and with a new respect. Wilt knew the liberal conscience too well not to suppose that he would appear anything less than a martyr when he went back. And a hero. They would bend over backwards to convince themselves that they hadn't thought him as guilty as hell. He'd get promotion too, not for being a good teacher but because they would need to salve their fragile consciences. Talk about killing the fatted calf.

Chapter 14

At the Tech there was no question of killing the fatted calf, at least not for Henry Wilt. The imminence of the CNAA visitation on Friday, coinciding as it apparently would with the resurrection of the late Mrs Wilt, was causing something approaching panic. The Course Board met in almost continuous session and memoranda circulated so furiously that it was impossible to read one before the next arrived.

'Can't we postpone the visit?' Dr Cox asked. 'I can't have them in my office discussing bibliographies with bits of Mrs Wilt being dug out of the ground outside the window.'

'I have asked the police to make themselves as inconspicuous as possible,' said Dr Mayfield.

'With conspicuous lack of success so far,' said Dr Board. 'They couldn't be more in evidence. There are ten of them peering down that hole at this very moment.'

The Vice-Principal struck a brighter note. 'You'll be glad to hear that we've managed to restore power to the canteen,' he told the meeting, 'so we should be able to lay on a good lunch.'

'I just hope I feel up to eating,' said Dr Cox. 'The shocks of the last few days have done nothing to improve my appetite and when I think of poor Mrs Wilt . . .'

'Try not to think of her,' said the Vice-Principal, but Dr Cox shook his head.

'You try not to think of her with a damned great boring machine grinding away outside your office window all day.'

'Talking about shocks,' said Dr Board, 'I still can't understand how the driver of that mechanical corkscrew managed to escape electrocution when they cut through the power cable.'

'Considering the problems we are faced with, I hardly think that's a relevant point just at present,' said Dr Mayfield. 'What we have got to stress to the members of the CNAA committee is that this degree is an integrated course with a fundamental substructure grounded thematically on a concomitance of cultural and sociological factors in no way unsuperficially disparate and with a solid quota of academic content to give students an intellectual and cerebral . . .'

'Haemorrhage?' suggested Dr Board.

Dr Mayfield regarded him balefully. 'I really do think this is no time for flippancy,' he said angrily. 'Either we are committed to the Joint Honours degree or we are not. Furthermore we have only until tomorrow to structure our tactical approach to the visitation committee. Now, which is it to be?'

'Which is what to be?' asked Dr Board. 'What has our commitment or lack of it to do with structuring, for want of several far better words, our so-called tactical approach to a committee which, since it is coming all the way from London to us and not vice versa, is presumably approaching us?'

'Vice-Principal,' said Dr Mayfield, 'I really must protest. Dr Board's attitude at this late stage in the game is quite incomprehensible. If Dr Board . . .'

'Could even begin to understand one tenth of the jargon Dr Mayfield seems to suppose is English he might be in a better position to express his opinion,' interrupted Dr Board. 'As it is, "incomprehensible" applies to Dr Mayfield's syntax, not to my attitude. I have always maintained . . .'

'Gentlemen,' said the Vice-Principal, 'I think it would be best if we avoided inter-departmental wrangles at this point in time and got down to business.'

There was a silence broken finally by Dr Cox. 'Do you think the police could be persuaded to erect a screen round that hole?' he asked.

'I shall certainly suggest that to them,' said Dr Mayfield. They passed on to the matter of entertainment.

'I have arranged for there to be plenty of drinks before lunch,' said the Vice-Principal, 'and in any case lunch will be judiciously delayed to allow them to get into the right mood so the afternoon sessions should be cut short and proceed, hopefully, more smoothly.'

'Just so long as the Catering Department doesn't serve Toad in the Hole,' said Dr Board.

The meeting broke up acrimoniously.

So did Mr Morris' encounter with the Crime Reporter of the *Sunday Post*.

'Of course I didn't tell the police that I employed homicidal maniacs as a matter of policy,' he shouted at the reporter. 'And in any case what I said was, as I understood it, to be treated in the strictest confidence.'

'But you did say you thought Wilt was insane and that quite a number of Liberal Studies lecturers were off their heads?'

Mr Morris looked at the man with loathing. 'To put the record straight, what I said was that some of them were . . .'

'Off their rockers?' suggested the reporter.

'No, not off their rockers,' shouted Mr Morris. 'Merely, well, shall we say, slightly unbalanced.'

'That's not what the police say you said. They say quote . . .'

'I don't care what the police say I said. I know what I said and what I didn't and if you're implying . . .'

'I'm not implying anything. You made a statement that half your staff are nuts and I'm trying to verify it.'

'Verify it?' snarled Mr Morris. 'You put words into my mouth I never said and you call that verifying it?'

'Did you say it or not? That's all I'm asking. I mean if you express an opinion about your staff . . .'

'Mr MacArthur, what I think about my staff is my own affair. It has absolutely nothing to do with you or the rag you represent.'

'Three million people will be interested to read your opinion on Sunday morning,' said Mr MacArthur, 'and I wouldn't be at all surprised if this Wilt character didn't sue you if he ever gets out of the copshop.'

'Sue me? What the hell could he sue me for?'

'Calling him a homicidal maniac for a start. Banner headlines HEAD OF LIBERAL STUDIES CALLS LECTURER HOMICIDAL MANIAC should be good for fifty thousand. I'd be surprised if he got less.'

Mr Morris contemplated destitution. 'Even your paper would never print that,' he muttered, 'I mean Wilt would sue you too.'

'Oh we're used to libel actions. They're run-of-the-mill for us. We pay for them out of petty cash. Now if you'd be a bit more cooperative . . .' He left the suggestion in mid-air for Mr Morris to digest.

'What do you want to know?' he asked miserably.

'Got any juicy drug scene stories for us?' asked Mr Mac-

Arthur. 'You know the sort of thing. LOVE ORGIES IN LECTURES. That always gets the public. Teenyboppers having it off and all that. Give us a good one and we'll let you off the hook about Wilt.'

'Get out of my office!' yelled Mr Morris.

Mr MacArthur got up. 'You're going to regret this,' he said and went downstairs to the students' canteen to dig up some dirt on Mr Morris.

'Not tests,' said Wilt adamantly. 'They're deceptive.'

'You think so?' said Dr Pittman, consultant psychiatrist at the Fenland Hospital and professor of Criminal Psychology at the University. Being plagiocephalic didn't help either.

'I should have thought it was obvious,' said Wilt. 'You show me an ink-blot and I think it looks like my grandmother lying in a pool of blood, do you honestly think I'm going to be fool enough to say so? I'd be daft to do that. So I say a butterfly sitting on a geranium. And every time it's the same. I think what it does look like and then say something completely different. Where does that get you?'

'It is still possible to infer something from that,' said Dr Pittman.

'Well, you don't need a bloody ink-blot to infer, do you?' said Wilt. Dr Pittman made a note of Wilt's interest in blood. 'You can infer things from just looking at the shape of people's heads.'

Dr Pittman polished his glasses grimly. Heads were not things he liked inferences to be drawn from. 'Mr Wilt,' he said, 'I am here at your request to ascertain your sanity and in particular to give an opinion as to whether or not I consider you capable of murdering your wife and disposing of her body in a singularly revolting and callous fashion. I shall not allow anything you may say to influence my ultimate and objective findings.'

Wilt looked perplexed. 'I must say you're not giving yourself much room for manoeuvre. Since we've dispensed with mechanical aids like tests I should have thought what I had to say would be the only thing you could go on. Unless of course you're going to read the bumps on my head. Isn't that a bit old fashioned?'

'Mr Wilt,' said Dr Pittman, 'the fact that you clearly have a sadistic streak and take pleasure in drawing attention to other people's physical infirmities in no way disposes me to conclude you are capable of murder . . .'

'Very decent of you,' said Wilt, 'though frankly I'd have thought anyone was capable of murder given the right, or to be precise the wrong, circumstances.'

Dr Pittman stifled the impulse to say how right he was. Instead he smiled prognathously. 'Would you say you were a rational man, Henry?' he asked.

Wilt frowned. 'Just stick to Mr Wilt if you don't mind. This may not be a paid consultation but I prefer a little formality.'

Dr Pittman's smile vanished. 'You haven't answered my question.'

'No, I wouldn't say I was a rational man,' said Wilt.

'An irrational one perhaps?'

'Neither the one wholly nor the other wholly. Just a man.'

'And a man is neither one thing nor the other?'

'Dr Pittman, this is your province not mine but in my opinion man is capable of reasoning but not of acting within wholly rational limits. Man is an animal, a developed animal, though come to think of it all animals are developed if we are to believe Darwin. Let's just say man is a domesticated animal with elements of wildness about him . . .'

'And what sort of animal are you, Mr Wilt?' said Dr Pittman. 'A domesticated animal or a wild one?'

'Here we go again. These splendidly simple dual categories that seem to obsess the modern mind. Either/Or Kierkegaard as that bitch Sally Pringsheim would say. No, I am not wholly domesticated. Ask my wife. She'll express an opinion on the matter.'

'In what respect are you undomesticated?'

'I fart in bed, Dr Pittman. I like to fart in bed. It is the trumpet call of the anthropoid ape in me asserting its territorial imperative in the only way possible.'

'In the only way possible?'

'You haven't met Eva,' said Wilt. 'When you do you'll see that assertion is her forte not mine.'

'You feel dominated by Mrs Wilt?'

'I *am* dominated by Mrs Wilt.'

'She bullies you? She assumes the dominant role?'

'Eva is, Dr Pittman. She doesn't have to assume anything. She just is.'

'Is what?'

'Now there's the rub,' said Wilt. 'What's today? You lose track of time in this place.'

'Thursday.'

'Well, today being Thursday, Eva is Bernard Leach.'

'Bernard Leach?'

'The potter, Dr Pittman, the famous potter,' said Wilt. 'Now tomorrow she'll be Margot Fonteyn and on Saturday we play bridge with the Mottrams so she'll be Omar Sharif. On Sunday she's Elizabeth Taylor or Edna O'Brien depending on what the Colour Supplements have in store for me and in the afternoon we go for a drive and she's Eva Wilt. It's about the only time in the week I meet her and that's because I'm driving and she's got nothing to do but sit still and nag the pants off me.'

'I begin to see the pattern,' said Dr Pittman. 'Mrs Wilt was . . . is given to role-playing. This made for an unstable relationship in which you couldn't establish a distinctive and assertive role as a husband . . .'

'Dr Pittman,' said Wilt, 'a gyroscope may, indeed must, spin but in doing so it achieves a stability that is virtually unequalled. Now if you understand the principle of the gyroscope you may begin to understand that our marriage does not lack stability. It may be damned uncomfortable coming home to a centrifugal force but it bloody well isn't unstable.'

'But just now you told me that Mrs Wilt did not assume a dominant role. Now you tell me she is a forceful character.'

'Eva is not forceful. She is a force. There's a difference. And as for character, she has so many and so varied it's difficult to keep up with them all. Let's just say she throws herself into whoever she is with an urgency and compulsiveness that is not always appropriate. You remember that series of Garbo pictures they showed on TV some years back? Well, Eva was La Dame Aux Camélias for three days after that and she made dying of TB look like St Vitus' dance. Talk about galloping consumption.'

'I begin to get the picture,' said Dr Pittman making a note that Wilt was a pathological liar with sado-masochistic tendencies.

'I'm glad somebody does,' said Wilt. 'Inspector Flint thinks I murdered her and the Pringsheims in some sort of bloodlust and disposed of their bodies in some extraordinary fashion. He mentioned acid. I mean it's crazy. Where on earth does one get nitric acid in the quantities necessary to dissolve three dead bodies, and one of them overweight at that? I mean it doesn't bear thinking about.'

'It certainly doesn't,' said Dr Pittman.

'In any case do I look like a murderer?' continued Wilt cheerfully. 'Of course I don't. Now if he'd said Eva had slaughtered the brutes, and in my opinion someone should have done years ago, I'd have taken him seriously. God help the poor sods who happen to be around when Eva takes it into her head she's Lizzie Borden.'

Dr Pittman studied him predaciously.

'Are you suggesting that Dr and Mrs Pringsheim were murdered by your wife?' he asked. 'Is that what you're saying?'

'No,' said Wilt, 'I am not. All I'm saying is that when Eva does things she does them wholeheartedly. When she cleans the house she cleans it. Let me tell you about the Harpic. She's got this thing about germs . . .'

'Mr Wilt,' said Dr Pittman hastily, 'I am not interested in what Mrs Wilt does with the Harpic. I have come here to understand you. Now then, do you make a habit of copulating with a plastic doll? Is this a regular occurrence?'

'Regular?' said Wilt. 'Do you mean a normal occurrence or a recurring one? Now your notion of what constitutes a normal occurrence may differ from mine . . .'

'I mean, do you do it often?' interrupted Dr Pittman.

'Do it?' said Wilt. 'I don't do it at all.'

'But I understood you to have placed particular emphasis on the fact that this doll had a vagina?'

'Emphasis? I didn't have to emphasize the fact. The beastly thing was plainly visible.'

'You find vaginas beastly?' said Dr Pittman stalking his prey into the more familiar territory of sexual aberration.

'Taken out of context, yes,' said Wilt sidestepping, 'and with plastic ones you can leave them in context and I still find them nauseating.'

By the time Dr Pittman had finished the interview he was

uncertain what to think. He got up wearily and made for the door.

'You've forgotten your hat, doctor,' said Wilt holding it out to him. 'Pardon my asking but do you have them specially made for you?'

'Well?' said Inspector Flint when Dr Pittman came into his office. 'What's the verdict?'

'Verdict? That man should be put away for life.'

'You mean he's a homicidal maniac?'

'I mean that no matter how he killed her Mrs Wilt must have been thankful to go. Twelve years married to that man . . . Good God, it doesn't bear thinking about.'

'Well, that doesn't get us much forrader,' said the Inspector, when the psychiatrist had left having expressed the opinion that while Wilt had the mind of an intellectual jackrabbit he couldn't in all honesty say that he was criminally insane. 'We'll just have to see what turns up tomorrow.'

Chapter 15

What turned up on Friday was seen not only by Inspector Flint, Sergeant Yates, twelve other policemen, Barney and half a dozen construction workers, but several hundred Tech students standing on the steps of the Science block, most of the staff and by all eight members of the CNAA visitation committee who had a particularly good view from the windows of the mock hotel lounge used by the Catering Department to train waiters and to entertain distinguished guests. Dr Mayfield did his best to distract their attention.

'We have structured the foundation course to maximize student interest,' he told Professor Baxendale, who headed the committee, but the professor was not to be diverted. His interest was maximized by what was being unstructured from the foundations of the new Admin block.

'How absolutely appalling,' he muttered as Judy protruded from the hole. Contrary to Wilt's hopes and expectations she had not burst. The liquid concrete had sealed her in too well for that and if in life she had resembled in many particulars a real live woman, in death she had all the attributes of a real dead one. As the corpse of a murdered woman she was entirely convincing. Her wig was matted and secured to her head at an awful angle by the concrete. Her clothes clung to her and cement to them while her legs had evidently been contorted to the point of mutilation and her outstretched arm had, as Barney had foretold, a desperate appeal about it that was most affecting. It also made it exceedingly difficult to extricate her from the hole. The legs didn't help, added to which the concrete had given her a substance and stature approximate to that of Eva Wilt.

'I suppose that's what they mean by rigor mortice,' said Dr Board, as Dr Mayfield desperately tried to steer the conversation back to the Joint Honours degree.

'Dear Lord,' muttered Professor Baxendale. Judy had eluded the efforts of Barney and his men and had slumped back down the hole. 'To think what she must have suffered. Did you see that damned hand?'

Dr Mayfield had. He shuddered. Behind him Dr Board sniggered. 'There's a divinity that shapes our ends, rough-hew them how we will,' he said gaily. 'At least Wilt has saved himself the cost of a gravestone. All they'll have to do is prop her up with Here Stands Eva Wilt, Born So and So, Murdered last Saturday carved across her chest. In life monumental, in death a monument.'

'I must say, Board,' said Dr Mayfield, 'I find your sense of humour singularly ill-timed.'

'Well they'll never be able to cremate her, that's for certain,' continued Dr Board. 'And the undertaker who can fit that little lot into a coffin will be nothing short of a genius. I suppose they could always take a sledgehammer to her.'

In the corner Dr Cox fainted.

'I think I'll have another whisky if you don't mind,' said Professor Baxendale weakly. Dr Mayfield poured him a double. When he turned back to the window Judy was protruding once more from the hole.

'The thing about embalming,' said Dr Board, 'is that it costs so much. Now I'm not saying that thing out there is a perfect likeness of Eva Wilt as I remember her . . .'

'For heaven's sake, do you have to go on about it?' snarled Dr Mayfield, but Dr Board was not to be stopped. 'Quite apart from the legs there seems to be something odd about the breasts. I know Mrs Wilt's were large but they do seem to have inflated. Probably due to the gases. They putrefy, you know, which would account for it.'

By the time the committee went into lunch they had lost all appetite for food and most of them were drunk.

Inspector Flint was less fortunate. He didn't like being present at exhumations at the best of times and particularly when the corpse on whose behalf he was acting showed such a marked inclination to go back where she came from. Besides he was in two minds whether it was a corpse or not. It looked like a corpse and it certainly behaved like a corpse, albeit a very heavy one, but there was something about the knees that suggested that all was not anatomically as it should have been with whatever it was they had dug up. There was a double-jointedness and a certain lack of substance where the legs stuck forwards at right angles that seemed to indicate that Mrs Wilt had lost not only her life but both kneecaps as well. It was this mangled quality that made Barney's job so difficult and exceedingly distasteful. After the body had dropped down the hole for the fourth time Barney went down himself to assist from below.

'If you sods drop her,' he shouted from the depths, 'you'll have two dead bodies down here so hang onto that rope whatever happens. I'm going to tie it round her neck.'

Inspector Flint peered down the shaft. 'You'll do no such thing,' he shouted, 'we don't want her decapitated. We need her all in one piece.'

'She is all in one bloody piece,' came Barney's muffled reply, 'that's one thing you don't have to worry about.'

'Can't you tie the rope around something else?'

'Well I could,' Barney conceded, 'but I'm not going to. A leg is more likely to come off than her head and I'm not going to be underneath her when it goes.'

'All right,' said the Inspector, 'I just hope you know what you're doing, that's all.'

'I'll tell you one thing. The sod who put her down here knew what he was doing and no mistake.'

But this fifth attempt failed, like the previous four, and Judy was lowered into the depths where she rested heavily on Barney's foot.

'Go and get that bloody crane,' he shouted, 'I can't stand much more of this.'

'Nor can I,' muttered the Inspector, who still couldn't make up his mind what it was he was supposed to be disinterring; a doll dressed up to look like Mrs Wilt or Mrs Wilt dressed up to look like something some demented sculptor forgot to finish. What few doubts he had had about Wilt's sanity had been entirely dispelled by what he was presently witnessing. Any man who could go to the awful lengths Wilt had gone to render, and the word was entirely apposite whichever way you took it, either his wife or a plastic doll with a vagina, both inaccessible and horribly mutilated must be insane.

Sergeant Yates put his thoughts into words. 'You're not

going to tell me now that the bastard isn't off his rocker,' he said, as the crane was moved into position and the rope lowered and attached to Judy's neck.

'All right, now take her away,' shouted Barney.

In the dining-room only Dr Board was enjoying his lunch. The eight members of the CNAA committee weren't. Their eyes were glued to the scene below.

'I suppose it could be said she was *in statue pupillari*,' said Dr Board, helping himself to some more Lemon Meringue, 'in which case we stand *in loco parentis*. Not a pleasant thought, gentlemen. Not that she was ever a very bright student. I once had her for an Evening Class in French literature. I don't know what she got out of *Fleurs du Mal* but I do remember thinking that Baudelaire . . .'

'Dr Board,' said Dr Mayfield drunkenly, 'for a so-called cultured man you are entirely without feeling.'

'Something I share with the late Mrs Wilt, by the look of things,' said Dr Board, glancing out of the window, 'and while we are still on the subject, things seem to be coming to a head. They do indeed.'

Even Dr Cox, recently revived and coaxed into having some mutton, looked out of the window. As the crane slowly winched Judy into view the Course Board and the Committee rose and went to watch. It was an unedifying sight. Near the top of the shaft Judy's left leg caught in a crevice while her outstretched arm embedded itself in the clay.

'Hold it,' shouted Barney indistinctly, but it was too late. Unnerved by the nature of his load or in the mistaken belief that he had been told to lift harder, the crane driver hoisted away. There was a ghastly cracking sound as the noose tightened and the next moment Judy's concrete head, capped by Eva Wilt's wig, looked as if it was about to fulfil Inspector Flint's prediction that she would be decapitated. In the event he need not have worried. Judy was made of sterner stuff than might have been expected. As the head continued to rise and the body to remain firmly embedded in the shaft Judy's neck rose to the occasion. It stretched.

'Dear God,' said Professor Baxendale frantically, 'will it never end?'

Dr Board studied the phenomenon with increasing interest. 'It doesn't look like it,' he said. 'Mind you we do make a point of stretching our students, eh Mayfield?'

But Dr Mayfield made no response. As Judy took on the configuration of an ostrich that had absentmindedly buried its head in a pail of cement he knew that the Joint Honours degree was doomed.

'I'll say this for Mrs Wilt,' said Dr Board, 'she do hold on. No one could call her stiff-necked. Attenuated possibly. One begins to see what Modigliani was getting at.'

'For God's sake stop,' yelled Dr Cox hysterically, 'I think I'm going off my head.'

'Which is more than can be said for Mrs Wilt,' said Dr Board callously.

He was interrupted by another awful crack as Judy's body finally gave up the struggle with the shaft. With a shower of clay it careered upwards to resume a closer relationship with the head and hung naked, pink and, now that the clothes and the concrete had been removed, remarkably lifelike at the end of the rope some twenty feet above the ground.

'I must say,' said Dr Board, studying the vulva with relish, 'I've never had much sympathy with necrophilia before but I do begin to see its attractions now. Of course it's only of historical interest but in Elizabethan times it was one of the perks of an executioner . . .'

'Board,' screamed Dr Mayfield, 'I've known some fucking swine in my time . . .'

Dr Board helped himself to some more coffee. 'I believe the slang term for it is liking your meat cold.'

Underneath the crane Inspector Flint wiped the mud from his face and peered up at the awful object swinging above him. He could see now that it was only a doll. He could also see why Wilt had wanted to bury the beastly thing.

'Get it down. For God's sake get it down,' he bawled, as the press photographers circled round him. But the crane driver had lost his nerve. He shut his eyes, pulled the wrong lever and Judy began a further ascent.

'Stop it, stop it, that's fucking evidence,' screamed the Inspector, but it was already too late. As the rope wound through the final pulley Judy followed. The concrete cap disintegrated, her head slid between the rollers and her body began to swell. Her legs were the first to be affected.

'I've often wondered what elephantiasis looked like,' said Dr Board, 'Shelley had a phobia about it, I believe.'

Dr Cox certainly had. He was gibbering in a corner and the Vice-Principal was urging him to pull himself together.

'An apt expression,' observed Dr Board, above the gasps of horror as Judy, now clearly twelve months pregnant, continued her transformation. 'Early Minoan, wouldn't you say Mayfield?'

But Dr Mayfield was past speech. He was staring dementedly at a rapidly expanding vagina some fourteen inches long and eight wide. There was a pop and the thing became a penis, an enormous penis that swelled and swelled. He was going mad. He knew he was.

'Now that,' said Dr Board, 'takes some beating. I've heard about sex-change operations for men but . . .'

'Beating?' screamed Dr Mayfield, 'Beating? You can stand there cold-bloodedly and talk about . . .'

There was a loud bang. Judy had come to the end of her tether. So had Dr Mayfield. The penis was the first thing to go. Dr Mayfield the second. As Judy deflated he hurled himself at Dr Board only to sink to the ground gibbering.

Dr Board ignored his colleague. 'Who would have thought the old bag had so much wind in her?' he murmured, and finished his coffee. As Dr Mayfield was led out by the Vice-Principal, Dr Board turned to Professor Baxendale.

'I must apologize for Mayfield,' he said, 'I'm afraid this Joint Honours degree has been too much for him and to tell the truth I have always found him to be fundamentally unsound. A case of dementia post Cox I daresay.'

Inspector Flint drove back to the Police Station in a state bordering on lunacy.

'We've been made to look idiots,' he snarled at Sergeant Yates. 'You saw them laughing. You heard the bastards.' He was particularly incensed by the press photographers who had asked him to pose with the limp remnants of the plastic doll.

'We've been held up to public ridicule. Well, my God, somebody's going to pay.'

He hurled himself out of the car and lunged down the passage to the Interview Room. 'Right, Wilt,' he shouted, 'you've had your little joke and a bloody nasty one it was too. So now we're going to forget the niceties and get to the bottom of this business.'

Wilt studied the torn piece of plastic. 'Looks better like that if you ask me,' he said. 'More natural if you know what I mean.'

'You'll look bloody unnatural if you don't answer my questions,' yelled the Inspector. 'Where is she?'

'Where is who?' said Wilt.

'Mrs Fucking Wilt. Where did you put her?'

'I've told you. I didn't put her anywhere.'

'And I'm telling you you did. Now either you're going to tell me where she is or I'm going to beat it out of you.'

'You can beat me up if you like,' said Wilt, 'but it won't do you any good.'

'Oh yes it will,' said the Inspector and took off his coat.

'I demand to see a solicitor,' said Wilt hastily.

Inspector Flint put his jacket on again. 'I've been waiting to hear you say that. Henry Wilt, I hereby charge you with . . .'

Chapter 16

In the reeds Eva greeted the dawn of another day by blowing up the airbed for the tenth time. It had either sprung a leak or developed a fault in the valve. Whichever it was it had made her progress exceedingly slow and had finally forced her to take refuge in the reeds away from the channel. Here, wedged between the stems, she had spent a muddy night getting off the airbed to blow it up and getting back on to try and wash off the sludge and weeds that had adhered to her when she got off. In the process she had lost the bottom half of her lemon loungers and had torn the top half so that by dawn she resembled less the obsessive housewife of 34 Parkview Avenue than a finalist in the heavyweight division of the Ladies Mudwrestling Championship. In addition she was exceedingly cold and was glad when the sun came up bringing with it the promise of a hot summer day. All she had to do now was to find her way to land or open water and get someone to . . . At this point Eva became aware that her appearance was likely to cause some embarrassment. The lemon loungers had been sufficiently outré to make her avoid walking down the street when she had had them on; with them largely off she certainly didn't want to be seen in public. On the other hand she couldn't stay in the reeds all day. She plunged on, dragging the airbed behind her, half swimming but for the most part trudging through mud and water. At last she came out of the reeds into open water and found herself looking across a stretch to a house, a garden that sloped down to the water's edge, and a church. It seemed a long way across but there was no boat in sight. She would have to swim across and just hope that the woman who lived there was sympathetic and better still large enough to lend her some clothes until she got home. It was at this point that Eva discovered that she had left her handbag somewhere in the reeds. She remembered having it during the night but it must have fallen off the airbed when she was blowing it up. Well she couldn't go back and look for it now. She would just have to go on without it and ring Henry up

and tell him to come out in the car and get her. He could bring
some clothes too. Yes, that was it. Eva Wilt climbed onto the
airbed and began to paddle across. Halfway over the airbed
went down for the eleventh time. Eva abandoned it and
struggled on in the lifejacket. But that too impeded her progress
and she finally decided to take it off. She trod water and tried to
undo it and after a struggle managed to get it off. In the process
the rest of the lemon loungers disintegrated so that by the time
she reached the bank Eva Wilt was exhausted and quite naked.
She crawled into the cover of a willow tree and lay panting on
the ground. When she had recovered she stood up and looked
around. She was at the bottom of the garden and the house was
a hundred yards away up the hill. It was a very large house by
Eva's standards, and not the sort she would feel at home in at
the best of times. For one thing it appeared to have a courtyard
with stables at the back and to Eva, whose knowledge of large
country houses was confined to what she had seen on TV, there
was the suggestion of servants, gentility and a social formality
that would make her arrival in the nude rather heavy going. On
the other hand the whole place looked decidedly run down.
The garden was overgrown and unkempt; ornamental bushes
which might once have been trimmed to look like birds and
animals had reverted to strange and vaguely monstrous shapes;
rusted hoops leant half-hidden in the grass of an untended
croquet lawn; a tennis net sagged between posts and an abandoned greenhouse boasted a few panes of lichened glass. Finally
there was a dilapidated boathouse and a rowing boat. All in all
the domain had a sinister and imposing air to it which wasn't
helped by the presence of a small church hidden among trees to
the left and a neglected graveyard beyond an old iron fence. Eva
peered out from the weeping willow and was about to leave its
cover when the French windows opened and a man came out
onto the terrace with a pair of binoculars and peered through
them in the direction of Eel Stretch. He was wearing a black
cassock and a dog collar. Eva went back behind the tree and
considered the awkwardness of her situation and lack of attire.
It was all extremely embarrassing. Nothing on earth would
make her go up to the house, the Vicarage, with nothing on.
Parkview Avenue hadn't prepared her for situations of this
sort.

Rossiter Grove hadn't prepared Gaskell for the situation he found when Sally woke him with 'Noah baby, it's drywise topside. Time to fly the coop.'

He opened the cabin door and stepped outside to discover that Eva had already flown and had taken the airbed and the lifejackets with her.

'You mean you left her outside all night?' he said. 'Now we're really up Shit Creek. No paddle, no airbed, no goddam lifejackets, no nothing.'

'I didn't know she'd do something crazy like take off with everything,' said Sally.

'You leave her outside in the pouring rain all night she's got to do something. She's probably frozen to death by now. Or drowned.'

'She tried to kill me. You think I was going to let her in when she's tried to do that. Anyhow it's all your fault for shooting your mouth off about that doll.'

'You tell that to the law when they find her body floating downstream. You just explain how come she goes off in the middle of a storm.'

'You're just trying to scare me,' said Sally. 'I didn't make her go or anything.'

'It's going to look peculiar if something has happened to her is all I'm saying. And you tell me how we're going to get off of here now. You think I'm going swimming without a lifejacket you're mistaken. I'm no Spitz.'

'My hero,' said Sally.

Gaskell went into the cabin and looked in the cupboard by the stove. 'And another thing. We've got a food problem. And water. There's not much left.'

'You got us into this mess. You think of a way out,' said Sally.

Gaskell sat down on the bunk and tried to think. There had to be some way of letting people know they were there and in trouble. They couldn't be far from land. For all he knew dry land was just the other side of the reeds. He went out and climbed on top of the cabin but apart from the church spire in the distance he could see nothing beyond the reeds. Perhaps if they got a piece of cloth and waved it someone would spot it. He went down and fetched a pillow case and spent twenty minutes waving it above his head and shouting. Then he returned to the cabin and got out the chart and pored over it in a vain attempt to discover where they were. He was just folding the map up when he spotted the pieces of Scrabble still lying on the table. Letters. Individual letters. Now if they had something that would float up in the air with letters on it. Like a kite. Gaskell considered ways of making a kite and gave it up. Perhaps the best thing after all was to make smoke signals. He fetched an empty can from the kitchen and filled it with fuel oil from beside the engine and soaked a handkerchief in it and clambered up on the cabin roof. He lit the handkerchief and tried to get the oil to burn but when it did there was very little smoke and the tin got too hot to hold. Gaskell kicked it into the water where it fizzled out.

'Genius baby,' said Sally, 'you're the greatest.'

'Yea, well if you can think of something practical let me know.'

'Try swimming.'

'Try drowning,' said Gaskell.

'You could make a raft or something.'

'I could hack this boat of Scheimacher's up. That's all we need.'

'I saw a movie once where there were these gauchos or Romans or something and they came to a river and wanted to cross and they used pigs' bladders,' said Sally.

'Right now all we don't have is a pig,' said Gaskell.

'You could use the garbage bags in the kitchen,' said Sally. Gaskell fetched a plastic bag and blew it up and tied the end with string. Then he squeezed it. The bag went down.

Gaskell sat down despondently. There had to be some simple way of attracting attention and he certainly didn't want to swim out across that dark water clutching an inflated garbage bag. He fiddled with the pieces of Scrabble and thought once again about kites. Or balloons. Balloons.

'You got those rubbers you use?' he asked suddenly.

'Jesus, at a time like this you get a hard on,' said Sally. 'Forget sex. Think of some way of getting us off here.'

'I have,' said Gaskell, 'I want those skins.'

'You going to float downriver on a pontoon of condoms?'

'Balloons,' said Gaskell. 'We blow them up and paint letters on them and float them in the wind.'

'Genius baby,' said Sally and went into the toilet. She came out with a sponge bag. 'Here they are. For a moment there I thought you wanted me.'

'Days of wine and roses,' said Gaskell, 'are over. Remind me to divorce you.' He tore a packet open and blew a contraceptive up and tied a knot in its end.

'On what grounds?'

'Like you're a lesbian,' said Gaskell and held up the dildo. 'This and kleptomania and the habit you have of putting other men in dolls and knotting them. You name it, I'll use it. Like you're a nymphomaniac.'

'You wouldn't dare. Your family would love it, the scandal.'

'Try me,' said Gaskell and blew up another condom.

'Plastic freak.'

'Bull dyke.'

Sally's eyes narrowed. She was beginning to think he meant what he said about divorce and if Gaskell divorced her in England what sort of alimony would she get? Very little. There were no children and she had the idea that British courts were mean in matters of money. So was Gaskell and there was his family too. Rich and mean. She sat and eyed him.

'Where's your nail varnish?' Gaskell asked when he had finished and twelve contraceptives cluttered the cabin.

'Drop dead,' said Sally and went out on deck to think. She stared down at the dark water and thought about rats and death and being poor again and liberated. The rat paradigm. The world was a rotten place. People were objects to be used and discarded. It was Gaskell's own philosophy and now he was discarding her. And one slip on this oily deck could solve her problems. All that had to happen was for Gaskell to slip and drown and she would be free and rich and no one would ever know. An accident. Natural death. But Gaskell could swim and there had to be no mistakes. Try it once and fail and she wouldn't be able to try again. He would be on his guard. It had to be certain and it had to be natural.

Gaskell came out on deck with the contraceptives. He had tied them together and painted on each one a single letter with nail varnish so that the whole read HELP SOS HELP. He climbed up on the cabin roof and launched them into the air. They floated up for a moment, were caught in the light breeze and sagged sideways down onto the water. Gaskell pulled them in on the string and tried again. Once again they floated down onto the water.

'I'll wait until there's some more wind,' he said, and tied the string to the rail where they bobbed gently. Then he went into the cabin and lay on the bunk.

'What are you going to do now?' Sally asked.

'Sleep. Wake me when there's a wind.'

He took off his glasses and pulled a blanket over him.

Outside Sally sat on a locker and thought about drowning. In bed.

'Mr Gosdyke,' said Inspector Flint, 'you and I have had dealings for a good many years now and I'm prepared to be frank with you. I don't know.'

'But you've charged him with murder,' said Mr Gosdyke.

'He'll come up for remand on Monday. In the meantime I am going on questioning him.'

'But surely the fact that he admits burying a lifesize doll . . .'

'Dressed in his wife's clothes, Gosdyke. In his wife's clothes. Don't forget that.'

'It still seems insufficient to me. Can you be absolutely sure that a murder has been committed?'

'Three people disappear off the face of the earth without a trace. They leave behind them two cars, a house littered with unwashed glasses and the leftovers of a party . . . you should see that house . . . a bathroom and landing covered with blood . . .'

'They could have gone in someone else's car.'

'They could have but they didn't. Dr Pringsheim didn't like being driven by anyone else. We know that from his colleagues at the Department of Biochemistry. He had a rooted objection to British drivers. Don't ask me why but he had.'

'Trains? Buses? Planes?'

'Checked, rechecked and checked again. No one answering to their description used any form of public or private transport out of town. And if you think they went on a bicycle ride, you're wrong again. Dr Pringsheim's bicycle is in the garage. No, you can forget their going anywhere. They died and Mr Smart Alec Wilt knows it.'

'I still don't see how you can be so sure,' said Mr Gosdyke.

Inspector Flint lit a cigarette. 'Let's just look at his actions, his admitted actions and see what they add up to,' he said. 'He gets a lifesize doll . . .'

'Where from?'

'He says he was given it by his wife. Where he got it from doesn't matter.'

'He says he first saw the thing at the Pringsheims' house.'

'Perhaps he did. I'm prepared to believe that. Wherever he got it, the fact remains that he dressed it up to look like Mrs Wilt. He puts it down that hole at the Tech, a hole he knows is going to be filled with concrete. He makes certain he is seen by the caretaker when he knows that the Tech is closed. He leaves a bicycle covered with his fingerprints and with a book of his in the basket. He leaves a trail of notes to the hole. He turns up at Mr Braintree's house at midnight covered with mud and says he's had a puncture when he hasn't. Now you're not going to tell me that he hadn't got something in mind.'

'He says he was merely trying to dispose of that doll.'

'And he tells me he was rehearsing his wife's murder. He's admitted that.'

'Yes, but only in fantasy. His story to me is that he wanted to get rid of that doll,' Mr Gosdyke persisted.

'Then why the clothes, why blow the thing up and why leave it in such a position it was bound to be spotted when the concrete was poured down? Why didn't he cover it with earth if he didn't want it to be found? Why didn't he just burn the bloody thing or leave it by the roadside? It just doesn't make sense unless you see it as a deliberate plan to draw our attention away from the real crime.' The Inspector paused. 'Well now, the way I see it is that something happened at that party we don't know anything about. Perhaps Wilt found his wife in bed with Dr Pringsheim. He killed them both. Mrs Pringsheim puts in an appearance and he kills her too.'

'How?' said Mr Gosdyke. 'You didn't find that much blood.'

'He strangled her. He strangled his own wife. He battered Pringsheim to death. Then he hides the bodies somewhere, goes home and lays the doll trail. On Sunday he disposes of the real bodies . . .'

'Where?'

'God alone knows, but I'm going to find out. All I know is

that a man who can think up a scheme like this one is bound to
have thought of somewhere diabolical to put the real victims. It
wouldn't surprise me to learn that he spent Sunday making
illegal use of the crematorium. Whatever he did you can be sure
he did it thoroughly.'

But Mr Gosdyke remained unconvinced. 'I wish I knew how
you could be so certain,' he said.

'Mr Gosdyke,' said the Inspector wearily, 'you have spent
two hours with your client. I have spent the best part of the
week and if I've learnt one thing from the experience it is this,
that sod in there knows what he is doing. Any normal man in his
position would have been worried and alarmed and downright
frightened. Any innocent man faced with a missing wife and the
evidence we've got of murder would have had a nervous
breakdown. Not Wilt. Oh no, he sits in there as bold as you
please and tells me how to conduct the investigation. Now if
anything convinces me that that bastard is as guilty as hell that
does. He did it and I know it. And what is more, I'm going to
prove it.'

'He seems a bit worried now,' said Mr Gosdyke.

'He's got reason to be,' said the Inspector, 'because by
Monday morning I'm going to get the truth out of him even if
it kills him and me both.'

'Inspector,' said Mr Gosdyke getting to his feet, 'I must warn
you that I have advised my client not to say another word and
if he appears in Court with a mark on him . . .'

'Mr Gosdyke, you should know me better than that. I'm not
a complete fool and if your client has any marks on him on
Monday morning they will not have been made by me or any of
my men. You have my assurance on that.'

Mr Gosdyke left the Police Station a puzzled man. He had to
admit that Wilt's story hadn't been a very convincing one.
Mr Gosdyke's experience of murderers was not extensive but
he had a shrewd suspicion that men who confessed openly that
they had entertained fantasies of murdering their wives ended
by admitting that they had done so in fact. Besides his attempt
to get Wilt to agree that he'd put the doll down the hole as a
practical joke on his colleagues at the Tech had failed hopelessly.
Wilt had refused to lie and Mr Gosdyke was not used to clients
who insisted on telling the truth.

Inspector Flint went back into the Interview Room and looked at Wilt. Then he pulled up a chair and sat down.

'Henry,' he said with an affability he didn't feel, 'you and I are going to have a little chat.'

'What, another one?' said Wilt. 'Mr Gosdyke has advised me to say nothing.'

'He always does,' said the Inspector sweetly, 'to clients he knows are guilty. Now are you going to talk?'

'I can't see why not? I'm not guilty and it helps to pass the time.'

Chapter 17

It was Friday and as on every other day in the week the little church at Waterswick was empty. And as on every other day of the week the Vicar, the Reverend St John Froude, was drunk. The two things went together, the lack of a congregation and the Vicar's insobriety. It was an old tradition dating back to the days of smuggling when Brandy for the Parson had been about the only reason the isolated hamlet had a vicar at all. And like so many English traditions it died hard. The Church authorities saw to it that Waterswick got idiosyncratic parsons whose awkward enthusiasms tended to make them unsuitable for more respectable parishes and they, to console themselves for its remoteness and lack of interest in things spiritual, got alcoholic. The Rev St John Froude maintained the tradition. He attended to his duties with the same Anglo-Catholic Fundamentalist fervour that had made him so unpopular in Esher and turned an alcoholic eye on the activities of his few parishioners who, now that brandy was not so much in demand, contented themselves with the occasional boatload of illegal Indian immigrants.

Now as he finished a breakfast of eggnog and Irish coffee and considered the iniquities of his more egregious colleagues as related in the previous Sunday's paper he was startled to see something wobbling above the reeds on Eel Stretch. It looked like balloons, white sausage-shaped balloons that rose briefly and then disappeared. The Rev St John Froude shuddered, shut his eyes, opened them again and thought about the virtues of abstinence. If he was right and he didn't know whether he wanted to be or not, the morning was being profaned by a cluster of contraceptives, inflated contraceptives, wobbling erratically where by the nature of things no contraceptive had ever wobbled before. At least he hoped it was a cluster. He was so used to seeing things in twos when they were in fact ones that he couldn't be sure if what looked like a cluster of inflated contraceptives wasn't just one or better still none at all.

He reeled off to his study to get his binoculars and stepped out onto the terrace to focus them. By that time the manifestation had disappeared. The Rev St John Froude shook his head mournfully. Things and in particular his liver had reached a pretty pickle for him to have hallucinations so early in the morning. He went back into the house and tried to concentrate his attention on a case involving an Archdeacon in Ongar who had undergone a sex-change operation before eloping with his verger. There was matter there for a sermon if only he could think of a suitable text.

At the bottom of the garden Eva Wilt watched his retreat and wondered what to do. She had no intention of going up to the house and introducing herself in her present condition. She needed clothes, or at least some sort of covering. She looked around for something temporary and finally decided on some ivy climbing up the graveyard fence. With one eye on the Vicarage she emerged from the willow tree and scampered across to the fence and through the gate into the churchyard. There she ripped some ivy off the trunk of a tree and, carrying it in front of her rather awkwardly, made her way surreptitiously up the overgrown path towards the church. For the most part her progress was masked from the house by the trees but once or twice she had to crouch low and scamper from tombstone to tombstone in full view of the Vicarage. By the time she reached the church porch she was panting and her sense of impropriety had been increased tenfold. If the prospect of presenting herself at the house in the nude offended her on grounds of social decorum, going into a church in the raw was positively sacrilegious. She stood in the porch and tried frantically to steel herself to go in. There were bound to be surplices for the choir in the vestry and dressed in a surplice she could go up to the house. Or could she? Eva wasn't sure about the significance of surplices and the Vicar might be angry. Oh dear it was all so awkward. In the end she opened the church door and went inside. It was cold and damp and empty. Clutching the ivy to her she crossed to the vestry door and tried it. It was locked. Eva stood shivering and tried to think. Finally she went outside and stood in the sunshine trying to get warm.

In the Staff Room at the Tech, Dr Board was holding court. 'All things considered I think we came out of the whole business rather creditably,' he said. 'The Principal has always said he wanted to put the college on the map and with the help of friend Wilt it must be said he has succeeded. The newspaper coverage has been positively prodigious. I shouldn't be surprised if our student intake jumped astonishingly.'

'The committee didn't approve our facilities,' said Mr Morris, 'so you can hardly claim their visit was an unqualified success.'

'Personally I think they got their money's worth,' said Dr Board. 'It's not every day you get the chance to see an exhumation and an execution at the same time. The one usually precedes the other and certainly the experience of seeing what to all intents and purposes was a woman turn in a matter of seconds into a man, an instantaneous sex change, was, to use a modern idiom, a mind-blowing one.'

'Talking of poor Mayfield,' said the Head of Geography, 'I understand he's still at the Mental Hospital.'

'Committed?' asked Dr Board hopefully.

'Depressed. And suffering from exhaustion.'

'Hardly surprising. Anyone who can use language . . . abuse language like that is asking for trouble. Structure as a verb, for example.'

'He had set great store by the Joint Honours degree and the fact that it has been turned down . . .'

'Quite right too,' said Dr Board. 'The educative value of stuffing second-rate students with fifth-rate ideas on subjects as diverse as Medieval Poetry and Urban Studies escapes me. Far better that they should spend their time watching the police dig up the supposed body of a woman coated in concrete, stretch her neck, rip all her clothes off her, hang her and finally blow her up until she explodes. Now that is what I call a truly educational experience. It combines archaeology with criminology, zoology with physics, anatomy with economic theory, while maintaining the students' undivided attention all the time. If we must have Joint Honours degrees let them be of that vitality. Practical too. I'm thinking of sending away for one of those dolls.'

'It still leaves unresolved the question of Mrs Wilt's disappearance,' said Mr Morris.

'Ah, dear Eva,' said Dr Board wistfully. 'Having seen so

much of what I imagined to be her I shall, if I ever have the pleasure of meeting her again, treat her with the utmost courtesy. An amazingly versatile woman and interestingly proportioned. I think I shall christen my doll Eva.'

'But the police still seem to think she is dead.'

'A woman like that can never die,' said Dr Board. 'She may explode but her memory lingers on indelibly.'

In his study the Rev St John Froude shared Dr Board's opinion. The memory of the large and apparently naked lady he had glimpsed emerging from the willow tree at the bottom of his garden like some disgustingly oversized nymph and scuttling through the churchyard was not something he was ever likely to forget. Coming so shortly after the apparition of the inflated contraceptives it leant weight to the suspicion that he had been overdoing things on the alcohol side. Abandoning the sermon he had been preparing on the apostate Archdeacon of Ongar— he had had 'By their fruits ye shall know them' in mind as a text—he got up and peered out of the window in the direction of the church and was wondering if he shouldn't go down and see if there wasn't a large fat naked lady there when his attention was drawn to the reeds across the water. They were there again, those infernal things. This time there could be no doubt about it. He grabbed his binoculars and stared furiously through them. He could see them much more clearly than the first time and much more ominously. The sun was high in the sky and a mist rose over Eel Stretch so that the contraceptives had a luminescent sheen about them, an insubstantiality that was almost spiritual in its implications. Worse still, there appeared to be something written on them. The message was clear if incomprehensible. It read PEESOP. The Rev St John Froude lowered his binoculars and reached for the whisky bottle and considered the significance of PEESOP etched ectoplasmically against the sky. By the time he had finished his third hurried glass and had decided that spiritualism might after all have something to be said for it though why you almost always found yourself in touch with a Red Indian who was acting by proxy for an aunt which might account for the mis- spelling of Peasoup while removing some of the less attractive ingredients from the stuff, the wind had changed the letters round. This time when he looked the message read EELPOPS. The Vicar shuddered. What eel was popping and how?

'The sins of the spirit,' he said reproachfully to his fourth glass of whisky before consulting the oracle once more. POSHELLS was followed by HEPOLP to be succeeded by SHHLPSPO which was even worse. The Rev St John Froude thrust his binoculars and the bottle of whisky aside and went down on his knees to pray for deliverance, or at least for some guidance in interpreting the message. But every time he got up to see if his wish had been granted the combination of letters was as meaningless as ever or downright threatening. What, for instance, did HELLSPO signify? Or SLOSHHEEL? Finally, determined to discover for himself the true nature of the occurrence, he put on his cassock and wove off down the garden path to the boathouse.

'They shall rue the day,' he muttered as he climbed into the rowing boat and took the oars. The Rev St John Froude held firm views on contraception. It was one of the tenets of his Anglo-Catholicism.

In the cabin cruiser Gaskell slept soundly. Around him Sally made her preparations. She undressed and changed into the plastic bikini. She took a silk square from her bag and put it on the table and she fetched a jug from the kitchen and leaning over the side filled it with water. Finally she went into the toilet and made her face up in the mirror. When she emerged she was wearing false eyelashes, her lips were heavily red and pancake make-up obscured her pale complexion. She was carrying a bathing-cap. She crossed to the door of the galley and put an arm up and stuck her hip out.

'Gaskell baby,' she called.

Gaskell opened his eyes and looked at her. 'What the hell gives?'

'Like it, baby?'

Gaskell put on his glasses. In spite of himself he did like it. 'You think you're going to wheedle round me, you're wrong...'

Sally smiled. 'Conserve the verbiage. You turn me on, biodegradable baby.' She moved forward and sat on the bunk beside him.

'What are you trying to do?'

'Make it up, babykink. You deserve a curve.' She fondled him gently. 'Like the old days. Remember?'

Gaskell remembered and felt weak. Sally leant forward and pressed him down onto the bunk.

'Surrogate Sally,' she said and unbuttoned his shirt.

Gaskell squirmed. 'If you think . . .'

'Don't think, kink,' said Sally and undid his jeans. 'Only erect.'

'Oh God,' said Gaskell. The perfume, the plastic, the mask of a face and her hands were awakening ancient fantasies. He lay supine on the bunk staring at her while Sally undressed him. Even when she rolled him over on his face and pulled his hands behind his back he made no resistance.

'Bondage baby,' she said softly and reached for the silk square.

'No, Sally, no,' he said weakly. Sally smiled grimly and tied his hands together, winding the silk between his wrists carefully before tightening it. When she had finished Gaskell whimpered. 'You're hurting me.'

Sally rolled him over. 'You love it,' she said and kissed him. She sat back and stroked him gently. 'Harder, baby, real hard. Lift me lover sky high.'

'Oh Sally.'

'That's my baby and now the waterproof.'

'There's no need. I like it better without.'

'But I do, G. I need it to prove you loved me till death did us part.' She bent over and rolled it down.

Gaskell stared up at her. Something was wrong.

'And now the cap.' She reached over and picked up the bathing-cap.

'The cap?' said Gaskell. 'Why the cap? I don't want that thing on.'

'Oh but you do, sweetheart. It makes you look girlwise.' She fitted the cap over his head. 'Now into Sallia inter alia.' She undid the bikini and lowered herself onto him. Gaskell moaned and stared up at her. She was lovely. It was a long time since she had been so good. But he was still frightened. There was a look in her eyes he hadn't seen before. 'Untie me,' he pleaded, 'you're hurting my arm.'

But Sally merely smiled and gyrated. 'When you've come and gone, G baby. When you've been.' She moved her hips. 'Come, bum, come quick.'

Gaskell shuddered.

'Finished?'

He nodded. 'Finished,' he sighed.

'For good, baby, for good,' said Sally. 'That was it. You're past the last.'

'Past the last?'

'You've come and gone, G, come and gone. It's Styxside for you now.'

'Stickside?'

'S for Sally, T for Terminal, Y for You and X for Exit. All that's left is this.' She reached over and picked up the jug of muddy water. Gaskell turned his head and looked at it.

'What's that for?'

'For you, baby. Mudders milk.' She moved up his body and sat on his chest. 'Open your mouth.'

Gaskell Pringsheim stared up at her frantically. He began to writhe. 'You're mad. You're crazy.'

'Now just lie quietly and it won't hurt. It will soon be over, lover. Natural death by drowning. In bed. You're making history.'

'You bitch, you murderous bitch. . . .'

'Cerberuswise,' said Sally, and poured the water into his mouth. She put the jug down and pulled the cap down over his face.

The Rev St John Froude rowed surprisingly steadily for a man with half a bottle of whisky inside him and wrath in his heart, and the nearer he got to the contraceptives the greater his wrath became. It wasn't simply that he had been given a quite unnecessary fright about the state of his liver by the sight of the things (he could see now that he was close to them that they were real), it was rather that he adhered to the doctrine of sexual non-intervention. God, in his view, had created a perfect world if the book of Genesis was to be believed and it had been going downhill ever since. And the book of Genesis *was* to be believed or the rest of the Bible made no sense at all. Starting from this fundamentalist premise the Rev St John Froude had progressed erratically by way of Blake, Hawker, Leavis and a number of obscurantist theologians to the conviction that the miracles of modern science were the works of the devil, that salvation lay in eschewing every material advance since the Renaissance, and one or two before, and that nature was infinitely less red in tooth and claw than modern mechanized man. In short he was convinced that the end of the world was at hand in the shape of a nuclear holocaust and that it was his duty as a Christian to announce the fact. His sermons on the subject had been of such a vividly horrendous fervour as to lead to his exile in Waterswick. Now as he rowed up the channel into Eel Stretch he fulminated silently against contraception, abortion and the evils of sexual promiscuity. They were all symptoms and causes and causative symptoms of the moral chaos which life on earth had become. And finally there were trippers. The Rev St John Froude loathed trippers. They fouled the little Eden of his parish with their boats, their transistors, and their unabashed enjoyment of the present. And trippers who desecrated the prospect from his study window with inflated contraceptives and meaningless messages were an abomination. By the time he came in sight of the cabin cruiser he was in no mood to be trifled with. He rowed furiously across to the boat, tied up to the rail and, lifting his cassock over his knees, stepped aboard.

In the cabin Sally stared down at the bathing-cap. It deflated and inflated, expanded and was sucked in against Gaskell's face and Sally squirmed with pleasure. She was the liberatedest woman in the world, but the liberatedest. Gaskell was dying and she would be free to be with a million dollars in the kitty. And no one would ever know. When he was dead she would take the cap off and untie him and push his body over the side into the water. Gaskell Pringsheim would have died a natural death by drowning. And at that moment the cabin door opened and she looked up at the silhouette of the Rev St John Froude in the cabin doorway.

'What the hell . . .' she muttered and leapt off Gaskell.

The Rev St John Froude hesitated. He had come to say his piece and say it he would but he had clearly intruded on a very naked woman with a horribly made-up face in the act of making love to a man who as far as a quick glance enabled him to tell had no face at all.

'I . . .' he began and stopped. The man on the bunk had rolled onto the floor and was writhing there in the most extraordinary fashion. The Rev St John Froude stared down at him aghast. The man was not only faceless but his hands were tied behind his back.

'My dear fellow,' said the Vicar, appalled at the scene and looked up at the naked woman for some sort of explanation. She was staring at him demonically and holding a large kitchen knife. The Rev St John Froude stumbled back into the cockpit as the woman advanced towards him holding the knife in front of her with both hands. She was clearly quite demented. So was the man on the floor. He rolled about and dragged his head from side to side. The bathing-cap came off but the Rev St John Froude was too busy scrambling over the side into his rowing boat to notice. He cast off as the ghastly woman lunged towards him and began to row away, his original mission entirely forgotten. In the cockpit Sally stood screaming abuse at him and behind her a shape had appeared in the cabin door. The Vicar was grateful to see that the man had a face now, not a nice face, a positively horrible face but a face for all that, and he was coming up behind the woman with some hideous intention. The next moment the intention was carried out. The man hurled himself at her, the knife dropped onto the deck, the woman scrabbled at the side of the boat and then slid forward into the water. The Rev St John Froude waited no longer. He rowed vigorously away. Whatever appalling orgy of sexual perversion he had interrupted he wanted none of it and painted women with knives who called him a mother-fucking son of a cuntsucker among other things didn't elicit his sympathy when the object of their obscene passions pushed them into the water. And in any case they were Americans. The Rev St John Froude had no time for Americans. They epitomized everything he found offensive about the modern world. Imbued with a new disgust for the present and an urge to hit the whisky he rowed home and tied up at the bottom of the garden.

Behind him in the cabin cruiser Gaskell ceased shouting. The priest who had saved his life had ignored his hoarse pleas for further help and Sally was standing waist-deep in water beside the boat. Well she could stay there. He went back into the cabin, turned so that he could lock the door with his tied hands and then looked around for something to cut the silk scarf with. He was still very frightened.

'Right,' said Inspector Flint, 'so what did you do then?'
'Got up and read the Sunday papers.'
'After that?'
'I ate a plate of All-Bran and drank some tea.'
'Tea? You sure it was tea? Last time you said coffee.'
'Which time?'
'The last time you told it.'
'I drank tea.'
'What then?'
'I gave Clem his breakfast.'
'What sort?'
'Chappie.'
'Last time you said Bonzo.'
'This time I say Chappie.'
'Make up your mind. Which sort was it?'
'What the fuck does it matter which sort it was?'
'It matters to me.'
'Chappie.'
'And when you had fed the dog.'
'I shaved.'
'Last time you said you had a bath.'
'I had a bath and then I shaved. I was trying to save time.'
'Forget the time, Wilt, we've got all the time in the world.'
'What time is it?'
'Shut up. What did you do then?'
'Oh for God's sake, what does it matter. What's the point of going over and over the same things?'
'Shut up.'
'Right,' said Wilt, 'I will.'
'When you had shaved what did you do?'
Wilt stared at him and said nothing.
'When you had shaved?'
But Wilt remained silent. Finally Inspector Flint left the room and sent for Sergeant Yates.

'He's clammed up,' he said wearily. 'So what do we do now?'

'Try a little physical persuasion?'

Flint shook his head. 'Gosdyke's seen him. If he turns up in Court on Monday with so much as a hair out of place, he'll be all over us for brutality. There's got to be some other way. He must have a weak spot somewhere but I'm damned if I can find it. How does he do it?'

'Do what?'

'Keep talking and saying nothing. Not one bloody useful thing. That sod's got more opinions on every topic under the flaming sun than I've got hairs on my head.'

'If we keep him awake for another forty-eight hours he's bound to crack up.'

'He'll take me with him,' said Flint. 'We'll both go into court in straitjackets.'

In the Interview Room Wilt put his head on the table. They would be back in a minute with more questions but a moment's sleep was better than none. Sleep. If only they would let him sleep. What had Flint said? 'The moment you sign a confession, you can have all the sleep you want.' Wilt considered the remark and its possibilities. A confession. But it would have to be plausible enough to keep them occupied while he got some rest and at the same time so impossible that it would be rejected by the court. A delaying tactic to give Eva time to come back and prove his innocence. It would be like giving Gasfitters Two *Shane* to read while he sat and thought about putting Eva down the pile shaft. He should be able to think up something complicated that would keep them frantically active. How had he killed them? Beat them to death in the bathroom? Not enough blood. Even Flint had admitted that much. So how? What was a nice gentle way to go? Poor old Pinkerton had chosen a peaceful death when he stuck a tube up the exhaust pipe of his car . . . That was it. But why? There had to be a motive. Eva was having it off with Dr Pringsheim? With that twit? Not in a month of Sundays. Eva wouldn't have looked twice at Gaskell. But Flint wasn't to know that. And what about that bitch Sally? All three having it off together? Well at least it would explain why he killed them all and it would provide the sort of motive Flint would understand. And

besides it was right for that kind of party. So he got this pipe . . .
What pipe? There was no need for a pipe. They were in the
garage to get away from everyone else. No, that wouldn't do.
It had to be the bathroom. How about Eva and Gaskell doing
it in the bath? That was better. He had bust the door down in a
fit of jealousy. Much better. Then he had drowned them. And
then Sally had come upstairs and he had had to kill her too.
That explained the blood. There had been a struggle. He hadn't
meant to kill her but she had fallen in the bath. So far so good.
But where had he put them? It had to be something good. Flint
wasn't going to believe anything like the river. Somewhere that
made sense of the doll down the hole. Flint had it firmly fixed
in his head that the doll had been a diversionary tactic. That
meant that time entered into their disposal.

Wilt got up and asked to go to the toilet. As usual the
constable came with him and stood outside the door.

'Do you have to?' said Wilt. 'I'm not going to hang myself
with the chain.'

'To see you don't beat your meat,' said the constable
coarsely.

Wilt sat down. Beat your meat. What a hell of an expression.
It called to mind Meat One. Meat One? It was a moment of
inspiration. Wilt got up and flushed the toilet. Meat One would
keep them busy for a long time. He went back to the pale green
room where the light buzzed. Flint was waiting for him.

'You going to talk now?' he asked.

Wilt shook his head. They would have to drag it out of him
if his confession was to be at all convincing. He would have to
hesitate, start to say something, stop, start again, appeal to
Flint to stop torturing him, plead and start again. This trout
needed tickling. Oh well, it would help to keep him awake.

'Are you going to start again at the beginning?' he asked.

Inspector Flint smiled horribly. 'Right at the beginning.'

'All right,' said Wilt, 'have it your own way. Just don't keep
asking me if I gave the dog Chappie or Bonzo. I can't stand all
that talk about dog food.'

Inspector Flint rose to the bait. 'Why not?'

'It gets on my nerves,' said Wilt, with a shudder.

The Inspector leant forward. 'Dog food gets on your nerves?'
he said.

Wilt hesitated pathetically. 'Don't go on about it,' he said. 'Please don't go on.'

'Now then which was it, Bonzo or Chappie?' said the Inspector, scenting blood.

Wilt put his head in his hands. 'I won't say anything. I won't. Why must you keep asking me about food? Leave me alone.' His voice rose hysterically and with it Inspector Flint's hopes. He knew when he had touched the nerve. He was on to a good thing.

Chapter 18

'Dear God,' said Sergeant Yates, 'but we had pork pies for lunch yesterday. It's too awful.'

Inspector Flint rinsed his mouth out with black coffee and spat into the washbasin. He had vomited twice and felt like vomiting again.

'I knew it would be something like that,' he said with a shudder, 'I just knew it. A man who could pull that doll trick had to have something really filthy up his sleeve.'

'But they may all have been eaten by now,' said the Sergeant. Flint looked at him balefully.

'Why the hell do you think he laid that phoney trail?' he asked. 'To give them plenty of time to be consumed. His expression "consumed", not mine. You know what the shelf life of a pork pie is?'

Yates shook his head.

'Five days. Five days. So they went out on Tuesday which leaves us one day to find them or what remains of them. I want every pork pie in East Anglia picked up. I want every fucking sausage and steak and kidney pie that went out of Sweetbreads Meat Factory this week found and brought in. And every tin of dog food.'

'Dog food?'

'You heard me,' said Inspector Flint staggering out of the washroom. 'And while you're about it you'd better make it cat food too. You never know with Wilt. He's capable of leading us up the garden path in one important detail.'

'But if they went into pork pies what's all this about dog food?'

'Where the hell do you think he put the odds and ends and I do mean ends?' Inspector Flint asked savagely. 'You don't imagine he was going to have people coming in and complaining they'd found a tooth or a toenail in the Sweetbreads pie they had bought that morning. Not Wilt. That swine thinks of everything. He drowns them in their own bath. He puts them in plastic garbage bags and locks the bags in the garage while he goes home and sticks the doll down that fucking hole. Then on Sunday he goes back and picks them up and spends the day at the meat factory all by himself . . . Well if you want to know what he did on Sunday you can read all about it in his statement. It's more than my stomach can stand.'

The Inspector went back hurriedly into the washroom. He'd been living off pork pies since Monday. The statistical chances of his having partaken of Mrs Wilt were extremely high.

When Sweetbreads Meat and Canning Factory opened at eight, Inspector Flint was waiting at the gate. He stormed into the manager's office and demanded to speak to him.

'He's not here yet,' said the secretary. 'Is there anything I can do for you?'

'I want a list of every establishment you supply with pork pies, steak and kidney pies, sausages and dog food,' said the Inspector.

'I couldn't possibly give you that information,' said the secretary. 'It's extremely confidential.'

'Confidential? What the hell do you mean confidential?'

'Well I don't know really. It's just that I couldn't take it on myself to provide you with inside information. . . .' She stopped. Inspector Flint was staring at her with a quite horrible expression on his face.

'Well, miss,' he said finally, 'while we're on the topic of inside information, it may interest you to know that what has been inside your pork pies is by way of being inside information. Vital information.'

'Vital information? I don't know what you mean. Our pies contain perfectly wholesome ingredients.'

'Wholesome?' shouted the Inspector. 'You call three human bodies wholesome? You call the boiled, bleached, minced and cooked remains of three murdered bodies wholesome?'

'But we only use . . .' the secretary began and fell sideways off her chair in a dead faint.

'Oh for God's sake,' shouted the Inspector, 'you'd think a silly bitch who can work in an abattoir wouldn't be squeamish. Find out who the manager is and where he lives and tell him to come down here at the double.'

He sat down in a chair while Sergeant Yates rummaged in the desk. 'Wakey, wakey,' he said, prodding the secretary with his foot. 'If anyone has got a right to lie down on the job, it's me. I've been on my feet for three days and nights and I've been an accessory after the fact of murder.'

'An accessory?' said Yates. 'I don't see how you can say that.'

'Can't you? Well what would you call helping to dispose of parts of a murder victim? Concealing evidence of a crime?'

'I never thought of it that way,' said Yates.

'I did,' said the Inspector, 'I can't think of anything else.'

In his cell Wilt stared up at the ceiling peacefully. He was astonished that it had been so easy. All you had to do was tell people what they wanted to hear and they would believe you no matter how implausible your story might be. And three days and nights without sleep had suspended Inspector Flint's disbelief with a vengeance. Then again Wilt's hesitations had been timed perfectly and his final confession a nice mixture of conceit and matter-of-factness. On the details of the murder he had been coldly precise and in describing their disposal he had been a craftsman taking pride in his work. Every now and then when he got to a difficult spot he would veer away into a manic arrogance at once boastful and cowardly with 'You'll never be able to prove it. They'll have disappeared without trace now.' And the Harpic had come in useful once again, adding a macabre touch of realism about evidence being flushed down thousands of U-bends with Harpic being poured after it like salt from a salt cellar. Eva would enjoy that when he told her about it, which was more than could be said for Inspector Flint. He hadn't even seen the irony of Wilt's remark that while he had been looking for the Pringsheims they had been under his nose all the time. He had been particularly upset by the crack about gut reactions and the advice to stick to health foods in future. Yes, in spite of his tiredness Wilt had enjoyed himself watching the Inspector's bloodshot eyes turn from glee and gloating self-satisfaction to open amazement and finally undisguised nausea. And when finally Wilt had boasted that they would never be able to bring him to trial without the evidence, Flint had responded magnificently.

'Oh yes, we will,' he had shouted hoarsely, 'if there is one

single pie left from that batch we'll get it and when we do the
Lab boys will . . .'

'Find nothing but pork in it,' said Wilt before being dragged
off to his cell. At least that was the truth and if Flint didn't
believe it that was his own fault. He had asked for a confession
and he had got one by courtesy of Meat One, the apprentice
butchers who had spent so many hours of Liberal Studies
explaining the workings of Sweetbreads Meat Factory to him
and had actually taken him down there one afternoon to show
him how it all worked. Dear lads. And how he had loathed them
at the time. Which only went to show how wrong you could be
about people. Wilt was just wondering if he had been wrong
about Eva and perhaps she was dead when he fell asleep.

In the churchyard Eva watched the Rev St John Froude walk
down to the boathouse and start rowing towards the reeds. As
soon as he had disappeared she made her way up the path
towards the house. With the Vicar out of the way she was
prepared to take the risk of meeting his wife. She stole through
the doorway into the courtyard and looked about her. The
place had a dilapidated air about it and a pile of empty bottles
in one corner, whisky and gin bottles, seemed to indicate that
he might well be unmarried. Still clutching her ivy, she went
across to the door, evidently the kitchen door, and knocked.
There was no answer. She crossed to the window and looked
inside. The kitchen was large, distinctly untidy and had all the
hallmarks of a bachelor existence about it. She went back to the
door and knocked again and she was just wondering what to do
now when there was the sound of a vehicle coming down the
drive.

Eva hesitated for a second and then tried the door. It was
unlocked. She stepped inside and shut the door as a milk van
drove into the courtyard. Eva listened while the milkman put
down several bottles and then drove away. Then she turned and
went down the passage to the front hall. If she could find the
phone she could ring Henry and he could come out in the car
and fetch her. She would go back to the church and wait for him
there. But the hall was empty. She poked her head into several
rooms with a good deal of care and found them largely bare of
furniture or with dustcovers over chairs and sofas. The place

was incredibly untidy too. Definitely the Vicar was a bachelor.
Finally she found his study. There was a phone on the desk. Eva
went over and lifted the receiver and dialled Ipford 66066.
There was no reply. Henry would be at the Tech. She dialled the
Tech number and asked for Mr Wilt.

'Wilt?' said the girl on the switchboard. 'Mr Wilt?'

'Yes,' said Eva in a low voice.

'I'm afraid he's not here,' said the girl.

'Not there? But he's got to be there.'

'Well he isn't.'

'But he's got to be. It's desperately important I get in touch
with him.'

'I'm sorry but I can't help you,' said the girl.

'But . . .' Eva began and glanced out of the window. The
Vicar had returned and was walking up the garden path
towards her. 'Oh God,' she muttered and put the phone down
hurriedly. She turned and rushed out of the room in a state of
panic. Only when she had made her way back along the passage
to the kitchen did it occur to her that she had left her ivy behind
in the study. There were footsteps in the passage. Eva looked
frantically around, decided against the courtyard and went up a
flight of stone steps to the first floor. There she stood and
listened. Her heart was palpitating. She was naked and alone in
a strange house with a clergyman and Henry wasn't at the Tech
when he should have been and the girl on the switchboard had
sounded most peculiar almost as though there was something
wrong with wanting to speak to Henry. She had no idea what
to do.

In the kitchen the Rev St John Froude had a very good idea
what he wanted to do: expunge for ever the vision of the inferno
to which he had been lured by those vile things with their
meaningless messages floating across the water. He dug a fresh
bottle of Teachers out of the cupboard and took it back to his
study. What he had witnessed had been so grotesque, so
evidently evil, so awful, so prescient of hell itself that he was in
two minds whether it had been real or simply a waking nightmare. A man without a face, whose hands were tied behind his
back, a woman with a painted face and a knife, the language . . .
The Rev St John Froude opened the bottle and was about to

pour a glass when his eye fell on the ivy Eva had left on the
chair. He put the bottle down hastily and stared at the leaves.
Here was another mystery to perplex him. How had a clump of
ivy got onto the chair in his study? It certainly hadn't been there
when he had left the house. He picked it up gingerly and put it
on his desk. Then he sat down and contemplated it with a
growing sense of unease. Something was happening in his world
that he could not understand. And what about the strange
figure he had seen flitting between the tombstones? He had quite
forgotten her. The Rev St John Froude got up and went out
onto the terrace and down the path to the church.

'On a Sunday?' shouted the manager of Sweetbreads. 'On a
Sunday? But we don't work on a Sunday. There's nobody here.
The place is shut.'

'It wasn't last Sunday and there was someone here, Mr
Kidney,' said the Inspector.

'Kidley, please,' said the manager, 'Kidley with an L.'

The Inspector nodded. 'OK Mr Kidley, now what I'm telling
you is that this man Wilt was here last Sunday and he . . .'

'How did he get in?'

'He used a ladder against the back wall from the car park.'

'In broad daylight? He'd have been seen.'

'At two o'clock in the morning, Mr Kidney.'

'Kidley, Inspector, Kidley.'

'Look Mr Kidley, if you work in a place like this with a
name like that you're asking for it.'

Mr Kidley looked at him belligerently. 'And if you're telling
me that some bloody maniac came in here with three dead bodies
last Sunday and spent the day using our equipment to convert
them into cooked meat edible for human consumption under
the Food Regulations Act I'm telling you that that comes
under the head of . . . Head? What did he do with the heads?
Tell me that?'

'What do you do with heads, Mr Kidley?' asked the
Inspector.

'That rather depends. Some of them go with the offal into
the animal food bins . . .'

'Right. So that's what Wilt said he did with them. And you
keep those in the No. 2 cold storage room. Am I right?'

Mr Kidley nodded miserably. 'Yes,' he said, 'we do.' He paused and gaped at the Inspector. 'But there's a world of difference between a pig's head and a . . .'

'Quite,' said the Inspector hastily, 'and I daresay you think someone was bound to spot the difference.'

'Of course they would.'

'Now I understand from Mr Wilt that you have an extremely efficient mincing machine . . .'

'No,' shouted Mr Kidley desperately. 'No, I don't believe it. It's not possible. It's . . .'

'Are you saying he couldn't possibly have . . .'

'I'm not saying that. I'm saying he shouldn't have. It's monstrous. It's horrible.'

'Of course it's horrible,' said the Inspector. 'The fact remains that he used that machine.'

'But we keep our equipment meticulously clean.'

'So Wilt says. He was definite on that point. He says he cleaned up carefully afterwards.'

'He must have done,' said Mr Kidley. 'There wasn't a thing out of place on Monday morning. You heard the foreman say so.'

'And I also heard this swine Wilt say that he made a list of where everything came from before he used it so that he could put it back exactly where he'd found it. He thought of everything.'

'And what about our reputation for hygiene? He didn't think of that, did he? For twenty-five years we've been known for the excellence of our products and now this has to happen. We've been at the head of . . .' Mr Kidley stopped suddenly and sat down.

'Now then,' said the Inspector, 'what I have to know is who you supply to. We're going to call in every pork pie and sausage . . .'

'Call them in? You can't call them in,' screamed Mr Kidley, 'they've all gone.'

'Gone? What do you mean they've gone?'

'What I say. They've gone. They've either been eaten or destroyed by now.'

'Destroyed? You're not going to tell me that there aren't any left. It's only five days since they went out.'

Mr Kidley drew himself up. 'Inspector, this is an old-fashioned firm and we use traditional methods and a Sweetbreads pork pie is a genuine pork pie. It's not one of your ersatz pies with preservatives that . . .'

It was Inspector Flint's turn to slump into a chair. 'Am I to understand that your fucking pies don't keep?' he asked.

Mr Kidley nodded. 'They are for immediate consumption,' he said proudly. 'Here today, gone tomorrow. That's our motto. You've seen our advertisements of course.'

Inspector Flint hadn't.

'Today's pie with yesterday's flavour, the traditional pie with the family filling.'

'You can say that again,' said Inspector Flint.

Mr Gosdyke regarded Wilt sceptically and shook his head. 'You should have listened to me,' he said, 'I told you not to talk.'

'I had to say something,' said Wilt. 'They wouldn't let me sleep and they kept asking me the same stupid questions over and over again. You've no idea what that does to you. It drives you potty.'

'Frankly, Mr Wilt, in the light of the confession you have made I find it hard to believe there was any need to. A man who can, of his own free will, make a statement like this to the police is clearly insane.'

'But it's not true,' said Wilt, 'it's all pure invention.'

'With a wealth of such revolting detail? I must say I find that hard to believe. I do indeed. The bit about hips and thighs . . . It makes my stomach turn over.'

'But that's from the Bible,' said Wilt, 'and besides I had to put in the gory bits or they wouldn't have believed me. Take the part where I say I sawed their . . .'

'Mr Wilt, for God's sake . . .'

'Well, all I can say is you've never taught Meat One. I got it all from them and once you've taught them life can hold few surprises.'

Mr Gosdyke raised an eyebrow. 'Can't it? Well I think I can disabuse you of that notion,' he said solemnly. 'In the light of this confession you have made against my most earnest advice, and as a result of my firm belief that every word in it is true, I am no longer prepared to act on your behalf.' He collected his papers and stood up. 'You will have to get someone else.'

'But, Mr Gosdyke, you don't really believe all that nonsense about putting Eva in a pork pie, do you?' Wilt asked.

'Believe it? A man who can conceive of such a disgusting thing is capable of anything. Yes I do and what is more so do the police. They are this moment scouring the shops, the pubs and the supermarkets and dustbins of the entire county in search of pork pies.'

'But if they find any it won't do any good.'

'It may also interest you to know that they have impounded five thousand cans of Dogfill, an equal number of Catkin and have begun to dissect a quarter of a ton of Sweetbreads Best Bangers. Somewhere in that little lot they are bound to find some trace of Mrs Wilt, not to mention Dr and Mrs Pringsheim.'

'Well, all I can say is that I wish them luck,' said Wilt.

'And so do I,' said Mr Gosdyke disgustedly and left the room. Behind him Wilt sighed. If only Eva would turn up. Where the hell could she have got to?

At the Police Laboratories Inspector Flint was getting restive. 'Can't you speed things up a bit?' he asked.

The Head of the Forensic Department shook his head. 'It's like looking for a needle in a haystack,' he said, glancing significantly at another batch of sausages that had just been brought in. 'So far not a trace. This could take weeks.'

'I haven't got weeks,' said the Inspector, 'he's due in Court on Monday.'

'Only for remand and in any case you've got his statement.' But Inspector Flint had his doubts about that. He had been looking at that statement and had noticed a number of discrepancies about it which fatigue, disgust and an overwhelming desire to get the filthy account over and done with before he was sick had tended to obscure at the time. For one thing Wilt's scrawled signature looked suspiciously like Little Tommy Tucker when examined closely and there was a QNED beside it, which Flint had a shrewd idea meant Quod Non Erat Demonstrandum, and in any case there were rather too many references to pigs for his policeman's fancy and fuzzy pigs at that. Finally the information that Wilt had made a special request for two pork pies for lunch and had specified Sweet-breads in particular suggested an insane cannibalism that might fit in with what he had said he had done but seemed to be carrying things too far. The word 'provocation' sprang to mind and since the episode of the doll Flint had been rather conscious of bad publicity. He read through the statement again and couldn't make up his mind about it. One thing was quite certain. Wilt knew exactly how Sweetbreads factory worked. The wealth of detail he had supplied proved that. On the other hand Mr Kidley's incredulity about the heads and the mincing machine had seemed, on inspection, to be justified. Flint had looked gingerly at the beastly contraption and had found it difficult to believe that even Wilt in a fit of homicidal mania could have . . . Flint put the thought out of his mind. He decided to have another little chat with Henry Wilt. Feeling like death warmed up he went back to the Interview Room and sent for Wilt.

'How's it going?' said Wilt when he arrived. 'Had any luck with the frankfurters yet? Of course you could always try your hand at black puddings . . .'

'Wilt,' interrupted the Inspector, 'why did you sign that statement Little Tommy Tucker?'

Wilt sat down. 'So you've noticed that at last, have you? Very observant of you I must say.'

'I asked you a question.'

'So you did,' said Wilt. 'Let's just say I thought it was appropriate.'

'Appropriate?'

'I was singing, I think that's the slang term for it isn't it, for my sleep, so naturally . . .'

'Are you telling me you made all that up?'

'What the hell do you think I did? You don't seriously think I would inflict the Pringsheims and Eva on an unsuspecting public in the form of pork pies, do you? I mean there must be some limits to your credulity.'

Inspector Flint glared at him. 'My God, Wilt,' he said, 'if I find you've deliberately fabricated a story . . .'

'You can't do very much more,' said Wilt. 'You've already charged me with murder. What more do you want? You drag me in here, you humiliate me, you shout at me, you keep me

awake for days and nights bombarding me with questions about
dog food, you announce to the world that I am helping you in
your enquiries into a multiple murder thus leading every
citizen in the country to suppose that I have slaughtered my
wife and a beastly biochemist and . . .'

'Shut up,' shouted Flint, 'I don't care what you think. It's
what you've done and what you've said you've done that
worries me. You've gone out of your way to mislead me. . . .'

'I've done nothing of the sort,' said Wilt. 'Until last night I
had told you nothing but the truth and you wouldn't accept it.
Last night I handed you, in the absurd shape of a pork pie, a
lie you wanted to believe. If you crave crap and use illegal
methods like sleep deprivation to get it you can't blame me
for serving it up. Don't come in here and bluster. If you're
stupid that's your problem. Go and find my wife.'

'Someone stop me from killing the bastard,' yelled Flint, as
he hurled himself from the room. He went to his office and sent
for Sergeant Yates. 'Cancel the pie hunt. It's a load of bull,' he
told him.

'Bull?' said the Sergeant uncertainly.

'Shit,' said Flint. 'He's done it again.'

'You mean . . .'

'I mean that that little turd in there has led us up the garden
path again.'

'But how did he know about the factory and all that?'

Flint looked up at him pathetically. 'If you want to know why
he's a walking encyclopedia, you go and ask him yourself.'

Sergeant Yates went out and returned five minutes later.
'Meat One,' he announced enigmatically.

'Meet won?'

'A class of butchers he used to teach. They took him round
the factory.'

'Jesus,' said Flint, 'is there anybody that little swine hasn't
taught?'

'He says they were most instructive.'

'Yates, do me a favour. Just go back and find out all the
names of the classes he's taught. That way we'll know what to
expect next.'

'Well I have heard him mention Plasterers Two and Gasfitters
One . . .'

'All of them, Yates, all of them. I don't want to be caught out with some tale about Mrs Wilt being got rid of in the Sewage Works because he once taught Shit Two.' He picked up the evening paper and glanced at the headlines. POLICE PROBE PIES FOR MISSING WIFE.

'Oh my God,' he groaned. 'This is going to do our public image no end of good.'

At the Tech the Principal was expressing the same opinion at a meeting of the Heads of Departments.

'We've been held up to public ridicule,' he said. 'First it is popularly supposed that we make a habit of employing lecturers who bury their unwanted wives in the foundations of the new block. Secondly we have lost all chance of attaining Polytechnic status by having the Joint Honours degree turned down by the CNAA on the grounds that those facilities we do provide are not such as befit an institution of higher learning. Professor Baxendale expressed himself very forcibly on that point and particularly on a remark he heard from one of the senior staff about necrophilia . . .'

'I merely said . . .' Dr Board began.

'We all know what you said, Dr Board. And it may interest you to know that Dr Cox in his lucid moments is still refusing cold meat. Dr Mayfield has already tendered his resignation. And now to cap it all we have this.'

He held up a newspaper, across the top of whose second page there read SEX LECTURES STUN STUDENTS.

'I hope you have all taken good note of the photograph,' said the Principal bitterly, indicating a large and unfortunately angled picture of Judy hanging from the crane. 'The article goes on . . . well never mind. You can read it for yourselves. I would merely like answers to the following questions. Who authorized the purchase of thirty copies of *Last Exit From Brooklyn* for use with Fitters and Turners?'

Mr Morris tried to think who had taken FTs. 'I think that must have been Watkins,' he said. 'He left us last term. He was only a part-time lecturer.'

'Thank God we were spared him full-time,' said the Principal. 'Secondly which lecturer makes a habit of advocating to Nursery Nurses that they wear . . . er . . . Dutch Caps all the time?'

'Well Mr Sedgwick is very keen on them,' said Mr Morris.
'Nursery Nurses or Dutch Caps?' enquired the Principal.
'Possibly both together?' suggested Dr Board sotto voce.
'He's got this thing against the Pill,' said Mr Morris.
'Well please ask Mr Sedgwick to see me in my office on Monday at ten. I want to explain the terms under which he is employed here. And finally, how many lecturers do you know of who make use of Audio Visual Aid equipment to show blue movies to the Senior Secs?'

Mr Morris shook his head emphatically. 'No one in my department,' he said.

'It says here that blue movies have been shown,' said the Principal, 'in periods properly allocated to Current Affairs.'

'Wentworth did show them *Women in Love*,' said the Head of English.

'Well never mind. There's just one more point I want to mention. We are not going to conduct an Evening Class in First Aid with particular reference to the Treatment of Abdominal Hernia for which it was proposed to purchase an inflatable doll. From now on we are going to have to cut our coats to suit our cloth.'

'On the grounds of inflation?' asked Dr Board.

'On the grounds that the Education Committee has been waiting for years for an opportunity to cut back our budget,' said the Principal. 'That opportunity has now been given them. The fact that we have been providing a public service by keeping, to quote Mr Morris, "a large number of mentally unbalanced and potentially dangerous psychopaths off the streets" unquote seems to have escaped their notice.'

'I presume he was referring to the Day Release Apprentices,' said Dr Board charitably.

'He was not,' said the Principal. 'Correct me if I am wrong, Morris, but hadn't you in mind the members of the Liberal Studies Department?'

The meeting broke up. Later that day Mr Morris sat down to compose his letter of resignation.

Chapter 19

From the window of an empty bedroom on the first floor of the Vicarage, Eva Wilt watched the Rev St John Froude walk pensively down the path to the church. As soon as he had passed out of sight she went downstairs and into the study. She would phone Henry again. If he wasn't at the Tech he must be at home. She crossed to the desk and was about to pick up the phone when she saw the ivy. Oh dear, she had forgotten all about the ivy and she had left it where he was bound to have seen it. It was all so terribly embarrassing. She dialled 34 Parkview Avenue and waited. There was no reply. She put the phone down and dialled the Tech. And all the time she watched the gate into the churchyard in case the Vicar should return.

'Fenland College of Arts and Technology,' said the girl on the switchboard.

'It's me again,' said Eva, 'I want to speak to Mr Wilt.'

'I'm very sorry but Mr Wilt isn't here.'

'But where is he? I've dialled home and . . .'

'He's at the Police Station.'

'He's what?' Eva said.

'He's at the Police Station helping the police with their enquiries . . .'

'Enquiries? What enquiries?' Eva shrieked.

'Didn't you know?' said the girl. 'It's been in all the papers. He's been and murdered his wife . . .'

Eva took the phone from her ear and stared at it in horror. The girl was still speaking but she was no longer listening. Henry had murdered his wife. But she was his wife. It wasn't possible. She couldn't have been murdered. For one horrible moment Eva Wilt felt sanity slipping from her. Then she put the receiver to her ear again.

'Are you there?' said the girl.

'But I am his wife,' Eva shouted. There was a long silence at the other end and she heard the girl telling someone that there

was a crazy woman on the line who said she was Mrs Wilt and
what ought she to do.

'I tell you I am Mrs Wilt. Mrs Eva Wilt,' she shouted but the
line had gone dead. Eva put the phone down weakly. Henry at
the Police Station . . . Henry had murdered her . . . Oh God.
The whole world had gone mad. And here she was naked in
a vicarage at . . . Eva had no idea where she was. She dialled 999.

'Emergency Services. Which department do you require?'
said the operator.

'Police,' said Eva. There was a click and a man's voice came
on.

'Police here.'

'This is Mrs Wilt,' said Eva.

'Mrs Wilt?'

'Mrs Eva Wilt. Is it true that my husband has murdered . . . I
mean has my husband . . . oh dear I don't know what to say.'

'You say you're Mrs Wilt, Mrs Eva Wilt?' said the man.

Eva nodded and then said, 'Yes.'

'I see,' said the man dubiously. 'You're quite sure you're
Mrs Wilt?'

'Of course I'm sure. That's what I'm ringing about.'

'Might I enquire where you're calling from?'

'I don't know,' said Eva. 'You see I'm in this house and I've
got no clothes and . . . oh dear.' The Vicar was coming up the
path onto the terrace.

'If you could just give us the address.'

'I can't stop now,' said Eva and put the phone down. For a
moment she hesitated and then grabbing the ivy from the desk
she rushed out of the room.

'I tell you I don't know where she is,' said Wilt, 'I expect
you'll find her under missing persons. She has passed from the
realm of substantiality into that of abstraction.'

'What the hell do you mean by that?' asked the Inspector,
reaching for his cup of coffee. It was eleven o'clock on Saturday
morning but he persisted. He had twenty-eight hours to get to
the truth.

'I always warned her that Transcendental Meditation carried
potential dangers,' said Wilt, himself in a no-man's-land
between sleeping and waking. 'But she would do it.'

'Do what?'

'Meditate transcendentally. In the lotus position. Perhaps she has gone too far this time. Possibly she has transmogrified herself.'

'Trans what?' said Inspector Flint suspiciously.

'Changed herself in some magical fashion into something else.'

'Jesus, Wilt, if you start on those pork pies again . . .'

'I was thinking of something more spiritual, Inspector, something beautiful.'

'I doubt it.'

'Ah, but think. Here am I sitting in this room with you as a direct result of going for walks with the dog and thinking dark thoughts about murdering my wife. From those hours of idle fancy I have gained the reputation of being a murderer without committing a murder. Who is to say but that Eva whose thoughts were monotonously beautiful has not earned herself a commensurately beautiful reward? To put it in your terms, Inspector, we get what we ask for.'

'I fervently hope so, Wilt,' said the Inspector.

'Ah,' said Wilt, 'but then where is she? Tell me that. Mere speculation will not do . . .'

'Me tell you?' shouted the Inspector upsetting his cup of coffee. 'You know which hole in the ground you put her in or which cement mixer or incinerator you used.'

'I was speaking metaphorically . . . I mean rhetorically,' said Wilt. 'I was trying to imagine what Eva would be if her thoughts such as they are took on the substance of reality. My secret dream was to become a ruthless man of action, decisive, unhindered by moral doubts or considerations of conscience, a Hamlet transformed into Henry the Fifth without the patriotic fervour that inclines one to think that he would not have approved of the Common Market, a Caesar . . .'

Inspector Flint had heard enough. 'Wilt,' he snarled, 'I don't give a damn what you wanted to become. What I want to know is what has become of your wife.'

'I was just coming to that,' said Wilt. 'What we've got to establish first is what I am.'

'I know what you are, Wilt. A bloody word merchant, a verbal contortionist, a fucking logic-chopper, a linguistic

Houdini, an encyclopedia of unwanted information . . .'
Inspector Flint ran out of metaphors.

'Brilliant, Inspector, brilliant. I couldn't have put it better
myself. A logic-chopper, but alas not a wife one. If we follow
the same line of reasoning Eva in spite of all her beautiful
thoughts and meditations has remained as unchanged as I. The
ethereal eludes her. Nirvana slips ever from her grasp. Beauty
and truth evade her. She pursues the absolute with a fly-
swatter and pours Harpic down the drains of Hell itself . . .'

'That's the tenth time you have mentioned Harpic,' said the
Inspector, suddenly alive to a new dreadful possibility. 'You
didn't . . .'

Wilt shook his head. 'There you go again. So like poor Eva.
The literal mind that seeks to seize the evanescent and clutches
fancy by its non-existent throat. That's Eva for you. She will
never dance Swan Lake. No management would allow her to
fill the stage with water or install a double bed and Eva would
insist.'

Inspector Flint got up. 'This is getting us nowhere fast.'

'Precisely,' said Wilt, 'nowhere at all. We are what we are
and nothing we can do will alter the fact. The mould that forms
our natures remains unbroken. Call it heredity, call it chance . . .'

'Call it a load of codswallop,' said Flint and left the room.
He needed his sleep and he intended to get it.

In the passage he met Sergeant Yates.

'There's been an emergency call from a woman claiming to
be Mrs Wilt,' the Sergeant said.

'Where from?'

'She wouldn't say where she was,' said Yates. 'She just said
she didn't know and that she had no clothes on . . .'

'Oh one of those,' said the Inspector. 'A bloody nutter. What
the hell are you wasting my time for? As if we didn't have
enough on our hands without that.'

'I just thought you'd want to know. If she calls again we'll
try and get a fix on the number.'

'As if I cared,' said Flint and hurried off in search of his lost
sleep.

The Rev St John Froude spent an uneasy day. His investigation of the church had revealed nothing untoward and there was

no sign that an obscene ritual (a Black Mass had crossed his mind) had been performed there. As he walked back to the Vicarage he was glad to note that the sky over Eel Stretch was empty and that the contraceptives had disappeared. So had the ivy on his desk. He regarded the space where it had been with apprehension and helped himself to whisky. He could have sworn there had been a sprig of ivy there when he had left. By the time he had finished what remained in the bottle his mind was filled with weird fancies. The Vicarage was strangely noisy. There were odd creaks from the staircase and inexplicable sounds from the upper floor as if someone or something was moving stealthily about but when the Vicar went to investigate the noises ceased abruptly. He went upstairs and poked his head into several empty bedrooms. He came down again and stood in the hall listening. Then he returned to his study and tried to concentrate on his sermon, but the feeling that he was not alone persisted. The Rev St John Froude sat at his desk and considered the possibility of ghosts. Something very odd was going on. At one o'clock he went down the hall to the kitchen for lunch and discovered that a pint of milk had disappeared from the pantry and that the remains of an apple pie that Mrs Snape who did his cleaning twice weekly had brought him had also vanished. He made do with baked beans on toast and tottered upstairs for his afternoon nap. It was while he was there that he first heard the voices. Or rather one voice. It seemed to come from his study. The Rev St John Froude sat up in bed. If his ears weren't betraying him and in view of the morning's weird events he was inclined to believe that they were he could have sworn someone had been using his telephone. He got up and put on his shoes. Someone was crying. He went out onto the landing and listened. The sobbing had stopped. He went downstairs and looked in all the rooms on the ground floor but, apart from the fact that a dust cover had been removed from one of the armchairs in the unused sitting-room, there was no sign of anyone. He was just about to go upstairs again when the telephone rang. He went into the study and answered it.

'Waterswick Vicarage,' he mumbled.

'This is Fenland Constabulary,' said a man. 'We've just had a call from your number purporting to come from a Mrs Wilt.'

'Mrs Wilt?' said the Rev St John Froude. 'Mrs Wilt? I'm

afraid there must be some mistake. I don't know any Mrs
Wilt.'

'The call definitely came from your phone, sir.'

The Rev St John Froude considered the matter. 'This is all
very peculiar,' he said, 'I live alone.'

'You are the Vicar?'

'Of course I'm the Vicar. This is the Vicarage and I am the
Vicar.'

'I see, sir. And your name is?'

'The Reverend St John Froude. F . . . R . . . O . . . U . . .
D . . . E.'

'Quite sir, and you definitely don't have a woman in the
house.'

'Of course I don't have a woman in the house. I find the
suggestion distinctly improper. I am a . . .'

'I'm sorry, sir, but we just have to check these things out.
We've had a call from Mrs Wilt, at least a woman claiming to
be Mrs Wilt, and it came from your phone . . .'

'Who is this Mrs Wilt? I've never heard of a Mrs Wilt.'

'Well sir, Mrs Wilt . . . it's a bit difficult really. She's supposed
to have been murdered.'

'Murdered?' said the Rev St John Froude. 'Did you say
"murdered"?'

'Let's just say she is missing from home in suspicious circumstances. We're holding her husband for questioning.'

The Rev St John Froude shook his head. 'How very unfortunate,' he murmured.

'Thank you for your help, sir,' said the Sergeant. 'Sorry to
have disturbed you.'

The Rev St John Froude put the phone down thoughtfully.
The notion that he was sharing the house with a disembodied
and recently murdered woman was not one that he had wanted
to put to his caller. His reputation for eccentricity was already
sufficiently widespread without adding to it. On the other hand
what he had seen on the boat in Eel Stretch bore, now that he
came to think of it, all the hallmarks of murder. Perhaps in
some extraordinary way he had been a witness to a tragedy that
had already occurred, a sort of post-mortem déja vu if that
was the right way of putting it. Certainly if the husband were
being held for questioning the murder must have taken place

before . . . In which case . . . The Rev St John Froude stumbled
through a series of suppositions in which Time with a capital T,
and appeals for help from beyond the grave figured largely.
Perhaps it was his duty to inform the police of what he had
seen. He was just hesitating and wondering what to do when he
heard those sobs again and this time quite distinctly. They came
from the next room. He got up, braced himself with another
shot of whisky and went next door. Standing in the middle of
the room was a large woman whose hair straggled down over
her shoulders and whose face was ravaged. She was wearing
what appeared to be a shroud. The Rev St John Froude stared
at her with a growing sense of horror. Then he sank to his knees.

'Let us pray,' he muttered hoarsely.

The ghastly apparition slumped heavily forward clutching the
shroud to its bosom. Together they kneeled in prayer.

'Check it out? What the hell do you mean "check it out"?'
said Inspector Flint who objected strongly to being woken in the
middle of the afternoon when he had had no sleep for thirty-six
hours and was trying to get some. 'You wake me with some
damned tomfoolery about a vicar called Sigmund Freud . . .'

'St John Froude,' said Yates.

'I don't care what he's called. It's still improbable. If the
bloody man says she isn't there, she isn't there. What am I
supposed to do about it?'

'I just thought we ought to get a patrol car to check, that's
all.'

'What makes you think . . .'

'There was definitely a call from a woman claiming to be
Mrs Wilt and it came from that number. She's called twice
now. We've got a tape of the second call. She gave details of
herself and they sound authentic. Date of birth, address, Wilt's
occupation, even the right name of their dog and the fact that
they have yellow curtains in the lounge.'

'Well, any fool can tell that. All they've got to do is walk past
the house.'

'And the name of the dog. It's called Clem. I've checked that
and she's right.'

'She didn't happen to say what she'd been doing for the past
week did she?'

'She said she'd been on a boat,' said Yates. 'Then she rang off.'

Inspector Flint sat up in bed. 'A boat? What boat?'

'She rang off. Oh and another thing, she said she takes a size ten shoe. She does.'

'Oh shit,' said Flint. 'All right, I'll come on down.' He got out of bed and began to dress.

In his cell Wilt stared at the ceiling. After so many hours of interrogation his mind still reverberated with questions. 'How did you kill her? Where did you put her? What did you do with the weapon?' Meaningless questions continually reiterated in the hope they would finally break him. But Wilt hadn't broken. He had triumphed. For once in his life he knew himself to be invincibly right and everyone else totally wrong. Always before he had had doubts. Plasterers Two might after all have been right about there being too many wogs in the country. Perhaps hanging was a deterrent. Wilt didn't think so but he couldn't be absolutely certain. Only time would tell. But in the case of Regina *versus* Wilt *re* the murder of Mrs Wilt there could be no question of his guilt. He could be tried, found guilty and sentenced, it would make no difference. He was innocent of the charge and if he was sentenced to life imprisonment the very enormity of the injustice done to him would compound his knowledge of his own innocence. For the very first time in his life Wilt knew himself to be free. It was as though the original sin of being Henry Wilt, of 34 Parkview Avenue, Ipford, lecturer in Liberal Studies at the Fenland College of Arts and Technology, husband of Eva Wilt and father of none, had been lifted from him. All the encumbrances of possessions, habits, salary and status, all the social conformities, the niceties of estimation of himself and other people which he and Eva had acquired, all these had gone. Locked in his cell Wilt was free to be. And whatever happened he would never again succumb to the siren calls of self-effacement. After the flagrant contempt and fury of Inspector Flint, the abuse and the opprobrium heaped on him for a week, who needed approbation? They could stuff their opinions of him. Wilt would pursue his independent course and put to good use his evident gifts of inconsequence. Give him a life sentence and a progressive prison governor and Wilt would drive the man mad within a month by the sweet reasonableness of his refusal to obey the prison rules. Solitary confinement and a regime of bread and water, if such punishments still existed, would not deter him. Give him his freedom and he would apply his new-found talents at the Tech. He would sit happily on committees and reduce them to dissensions by his untiring adoption of whatever argument was most contrary to the consensus opinion. The race was not to the swift after all, it was to the indefatigably inconsequential and life was random, anarchic and chaotic. Rules were made to be broken and the man with the grasshopper mind was one jump ahead of all the others. Having established this new rule, Wilt turned on his side and tried to sleep but sleep wouldn't come. He tried his other side with equal lack of success. Thoughts, questions, irrelevant answers and imaginary dialogues filled his mind. He tried counting sheep but found himself thinking of Eva. Dear Eva, damnable Eva, ebullient Eva and Eva the irrepressibly enthusiastic. Like him she had sought the Absolute, the Eternal Truth which would save her the bother of ever having to think for herself again. She had sought it in Pottery, in Transcendental Meditation, in Judo, on trampolines and most incongruously of all in Oriental Dance. Finally she had tried to find it in sexual emancipation, Women's Lib and the Sacrament of the Orgasm in which she could forever lose herself. Which, come to think of it, was what she appeared to have done. And taken the bloody Pringsheims with her. Well she would certainly have some explaining to do when and if she ever returned. Wilt smiled to himself at the thought of what she would say when she discovered what her latest infatuation with the Infinite had led to. He'd see to it that she had cause to regret it to her dying day.

On the floor of the sitting-room at the Vicarage Eva Wilt struggled with the growing conviction that her dying day was already over and done with. Certainly everyone she came into contact with seemed to think she was dead. The policeman she had spoken to on the phone had seemed disinclined to believe her assertion that she was alive and at least relatively well and had demanded proofs of her identity in the most disconcerting fashion. Eva had retreated stricken from the encounter with her confidence in her own continuing existence seriously undermined and it had only needed the reaction of the Rev St John Froude to her appearance in his house to complete her misery. His frantic appeals to the Almighty to rescue the soul of our dear departed, one Eva Wilt, deceased, from its present shape and unendurable form had affected Eva profoundly. She knelt on the carpet and sobbed while the Vicar stared at her over his glasses, shut his eyes, lifted up a shaky voice in prayer, opened his eyes, shuddered and generally behaved in a manner calculated to cause gloom and despondency in the putative corpse and when in a last desperate attempt to get Eva Wilt, deceased, to take her proper place in the heavenly choir he cut short a prayer about 'Man that is born of Woman hath but a short time to live and is full of misery' and struck up 'Abide with me' with many a semi-quaver, Eva abandoned all attempt at self-control and wailed 'Fast falls the eventide' most affectingly. By the time they had got to 'I need thy presence every passing hour' the Rev St John Froude was of an entirely contrary opinion. He staggered from the room and took sanctuary in his study. Behind him Eva Wilt, espousing her new role as deceased with all the enthusiasm she had formerly bestowed on trampolines, judo and pottery, demanded to know where death's sting was and where, grave, thy victory. 'As if I bloody knew,' muttered the Vicar and reached for the whisky bottle only to find that it too was empty. He sat down and put his hands over his ears to shut out the dreadful noise. On the whole 'Abide with me' was the last hymn he should have chosen. He'd have been better off with 'There is a green hill far away'. It was less open to misinterpretation.

When at last the hymn ended he sat relishing the silence and was about to investigate the possibility that there was another bottle in the larder when there was a knock on the door and Eva entered.

'Oh Father I have sinned,' she shrieked, doing her level best to wail and gnash her teeth at the same time. The Rev St John Froude gripped the arms of his chair and tried to swallow. It was not easy. Then overcoming the reasonable fear that delirium tremens had come all too suddenly he managed to speak. 'Rise, my child,' he gasped as Eva writhed on the rug before him, 'I will hear your confession.'

Chapter 20

Inspector Flint switched the tape recorder off and looked at Wilt.
'Well?'

'Well what?' said Wilt.

'Is that her? Is that Mrs Wilt?'

Wilt nodded. 'I'm afraid so.'

'What do you mean you're afraid so? The damned woman is alive. You should be fucking grateful. Instead of that you sit there saying you're afraid so.'

Wilt sighed. 'I was just thinking what an abyss there is between the person as we remember and imagine them and the reality of what they are. I was beginning to have fond memories of her and now . . .'

'You ever been to Waterswick?'

Wilt shook his head. 'Never.'

'Know the Vicar there?'

'Didn't even know there was a vicar there.'

'And you wouldn't know how she got there?'

'You heard her,' said Wilt. 'She said she'd been on a boat.'

'And you wouldn't know anyone with a boat, would you?'

'People in my circle don't have boats, Inspector. Maybe the Pringsheims have a boat.'

Inspector Flint considered the possibility and rejected it. They had checked the boatyards out and the Pringsheims didn't have a boat and hadn't hired one either.

On the other hand the possibility that he had been the victim of some gigantic hoax, a deliberate and involved scheme to make him look an idiot, was beginning to take shape in his mind. At the instigation of this infernal Wilt he had ordered the exhumation of an inflatable doll and had been photographed staring lividly at it at the very moment it changed sex. He had instituted a round-up of pork pies unprecedented in the history of the country. He wouldn't be at all surprised if Sweetbreads instituted legal proceedings for the damage done to their previously unspotted reputation. And finally he had held an apparently innocent man for questioning for a week and would doubtless be held responsible for the delay and additional cost in building the new Administration block at the Tech. There were, in all probability, other appalling consequences to be considered, but that was enough to be going on with. And he had nobody to blame but himself. Or Wilt. He looked at Wilt venomously.

Wilt smiled. 'I know what you're thinking,' he said.

'You don't,' said the Inspector. 'You've no idea.'

'That we are all the creatures of circumstance, that things are never what they seem, that there's more to this than meets . . .'

'We'll see about that,' said the Inspector.

Wilt got up. 'I don't suppose you'll want me for anything else,' he said. 'I'll be getting along home.'

'You'll be doing no such thing. You're coming with us to pick up Mrs Wilt.'

They went out into the courtyard and got into a police car. As they drove through the suburbs, past the filling stations and factories and out across the fens Wilt shrank into the back seat of the car and felt the sense of freedom he had enjoyed in the Police Station evaporate. And with every mile it dwindled further and the harsh reality of choice, of having to earn a living, of boredom and the endless petty arguments with Eva, of bridge on Saturday nights with the Mottrams and drives on Sundays with Eva, reasserted itself. Beside him, sunk in sullen silence, Inspector Flint lost his symbolic appeal. No longer the mentor of Wilt's self-confidence, the foil to his inconsequentiality, he had become a fellow sufferer in the business of living, almost a mirror-image of Wilt's own nonentity. And ahead, across this flat bleak landscape with its black earth and cumulus skies, lay Eva and a lifetime of attempted explanations and counter-accusations. For a moment Wilt considered shouting 'Stop the car. I want to get out', but the moment passed. Whatever the future held he would learn to live with it. He had not discovered the paradoxical nature of freedom only to succumb once more to the servitude of Parkview Avenue, the Tech and Eva's trivial enthusiasms. He was Wilt, the man with the grasshopper mind.

Eva was drunk. The Rev St John Froude's automatic reaction

to her appalling confession had been to turn from whisky to
150% Polish spirit which he kept for emergencies and Eva, in
between agonies of repentance and the outpourings of lurid
sins, had wet her whistle with the stuff. Encouraged by its
effect, by the petrified benevolence of the Vicar's smile and
by the growing conviction that if she was dead eternal life
demanded an act of absolute contrition while if she wasn't
it allowed her to avoid the embarrassment of explaining what
precisely she was doing naked in someone else's house, Eva
confessed her sins with an enthusiasm that matched her deepest
needs. This was what she had sought in judo and pottery and
Oriental dance, an orgiastic expiation of her guilt. She confessed
sins she had committed and sins she hadn't, sins that had
occurred to her and sins she had forgotten. She had betrayed
Henry, she had wished him dead, she had lusted after other
men, she was an adulterated woman, she was a lesbian, she was
a nymphomaniac. And interspersed with these sins of the flesh
there were sins of omission. Eva left nothing out. Henry's cold
suppers, his lonely walks with the dog, her lack of appreciation
for all he had done for her, her failure to be a good wife, her
obsession with Harpic . . . everything poured out. In his chair
the Rev St John Froude sat nodding incessantly like a toy dog
in the back window of a car, raising his head to stare at her
when she confessed to being a nymphomaniac and dropping it
abruptly at the mention of Harpic, and all the time desperately
trying to understand what had brought a fat naked—the shroud
kept falling off her—lady, no definitely not lady, woman to his
house with all the symptoms of religious mania upon her.

'My child, is that all?' he muttered when Eva finally exhausted
her repertoire.

'Yes, Father,' sobbed Eva.

'Thank God,' said the Rev St John Froude fervently and
wondered what to do next. If half the things he had heard were
true he was in the presence of a sinner so depraved as to make
the ex-Archdeacon of Ongar a positive saint. On the other hand
there were incongruities about her sins that made him hesitate
before granting absolution. A confession full of falsehoods was
no sign of true repentance.

'I take it that you are married,' he said doubtfully, 'and that
Henry is your lawful wedded husband?'

'Yes,' said Eva. 'Dear Henry.'

Poor sod, thought the Vicar but he was too tactful to say so. 'And you have left him?'

'Yes.'

'For another man?'

Eva shook her head. 'To teach him a lesson,' she said with sudden belligerence.

'A lesson?' said the Vicar, trying frantically to imagine what sort of lesson the wretched Mr Wilt had learnt from her absence. 'You did say a lesson?'

'Yes,' said Eva, 'I wanted him to learn that he couldn't get along without me.'

The Rev St John Froude sipped his drink thoughtfully. If even a quarter of her confession was to be believed her husband must be finding getting along without her quite delightful. 'And now you want to go back to him?'

'Yes,' said Eva.

'But he won't have you?'

'He can't. The police have got him.'

'The police?' said the Vicar. 'And may one ask what the police have got him for?'

'They say he's murdered me,' said Eva.

The Rev St John Froude eyed her with new alarm. He knew now that Mrs Wilt was out of her mind. He glanced round for something to use as a weapon should the need arise and finding nothing better to choose from than a plaster bust of the poet Dante and the bottle of Polish spirit, picked up the latter by its neck. Eva held her glass out.

'Oh you are awful,' she said. 'You're getting me tiddly.'

'Quite,' said the Vicar and put the bottle down again hastily. It was bad enough being alone in the house with a large, drunk, semi-naked woman who imagined that her husband had murdered her and who confessed to sins he had previously only read about without her jumping to the conclusion that he was deliberately trying to make her drunk. The Rev St John Froude had no desire to figure prominently in next Sunday's *News of the World*.

'You were saying that your husband murdered . . .' He stopped. That seemed an unprofitable subject to pursue.

'How could he have murdered me?' asked Eva. 'I'm here in the flesh, aren't I?'

'Definitely,' said the Vicar. 'Most definitely.'

'Well then,' said Eva. 'And anyway Henry couldn't murder anyone. He wouldn't know how. He can't even change a fuse in a plug. I have to do everything like that in the house.' She stared at the Vicar balefully. 'Are you married?'

'No,' said the Rev St John Froude, wishing to hell that he was.

'What do you know about life if you aren't married?' asked Eva truculently. The Polish spirit was getting to her now and with it there came a terrible sense of grievance. 'Men. What good are men? They can't even keep a house tidy. Look at this room. I ask you.' She waved her arms to emphasize the point and the dustcover dropped. 'Just look at it.' But the Rev St John Froude had no eyes for the room. What he could see of Eva was enough to convince him that his life was in danger. He bounded from the chair, trod heavily on an occasional table, overturned the wastepaper basket and threw himself through the door into the hall. As he stumbled away in search of sanctuary the front door bell rang. The Rev St John Froude opened it and stared into Inspector Flint's face.

'Thank God, you've come,' he gasped, 'she's in there.'

The Inspector and two uniformed constables went across the hall. Wilt followed uneasily. This was the moment he had been dreading. In the event it was better than he had expected. Not so for Inspector Flint. He entered the study and found himself confronted by a large naked woman.

'Mrs Wilt . . .' he began but Eva was staring at the two uniformed constables.

'Where's my Henry?' Eva shouted. 'You've got my Henry.' She hurled herself forward. Unwisely the Inspector attempted to restrain her.

'Mrs Wilt, if you'll just . . .' A blow on the side of his head ended the sentence.

'Keep your hands off me,' yelled Eva, and putting her knowledge of Judo to good use hurled him to the floor. She was about to repeat the performance with the constables when Wilt thrust himself forward.

'Here I am, dear,' he said. Eva stopped in her tracks. For a moment she quivered and, seen from Inspector Flint's viewpoint, appeared to be about to melt. 'Oh Henry,' she said, 'what have they been doing to you?'

'Nothing at all, dear,' said Wilt. 'Now get your clothes on. We're going home.' Eva looked down at herself, shuddered and allowed him to lead her out of the room.

Slowly and wearily Inspector Flint got to his feet. He knew now why Wilt had put that bloody doll down the hole and why he had sat so confidently through days and nights of interrogation. After twelve years of marriage to Eva Wilt the urge to commit homicide if only by proxy would be overwhelming. And as for Wilt's ability to stand up to cross-examination . . . it was self-evident. But the Inspector knew too that he would never be able to explain it to anyone else. There were mysteries of human relationships that defied analysis. And Wilt had stood there calmly and told her to get her clothes on. With a grudging sense of admiration Flint went out into the hall. The little sod had guts, whatever else you could say about him.

They drove back to Parkview Avenue in silence. In the back seat Eva, wrapped in a blanket, slept with her head lolling on Wilt's shoulder. Beside her Henry Wilt sat proudly. A woman who could silence Inspector Flint with one swift blow to the head was worth her weight in gold and besides that scene in the study had given him the weapon he needed. Naked and drunk in a vicar's study . . . There would be no questions now about why he had put that doll down the hole. No accusations, no recriminations. The entire episode would be relegated to the best forgotten. And with it would go all doubts about his virility or his ability to get on in the world. It was checkmate. For a moment Wilt almost lapsed into sentimentality and thought of love before recalling just how dangerous a topic that was. He would be better off sticking to indifference and undisclosed affection. 'Let sleeping dogs lie,' he muttered.

It was an opinion shared by the Pringsheims. As they were helped from the cruiser to a police launch, as they climbed ashore, as they explained to a sceptical Inspector Flint how they had come to be marooned for a week in Eel Stretch in a boat that belonged to someone else, they were strangely uncommunicative. No they didn't know how the door of the bathroom had been bust down. Well maybe there had been an accident. They had been too drunk to remember. A doll? What doll? Grass?

You mean marijuana? They had no idea. In their house?

Inspector Flint let them go finally. 'I'll be seeing you again when the charges have been properly formulated,' he said grimly. The Pringsheims left for Rossiter Grove to pack. They flew out of Heathrow next morning.

Chapter 21

The Principal sat behind his desk and regarded Wilt incredulously. 'Promotion?' he said. 'Did I hear you mention the word "promotion"?'

'You did,' said Wilt. 'And what is more you also heard "Head of Liberal Studies" too.'

'After all you've done? You mean to say you have the nerve to come in here and demand to be made Head of Liberal Studies?'

'Yes,' said Wilt.

The Principal struggled to find words to match his feelings. It wasn't easy. In front of him sat the man who was responsible for the series of disasters that had put an end to his fondest hopes. The Tech would never be a Poly now. The Joint Honours degree's rejection had seen to that. And then there was the adverse publicity, the cut in the budget, his battles with the Education Committee, the humiliation of being heralded as the Principal of Dollfuckers Hall . . .

'You're fired!' he shouted.

Wilt smiled. 'I think not,' he said. 'Here are my terms . . .'

'Your what?'

'Terms,' said Wilt. 'In return for my appointment as Head of Liberal Studies, I shall not institute proceedings against you for unfair dismissal with all the attendant publicity that would entail. I shall withdraw my case against the police for unlawful arrest. The contract I have here with the *Sunday Post* for a series of articles on the true nature of Liberal Studies—I intend to call them Exposure to Barbarism—will remain unsigned. I will cancel the lectures I had promised to give for the Sex Education Centre. I will not appear on *Panorama* next Monday. In short I will abjure the pleasures and rewards of public exposure . . .'

The Principal raised a shaky hand. 'Enough,' he said, 'I'll see what I can do.'

Wilt got to his feet. 'Let me know your answer by lunchtime,' he said. 'I'll be in my office.'

'Your office?' said the Principal.

'It used to belong to Mr Morris,' said Wilt and closed the door. Behind him the Principal picked up the phone. There had been no mistaking the seriousness of Wilt's threats. He would have to hurry.

Wilt strolled down the corridor to the Liberal Studies Department and stood looking at the books on the shelves. There were changes he had in mind. *The Lord of the Flies* would go and with it *Shane*, *Women in Love*, Orwell's *Essays* and *Catcher in the Rye*, all those symptoms of intellectual condescension, those dangled worms of sensibility. In future Gasfitters One and Meat Two would learn the how of things not why. How to read and write. How to make beer. How to fiddle their income tax returns. How to cope with the police when arrested. How to make an incompatible marriage work. Wilt would give the last two lessons himself. There would be objections from the staff, even threats of resignation, but it would make no difference. He might well accept several resignations from those who persisted in opposing his ideas. After all you didn't require a degree in English literature to teach Gasfitters the how of anything. Come to think of it, they had taught him more than they had learnt from him. Much more. He went into Mr Morris' empty office and sat down at the desk and composed a memorandum to Liberal Studies Staff. It was headed Notes on a System of Self-Teaching for Day Release Classes. He had just written 'non-hierarchical' for the fifth time when the phone rang. It was the Principal.

'Thank you,' said the new Head of Liberal Studies.

Eva Wilt walked gaily up Parkview Avenue from the doctor's office. She had made breakfast for Henry and Hoovered the front room and polished the hall and cleaned the windows and Harpicked the loo and been round to the Harmony Community Centre and helped with Xeroxing an appeal for a new play group and done the shopping and paid the milkman and been to the doctor to ask if there was any point in taking a course of fertility drugs and there was. 'Of course we'll have to do tests,' the doctor had told her, 'but there's no reason to think they'd prove negative. The only danger is that you might have sextuplets.' It wasn't a danger to Eva. It was what she had always wanted, a house full of children. And all at once. Henry would be pleased. And so the sun shone brighter, the sky was bluer, the flowers in the gardens were rosier and even Parkview Avenue itself seemed to have taken on a new and brighter aspect. It was one of Eva Wilt's better days.